In the Nameless Wood.
Explorations in the Philological Hinterland
of Tolkien's Literary Creations

D1620010

J.S. Ryan

In the Nameless Wood
Explorations in the Philological Hinterland of Tolkien's Literary Creations

WALKING TREE PUBLISHERS

2013

Cormarë Series No. 30

Series Editors: Peter Buchs • Thomas Honegger • Andrew Moglestue • Johanna Schön

Editor responsible for this volume: Peter Buchs

Library of Congress Cataloging-in-Publication Data

Ryan, J.S.
In the Nameless Wood. Explorations in the Philological Hinterland of Tolkien's Literary
Creations
ISBN 978-3-905703-30-6

Subject headings:
Tolkien, J. R. R. (John Ronald Reuel), 1892-1973 – Biography and interpretation
Tolkien, J. R. R. (John Ronald Reuel), 1892-1973 – Language and style
Mythopoeic fiction, English – neo-mediaeval legend and story
Middle-earth (cosmology of last things)
Recension of Roman and European history and culture

Cormarë Series No. 30

First published 2013

© Walking Tree Publishers, Zurich and Jena, 2013

Front cover picture taken of trail in Lolo National Forest, Idaho, USA, by Ellen Isaacs
© Unlisted Images / Fotosearch.com
Back cover picture taken in the Forêt de Fontainebleau, France, by Auria Buchs-Alves

Illustrations by Anke Eissmann

Set in Adobe Garamond Pro and Shannon by Walking Tree Publishers
Printed by Lightning Source in the United Kingdom and United States

In Memory of

Frederick T. Wainwright (1917-1961)

and of Nora Kershaw Chadwick (1891-1972),

both inspirational scholars of
Europe's Migration Ages and Dark Age Britain, and
significant recoverers of their country's
richly storied cultures and landscapes

Contents

Part D
Twentieth Century Oxford & England

Appendix

Preface

When in the summer of 2009 I wrote the 'Preface' to our first volume of select essays by Professor J.S. Ryan, I already mentioned that it did "not contain everything that Professor Ryan and the Walking Tree Publishers deemed worthy of issuing now" and I hoped that a second volume of his essays would see the light of day within a year. Whereas the first statement remains as true as ever, the second was far too optimistic. When Professor Ryan and I were to have a look at what we wanted to include in such a second volume, it became soon clear that we were to go treasure-hunting again as the twenty-two essays that would make it into the final list of items were to be found in no less than twelve different journals or other publications, quite a few of which have been discontinued in the mean-time, and for which no contact address could be found. Had it not been for some institutional collectors of all publications Tolkienian, like The Marion E. Wade Center at Wheaton College, Illinois and The Tolkien Society, the present endeavour would not have come to a successful conclusion.

Now, here it is, this second volume of Tolkien-focussed essays by Professor Ryan. As can be expected, it is not wholly different from its predecessor, both in its strengths and – as the more critical reviewers may well remind us – in its limitations. Again it contains a fair number of essays where Professor Ryan digs deep into the etymological truth behind one particular word or a group of related words and will thereby offer the reader new insights into what J.R.R. Tolkien had or might have had in mind when giving a certain person or people his, her or its name. These essays will not necessarily tell us everything there is to know about the matter, but often point to some analogy or potentially interesting context, opening vistas for other authors and scholars to pursue. Another group of essays is concerned solely with the archaeological digging at Lydney, for which Professor Tolkien worked on the etymology of names, and the ancient and Roman period mining in the West Country and the Midlands, and how this preoccupation translated into his literary œuvre. A third group is concerned with the influence of Tolkien's main study matter, the literature of the early and the high Middle Ages, on his literary works. Behind all, however, there is again a focus on the one subject matter that many reviewers see as Professor Ryan's most important contribution to Tolkien studies, that is his personal experience of Tolkien the Man. This is emphasized also by the one item that Professor Ryan wrote especially for this collection and which constitutes the Appendix.

When editing the material included in this book and cross-checking its many references and quotations, I have been positively surprised how much of our work has been facilitated by the increasing amount of related material now available online – compared to three to four years ago. Next to the quote-checking function in Google Book, we found the fast growing number of scholarly work available on the internet either in text format such as in the Gutenberg Project or as print scans such as Ernest Weekley's *An Etymological Dictionary of Modern English*, as well as the very useful online version of Joseph Wright's *English Dialect Dictionary* by the University of Innsbruck. It would be a brilliant idea to make likewise available the more obscure texts by Professor J.R.R. Tolkien for general study.

I would like to end this 'Preface' by thanking all the many people who provided those invaluable services without which we never would have been able to bring this volume to its conclusion. First of all, I'd like to mention Stephanie Luther from the Friedrich-Schiller-Universität (FSU) Jena who accompanied the editing process from the beginning to the end and who proved a most valued collaborator on the project. I would also like to thank my colleagues from Walking Tree Publishers, Andrew Moglestue, Johanna Schön and Thomas Honegger for their unwavering support both moral and technical and the wonderful interns-team at the FSU Jena, which has accompanied the book over the many years, starting with Doreen Triebel, but equally including Simone Hermann and Margaret Brown. I was also happy to witness the remarkable support throughout the academic and publishing world when inquiring about additional material. Very rarely did an inquiry meet with silence or outright refusal – on the contrary. Without the support of the various editors of publications where Professor Ryan's essays first were published, but also of Laura Schmidt, Archivist at the Marion E. Wade Center at Wheaton College, Illinois, and Pat Reynolds, the Archivist of The Tolkien Society, this book would not have been possible. Further aid was received from Anne Mouron of the Bodleian Library, Beth and Agnes from the *Cherwell*, Declan McCarthy of The Ashmolean, Peter Gilliver and Jeremy Marshall of the *O.E.D.*, Petra Hofmann of Merton College, Su Lockley of the Oxford Union Society Library, Heather Rowland of the Society of Antiquaries of London, Isabel Holroyd of the *Journal of the British Archaeological Association*, Rose Trupiano of the Raynor Memorial Libraries at Marquette University in Milwaukee, Wisconsin, Reinhard Heuberger at the University of Innsbruck, Christian Delcourt and Juliette Dor of the Association des Romanistes de l'Université de Liège, James Yardley of Little St. Mary's Church, Cambridge, Bernd Greisinger, who gave me access to his immense Tolkien collection, Anke Eissmann for her artwork and Robert Haworth, Denis Bridoux, Jason Fisher, Johan Vanhecke, Michael Drout and Vincent Ferré who provided me with specialist knowledge when I was stuck in my research.

We wish the readers of these lines as much enjoyment and enlightenment from the twenty-three essays of the present collection as we had compiling, researching and editing them. May they provide further 'Light of Knowledge' to Tolkien and Arda Studies.

Zollikofen, August 2013   Peter Buchs

T his book is one which, in its sensitive style of publication and in its nuanced mediaeval series, gives its writer enormous pleasure for a number of reasons, for it is a gathering up, a clustering and the clarifying in 2013 of a number of my earlier research essays concerned with the life, purposes and achievements of one of my own early academic mentors, the late Professor J.R.R. Tolkien. And much like my earlier collection *Tolkien's View: Windows into his World* (2009) – one also selected and published in the Cormarë Series – this volume offers a number of research and reflective pieces, very largely more evolved versions and modifications of items issued variously and much earlier.

Although confident in their several stances and conclusions, these essays are still very much text based, and often contain – or are, to some degree, shaped by – a measure of personal knowledge derived from my close acquaintance with J.R.R. Tolkien when I was a student very close to him in the School of English within the University of Oxford. These several pieces are now developed further in various ways, not least in appreciative response to the interest expressed in their now being re-issued together, and in Europe, by the Editors of the Walking Tree Publishers. In each instance, these leading Tolkien scholars have advised perceptively on first the selection of items, and then on their clustering, and as to clarifications deemed appropriate in view of the passage of time since first issue, or from the further development of my cultural appraisals.

While each individual essay has had its earlier appearance, and so its first readership indicated more clearly – for they have been published by differing research series and varied readers' interests, as in the United States of America, Australia, Norway, Germany, England and Scotland – most have now been adapted and/or expanded in various ways that should make them more accessible, and, certainly, more relevant to current scholarship. However, the present selection and their helpful ordering have alike been the particular work of my

editor, Peter Buchs, to whom I am most grateful for his patience, his collecting up of the writings, and, especially, for his suggested clusterings and for the
so thematic and more illuminating foci for the present sections. I also wish
to extend my congratulations again to Anke Eissmann for the way in which
she has produced motifs so sensitively appropriate to various header and like
spaces in our text. The work is imaginative, illuminating and integrative to
every reader's responses to the Tolkienian corpus and to its ongoing impact on
readers worldwide.

Further, the opening essay and the 'Appendix' contain very much fresh work
and new overviews. However, it may be noted that many of the American pieces
now revised were deemed as significant when I was awarded a Doctorate of
Hobbit Letters by the American Tolkien Society in 1992, Tolkien's centennial
year, for my then contributions to the field of Tolkien scholarship, while others
have been included in collections assembled by Professor Neil Isaacs. Moreover,
as in the first part of the earlier volume, this present collection contains a quite
fresh opening section – as well as a long 'Appendix', this entitled 'J.R.R. Tolkien
and the *Ancrene Riwle*, or Two Fine and Courteous Mentors to Women's Spirit'.
Thus, there are in all some twenty-one essays, as well as the 'Prequel' – that
fine Tolkienian term – and a lengthy and very serious 'Appendix'.

The present opening essay – with its reference to the northern hemisphere's
menacing and timeless wood and to the path of both danger and destiny within
and along it – gives the reader my ever clarifying perception of the grand, central,
and eschatological themes of the smaller Tolkien corpus of his most polished
work, as it had been issued in his own lifetime. For these best known works
from his numerous texts and (unfinished) variant editions and manuscripts are,
alike, concerned with his own and everyman's journey, through this mortal
world, and with his convictions as to how, so moving forward, we may grow to
the deepest understanding of our role as we prepare to receive 'the Gift of the
One to the many'. Thus the initial piece, like the title for the collection, is one
to assist us dwellers on Middle Earth so that we may all reflect on the past of
(Western) European man, and the better understand how Tolkien has made
available for us his views as to the life lived and the necessary eschatology for
all, an eschatology which is also subtly present in so many of his more finalised
creative story tellings.

Further, we may stress at the outset that Tolkien the classical scholar and Tolkien the lexicographer have merged with Tolkien the writer in so many of his tales of his world of Middle-earth as was explained earlier by my editor, Peter Buchs of Zollikofen, Switzerland – in his 'Preface' to my *Tolkien's View: Windows into his World*.

Introduction and Background

As I had indicated some three years ago in the first part of this re-presenting of a lifetime of related research, both my dominions' background in New Zealand and Australia, and my Dark Age studies in Britain, as well as my membership of Merton College in Oxford, and of Peterhouse in Cambridge had given me many opportunities to meet with Tolkien's friends and colleagues,[1] and to en-counter him – formally and informally – on numerous occasions. And I had had many easy and informal meetings with a number of his 'circle', especially his fellow Inklings, notably:

Dr Humphrey Harvard, my own college doctor in Oxford, a serious Roman Catholic, and the author of the 'Inklings' text, *The Problem of Pain*;

Dr – later Professor – 'Jack' Bennett, New Zealand nurtured mediaevalist of such English letters,[2] but with an Oxford doctorate in Norse studies, and a deep interest in Christian worship and in the mediaeval church; and

Hugo Dyson, he often met by me both socially and academically in Merton College;

while I had variously encountered Professor Garrod, Geoffrey Muir, and many classicist members of the Merton Senior Common Room.

I had also been tutored by E. O. G. Turvillle-Petre, a committed Roman Catholic, the long time lecturer, and then Reader in Old Norse within that university, and a most profound scholar of Scandinavian landscapes, ancient

---

1 There were also those members of Faculty who had crossed over from Oxford to Cambridge, to be professors there, like Dorothy Whitelock (in Old English) and J.A.W. Bennett ('Jack') (in Mediaeval Studies).

2 In actuality, I was also able to do some sub-editing work with him for the Mediaeval Society, of whose journal, *Medium Aevum*, he was long the editor.

and more recent, as well as a powerful mediaevalist who had researched Norse texts under Tolkien himself.

And as is mentioned in *Tolkien's View* (2009: xi), I had numerous subsequent contacts with the Cambridge friends to Tolkien, mainly historians and committed Christians, they particularly in the Senior Common Room of Peterhouse, as well as with the Dominicans in Blackfriars, Cambridge. I should also include here Professor Sir Harold Bailey of Queen's College for his reflections on Tolkien and 'path' offered me in the spring of 1966.

*   *   *

As with the earlier collection, *Tolkien's View*, it is again the case that these of my many essays now presented have been selected most carefully by my scholar publishers. Again, too, they have put in order these further pieces which they have collected up after obtaining the necessary permissions. This publication, pleasingly, also enables me to give appropriate emphasis to other mentors – to Tolkien's early student in Leeds, Hugh Smith, long the doyen of the study of English place names and landscapes; to Frederick Wainwright, the brilliant archaeologist of West Mercia, and for whom I had worked on a post-Alfredian site, and to Mrs Nora Chadwick's very early sharing with me her awareness of the significance of Lydney for so much of Tolkien's settings, and plots. She was also quietly alert to his speculations on the significance of the late Roman 'Christianity' at Lydney, especially as it might relate to the deeper meaning of Aragorn, the ideal and selfless 'Healer-King'.

*   *   *

In Australia, at the University of New England, I must express my appreciation to Professors Jennie Shaw and Lynda Garland for giving me the opportunity to complete this work with suitable revisions and a firmer structure for the whole, at much the time that I was refining my *Tolkien: Cult or Culture?* (as issued last year by the Heritage Futures Research Centre, University of New England, in 2012).

Finally, it is again my great pleasure to thank Thomas Honegger and all the Board of Editors of the Walking Tree Publishers in Germany and Switzerland,

and, once again, Peter Buchs, the most understanding and supportive editor for his patience at the unavoidable delays with which I have confronted him.

Epilogue

As was the case with *Tolkien's View*'s 'Preface', I now wish to close with some reference to the volume's selected covers, the front suggesting the menace and hostility of the unknown future, 'the wood' that lies ahead of all mortal men and women, even as the rear cover takes the reader, like the adventurer, further on, to a prospect of light, hope, and so a form of divine benison; for Tolkien's final message to the quester along the paths of Middle-earth was ever one of faith, of hope and of the possibility for Divine Charity (*caritas*) for all. He had reflected long on the Christian pattern of selfless living for others, creating his profoundly eschatological tales to give every man and woman who might read them a or even the way to interpret and respond to the landscapes and 'settings' of Middle-earth, and so to win eternity for their immortal souls.

*   *   *

While much of the popular – and even the academic – Tolkien scholarship of the early twenty-first century may well seem querulous, hostile, and unduly reader-reflecting, that is not the stance of the present Tolkien student and researcher.

Accordingly, my more assertive 'Appendix' has been written to endeavour to correct and clarify the ever more numerous stereotypical and journalistic views of Tolkien the man and the writer. For his faith and art – and the two cannot be separated – have made him at once one of the most controversial, and yet the most read, beloved and significant of writers for all on Middle-earth at the beginning of the Third Christian millenium.

August 2013

J.S. Ryan
University of New England
Armidale, New South Wales
Australia

List of Abbreviations and References

Ancrene Wisse	'Ancrene Wisse and Hali Meiðhad'
AW	*Ancrene Wisse*
BLT II	*The Book of Lost Tales, Part. II*
EDD	*English Dialect Dictionary*
E.E.T.S	Early English Text Society
EPNS	English Place-Name Society
E.R.E.	*Encyclopædia of Religion and Ethics*
Essays and Studies	*Essays and Studies by Members of the English Association*
FotR	*The Fellowship of the Ring*
Hobbit	*The Hobbit*
Letters	*The Letters of J.R.R. Tolkien*
MCE	*The Monsters and the Critics and Other Essays*
M.H. German	Middle High German
N.E.D.	*New English Dictionary*
OE	Old English
O.E.D.	*Oxford English Dictionary*
OHG	Old High German
O.H. German	Old High German
ON	Old Norse
PMLA	Proceedings of the Modern Language Association
R.A.F.	Royal Air Force
RotK	*The Return of the King*
Silmarillion	*The Silmarillion*
TL	*Tree and Leaf*
TT	*The Two Towers*
UT	*Unfinished Tales*
VCH	*Victoria County History*
YWES IV	*Year's Work in English Studies*, Vol IV
YWES V	*Year's Work in English Studies*, Vol. V
YWES VI	*Year's Work in English Studies*, Vol. VI

Prequel

'The Nameless Wood' and 'The Narrow Path'

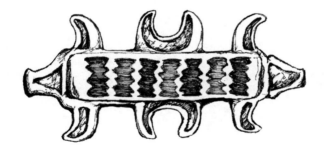

'The Nameless Wood' and 'The Narrow Path'

Myrkvið inn okunna, *Atlakviða*, 3,4. (Dronke 1969: 3)[1]

3/4 *Myrkvið*: the archetypal 'Black Forest', on the edges of habitation, beyond which lay the lands of alien peoples. A messenger riding from the Danube to the Rhine would, in fact, have to cross the great mountainous forests of central Europe, part of which, the Erzgebirge, was still called *Miriquidui* in the eleventh century (by Thietmar of Meresburg, *Chronicon* VI, § 8 MGH SS III. 807: *in Boemiam ... in silva, quae Miriquidui dicitur. (ibid.* 47)

The just cited half-line of Old Icelandic verse is a typical earlier mediaeval period reference to what is later called the 'Dark/Darkling wood'. This context – or the suggestive and ominous line – is an heroic medieval one, as spoken of by Kenfroth, the messenger of Atli, to the heroic Gunnar, referring to his impending dangerous journey, and it occurs in the short Norse poem that is usually styled 'The Greenland Lay of Atli'. These words may be translated thus – "[when certainly / if passing] through Myrkwood, the secret /unknown [...]" referring with caution to the vast forest which divided Atli's realm from

---

The Nameless Wood is the title of a cluster of essays from a Mythopoeic Society Conference at the University of New England, New South Wales, in 1986, and that was issued in a published version of papers delivered then. Much of this present text derives from the opening chapter, the published version of the welcoming address by the convenor, J.S. Ryan.

This text is much expanded from that one (Ryan 1986b: 11-24) and now brought up to date in various ways.

1 The initial quotation above must remind us of the description by Beorn in chapter VII of Tolkien's *The Hobbit* as to the way ahead of the adventuring company, and the area well to the east of 'the Last Homely House in the West':

All the time they ate, Beorn in his deep rolling voice told tales of the wild lands on this side of the mountains, and especially of the dark and dangerous wood, that lay outstretched far to North and South [...] barring their way to the East, the terrible forest of Mirkwood. (*Hobbit* 137)

and then his linked reference to:

a little-known pathway through Mirkwood that led almost straight towards the Lonely Mountain. (*idem.* 145)

that of the Gjukings. Thus the adumbrations of the phrase are those of dream-like menaces, or else are eschatological, shockingly dark and so intimating the presence of evil menace, even if there is no specifically Christian terminology used by the mediaeval poet or much later writer. Thus great danger or the terrible destructiveness of 'the other' are speedily envisioned by the hearer to, or the reader of, such a reference or tale.

In Norse tradition generally, as in this passage, the crossing or attempted entering of Mirkwood comes to signify penetrating the normal barriers, not merely those between one land and another, but those separating the world of reality from the other much more dangerous and ominous outer one, beyond the accepted bounds, and, of course, no longer protected by the household or other 'gods' of one's own nurturing culture. Further, as we should recall, the sons of Muspell and all the forces of destruction, when unleashed at the Ragnarøk, will also come riding demonically 'across/through Mirkwood', *Myrkvið yfir*, as we are told of so memorably in the Old Norse poem, *Lokasenna* (42/2).

It is also this same text which is echoed so closely in *The Hobbit*, when Tolkien, as the tale's narrator, speaks to his readers thus

> [...] they could see the forest coming as it were to meet them, or waiting for them like a black and frowning wall before them. [...] a silence began to draw in upon them [...] By the afternoon they had reached the eaves of Mirkwood [...].

> "Well, here is Mirkwood!" said Gandalf. "The greatest of the forests of the Northern world." (147)

Indeed, it may be noted of this passage that Gandalf in this text, especially in matters of explanation, is speaking in tones very much like those of an, or the, Oxford Professor of Old Icelandic – a role which Tolkien had himself been filling continuously since 1925.[2]

---

2 Although it is not so well known outside of mediaeval scholarship, J.R.R. Tolkien had also been the unsalaried Vigfusson Professor/Reader in Old Icelandic ever since his own teacher, William Craigie's departure for North America, and had already been giving all the lectures in this field since 1925. See Ryan (2009: 37ff).

And so to Return to some Reflections on the 'Nameless Wood' of the Germanic World, and of Western Germanic Stories recorded at Various Periods

It will be clear from the initially quoted and representative passage – and from the standard commentaries on it – that the very early (earliest?) literary use of an awesome phrase like 'unknown/nameless wood' can be related back to the fearful imaginations of the Germanic peoples in Central and Northern Europe as to the mysterious and savage regions to their immediate east, these constituting for them a vast, impenetrable, and ominous unknown. Further, and progressively in so much of Dark Age or mediaval European literature, the collocation of the menace and impenetrability of such a forest seems to be variously applied to and often used of: journeys beyond one's own proper region, as in French chivalric romance; variously, settings of great danger in Icelandic sagas;[3] in the several phases of Arthurian romance;[4] and, more generally, it is often applied, both then and much later, to the fearsome or desolate abode of hermits, of wild men, or of outlaws.[5]

In the case of England, the term/name 'The Edge'[6] is also often used to refer to hills and uplands that are wooded, lonely and even dangerous, sparsely inhabited, and so more obviously 'Wild'. Tolkien himself had extended this traditional usage to a whole atmospheric aura in his *The Hobbit*, where he makes Gandalf tell Bilbo and the party of dwarves that:

> There are no safe paths in this part of the world. Remember you are over the Edge of the Wild now. (149)

---

3 A helpful text here is G.W. Dasent's *Popular Tales from the Norse* (1859), in the later parts of the 'Introduction' to which, there is much discussion of the Wild Huntsman "and his ghastly following" (xxxiv), and other dangers of the night. This was a work closely studied by Tolkien as an undergraduate; see also Ryan 2009 (17-26).

4 The classic account of the earlier and considerable use of the same genre for English literature is still Chapter I, 'Romances', in *A Manual of the Writings in Middle English, 1050-1400*, by John Edwin Wells (1916). See also the relevant chapters in volume I, part 2 of *Middle English Literature*, by J.A.W. Bennett and Douglas Gray (1986), in the series, *Oxford History of English Literature*.

5 And compare, for example, Ray Cashman's 'The Heroic Outlaw in Irish Folklore and Popular Literature' in *Folklore* 111.2 (2000: 191-215).
   Arguably the sprawling and still unfenced 'bush' refuge of the bushranger figure in the middle third of the nineteenth century in Australia is a similar trope of danger and, for the city-dweller, at least, of much lawlessness.

6 The term is discussed in *The English Dialect Dictionary* by Joseph Wright, in Vol. II (1900: 236), under sense 3, to refer to the "ridge or summit of a hill or range of hills; a steep hill or hillside" particularly in the more northern and higher parts of England.

Clearly the same notion of what may occur beyond the usual limits of orderly and safe society is also to be found in the regions more distant from London, and, variously, using the term or referring to their elusive, fugitive and ancient woodlands denizen, 'the Green Man'. He is someone still remembered in parts of (southern) England, as is indicated by the frequency of the phrase as the appellation of a (rural) public house. Similarly, there was available to Tolkien – especially after his Lydney experiences[7] – an awareness of the peculiar fascination that the Forest of Dean has long had for so many in southern England.

All of this older lore of the more dangerous countryside or its further regions was also peculiarly fascinating to Victorian story-tellers as, more recently, it would prove to be to the neo-mediaeval fantasists,[8] who also make much use of the trope of the mysterious wayside inn encountered on the way to the un-known sphere ahead.

A Topography of the (Western European) Imagination

It will be very obvious to the modern and post-modern scholar that, in mediae-val times, the forests of central and northern Europe had been infinitely more extensive, more forbidding, mysterious and dangerous than in recent periods, and that they had a fierce and awful autonomy that was both threatening and deeply challenging to central authority and social order. Thus, in a similar fashion, even as many of those men were inspired by highwayman figures in both England and Ireland, so the notion of the awesome and once vast forests in their own country in an earlier age had been nicely caught up in the Icelanders' traditional term, *skogarmaðr*, 'man of the woods' for an 'outlaw', despite the landscape there having long been almost completely denuded.

---

7 See essay 6 in this book, especially in relation to Tolkien's own inscription-interpreting work for Mortimer Wheeler at Lydney, Gloucestershire, an area which was in the Forest of Dean, where there had been tensions between the foresters and the people particularly in the days of Charles I, while Cobbett would find a paper mill at the side of the Forest on a stream there. For useful background to post-mediaeval man's treatment of this Tolkien-beloved forest, see especially Humphrey Phelps' *The Forest of Dean* (1982).

8 Compare Tolkien's "before we can come to the Wilderland beyond" (*Hobbit* 56), with like passages in Ursula K. LeGuin's 'Vaster than Empires and More Slow' (1971), or in Diana Wynne Jones's *Hexwood* (1993). Yet other science fiction-type works envision various types of mysterious or terrifying 'forest-minds', as in Robert Holdstock's *Mythago Wood* (1984).

As so many of those ancient and primeval forests of the main European land mass have been sorely reduced, thus, too, the long time survivors of their class, like the Ardennes or the Black Forest, have now also lost much of their traditional legendary mystery. And so, linked with this notion of the forest, is that of 'the Edge', a local boundary between the known and so safe, and the 'other' that it would certainly be wiser and safer not to pass into. Interestingly, the phrase has had a recent renaissance, being used increasingly by folklorists and others to help create and 'identify' the spaces we may or may not claim as our own.[9]

The Wood's Mystery Remains

Yet we, albeit post-modern readers, are still all too well aware: of the (unknown) wood's powerful autonomy; of its transcendent reality; of its linked association with sleeping and dreaming; and with its world of treacherous appearances – in short, of its being a deceptive parallel dimension, and so eminently suitable for the creation of fantasy. And so often, too, its threatening darkness is used as a metaphor for the subconscious. From the very first reference to it, we continually sense its danger – especially that of losing one's way within it; its dangerous animals, even including the werewolf, about whom a lay of Marie de France tells us that he "lurks within the thick forest, mad, and horrible to see" (Mason 1932: 83);[10] its function of disorienting anyone straying there in the hazardous movement between worlds; its being a zone of the otherworld, a place transcending reality, one of appearances, or a world in some sort of parallel, and so such a large forest or wood must have seemed – and still seem – to be eminently suitable for the creation of fantasy.[11]

*   *   *

---

9 Consider here *Over the Edge: Pushing the Boundaries of Folklore and Ethno-Musicology*, a collection edited by Rhonda Dass *et al.* (2007), or the various publications of Heart of Albion Press in England, these better known collectively as 'Edge' volumes, and their style defined as one: 'Exploring new interpretations of past and place in archaeology, folklore and mythology'.

10 Also to be noted here, is Charles Perrault's so long popular folk tale, 'The Sleeping Beauty in the Wood' (1697), where the forest is a magical place with trees endowed with almost human yet complex, supernatural powers. We find the same awareness of the unknown in the Tolkienian re-activation and complex use of *warg* (see below).

11 J.K. Rowling of 'Harry Potter' fame was much influenced by the same forest, as she tells us in her autobiographical writings.

However, we may well wish to recall the later stages of this trope, especially whereby the wood became a typological or symbolic place, both after the age of the Romantic poets and then for the earlier country-haunted Victorians generally. For by that phase of the inevitable movement to urban dwelling, it was so very easy to deem the forest as the manifestation of man's fearful imagination, a place of powerful enchantment, much as is adumbrated in Shelley's heightened awareness of the mystery in that natural and seemingly immemorial setting, in 'Mont Blanc' (1816) –

> The wilderness has a mysterious tongue
>
> Which teaches awful doubt, or faith so mild [...]. (ll. 76-77)

While the words or concepts focused on in the title of this essay may seem somewhat arbitrary, they are, arguably, the most significant features often lurking behind the phrase, 'the nameless wood'. Further, as we will see in a moment, in both the Romantic Period and in Victorian England, there was a surprisingly close link of concepts and associations as between comparative philology, the native folklore and the mode of fantasy, the last by then an enigmatic genre. For it had somehow elected to tap into the national sub-conscious as to the way of life of the people before industrialism and so, before the rise of the dispiriting, sprawling, unhygienic, and imagination-crushing great cities.

However, let us return now to ancient tales of a brave champion or such a band questing and so, perforce, traversing such an unknown and terrifying forest in the Victorian writer's own land.

And in the 14th Century

A much earlier, famous and Tolkien-beloved account of – and continually lectured-on text about – what can well befall the traveller in a traditional English, Welsh, or other archetypal place of awe and often of terror is given, in the fourteenth-century poem *Sir Gawain and the Green Knight*. In it Gawain is described as riding alone through woods and hills in search of the challenging Green Knight. "At every ford or stream [...] it was a wonder if he did not find a foe [...], so evil and so fierce [...]. [D]ragons, [...] forest trolls, [...] bulls and bears [...], and ogres[12] who pursued him [...]; [...] had he not been bold and unflinching and served God, without doubt he would have been struck down and killed many a time." (Barron 1974: 69-71)[13] In other, less magical, Dark Age or mediaeval texts, the forest might well be a place for the reflective recluse, as it was for St. Guthlac in the centuries earlier, and for a clearly hermitic religious life, as is depicted in the Old English poem, *Guthlac*.[14]

Interestingly, – and a helpful clue to lost semantics and associations, – the older German, *walt*, the word for 'wood or forest', can also, simultaneously, mean 'wilderness, uninhabited place'. And yet there could well be a more pleasant aspect to the forest, especially in its outer regions, if there had been some measure of clearance for cultivation and so a tidy order, and where the nobles' much savoured pastime of hunting might be pursued. Much mediaeval use is also made of the romance and challenge of the forest, as a place for the true testing of oneself, or for a personal quest in order to achieve a stable adult identity; to overcome actual evil and restore it to the realm of possible threat; for the showing of the courage to meet the unknown,[15] and for an encounter with the Other World, or, for the searching of the soul, as in the case of the Grail-seeking Perceval.

Another comparative text, and one very familiar to Tolkien from his own student days[16] and memorably treating of the dangers in the wood, is Sir George Webbe Dasent's *Popular Tales from the Norse*, which, in its comparative 'Introduction' has much to say about the dangers of the great Western European forest, and so to pass on to the survival of the Wild Hunt in England, and to the rout of the terrifying Huntsman and of "his accursed crew [...] and his ghastly following"

---

12 See, for example, J.S. Ryan, 'Woses: Wild Men or "remnants of an Older Time"', in *Amon Hen* 65 (1983: 7-12), and also his essay 'German Mythology Applied: The literary Extension of the Folk Memory', in *Folklore* 77.1 (1966: 45-59); re-written for *Tolkien's View* (Ryan 2009: 199-213).

13 A *Gawain and the Green Knight*-type piece is to be found in the description of Bilbo's journey to the east in *The Hobbit*:

> there were hills in the distance rising higher and higher. There were castles on some of the hills, and many looked as if they had not been built for any good purpose. Also the weather [...] took a nasty turn. (41)

14 See Ryan (2009: 139-40) for some discussion of this.

15 See Professor Dennis Green's 'The Pathway to Adventure', in *Viator* 8 (1977: 145-88).

16 See the second essay in Ryan (2009).

(1859: xxxiv),[17] as well as making mention of other fearful folk materials, these persisting long in the various Germanic literatures.

Clearly, all these later 'forest tales' sought to remove the hero from the real and, perforce, stock-response world, in order to offer him, alone save for his horse, many shocking and testing adventures, though often causing him to pass through some transitional stage on the way from mundane reality to unreality, "to a world of enchantment in a manner which would invite, if not the audience's belief, at least their willing suspension of disbelief" (1977: 145), as the fine Cambridge mediaevalist of yesterday, D.H. Green[18] has put it. And the latter has also, – and variously – posed for us the question/issue of the mediaeval need for a knight to travel to a fabulous place, one removed from the conformist reality of the Arthurian court, to a location or situation of unexpected, wondrous, or even ominous possibility. Such a transition could well be attained by means of passage through an intermediate zone, such as the dense and uncultivated and menacing wood, with its terrible and testing adventures, and its *loca fabulosa*, whereby the knight has passed on and become disoriented, 'until ... '.

Continuing and Increasing Loss of Control over his Quest for the Traditional Hero

The forces that can, and often will get the (knightly) hero to such a point, are not usually in his choice, his passage thither perhaps being finally found for him by his horse, or by his own instinctive avoidance of low-slung boughs, or else by following a path that is not a way of his own choosing. In all of this 'the path' becomes a directing force, an agent; it quietly selects where he will go[19] and so, finally, exhausted, he, very likely, will come to a castle, where all is not at all what it seems. And often the guide who appears to him there will prove

---

17 See generally Dasent (1859: xxxiv-xxxvi), where the last vestiges in England of the dangers of continental forests are referred to in some detail.
18 The same situation occurs in various parts of Book I of Wolfram's *Parzival*, which is discussed in Essay 13 (pp. 167-81) of the present volume. One may also note the reference in *The Hobbit*, to "'After that the trouble would begin – .' 'A long time before that, if I know anything about the roads East,' [...]" (31). A little later, the hobbit, suddenly curious and now strangely emboldened, suggests – "you ought to go East and have a look round." (36)
19 Cp. From *The Hobbit*, "Up the hill they went; but there was no proper path to be seen [...]" (43).

to be a strangely dangerous tempter, for all his meekness, or even generousness and hospitality.

Certainly, all of this is foreign to the world left behind, and both the raucous and often unseen birds and the strangely confusing weather, too, – as we find also in *Sir Gawain and the Green Knight* – will all be found to have been sent to lure or test the wandering knight, now far from the comfortable and ostensibly 'courteous' or civilized court.[20] For there no such daunting challenges or dangerously and deceptively 'courteous' testing could ever arise. However, once the initial contact has been made with the realm of the fabulous, the transitional zone of the safe and the largely expected falls aside, – and away from the consideration of the narrator and of the reader, – since it has now served its purpose of severance and, perforce, of increasing the wanderer's or brash seeker's disorientation.

Of course, the questing hero, the knight, or the hobbit as an Everyman, in order to be tested, – and this often at several levels – must need to get through and beyond the disorienting and bewildering forest barrier, in order to have his trial, ordeal, or further confusing, self-probing and shockingly testing encounters. And in this progression he will find – and be lost on, or duly be lured along – paths steadily less familiar and bewildering. Simultaneously, the passage thither has already caused both the bemused suspension of ordinary belief in the reader, and provoked for her or him a pleasing confusion as to the several zones of his world and, similarly, for the listener/reader – of the more obviously heroic or Christian romance. And so the moral plain of danger, trial and temptation is reached and accepted that much more easily by the courtly listener or the modern reader.

But to return to Victorian times and to the notions prevalent there, especially for the scholar of story, set outside the realm of civilised society.

---

20 See W.T.H. Jackson, *The Literature of the Middle Ages* (1960: 10).

The Path and the Story Stress on its 'Narrowness' for the Victorian Writer, and, similarly, for the Later Reader

While many of the literary features focused on thus far describe the transition between the two worlds of the individual's quest story, there are other significant and speculative elements somehow linked to the phrase, 'the nameless wood'. For it was a particular feature of nineteenth century (English) high culture that there must then be a significantly close link between philology ('the science of words' – and so a knowledge of their ur-senses – or etymologies – as well as of their subsequent development), and of the painstaking recording or interpretation of the older folk-tales – these devices acting as a sense bridge between Western European mediaeval literature, and the writing of fantasy.[21]

For all of these associations had been available to the cultured and reflective writer, from the time of S.T. Coleridge at the beginning of the century, and then through William Barnes, the Dorset poet and philologist, to the youthful J.R.R. Tolkien[22] at its end. Similarly, the terror of being chased by unidentifiable beings in an unknown place also pervades H.G. Wells's strange scientific fantasy, *The Island of Dr Moreau* (1896).

For, inevitably, the 'forest' had acquired for Victorians and Georgians a composite identity, ambiguous, challenging, always one of menace, and often terrifying. Certainly the notion that the myth-associated aura of such often dialect-preserved senses of words were (half)-remembered by ordinary folk, and so – as in the dialect and legend-collecting activities of Joseph Wright c.1896 – still able to be recorded in timeless fairy tales, was a commonplace of Victorian antiquarian and dialectal research and of related thought.[23]

The central notion to this matter of sub-conscious memory of the perdurable elements and the linked story patterns was neatly summed up thus for us more

---

21 Compare Charles Perrault's 'The Sleeping Beauty in the Wood' (1697).
22 Tolkien's own philological career is well known, but not, perhaps, so familiar is the fact that the poet-author of 'Christobel' was also so trained. See the L.A. Willoughby paper, 'Coleridge as a Philologist', in *Transactions of the Philological Society* (1935: 75), and a related discussion of this in J.S. Ryan, *Tolkien: Cult or Culture* (1969). It is also significant that the same Oxford professor, Tolkien, was one of the longest-serving Vice-Presidents of that London-based Society (see below).
23 For some discussion of this, see the essay on Elizabeth Mary Lea's work in this area, as is discussed in J.S. Ryan (2009: 27-32). Elizabeth Wright also discussed this in her *The Life of Joseph Wright* (1932) in 2 vols.

than a century ago by the fine comparative scholar, Walter Johnson, in an expanded definition:

> By folk-memory we mean the conscious or unconscious remembrance, by a people collectively, of ideas connected with the retention of rites, and superstitions, habits and occupations. Such memory may be clear [...] [or] dim and fugitive, almost to the point of extinction; it may be distorted and misleading; [...] it [...] is, to a very great extent, correlated with [...] 'survivals', and [...] with that 'superstition' which [...] is etymologically a 'standing-over' of custom or ceremony [...]. (1908: 11)

And so to the core notion of the sole way through the wood or forest, and the traveller's dependence on the dangerous and, at first, seemingly innocuous 'path'.

An Interlude – an Actual English Forest often Threatened and Beloved by Tolkien

It is a commonplace of Merton anecdote of the 1950s and 1960s that almost all of the forest and forest-threatened notions in Tolkien's life were drawn from the Forest of Dean, one lying between the Severn and the Wye, a country on its own between England and Wales – see the attached map on the following page – and its homely story of man's abuse of it, and yet of its survival despite all odds.

Another aspect of the forest is that, long before, they provided timber-built trackways– often later converted to Roman roads – that have been dated back to the Late Bronze Age, according to pollen analysis. These 'ways' had been man's answer to nature and they tell us much about floodings at that time as can be seen in the relevant volumes of the *Victoria County History* and V.G. Childe's *Prehistoric Communities of the British Isles* (1940) and L.V. Grinsell's *The Archaeology of Wessex* (1958).

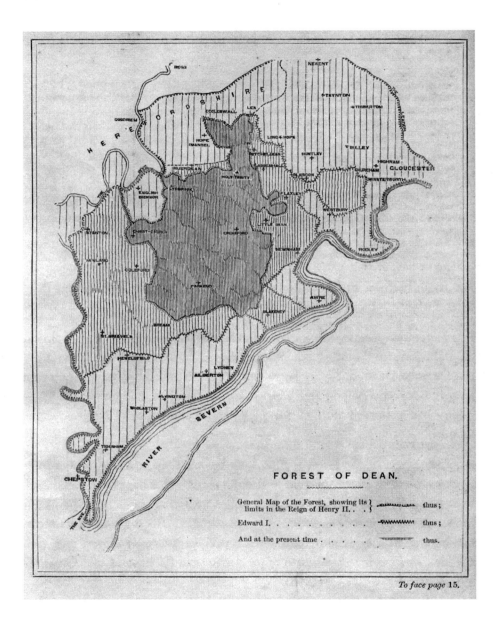

To face page 15.

Map of the Forest of Dean in H.G. Nicholls, 1858, *The Forest of Dean; an Historical and Descriptive Account, Derived from Personal Observation, and Other Sources, Public, Private, Legendary, and Local*, London: John Murray.

Old English pæð and its Early Indo-European/Story Recalled Associations

The very word *path* has long been a linguistic problem for philologists,[24] as much for its actual meaning as for its disputed and debated origins,[25] the *Shorter Oxford English Dictionary* only taking it back to Common West Germanic and giving it the sense "a way beaten or trodden by the feet of men or beasts, not expressly planned [...]" (Onions 1933: II, 1447). The alternative meaning (as cited there in its fn. 6) is found in 1903, in sense 2 of its entry in *The English Dialect Dictionary*, edited by Joseph Wright, Tolkien's early and inspirational language tutor, viz.:

> A steep and narrow way; a footpath on an acclivity; a wooded glen. (1903: 434)

and thus illustrated by the Scottish quotation:

> A peth is a road up a steep brae, but is not necessarily to be understood to be a narrow or foot path. (*ibid.*)

That reference volume's entry for the word also gave it a third sense : "A Roman road; *gen.* in place-names" – "Used as a synonym with ridge, way, and edge". And we may observe here the palpable interest in this third sense from such romantic Victorian storytellers as Charles Kingsley or Rudyard Kipling,[26] both

---

24 This complex of meanings or subtle senses to be found in the root of the word is clearly bound up with the Grimm's and Verner's Laws and their sound laws, and the changes in the various Indo-European languages. The matter was to be treated in exhaustive detail in the exciting article 'Path' by the etymologist professors, H.W. Bailey and Alan S.C. Ross, in *Transactions of the Philological Society*, 60.1 (November 1961: 107-42).
   There would also be a form of supplement to this study from Professor Theodora Bynon, in her related article 'Concerning the Etymology of English *path*' in Volume 65.1 of the same annual journal (1966: 67-87).

25 These are summed up for us by H.W. Bailey and Alan S.C. Ross in their above-mentioned article (1961: 107). See further in this present essay.
   By that time, the Australia-nurtured Bailey, a Fellow of the British Academy, had long been a Vice-President of that Society and had much linguistic association there and elsewhere with Professor Tolkien of Oxford. The Cambridge-based Sanskrit scholar, Sir Harold Bailey, – and a staunch champion of Tolkien as both philologist and story-teller, – had discussed this matter, the possible influence of such an etymology on his somewhat older colleague's writing, with the present writer in 1965 in the University of Cambridge in his rooms in Queen's College after an evening university linguistic meeting then held nearby. Interestingly, both Bailey and Tolkien had had considerable doubts as to the place of the new discipline, 'linguistics' in the university curriculum.

26 The latter, as in his *Puck of Pook's Hill* volume (1906), in his tales of Roman legionaries stationed in Britain in the 4th century. And see also the references to the attraction of the old Roman road to writers like Kenneth Grahame, as in the shorter essay in this present book on 'The Wild Wood'. See

of whom made artistic use of 'the path' as a likely or actually surviving, if
vestigial, Roman road that would open for the traveller or countryside walker
these forgotten pages from the 'book' of the history of his own land.

Yet another form of the wide-spread speculation as to the origins and conno-
tations of the word *path* had linked it with another problem p-word[27] of Old
English, *plega*, 'play', but a notion not found in W.W. Skeat's *Concise Etymological
Dictionary of the English Language* (1882: 42), where *battle*, Late Latin *battualia*
'fights', and **bat(t)uere*, 'to beat' are given. However, this sense or sense link is
to be found in the accessible T.G. Tucker's *A Concise Etymological Dictionary of
Latin* (1931: 31-33), where Latin *ballare* 'to dance' is linked with Greek *ball-* 'to
dance', while a different root grade, the stem **bel-*, is held to have given, with
metathesis, OE *plega*, a noun. In addition to that, Latin *batuere*, 'to beat', had
already been suggested to be a possible early form or cognate for *path*, the root
sense being 'the thing/place beaten down' by the feet, especially of those who
might be hastening along it.

In other words – and this is a notion central to our investigation of the nuances
involved here – the discipline of philology has been struggling since the early
Victorian period – and using both Grimm's Law and the various linguistic
assimilations possible, with the forms of the roots/etymons, the linked senses
of which are

PLAY – DANCE – BEAT – PATH.

The point to underscore here is that what was earlier in the twentieth century
deemed a 'speculative' etymology by philology is now much more willingly
accepted by the discipline, and so it is now able to avail itself of a notion long
familiar in folkloric studies, namely that this is a set of somehow linked forms
and sense associations. And Tolkien himself, on the eve of his 1915 army call-
up, had published his strangely haunting poem, 'Goblin Feet'[28] in which he

---

also my article ' "And What May Britain Be?" – the Fiction Field of Roman Britain' in *Orana* 14, nos.
3 and 4 (1978).

27 See, for example, John Earle, *The Philology of the English Tongue* (1892: 129). The 7th edition of
The Concise Oxford Dictionary (1982: 785) gives: OE *pleg(i)an, plægian* 'exercise' = M. Dutch *pleien*
'dance', [a word perhaps related] to O. Sax. *plegan*, O.H.G. *pflegan* 'attend to'.

28 See *Oxford Poetry* (1915: 64-65). The full text of the poem is given as an Appendix to this essay.
The considerable significance of this early and remarkably haunting little poem to Tolkien's later

juxtaposed – perhaps gently implied – a number of these very links and associations between these meanings:

> the road (l. 1)
> a slender band of grey (l. 4)
> I hear [...] the padding[29] feet (ll. 10-12)
> the crooked fairy lane (l. 18)
> They are fading round the turn (l. 23)
> And the echo of their padding feet is dying! (l. 25)

Ancient Paths

Another of the Victorian period's fields of scholarly interest that is relevant here
is the one beloved of antiquarians – that of the form, location and survival of the
dramatically straight ancient roads and paths, especially of and in the southern
and south eastern counties of England. This matter was neatly summed up
for us by R.G. Clay in his 'Some Prehistoric Ways', in the first-issued volume[30]
of the fine archaeological journal, *Antiquity* (1927: 54-65), from which these
observations may be noted:

> in early Neolithic times there were paths across the swamps (54);
>
> with the introduction of agriculture in later Neolithic days, tracks (i.e. ridge-
> ways[31]) would follow along the crests of the hills (54-55);
>
> the dawn of the Early Iron Age synchronized with the repeated immigrations
> of Celtic peoples,[32] such as the Belgae (55-56);

---

development was pointed out to me in 1964 by another humanities' Fellow of Merton College,
the classicist, antiquarian and doyen of English booksellers, Sir Basil Blackwell. However, in this
contextmay it not also be of a piece with a subtle etymological association, as between 'pad', 'beat',
and 'path'?

29 Cp. Old Frisian *pad*, 'path', Old Low German (Dutch) *pad* and the English cant word, *pad* (15th
cent.), probably from the Low German *pad*, as in *squire* or *gentleman of the pad* (hence *highpad*, and,
simply, *pad* 'highwayman', a term which survives in the more Modern English – if now somewhat
obsolescent – *footpad*).

30 Discussion in Pembroke College and elsewhere in the University in the 1950s and 1960s would
stress Tolkien's close interest in this fine journal, not least through his friendship with Professor R.G.
Collingwood, the archaeologist of Roman Britain. See below in relation to the excavation work at
Lydney in Gloucestershire by Mortimer Wheeler and his team.

31 Both 'ridgeway' and 'driftway' are significant concepts here, often being discussed in close detail in the
parish sections of the English Place Name Society's publications, these issued slowly, shire by shire.
There are several Tolkenian excited comments on like 1920s work on English toponymy as discussed
by me in Essay 8 of *Tolkien's View* (2009: 71-87).

32 Compare the treatment of this in chapters 5 and 6 of the novel by Tolkien's own very talented and
earlier student of Old English, the semantic and nuances-sensitive student, Penelope Lively, in her

[...] old tracks through natural passes in the hills, pre-existing fords and former clearings in the wooded valleys [...] developed [...] into more general use (56);

these ways, if traced for several miles, link up chains of camps (56)[33];

sunken roads [run] [...] through passes, over the edge of high terraces, thence to river fords (56); and

Hollow Ways or Sunken Roads [...] [may be observed to be] running up [...] in a slanting direction [...] to sites on the crest. (60)

Indeed, after close reference to these same very deep-cut paths, no more than ditches bounded by banks, Clay had then concluded that they

were cattle ways along which Celtic men drove their herds in single file from grazing ground to grazing ground without the danger of the animals [...] damaging the crops [...]. (64)

*   *   *

In 1961, Bailey and Ross (1961: 110) had quoted, prior to their very detailed publication on the matter, the senses[34] to be given to *peth* in the *Dictionary of the Older Scottish Tongue*, viz.:

2.a. A cleft, re-entrant or [...] water-course running up and down the slope of a steep hill, and so offering a passage to its top. Passing into:

b. A steep path or track leading to the top of a hill.

3: A path or way; a footpath.

They also showed the links between *path* and *pateo, -ere*, – 'lie open', 'extend up to'.[35] Further speculation linked *PAT- with the root, PENT- , the which may

---

haunting story, *The Driftway* (1972). This last extraordinarily atmospheric piece is a text where modern movement along an ancient road by persons in great stress then causes the associations and events of the ancient past there to again become available and felt agonizingly, – if only momentarily.

Both moderns, Africa-born and alike imaginative students of the Oxfordshire landscape – Lively and Tolkien – would seem to be suggesting some of the path and its memory-thought-associations to be found in various forest-landscape descriptions involving forests and paths, as in Caesar's *Gallic War*, but now applied to the rolling regional downs of Southern England in the hey-day of the British Empire.

33 I.e. mounds, barrows or hill-top occupation places. Compare the sequences around 'Weathertop' in J.R.R. Tolkien's *The Fellowship of the Ring* (1954). Cp. Clay (1927) and note the discussion of that same assault on that hill-top, as presented in J.S. Ryan (2009: 217 f).

34 These are very similar to those compounds or senses – well known to Tolkien – cited in J. Wright's *English Dialect Dictionary* (1900: 172-73), as in *drift-road, drift-way*, "a cattle-path or lane; a right of way for driving cattle" (1900: 172).

35 E.g. of an open space running up to the wall of a fortification. This was the style much more recently for the language in the more western settlement of the United States of America, where such spaces would be left clear, to prevent close-up attacks by Indian tribes, particularly on the protective forts

give the Old English *fandian*, 'to investigate'. This was further refined by the essay mentioned above by Theodora Bynon (1966: 67-87), which postulated as an original meaning for the etymon:

> [T]he concept of a cleft or cutting providing a passage across ground not otherwise easily passable such as a steep slope, dense woodland, cultivated fields. (1966: 77)

$$* \quad * \quad *$$

The conclusion to be drawn from the intriguing and both complex and comparative scholarship briefly outlined above is that there had been intense linguistic and topographic speculation in England for more than a century about the form origin and meaning range, various subliminal associations – and so as to the socio-cultural and landscape significance – of the Modern English word, *path*. The 'beat' sense, as indicated above, has also been variously included in some of the more adventurous etymological dictionaries. Eastern Indo-European origins for the word have been postulated, as by Bailey and Ross, or by the New Zealand-born linguist, Eric Partridge.[36] The stimulation for this persistent (and outsider) speculation and fascinated investigation of the relationship between words, customs of husbandry, and landscape would seem to be a complex mix of :

> a knowledge of journeying and landscape terms in the oldest recorded folk-tales;
>
> various archaeologists speculating about the use of popular names for known and so well-preserved ancient and traversing tracks or the ancient 'driftways';

and

> some realization that many of the concepts or senses caught up in the word *path* are very old, distinctly eastern in origin and had come west along the trade-routes from the east of Asia, and, so, perhaps, were/are not Indo-European at all.

---

as the settlers moved cautiously to the west from the earliest white settlements. See variously in the writings of J. Fenimore Cooper, as in his 1804-set novel, *The Prairie* (1827).

36 See his *Origins: A Short Etymological Dictionary of Modern English* (1958: 475), where the word is held to be akin to Avestan *patha*, Sanskrit *patha*, 'a way, a road' – and so is compared and linked to *FIND.

The Road and the Possible (Personal) Adventures to be Reached by or along it – for Later Victorians and Georgians

While the literature of Western Europe is full of such suggestive etymologies and contexts/imagery, the notion of the 'open-road', running freely across hill and valley, and so symbolizing the beckoning possibility of (personal) adventure, release, and freedom from the confines of town and society had appealed particularly to later 19th century writers. For R.L. Stevenson (1896: 5) had referred to "My mistress still the open road", Chesterton (1913) to the 'rolling English road', while H.G. Wells' Mr Polly (1910) had escaped to the 'open road'. And Kenneth Grahame, that quintessential Oxford man of that countryside, had had his creation, the ridiculously ostentatious Mr Toad, to expatiate fancifully to his friends on the limitless possibilities of

> [t]he open road, the dusty highway, the heath, the common, the hedgerows, the rolling downs! Camps, villages, towns [...]. (1968: 32)[37]

That enchanting journey was, immediately, one to a necessary freedom from (physical) confinement of the grimy cities, but, much earlier, it had been a spiritual one, a quest for the soul's salvation, as in Bunyan's *Pilgrim's Progress*, over a symbolic landscape, much as in the *Authorised Version* of the Bible, as in *The Gospel of St. Matthew*, Chapter VII.

A similar thought to these was present much earlier in the Old English verse epic, *Beowulf* (ll. 1409-1410), where, in the phrase, *enge anpaðas*, Levin Ludwig Schücking had demonstrated long ago[38] that the *an-* implies 'lonely' (i.e. rather than 'sole/single', as from *unus*), and *enge* something more like 'threatening, sinister', rather than 'narrow'.

The double meaning of 'way' – as both a (worldly) route and a method of personal progress in the metaphorical sense – is not merely to be found in the post-Renaissance period in Western European languages, but also in languages

---

37 See the essay on the Wild Wood included later in this present volume. There is also a whiff of the romance of gypsies, with their colourful caravans, and mysterious and unexpected comings and goings.
38 See Schücking (1915: 37 ff). However, there may be noted here these (quietly) underscored references from *The Hobbit* (58): "The only path was marked with white stones [...] it was a very slow business following the track [...]." Note also, a little later: " 'You are a little out of your way,' said the elf: 'that is, if you are making for the only path across the water [...].' " (*ibid.* 60-61)

far to the east. Thus the notions 'path' and 'a means of reaching a goal' are both to be found: in the Indian word *marga*; in the Germanic languages' word 'step'; and also in the Latin *peregrinus*, this later to be shortened and assimilated to become *pilgrim*, a root which meant originally no more than 'wanderer'. Similarly, *peregrinatio*, once only meaning 'wandering about', had then come to have a therapeutic sense, and so mean 'a purposeful journeying away from one's normal pursuits'. This 'pilgrim's way' had been and would be undertaken by those who could afford it, in order to obtain the spiritual and moral benefits believed stemming from some form of humble progression, sacrifice and testing, in some (distant) holy place.

On such journeys, Christian or secular, as in (the earlier dangerous) penetrations of the forest or the wilderness, the world of the supernatural would meet the world of men, or supernatural power (whether of God, demons or ghosts) would come into focus, as it would at the holy shrines themselves. While the skeptical modern mind is unable to accept that there are such easily accessible and powerfully numinous places, the intuitive religious mind believes implicitly in the supernatural world and in its worldly manifestation, by Divine Grace, at particular times and places.

And so, the Biblical Scholars' – and then the Romantic Mythmakers' – Turning from the Literal Sense of Path to one for the Individual's Metaphysical Journey in this Present Life

> Midway the journey of this life I was 'ware
> That I had strayed into a dark forest,
> And the right path appeared not anywhere.
>   Dante, *Inferno*, Canto I, opening lines.
>   (As translated by Laurence Binyon, 1928).

'Wood' and 'Forest' were and are very ancient concepts, the latter long deemed exceedingly dangerous. The word 'wood' could also mean 'a tree/the Cross' in Old English, as it does for Tyndale in his 1526 translation of *Revelation*, 22:2: "Off ether side of the ruyere was there wode off lyfe: which bare xij manner off fruites." The formal *O.E.D.* definition for the core word is one that is helpful here:

> A collection of trees growing more or less thickly together [...] of considerable extent, usually larger than a *grove* [...] and smaller than a *forest*; a piece of ground covered with trees, with or without undergrowth. (1989: 501)

And the same *Dictionary* records significant examples from the ninth century on. The 'forest' word's cognates seem restricted to the Germanic and Celtic languages.

The complex thought associations of 'forest' may not all apply to – or parallel – those of 'wood', but they may be tabled here since most came into English through Old French. Its Western Indo-European – and so later – progression of form and sense may be given, it running thus:

Latin (adv.) *foris* (outside);>

Late Latin *forestis* (used of >), i.e. wood outside the village, hence one available 'for the use of all'; >

Mediaeval Latin, *forestis*, a wood, forest;

Old, Middle French, *forest* (cp. Mod. Fr. *forêt*);

M. Lat. > O. Fr. *forestis silva*; related to *forum* in the Mediaeval Latin sense of 'court of the King's justice'.

Hence, from these semantic 'chainings' and so (progressive/associative) links or 'steps in the sense', it can be seen that the much smaller English 'woods' were and continued to be viewed – by the authorities or by the poorest in the land – much as the great continental forests or the officially declared Royal Hunting Forests[39] so dear to the Norman nobility, as places of both exclusive privilege and also – for the wretched of this world – a last sanctuary from the vicious and condoned social harassment.

---

39 As Manwood's privately circulated *A Brefe* [i.e. Brief] *Collection of the Lawes of the Forest* (1592) had defined it:

> [...] a certain Territorie of woody ground & fruitful pastures, privileged for wild beasts and foules of, Forest, Chase, and Warren, to rest and abide in, in the safe protection of the King for his princely delight and pleasure [...].

Something of a Recapitulation – The Dangerous Forest

And so it is that we may understand that the forest of larger (European) legend and of much of its folklore is a place often strange and eerie, a realm of Nature untamed by man, and one full of unearthly and potentially dangerous beings. The uncanny quality of all such woods is a significant part of the (residual) folklore of Europe, much as it was – much later – for the early white settlers in North America, or as it would be for the British schoolboys wrecked on a lonely island at some time in the mid-twentieth century, in William Golding's sobering fable[40] – not one of the terror of the forest, but of the murderous inner self that will out, if the constraints of 'civilization' should be suddenly removed.

It was seen to be – and long remained in the folk imagination – as a zone co-terminous with the world outside of the safety of the family and home – one of lawlessness, danger, malign foxes, ogres, witches and the like, although it could also always be a place of (perhaps last) refuge.[41]

In this discussed (ancient, and largely Dark Age and mediaeval) association, the forest could well be linked with the cluster of senses represented by:

Warg – Wearg – Earg – Werewolf.

This shorthand etymological (and probably closely linked) cluster from Old English indicates effectively the Western European – and largely – Germanic interlinked associations, namely, those of

Werewolf – Outlaw – Cursed Man – Coward.

While originally ancient/very early continental, this cluster provides many classic – and wood-related – motifs for Old Norse and Old Icelandic literature,[42] as well as for their derivatives, such as Tolkien's Middle-earth. Even older associations

---

40 *The Lord of the Flies* (1954), a text seemingly set during World War II, in which these boys have been evacuated from their bomb-threatened homes in England.

41 See J.S. Ryan, 'The Wild Wood – Place of Danger, Place of Protest', *Orana* 19.3 (1983b: 133-40), and its revised form included in this present volume.

42 See (1) J.S. Ryan, 'Warg, Wearg, Earg and Werewolf' in *Mallorn* 23 (1986c: 25-29), and, especially, (2) relevant parts on these themes in Inger M. Boberg, *Motif-Index of early Icelandic Literature* (1966).

of the Western European forests are to be found in odd recorded vestiges of
the Cult of Mithras in the Druidic religion of Britain.[43]

In Northern Europe, the tree-god cult of Othin and the various sacrifices of
men and animals by nines on the trees[44] of the sacred groves are yet other examples of an extension of the ancient tree worship. Something of the paralyzing
Roman fear of the great forests of Germany is recorded by Tacitus – as in his
famous remarks about the Hercynian forest in the *Germania* (chapters 30-31),
or in the even more menacing account of the forests associated with the Roman
commander, Varus, and the disaster always linked with his name (*Annals I*).

In the general 'Arthurian legend' of all periods, the forest was often the scene of
enchantment, of wonders and of testing encounters with beings of supernatural
power. Thus, – and again in *Sir Gawain and the Green Knight* – the hero would
meet in the Wilderness of the Wirral dragons, wolves, *woodwoses* (wild men of
the woods), bulls, bears, boars and ogres on the high fells. Yet other cycles of
romance would present the wild woods as:

> the testing place of the Grail Quest for spiritual perfection;
>
> the home of the Wild Hunt, originally Germanic, but, later, as in *Sir Orfeo*,
> associated with the courtly King of Fairyland;
>
> the place of retreat for Merlin;

as observed above

> the home of such outlaws as Robin Hood;[45] and

---

43 See the discussion of Tolkien's contribution to the Lydney excavation of a fourth century site in
   Gloucestershire, as discussed in Part B of this present volume.

44 Here we are dealing with the two Norse concepts, as meaning a deity, and as with the sense of a
   vertical beam of timber. These are linked in the *Hávamál*, as is discussed by me on p. 252 of my
   earlier essay collection, *Tolkien's View* (2009).
   The finest scholar of this notion in Oxford was Tolkien's most talented student, and real successor
   in the teaching of Old Norse, Professor E.O.G. Turville-Petre in his books, *Myth and Religion of the
   North: The Religion of Ancient Scandinavia* (1964) and his *Nine Norse Studies* (1972).

45 Fine scholarship of outlaws continues, as in

   a) Ohlgren, Thomas H. (ed.), 1998, *Medieval Outlaws: Ten Tales in Modern English*,
      Stroud: Sutton Publishing; and

   b) Seal, Graham, 2011, *Outlaw Heroes in Myth and History*, London, New York: Anthem
      Press.

   In the last work, Robin Hood is luminously discussed in Part Four: 'The Global Outlaw', pp. 165ff.

also for highwaymen – and even, in the Victorian period, for Oxford 'clerks' and tutors on cheerful wanderings, study and walking tours.[46]

And the Word 'Narrow'

The third strand in our title – 'narrow' – has been included now for several reasons, not the least of which is to dispel the seemingly bland contemporary sense of width to this word, one which is so often applied to 'the path'. While the word occurs in Old English, (*nearu, nearw-*), its Middle Dutch cognate, *nare*, has the sense 'unpleasant, dismal, sad, distressed, etc., and the *Oxford English Dictionary* has pointed out that it was 'of doubtful etymology'. One wonders exactly what associations were in Tolkien's mind when he presented us with his version of the dwarves and Bilbo entering Mirkwood:

> The entrance to the path was like a sort of arch leading into a gloomy tunnel [...]. The path itself was *narrow* [my emphasis] and wound in and out among the trunks. Soon the light at the gate[47] was like a little bright hole far behind [...]. (*Hobbit* 151)

And so Tolkien would add a further piece of (English) lore and literature in this *Sir Orfeo*-like reference with

> [...] they became aware of the dim blowing of horns in the wood and the sound as of dogs baying [...] it seemed they could hear the noise of a great hunt going by to the north of the path, though they saw no sign of it. (*ibid*. 156-57)

*   *   *

---

46 Tolkien was long famous in Oxford for his enthusiasm for participating in these weekend recreational activities between the two world wars, and something of this sort of walking for pleasure is the framework of the initial parts of the plot of C.S. Lewis's partly Oxford-region set fantasy, *That Hideous Strength* (1945).
One also recalls here the – surely author-revealing – comment on Bilbo:

> He loved maps, and in his hall there hung a large one of the Country Round with all his favourite walks marked on it in red ink. (*Hobbit* 30-31)

And Merton College in the 1950s was still practicing a form of this peripatetic learning in the reading weeks/spring vacation tutorial class retreats in the Vacation before the Degree Final Honours' Schools Examinations, these last always held in the English high summer.

47 We may be reasonably sure that he savoured the ambiguous sense of this word, especially after his post-war years in Yorkshire, where the word always has the primary sense of 'road' or 'way', often in the metaphorical sense.

However, more recent etymologists associate this same word, 'narrow', with the Indo-European intensive prefix in *S-*, thus linking our word with German *Schnur*, 'a cord'; Danish *snor*, 'a cord', and Avetsic *snavare*, 'a cord'. Thus, there is established a (likely) word cluster or collocation including Modern English *snare* (noun and verb), with its menacing and lethal sense of entrapment. When one recalls German *Narbe*, 'a scar' (lit. 'the drawing together of a wound'), or Lithuanian *narys*, 'a loop', it is clear that the original word-field contains such senses as 'unpleasant/trap/loop' [48] – several of which would seem to be found in folktales where the word is used frequently. As is pointed out by most dictionaries, the adjective 'straight' ('not bent') and the now archaic adjective *strait* ('tight, narrow'; 'strict'; 'limited in extent') have been confused in form and sense from an early date. Thus they contribute further to the rich philosophical and theological nuances of the seemingly artless account of adventure.

Note that the three commonest near-compounds in Old English are: *nearo-cræft*; *nearo-fāh*; and *nearo-thearf*, which are given the following first meanings in Bosworth and Toller's *An Anglo-Saxon Dictionary* (1898: 712-13):

'an art that imprisons';
'disastrously hostile'; and
'direly pressing need'.

These and many other compounds now lost enforce the meaning of the un-compounded noun *nearu*, there glossed as

1) confinement, durance, prison; and
2) 'a strait, a difficulty' [i.e. of a dangerously narrow boat passage].

Thus, there can be little doubt that *narrow* – both the noun and adjective – had possessed several pejorative senses in Old English, all of which would seem to have lingered long in the telling of old tales.

And so we may compare with the above this comment from *The Hobbit*:

They were high up in a narrow place, with a dreadful fall into a dim valley at one side of them. (69)

---

48 Compare the more menacing senses still retained and implied in the description of a dangerously 'tight' water-passage for vessels in entrance or exit, as in through 'the narrows/Narrows'.

Thus, we may postulate that 'wood', 'path', 'narrow', – and 'gate' are all key clues to the pattern of Tolkien's thoughts , one of 'a deep significance' [49] and that they have articulated so early in Tolkien's writing career, that of the heroic quest for all humanity, and so the (seemingly artless) chronicling of the struggle between good and evil forces for the possession of (a magic ring) of total power.

Now, a Form of Summary Perspective

This explorative essay is to be seen as one concerned to chart some aspects of a hugely significant trope in all older Germanic literature, that of a journey into the unknown in order to face the enemies of one's people, and of one's own life's purpose and meaning – even as it is also a seminal theme in the creative writings of J.R.R. Tolkien, with its underpinning significance for all who have or will dwell on Middle-earth. This is a very mind-grasping image, that of the dark and frightening forest to the east, and of the difficulty of any person finding 'a path' whereby one may enter its further zones – and so experience the dangers, magic and other challenging testings to one's selfhood that may well lurk there.[50]

It is also clear that the older and more ethereal beings, the elves of the woods, had left behind their earlier unfallen influence, so that "it seemed that some good magic lingered" (*ibid.* 176) and we, as reader-members of this Company, may also reach such spots, as those where "the Wood-Elves lingered in the twilight before the raising of the Sun and Moon" (*ibid.* 178).[51] Yet we readers must all pass on, to the water-gate, and beyond Lake-town, and to try to understand the wretchedly confused affairs of men before we must needs join the climactic and death-dealing Battle of the Five Armies – even as we must take sides in life's great battles.

---

49 This was the phrase that he had used of the heroic Old English epic poem, as early as 1937 in his famed *Beowulf* lecture, later published as '*Beowulf*: The Monsters and the Critics' (see 2006).
50 Compare the sentiment expressed early on in *The Hobbit*,

> There is nothing like looking, if you want to find something [...]. You certainly usually find something, if you look, but it is not always quite the something you were after. (69)

51 This was later changed to "the Wood-elves lingered in the twilight of our Sun and Moon" in the 1966-edition (178).

Further, we may make a close analysis of this formative story-construct – and indeed of this key to almost all of Tolkien's creative writing and its metaphysics – by our close examination of this text in the second (British) edition[52] of *The Hobbit*. Thus innumerable insights may be obtained by us readers from his scholarly and insightful authorial semantics and carefully conveyed spiritual nuances as to the purpose of our journeying, and the eschatological meaning of the decisions that we make during it.

In brief, by the middle of the twentieth century, Tolkien had already utilised and marshalled to his purpose oral literature, custom, and lore from across the older cultures of Western Europe, as well as imprinting in our perceptions such character types as the unlikely hero, Bilbo, his hugely satisfying folkloric antagonist, Smaug, and the mindlessly brutal goblins. In fact, his initial story is almost a richly textured, allusive and extended Germanic heroic lay, the precursor to the great prose epic conflict of the hobbits and other orders of rationality against total power. And then there would follow, as well as the innumerable (partly) crafted episodes in the corpus, – and in a style not unlike the mass of Homeric fragments – the heroically conceived and necessarily incomplete and still fragmentary history of Middle-earth.

Indeed, by his seemingly quirkish and insignificant protagonist having understood his mission, and so realising the inevitable need to destroy a magical and talismanic object, the One Ring of power, the mass of further ramified story becomes an ever more powerful allegory of the development of his reader as a simple and trusting Western Man, who progressively discovered and confronted the menaces unleashed in his society. Initially, the reader starts in some sort of exciting Victorian adventure, then the tone changes subtly to a confident Edwardian style of swagger to end in the tenseness, anarchy and despair that came to the author's England with the horrors of the Somme, reaching beyond the present to the deeply distressing mortal future of all mankind.

---

52 It is this text of 1951 which has the revisions necessitated by the changes in the symbolism, etc., which Tolkien made to equate with certain alterations made to the matter of the power of the One Ring over Frodo in his then as-yet-to be published epic, *The Lord of the Rings*.

The Tale of the Common Man from 'the Shires'

Clearly, Tolkien's handling of his protagonist hobbit is one of the world's great treatments and conceptions of the common man as hero, whether one considers Frodo or Sam to be the key figure – and embedded as he is in a symbolically interpreted and structurally derived pattern from the needful life and actions of so many earlier European representative figures. Separation, trials and misfortunes, and a return after adventure; all these perdurable patterns are here. However, this (Frodo-type wounded) hero[53] will not be able to enjoy his triumph in Middle-earth, and so he must pass beyond the seas and to the West.

Quite simply, this individual life's journeying on behalf of others was – and remains – the best known and so the most effective epic treatment of the nature of humanity and of Christian eschatology produced in the twentieth century. Whether we choose to follow the suggestion of the influence of Chesterton on the shape of this created universe[54] or not, it is very clear that Tolkien was far ahead of his generation in his view that the ancient forest-world, as given to mortals was both a testing and a utopian one, and its destruction by men and war an act of the utmost evil, whether or no we may choose to follow the Jungian aspects of these images.

Quite certainly, too, the ancient European notions of the spiritual significance of the forest[55] and of its groves are evoked so powerfully in *The Hobbit* and then in the celebrated prose epic, that Tolkien's neo-mediaeval and fable-like forests have become the century's great metaphor for the way in which mankind chooses to treat the world in which he has been placed. And in the process – whether

---

53 Some have likened the later scarified Frodo to the young Mertonian Group Captain, Geoffrey Leonard Cheshire of the R.A.F.'s Pathfinders and of his terrible spiritual hurt after being the official British observer of the nuclear bombing of Nagasaki in 1945.

54 See, for example, L.A. Zetler's powerful study, 'Chesterton and the Man in the Forest', *Chesterton Review* 1 (1974: 11-18).

55 Compare H.M. Chadwick's *The Cult of Othin* (1899), and the work of Tolkien's most illustrious Norse scholar and successor in this teaching, E.O.G. Turville-Petre, as in his similar but more clearly 'Catholic' and reflective writings on the ancient Germanic cosmology, particularly in his *Myth and Religion of the North: The Religion of Ancient Scandinavia* (1964). Interestingly – and with reference to the discussion of 'path' above – Professor Turville-Petre was long a colleague of A.S.C. Ross, the two of them associated, as in the record thereof, at the first Viking Congress, held in Lerwick, Scotland, in 1950 (see also the picture of its participants on the website of the Viking Congress – www.vikingcongress.com/pages/earlier-viking-congresses/1950).

hobbit or man – he reveals his understanding of the meaning of human life, or he fails the great test that has been put upon all men and women.

*   *   *

By grounding this core moral and eschatological text in the surrounding forest and oral traditions of Western Europe, and especially of the richly storied heritage of the English race, Tolkien had brilliantly bridged the literary worlds of both the half-remembered and the invented, of the more obviously Christian and of the nobly selfless and altruisic choices he deemed must be confronted by every mortal.

Not a Conclusion

This task of reflection on certain recurring concepts and of their teasing out and cultural interpretation has, off necessity, been attempted in somewhat brief compass, in order to underscore the more the focus and enormous significance of certain words and turns of Tolkienian phrase, particularly in *The Hobbit*. And this has been done both in their contexts, and as they are to be seen and interpreted in the light of the greater comparative philology and religious understanding that was the core of Tolkien's being. It is the most indicative key to all of Tolkien's writings as it is to the meaning and metaphysics of one person's life patterns, experiences and earthly, mortal choices.

For the grand theme of the most finished and symbolic of Tolkien's writings is the nature and (spiritual) meaning of conscience and of the response to the temptations of power. Sauron, the Nine, Saruman and Gollum were, alike, all shown to be unable to draw from the material universe the joy, the perception of which is the sign of a healthy spirit. Unlike Frodo, they had refused to give themselves to others, had become a law unto themselves, and in their hatred of the world of values, had eternalised their final choice. For this is the great drama as conceptualised by Tolkien and played out here in Middle-earth, along its 'paths', and as we, his readers and fellow-questers, endeavour to pass through its strangely beautiful 'woods'.

But to Return to *The Hobbit* after Approaching the Great Epic

It may well be contended that much of this so focussed corpus of Tolkien's writings is also an ethnology of: the progressing world of Europe both in the twentieth century and, earlier; the patterns and failures of Mediaeval Christendom; even as it is also the most heroic presentation of service, selflessness, adventure and personal growth in a quiet and modest member of the folk. For the core of the whole yet ever developing artistic creation of Middle-earth and, perforce, of its world view, is the notion, and finally the chosen practice of service to others and of pity, as is shown in a simple action by the wise king who, previously hesitant, had responded to the compassionate prayers of Bard, "for he was the lord of a good and kindly people" (*Hobbit* 265).

The Wood and the Path – for all Mortals

Never just a 'Georgian who survived World War I', it is Tolkien who has been the most profound twentieth-century explorer of mankind's 'path' and the most imaginative artist expounding it. For, himself by Divine Grace a survivor of Europe's Armageddon, the horror of the Somme, he would spend an enormous proportion of his further allotted life endeavouring to illustrate in the vast 'matter' of Middle-earth, in his sprawling and incomplete yet over-arching story what he deemed to be the proper course, the 'path' of humility and of sacrifice for all mankind in this fleeting sublunary setting.

Appendix One – Goblin Feet

I am off down the road
Where the fairy lanterns glowed
And the little pretty flittermice are flying:
A slender band of grey
It runs creepily away
And the hedges and the grasses are a-sighing.
The air is full of wings,

And of blundering beetle-things
That warn you with their whirring and their humming.
  O! I hear the tiny horns
  Of enchanted leprechauns
And the padding feet of many gnomes a-coming!

O! the lights: O! the gleams: O! the little tinkly sounds:
  O! the rustle of their noiseless little robes:
O! the echo of their feet – of their little happy feet:
  O! their swinging lamps in little starlit globes.

  I must follow in their train
  Down the crooked fairy lane
Where the coney-rabbits long ago have gone,
  And where silverly they sing
  In a moving moonlit ring
All a-twinkle with the jewels they have on.
  They are fading round the turn
  Where the glow-worms palely burn
And the echo of their padding feet is dying!
  O! it's knocking at my heart –
  Let me go! O! let me start!
For the little magic hours are all a–flying.

O! the warmth! O! the hum! O! the colours in the dark!
  O! the gauzy wings of golden honey-flies!
O! the music of their feet! – of their dancing goblin feet!
  O! the magic! O! the sorrow when it dies.

This poem is reprinted now from *Oxford Poetry* for 1915, as published by B.H. Blackwell in that same year. This item, pp. 64-65, is stated there to be 'from J.R.R. Tolkien of Exeter College', and it occurs after a Lay, 'Orford and Iseult', by D. Sayers, 'of Somerville College', pp. 50-58.

Appendix Two

Richard E. Blackwelder had collected up so many of the passages cited above in his *A Tolkien Thesaurus* (1990). Readers are referred to his sequential lists derived from the epic.

The following is a sequential selection from p. 173 of this work:

And take the hidden paths that run / Towards the Moon or (v) F.87/115

I wonder who made this path, and what for, said Merry F.197/249

Guided by Aragorn they struck a good path ... an ancient road F.299/374

He will not go astray – if there is any path to find. F.324/405

Maybe the paths that you each shall tread are already laid F.384/477

when I / shall take the hidden paths that run (v) R.308/381

The wood/woods references (on p. 273) are less dramatic, but to be noted are:

it was indeed ancient, a survivor of vast forgotten woods F.141/181

there was all one wood ... from here to the Mountains of Lune T.72/90

and Wild Men can go back to sleep in the wild woods R.107/130

look for Bilbo in the woods of the Shire. I shall be with him. R.267/330

Part A

The Ancient Middle East and its Associations

Indo-European Race-Memories and Race-Fears from the Ancient City of Uruk ... and so to Tolkien as the quietly Speculative Philologist

> The discoveries of Seton Lloyd and Fuad Safar have [...] traced the beginnings of Sumerian civilization back to the middle of the sixth millenium B.C. In the alluvial plain of ancient Sumer. (Mellaart 1970: 289)

> [...] many Sumerologists [...] are deterred from working on the literature and the ideas behind it [...]. After a spate of publication on the Epic of Gilgamesh in the 1920s and 1930s, little has been done [...]. (Kirk 1970: 84-85)

> Mythology is founded upon words, and the history of words, therefore, must explain it. (Sayce 1892: 303).

> [...] long ago as those times are now reckoned in years and lives of men, they were not very remote according to the memory of the Earth. [...] It is often difficult to discover from old [...] traditions precise information about things which people knew well and took for granted in their own day [...]. (*RotK* 385).

Preamble, and so, first to the City of *Uruk*

It is the contention of this reflective survey essay that a considerable cluster of monster, or demonic names – and thus of associated or derived words – owe, or are reasonably thought to owe, their seemingly distinct forms and later semantics to the name *Uruk*, that of the largest of the ancient Sumerian cities. It

This essay was first printed in the Norwegian journal *Angerthas* 22 (1988: 27-46), and is now largely reproduced with the permission of its then editors, and also expanded with some of the closer details of the earlier and related long note, 'Cultural Name Association: A Tolkienian Example from Gilgamesh', which had appeared in *Mallorn* 22 (1985: 21-23). Some thoughts on Saruman are found expanded further upon later in this collection, in essay 3.

was once much larger than *Ur, Eridu, Larsa, Nippur* or *Kish*, larger even than the older city of *Babylon*. *Uruk* was – and is – situated almost equidistant from the frontiers of Persia, Anatolia, Syria and Palestine, from the shores of the Black Sea and the Caspian, and so it might well be said to have been the hub of the ancient East. Once on the right or western bank of a branch of the Euphrates, the city shrank in size, until at last it came to its end after the destruction of the Parthian Kingdom there by the Sasanids in the 3rd century A.D.

Our first evidence of permanent settlements, dependent on agriculture and herding, goes back to the 8th millenium B.C. in the northern Mesopotamian hills, then to be followed by the extension of agriculture into the northern plains before 6000 B.C., and then again to the agricultural settlements in the south, the first of which, about 5000 B.C., occured at the site of Eridu, one of the holy cities of later Sumer. In the 5th and 4th millenia successive cultures, named after such sites as *Ur* and *Uruk*, mark stages in the Sumerian development of urban life and in the increasing influences in other regions of the Near East. Thus, direct contacts in the Uruk period extended out to Egypt and to the Iranian plateau. In the city itself monumental temples of unbaked brick accomodated the households of the gods and also the centres of religious and secular administration.[1] About 3500 B.C., there was invented pictographic writing, later formalized into a syllabic 'cuneiform' script in which the first literary and historical texts were written in the early 3rd millenium. Although the language of these documents was Sumerian, some of the personal names in it reveal the existence of a Semitic-speaking element in the population.

At the end of this Early Dynastic period the hegemony was traditionally associated with Kish in the northern alluvium, and about 2360 B.C., a Semitic court-official there usurped the throne, founded a new capital Agade nearby, took the name of Sargon[2] (the 'True King') and established the first Mesopotamian or Akkadian Empire. In Akkadian and Babylonian script the name 'Uruk' took the form 'Erech'.

---

1 A model to be associated with it is to be found in Tolkien's *The Lord of the Rings* in Barad-dûr, the ancient fortress of Sauron's might, crouched upon a great south-pointing inner spur of the Ash Mountains, with its "towers and battlements, tall as hills, founded upon a mighty mountain-throne" (*RotK* 224).
2 This is the probable cultural analogue of Tolkien's fictive Sauron, to whom all evil gravitated and who, from a fair beginning, then became 'The Dark Lord', the most terrible ruler in Middle-earth.

Some flavour of the might and power of Uruk is to be obtained from the poem named for Gilgamesh, the great hero of Sumerian and Babylonian mythology, who – potentially, at least – was the wisest, strongest, and most handsome of mortals – for he was two-thirds god and one third man – and had himself, as their king, built a monumental wall around the city, but, in so doing, had worked the inhabitants unmercifully, to the point where they prayed to the gods for relief. The text in which these events are narrated is an epic,[3] written down on a series of twelve clay tablets inscribed in the cuneiform script used by the Sumerians, the Babylonians and the people of Assyria. The fullest version that has come down to us was originally held in the great palace library of the King of Assyria, Ashurbanipal, who made a great collection of ancient texts in the years 660-630 B.C. Modern scholarship[4] postulates a much older Babylonian text on these matters, and one composed before 1800 B.C. However, the epic itself enables us to envisage a real king, Gilgamesh, as well as a world famous historical event, the Sumerian Deluge, the race memory of which has been preserved in the *Book of Genesis*.[5]

From the surviving poem we learn that the people prayed to the gods for a champion who would contend on their behalf against the oppressor within their city. The champion elected to liberate Erech was a hairy hunter named Enkidu, a Sumerian wild man who lived with wild animals – compare Tolkien's various passing references to and on 'wild men' – and who always protected them. In a later part of the story the high god, Anu, sent down from heaven an avenging bull to trample on the city,[6] but Enkidu killed it, spurning the gods' will and thereby sealing his own doom. Yet that act of slaughter had seemed justified, for the bull had then already slain some five hundred brave warriors of the city in but two terrible snorts.

---

3 Well-known and accesible translations are:

   a) *Gilgamesh: Epic of Old Babylonia*, by William Ellery Leonard (1934); and

   b) *The Epic of Gilgamesh*, transl. N.K. Sandars (1960).

4 See also W.G. Lambert and A.R. Millard, *Atra-Hasīs: The Babylonian Story of the Flood* (1969).

5 It may be argued that Tolkien's fictional and vaguely remembered pre-historic 'Wrack of Numenor' is an analogue of this.

6 This form of revenge and destruction is certainly – in some measure – analogous to the Ents and their deliberate destruction of Isengard as presented in the text of *The Lord of the Rings*.

While some may wonder whether Tolkien would have been familiar with the Sumerian epic, this is relatively easy to corroborate. All the twentieth century (Oxford) students of classical and Western European epic[7] have been much interested in the *Epic of Gilgamesh* and have compared or been expected to compare it with other ancient heroic poems. And there are also many articles on the poem in the (then) standard background work, the *Encyclopædia of Religion and Ethics*[8] (James Hastings (chief editor), 1908-26). It is, similarly, referred to several times in the following works by Tolkien's friends and epic theorist colleagues, namely W.F. Jackson Knight's *Roman Vergil* (1944),[9] Gilbert Highet's *The Classical Tradition* (1949), or in C.M. Bowra's magnificent *Heroic Poetry* (1952). The last volume by the then Master of Wadham College has several dozen references to the epic, and a number specifically to Erech and to its people.[10]

It is postulated now that the various more mobile (tribal) peoples, soon to progressively move west to occupy Europe, had noted this great city[11] so different from any shelter used in their still nomadic cultures. The highly significant and far scattering of these Indo-European peoples is variously dated between 3000 and 4000 years B.C. One of the earliest groups, the Hittites, made its home in Asia Minor, while the westward movement rapidly split the migrant peoples into different groups, each following its destiny wherever it would lead them into history, into differing language blocs, and, ultimately, into written and surviving records. Meantime, it is contended, the (fragmented) race-memory

---

7   See the references to "Sumerian precursors of Akkadian epic" and H.W.F. Saggs, in Hatto (1980b: IX-X).

8. The title is abbreviated to *E.R.E.* henceforth.

9   Knight's notion of 'epic structure' was a matter referred to from time to time by Tolkien in the seminar situation.

10 E.g., pp. 126, 185, 295, 339, 383, 510, 516, 560.

11 The *Mallorn*-editor of that publication time (1985: 23), Jenny Curtis, had then referred her readers to the following quotation in Daniel (1975: 200-01):

> It was in 1926 that the great pre-historic cemetery at Ur [see note 12 below], with its 'Royal Tombs' was excavated. The discovery of these tombs, with their splendid treasures [...] caused a sensation comparable only with [...] discoveries at Mycenae and those of [...] Tutankhamen's tomb. The [...] expedition [under Leonard Woolley] not only inaugurated the brilliant revival of excavation in Mesopotamia that took place in the twenties and early thirties; it was also responsible for widespread popular interest in Mesopotamian origins [...].

and then she had asked the question whether Tolkien could possibly have been unaware of at least part of the history/archaelogy/mythology of this area.

had reflected long on Uruk,[12] now far behind in the east, and on its walls, its culture, and on the religion which had caused its such stupendous temples to be erected.

Further, the site of Erech had been investigated by W.K. Loftus in the mid-Victorian period, and his experiences and thoughts are chronicled in his most popular proto-history, *Travels and Researches in Chaldaea and Susiana* (1857). Similarly there had been a series of meticulous excavations by German expeditions in 1912, 1928-39 and 1954-60. The results of all this field work are of outstanding importance for the early history of Mesopotamia, since the ancient clay tablets excavated there date from the fourth millenium B.C.

Of course, the final subtlety in the Tolkienian name comes from the form used. While the city was later occupied by the Greeks who called it *Orchoē*[13] and its Sumerian name was *Unu(g)*, it was known to the Akkadians as *Uruk*. The Akkadian language is often assigned to the eastern Semitic tongues, in contrast to Hebrew, Phoenician, Ugaritic, Arabic and Ethiopic in the western Semitic group. Whether Tolkien was curious about the ancient language – names and loan words from which appear in Sumerian – perhaps, even from the time of his early studies in comparative philology, there is no doubt that he would have been long familiar with its importance in the history of writing.[14]

And so Uruk does not seem to be an accidental name creation by Tolkien. Of course, there are further layers of association here, in that we have a parallel to – if not actual speculation about – the nature of the Sumerian warriors in Tolkien's highly militant orc group, much as the name Púkel-men may well be a pondering as to how the Celtic peoples and their cultural remains might have seemed to the Germanic peoples who supplanted them. Further, since Erech is mentioned in the Table of Nations (*Genesis* 10:10), it may be held that it is intended that the reflective reader of Tolkien should make a loose associa-

---

12 Uruk/Erech is represented today by the group of mounds known to the Arabs as *Warka*, a place which lies in Southern Babylonia, some 64 km NW of Ur and 6 km E of the present course of the Euphrates.

13 Clearly this name gives a further etymological association for *orc*, apart from OE *orc* and Latin *Orcus* (see Ryan 1966: 52-53, as also reprinted in Ryan 2009: 206). A similar etymology is given by T.A. Shippey (1982: 50, note). That etymology was corroborated by Tolkien himself (1975a: 171).

14 See R. Labat (1948). A more recent and accessible guide is Diringer (1962).

tion between Nimrod and Sauron. Nimrod is described in *Genesis* (10:8-12) as "the first on earth to be a mighty man. He was a mighty hunter before the Lord." According to some traditions[15] he was also the builder of the Tower of Babel, thus giving a further analogue to Sauron's defiant and obscene creation of Mordor.

Later Words of Fear

The names, toponyms and nouns derived from this original form Uruk, and with varying semantic extensions, may be held to include most or all of:

Uruk, Erech, Orchoë;

modern Arabic *Wark*;

Latin *Orcus, Orcades*, etc.;

Modern English *Ogre, Ogreish*;

(Old) French *Ogre, Ogresse, Ogre* (a Hungarian);

Byzantine Greek *Ogör*;

Old Spanish *huerco* (a devil, hell);

Hungarian *Ogur* (a Hungarian);

early Russian *Ugri* (pl.); cp. Medieval Latin (of Germany) *Ungarus* (i.e. Hungarian);

Italian *Orco* (demon, monster), and **Ogro*, Orgo* (dialectal variants);

Spanish *huerco, (h)uergo*.

Compare, too: Edmund Spenser's *Orgoglio* (cp. French *orgueil*, pride), from Italian *orco* and *orgoglio* (cp. Portug. *orguelhos, orgoillos*, Span. *orgulloso*); and J.R.R. Tolkien's *orc, Uruk(-hai), Erech*, etc; or –

the monstrous sense for *ogre*, first found in and perhaps invented by Charles Perrault in his *Contes* (1697) (it had already occured in Old French in the sense of 'pagan', originally 'Hungarian').

Until very recent times, it was not customary to speculate about possible links between these and other similar clusters of words and, apparently, various and simple proper names. Thus, even the scholarly compilation, *The Oxford*

---

15 Note the concluding remark by the former Manchester University scholar, W.L. Wardle, in his article on Nimrod: "In character there is a certain resemblance between Nimrod and the hero Gilgamesh." (*Encyclopædia Britannica* 1968b: 526c)

Dictionary of English Etymology, as edited by C.T. Onions, gives no more for *ogre* than:

> man-eating monster of popular story. [...] XVIII[th century] (*hogre*). – F[rench] *ogre* (Perrault's 'Contes', 1697); of unkn[own] origin; conjectured to have been based on a dial[ectal] var[iant] **ogro, *orgo* of It[alian] *orco* demon, monster = Sp[anish] *huerco, (h)uergo* – L[atin] *Orcus,* infernal deity [...]. (Onions 1966: 625)

This was in spite of the more imaginative if speculative etymology – and phonetically and philologically sound further supporting details – as provided in 1958 by Eric Partridge in his *Origins: A Short Etymological Dictionary of Modern English* (450). Although his ideas will be treated below at greater length, it may be noted that Byzantine Greek *Ogor* was linked with O. French *Ogre* and that the Greek form was held to have been borrowed into Hungarian, Russian and the Medieval Latin of Germany. In this last loan clustering, Partridge was following O. Bloch and W. von Wartburg, in their *Dictionnaire étymologique de la langue française* (1950).

A Similar Race Hatred

As in other linguistic puzzles of ethnic semantics – e.g. the disputed origin of *shark* – which J.R.R. Tolkien, by his gloss on his fictional character Saruman's nickname 'Sharkey' as being from Orkish, *sharkû,* 'old man' (*RotK* 365), enables the reader to link Saruman with either Arabic *sharqi,* 'eastern', *sharq,* 'east, rising sun', or with Arabic *sayk shaik* 'old man' – it is again possible to go beyond the more formal caution of Onions (1966: 817). Thus, Professor Ernest Weekley in his *An Etymological Dictionary of Modern English* (1921: 1328-29) had dared to speculate and thereby reflected on various early Dutch, Spanish and Florentine examples of **shark-* before its first recorded English use by John Hawkins in 1569, and postulating that the earlier sense was, indeed, a "greedy parasite", arguing that

> the word comes, perh. via Du[tch], from Ger[man] *schurk(e),* "a shark, sharper, rook, rake, rogue" [...], whence also *shirk* (q.v.), It[alian] *scrocco,* as in *mangiare a scrocco,* "to feede scotfree at another mans charge [...]". (1328)

and then adding:

This word may easily have been current among seamen before being recorded, and the quots. [of the word as an intransitive verb] suggest a naut[ical] nickname rather than a foreign word. (*ibid.*)

Since this was the major etymological dictionary for English published during Tolkien's earlier academic career, it is difficult to reject this last remark as being unlikely to be known to him. Thus we have the suggestion of a nickname for a ruthless predator of persons, one having a nautical background and as being current by c. 1600 amongst sailors off Sierra Leone, in the Lowlands, and also in the Mediterranean.

At this point, we must turn to another noun of more obvious Eastern origin, namely *Saracen*, the "name of nomadic peoples of the Syro-Arabic desert" (Onions 1966: 788). Following through the same dictionaries, we find for it:

Arab, Moslem; +pagan, infidel. XIII. – O[ld] F[rench] *Sar(r)azin, -cin* (mod. *Sarrasin*), corr. to Sp[anish] *Saraceno*, It[alian] *Saracino* – late L[atin] *Saracēnus* – late Gr[eek] *Sarakēnós*, perh. f. Arab. *sharqī* eastern, f. *sharq* sunrise, east (cf. SIROCCO). The name was in mediaeval times assoc. with Sarah, the wife of Abraham, or with the Hagarens, descendants of Hagar, Cf. SARSEN. (*ibid.*);

Lat. *saracenus*, a Saracen; lit. 'one of the eastern people.'; Arab. *sharqíy*, oriental, eastern; sunny [...] Cf. Arab. *sharq*, the east, the rising sun; id. From Arab. root *sharaqa*, it rose (Skeat 1882: 525)

Finally it may be appropriate to recall that *sheikh*, the title of address to an Arab leader is from Arabic *shaikh*, literally 'an old man', from *shakha*, 'to grow old'.

Tolkien's use of the name Saruman and of its colloquial form 'Sharkey', for a greedy Eastern leader who amassed great wealth and wrought brilliantly in metals and stone, reminds us of the figure Suruman, who is discussed in the 'Annals of Sargon', translated by Dr. Julius Oppert in the seventh, Assyrian volume of the original series of *Records of the Past: being English Translations of the Assyrian and Egyptian Monuments* (1876).[16] That vassal to the great king of Assyria had had to be subjugated when he challenged his lord.

---

16 These volumes were issued by the Society of Biblical Archaeology, of which the Oxford Professor of Comparative Philology, A.H. Sayce, was president. Sayce taught in Oxford until 1919 and Tolkien's studies (1911-1915; 1919-20) included papers on that subject, at a time when the basic guide was the much older man's *Principles of Comparative Philology* (1874). Tolkien's own books indicate familiarity with this seminal text, and with many other significant works of his mentor on the early cultures of the ancient Near East.

Thus, to continue this lexical analysis to a plausible conclusion, it may now be postulated:

> 1) that Modern English *shark* (of uncertain origin) seems to have been in English firstly a noun, of marine usage with the sense of 'prowler, predator'; and to have been widely used in the Mediterranean, possibly of Moorish or Levantine pirates;
>
> 2) that its original sense when adopted into Italian may well have been 'from the east', and so related to the other Italian borrowing, *sirocco* or *scirocco*, 'a hot desert wind', from Arabic *sharq*, 'east', from *sharaga* 'to rise' (of the sun);
>
> 3) that the related word *Saracen*, an English borrowing in the 13th century from Arabic, via French, is perhaps from Arabic *sharqi*, 'eastern', *sharq*, 'sunrise, east'; and
>
> 4) one may postulate a possible English Crusader colloquialism, **sharkey*, meaning 'the (old) Arab'.

It is also likely that the sense 'ruthless old man' was current at a vernacular level for centuries before its modern (British) use as a nickname for males with the surname Ward.[17]

Thus, as it will be suggested for the cluster derived from Uruk, the original neutral and descriptive sense, 'eastern', 'Arab', may well have deterriorated progressively in its semantics as may be found in the European languages, after its initial Mediterranean use as 'Easterner'[18] or 'old man', to come to mean 'voracious predator', the sense of the root in many Western European languages from c. 1550. The philologist Tolkien, by a novel footnote in one of his 'fictional' works, has given the clue to his own serious contribution to a considerable problem or 'gap' in both etymology and semantics.

Tolkien's Orcs

In his great prose epic, J.R.R. Tolkien 'created' a race, the orcs, which is described thus by J.E.A. Tyler in *The Tolkien Companion:*

---

17 See Leslie Dunkling, *The Guinness Book of Names* (1983: 99), where the association is linked with "a pirate so named". A 'Sharkey' pirate also appeared in a macabre story by A. Conan Doyle, 'The Blighting of Sharkey'.

18 Compare Ernest Weekley in his *An Etymological Dictionary of Modern English*, where in discussing the word 'Saracen' (1921: 1277), he observes that it, like 'Anatolia', originally meant merely, 'easterner'.

many of the denizens of age-old epic tales are similarly dismissed because our memory of them has become confused, and the feelings they once engendered [...] have been forgotten or diminished. [...] the real, darker origins of [orcs] may still be accurately traced. *Orc* is in fact derived from [...] orch and is to-day recalled somewhat in the Italian *Orco* or the French *Ogre*, both of which terms are classically applied to the blood-drinking, ferocious creatures whose appearance in even the most innocuous of folk-tales brings about a revival of ancient fears. As all will perceive, these are more accurate recollections of the foul and dangerous race of Orcs [...]. (Tyler 1976: 356-57)

Tyler goes on[19] to stress, of their manipulative breeding by the malign Morgoth, that "it is not now recalled with what ancient stock he worked" (*ibid*. 357) in the First Age. The same race persisted into the Second Age of Middle-earth's history – with greater ferocity and varying size –

Yet all were possessed of the same barbarous nature; and they were hideous, with jagged fangs, flared nostrils and slanting eyes which could see like gimlets in the dark [...]. (*ibid*. 358)

One of their leaders is given the name Azog[20] (*ibid*. 359). Elsewhere, Tyler stresses of the *Uruk-hai* that they

were a far superior breed, being taller and stronger, with great endurance, and an altogether higher level of intelligence. (*ibid*. 498)

Clearly Tyler, in glossing Tolkien, is concerned to show that the *orcs* and *Uruk-hai* are of the same race, a link which is warranted by the fact that they are, it is now postulated, (fictional) variants of the same ancient historic group, the men of Uruk in ancient Sumeria. Tolkien himself had, after the first use of the term 'goblin' in his *The Hobbit* (1937), preferred to name the race *orcs* and he added the following note in the 'Preface', in 1966, a note, which has since been printed in the Unwin editions:

Orc is not an English word. It occurs in one or two places but is usually trans-lated *goblin* (or *hobgoblin* for the larger kinds). *Orc* is the hobbits' form of the name given at that time to these creatures, and it is not connected at all with our *orc*, *ork*, applied to sea-animals of dolphin-kind. (1995: 1)

---

19 Tyler's synthesis is a composite one, drawn from many places in Tolkien's creative writings, but it is convenient to use his compendious definition here. A more exhaustive account may be found in David Day, *A Tolkien Bestiary* (1979:198-203).
20 It is, at very least, an 'Albanian sounding' anthroponym.

Tolkien's own more formal speculations about the word *orc* are presented for us in a note of his published posthumously:

> I originally took the word from Old English *orc* (*Beowulf* 112 *orc-n*[*eas*]) and the gloss *orc* = *Þyrs* ('ogre'), *heldeofol* ('hell-devil'). This is supposed not to be connected with modern English *orc*, *ork*, a name applied to various sea-beasts of the dolphin order. (Tolkien 1975a: 171)

The last sentence is interesting since it would seem to indicate that he was not sure in his own mind that the two roots were once separate. The Beowulfian passage[21] referred to is the problem half-line, *ylfe ond orcnēas*, and Professor T.A. Shippey has argued with some persuasiveness that

> [a] large part of Professor Tolkien's inspiration seems to have come from long brooding over such cruxes [and] [...] a thought-world once too familiar for explanation but now nearly too dead, (Shippey 1979a: 297)

but partly recoverable, not least because

> tiny, even pedantic points of philology can lead to the most certain and sweeping conclusions about that world *and the way that people lived in it.* (*ibid.*)

Non Tolkienian -Orc-, (-)Org-, -Ogr Lexis

While the thesis of the present article must remain incapable of exhaustive proof, such as scholars like C.T. Onions would have wished to be available by virtue of a wealth of surviving dated forms with fairly clear detoriation or perjorative semantic change, it is now possible to expatiate over various analogous or related forms and senses.

In English, the cluster of words on the root *ogre* include *ogress* (sb.), and the adjectives *ogreish* and *ogrish*. All come philologically from early Modern French *Ogre* (femine, *Ogresse*) which most relate to Latin *Orcus*, comparing Old Spanish *huerco*, *(h)uergo*, 'a devil, hell'. The words have each had the sense 'man-eating monster', but not necessarily in the bogey-form as encountered in popular story.

---

21 These words are to be found, with their context passages in the J. Bosworth and T.N. Toller compilation, *An Anglo-Saxon Dictionary* (1898: 764). *Orc-þyrs* is glossed as 'Orcus (the god of the infernal regions)'.

When discussing *ogre* and *Orcus*, etc., most dictionaries avoid the link with the *orc* or 'killer whale', as did Onions:

> **orc** † ferocious (sea-)monster; cetacean of the genus Orca. XVI.[th century] – [from] F[rench] *orque* or L[atin] *orca* 'kind of whale' (Pliny) – (from) Gr[eek] *óruga*, acc.[usative] of *órux* (Onions 1966: 631)

Tolkien did the same in the 'Preface' to his *The Hobbit* (1937) (*v. supra*). This is interesting in view of the fact that the Bosworth-Toller *An Anglo-Saxon Dictionary* glosses the Beowulfian *orcneas* (l. 112b) as 'sea-monsters', with the query "Cf. (?) *Icel.* orkn (örkn) *a kind of seal*" (1898: 764).

In his own more venturesome speculations concerning the ogre cluster, Partridge (1958), following Dauzat (1947), was concerned to stress the importance of the Byzantine Greek, *ogör* ('an Easterner'), which gave rise to Hungarian *Ogur* 'a Hungarian' and early Russian *Ugri* (pl.), 'Hungarians'. While it is not possible to discuss this use of the word *Ugri* (pl.) in Old Russian,[22] the documents of the 11th and 12th centuries are marked by regionalism, oral folk influence and eschatological materials, with much emphasis on the Devil-Evil as a characteristic of other races of man. In such contexts, it is difficult not to allow metaphysical and demonic associations to many of the references to Hungarians and Bulgarians. From this Russian name there arose the compounds Finno-Ugrian (used of the joint group of non Indo-European peoples to the immediate west) and the descriptive names Ugrian and Ugric, pertaining to a Ural-Altaic people, as in Ugro-Finnish. (Compare the older French notion (*v. supra*) of *ogre* as meaning 'a pagan').

Of related interest, but disputed origin, is the word *ugly* (adj.), 'horrible, terrible', which first appears in English in northern and eastern texts of the 13th century, and is held to come from Old Norse *uggligr*, 'to be feared', from *ugga* 'fear' (whence English dialectal *ug*, 'cause to fear, abhor'). Old Norse *ugga*, 'to fear' and *uggr*, 'fear, dread' are usually deemed to be of obscure origin, but metathesis and the change [k] > [g] would allow them to come from a Proto-

---

22 Convenient cultural summaries of the period may be found in Eremin (1966) or in the earlier parts of Kuskov (1977, transl. into English 1980).
  Similar poems, not always hostile to Hungarians, are to be found in the Yugoslav oral poetry relating to the times of the Despot Giorgje or Djuro (Brankovic), who reigned from 1427 to 1456. The Hungarian leader is called Ugrin Janko, or 'Janko the Hungarian', and is represented as being almost continually at enmity with the Despot Djuro.

Germanic *ork-, with a sense like 'fearful creature'. The 14th century *ugsome*, 'horrible', which was chiefly northern and Scottish, has had a further (literary) currency in modern times due to Sir Walter Scott, as in *The Antiquary*, "its useless ugsome carcase" (1816: 142).

Orcus, Orkney and Porcus

In Latin *Orcus* may denote either the kingdom of the dead or its ruler,[23] the two concepts often overlapping and blending. While one possible etymology gives the sense 'a storage vessel', this is hardly borne out by the early literary evidence in which Orcus is always a person. As king of the underworld he is often indistinguishable from Dis, but he can also be a menacing demon of death who attacks and destroys living men. The etymology of *Orcus* has long been held to be a problem. Thus T.G. Tucker's authoritative work, *A Concise Etymological Dictionary of Latin*, observes that the etymology is "obscure" (1931: 175).

The etymology of *Orkney* is another complex matter not simple of solution. While Strabo from Pytheas, c. 330 B.C., used the form *Orkas*, and Ptolemy c. 45 A.D. called the islands *Orchades*, Tacitus in the *Agricola* (98 A.D.) referred to them thus "incognitas [...] insulas, quas Orcadas vocant" (chapt. 10), Nennius used the form *Orc* and the *Anglo-Saxon Chronicle* in 1115 has the form *Orcanege* ('orc-islands'). The post-classical forms end in *ay*, *ey*, 'island', and most etymologists see the first element as 'the great fish, whale, or grampus', Latin *orca*, Norse *orc*, 'Orkn-'. A similar etymology for Orcades is also cautiously offered by Charles Tait, "[...] Ork probably means *Sea Pig* which could mean either a small whale or a seal" (2011: 130). Scholars of Gaelic have seen Orkney as coming from the Latin *orca*, 'a great fish', as with James B. Johnston in his *Place-Names of Scotland*[24]

> [a]t a very early stage *p* vanished from true Gaelic; witness [...] *orc*, a pig or sea-pig, i.e., whale, the L[atin] *porcus*, found in Orkney [...]. (1892: XXVI)

---

23 The personal sense is preferred in the Bosworth-Toller dictionary of Old English (*q.v.*).

24 The Rev. Johnston would have been well known to Tolkien as a worker on the *New Oxford English Dictionary* 1884-1915 and sporadically from 1926 until his death in 1953. Tolkien was on the staff 1918-20, and was consulted thereafter until its completion in 1933.

Tolkien, who knew both Johnston and his work, rejected the *orc-orca* link, as in his 'Preface' to *The Hobbit* (see 1995: 1).

A different etymology was followed by Edmund McClure in his *British Place-Names in their Historical Setting*, who has argued that since

> the term Orc in Orcades goes back to classical times [...] its meaning must be sought in the language of the earliest inhabitants. If these were Celts *orc*,[25] *oircnin* (glossed Porcellus) has the meaning of Pig in their language [...]. (1910: 225)

He then, however, ends with the caution "but the word is probably non-Aryan" (*ibid.*). It is interesting that *porcus* has the Old English cognate *fearh*. The last has a related abstract noun *fyrhti* = Gothic *faurhtei* = German *Furcht*, 'fear', "with the sense of bristling hair" (Tucker 1931: 191). This series of Old English cognates would have been familiar to Tolkien from their echoing in *Beowulf*[26] in another famed textual crux, the description of Beowulf and his men going out to face their adversary. The key lines are:

	Eofor-līc scionon
ofer hlēor-ber[*g*]an:	gehroden golde,
fāh ond fȳr-heard,	ferh-wearde hēold (ll. 303-05);

The 'diplomatic' translation, to which wording both Tolkien and Wrenn contributed,[27] is as follows:

> Above the cheek-guards shone the boar-images, covered with gold, gleaming and tempered. The fierce-hearted boar held guard [...]. (Hall and Wrenn 1940: 34-35)

There have always been problems with the use of *ferh*, 'boar' in poetry, "as otherwise it stands for the domestic pig" (*ibid.* 182), but "[a]s an auspicious animal, the boar might well guard the warriors" (*ibid.*). The last remark would seem to have indicated Wrenn's feeling that a metaphysical and even monstrous occult sense was possible for *ferh* (W.S. *fear*) in this clearly potent and violent and animalistic phrase.

---

25 Compare M. Irish, *Orc*.
26 Tolkien had lectured on the poem for many years and duly collaborated with his assistant, and later co-professor Charles Leslie Wrenn – an occasional 'Inkling', there largely for the Old English professional relationship with Tolkien – in the latter's edition of the poem in 1953.
27 In their joint revision, issued in both 1940 and 1950, of the J.R. Clark Hall translation of 1911.

Ariosto, Spenser and Tolkien

The root *orc-, *org- was of central significance to the Italian Ariosto (1474-1533) in his Renaissance epic, *Orlando Furioso*, particularly in the names of monstrous figures. Thus we encounter:

1) Orc, the, sea-monster with an appetite for fair damsels, unleashed by Proteus on Ebuda (Ariosto 1974: 614);

2) Orcus, blind monster akin to Polyphemus, who ravaged Norandin's bridal-party (*ibid.*);

3) Orgagna, sorceress of the enchanted garden (*ibid.*); and

4) Orrigilla, "a perfidious beauty who [...] leads her lover Grifon into trouble" (*ibid.* 615).

As Shippey observes,

in the sixteenth century the word [orc] was imported into English from Italian *orco*, meaning 'ogre' or 'giant'. (1979a: 293)

Perhaps its acquisition to English was due to Ariosto's name *Orc*, and to the related common noun, *orco*, meaning 'ogre' or 'giant'. Its best known literary occurrence is in the monstrous Orgoglio, a giant with 'the pride of brutality' who appears in Book I, Canto VII of Edmund Spenser's *The Faerie Queene* (1590).[28] There the Red Cross Knight descends into the dungeon of Orgoglio, an ugly, repulsive and frightening place, the master of which has a seven-headed dragon as a monster servant. The whole passage is invested with an atmosphere of terror and evil, borrowed from St. John the Divine's vision on Patmos. Orgoglio, a bladder of wind (and the child of Earth and Aeolus) cannot be defeated once and for all but lies ever in wait for the weak-hearted as the force of "melancholy and deadly depression" (Parker 1960: 92).[29]

---

28 See Pauline Parker, *The Allegory of the Faerie Queene* (1960: 35).
29 It does not seem necessary to take the extreme 'historical' view that Orgoglio is Philip II of Spain, and the dragon symbolizes the Marian persecutions.

And *Ungoliant* and other *org-like Words, some from Tolkien's Lexis

Another possible Tolkienian musing, perhaps related to Spenser's name, is his own *Ungoliant*, the great spider, whose descendant Shelob is described as the

> last child of Ungoliant to trouble the unhappy world. (*TT* 332)[30]

Of related sense – or recollection – is, or would seem to be, the (archaic) *orgulous*, from French *orgueilleux*, from *orgueil*, 'pride', a word held by E. Weekley (1921: 1014) to be of Teutonic origin.[31] It was revived by R. Southey in 1808 in *Chronicle of the Cid*, "They are of high blood and full orgullous [...]" (*ibid.* 239) and by Sir Walter Scott in *The Monastery*, "[...] punished for your outre-cuidance and orgulous presumption [...]" (Scott 1820: 228).

An associated root, or at least one of similar form, is that of Gorgon (for the head of Medusa on Athene's shiled), from the Greek γοργος, 'fearful, horrible, terrible' – which some scholars[32] also want to link with the Old Irish, *garg*, 'fierce'. The *-g-rg-* gave rise to the Modern Englisch verb, *gorganise*, 'to petrify' as in Tennyson's *Maud* (Tennyson 1859: 47). Tolkien used the element in another of his eastern names, that for the plateau of Mordor, *Gorgoroth*[33] 'the place of horror', which Robert Foster translates as 'haunted', and describes thus:

> The great plateau of north-western Mordor, a desolate area scarred with countless Orc-dug pits. (1978: 217)

The presumed link of *Orc* and *Gorgon* is made clear by Tolkien, if in fictional context, when he has the leader of the wild men in his *The Return of the King* (1955) call the Orcs *gorgûn* (1965: 106-108). In the posthumously published text, *The Silmarillion* (1977), he also has an ominous Mordor landscape feature, *Ered Gorgoroth*, 'The Mountains of Terror', also called 'the Gorgoroth' (1977: 81, 95, etc.).[34]

---

30 See H.G. Lotspeich, *Classical Mythology in the Poetry of Edmund Spenser* (1932).
31 *The Shorter Oxford English Dictionary on Historical Principles* related it to O.H. German *urguoli*, from *urguol*, 'renowned' (Onions 1933: II, 1384).
32 See, for example, W.W. Skeat, *A Concise Etymological Dictionary of the English Language* (1882: 218).
33 Cp. J.R.R. Tolkien, *The Fellowship of the Ring* (1965: 258).
34 The link between *Gorgoroth* and Greek *Gorgos* has been explicitly commented on by Robert Giddings and Elizabeth Holland in their *J.R.R. Tolkien: The Shores of Middle-Earth* (1981: 159).

We may note here, too, the awful figure of Demogorgon (in Shelley's *Prometheus Unbound*), whose name has a complex ancestry, being a blend of the monstrous terrifying Gorgous and the great Craftsmen, Demiourgos, who is said by Plato to have made the universe. He is mentioned in Lucan, *Bellum Civile* (6, 498), and later on invoked by the witch (6, 744f), and also in Statius, *Thebaid*, (4, 513f). He appears as Daemorgon in Boccaccio's *Genealogia deorum gentilium*, and first reaches English poetry in Spenser through Ariosto. In discussing the Shelleyan usage, J.F.C. Gutteling suggested that that Romantic poet was largely concerned with religion's power to terrorize the people (1924: 283-85).

Semantic Commonality

The essential point in these many postulated actual (or fictive) etymological links is to be found in the belief that the Sumerian culture – city walls, legends of the creation, the flood, the giants and the monsters – had been carried west by various races who had early contact with the Sumerian peoples. Some later legends preserved vestiges of original and new monster stories in their new (localized) myths, such as those of the *Beowulf* poet, Ariosto or Spenser. Survivals of ancient Sumerian legend were to be found in both lexis and proto-semantics, and later 19th century scholarship was clear on this point, which may be found espoused by Adam (1874) or by A.H. Sayce in his *The Principles of Comparative Philology* (1892).[35] This last work has much detail as to the influence of Akkadian on Semitic, Finno-Ugrian on Indo-European and on various other ancient linguistic groups who then moved south west or north west, and then into Western and Northern Europe. In short, the original sense for 'Uruk' as 'man of Uruk' or 'Easterner' began to change in the memory of non Semitic, non Sumerian man, as he moved away in both time and space from his original awesome encounters with the advanced powerful temple city of ancient Sumeria.

The earliest change of the city's actual name is that from Sumerian *Ulu(g)* and Akkadian *Uruk* to *Erech*, when it is mentioned in the Table of Nations (*Genesis*

---

35 First published in 1873, elsewhere quoted from the 4th edition (1892).

10:10) as one of the possessions of Nimrod[36] in the land of Shinar. The name Erech is used by Tolkien in the phrase, 'the Stone of Erech', referring to an enormous black spherical stone upon which a group of un-dead oath-breakers had sworn a fealty which they had not performed, and it is only by belatedly fulfilling their oath that they are able to achieve rest at last. This association must remind us of the ancient 'lamentation for oath-breaking' of the men of Erech, attested in Babylonian inscriptions.

The original site of Uruk was occupied for several millenia and has been much investigated since c. 1850. The Greek name for the much later city was *Orchoë*, and the modern Arabic name for the group of mounds there is *Warka*. While the site was investigated by W.K. Loftus in the mid-19th century – as chronicled in his popular *Travels and Researches in Chaldaea and Susiana* (1857) – there were a series of important German excavations in 1912, 1928-39 and 1954-60. Two convenient studies of this work are:

1) Walter Andrae, 'The Story of Uruk', *Antiquity* X.38 (1936: 133-45); and

2) R. North, 'Status of the Wark Excavations', *Orientalia*, N.S., vol. 26 (1957: 185-256).

As Andrae pointed out:

1) "It is not too much to claim for Uruk that it exhibits a clear sequence of four millenia of culture" (1936: 144);

2) "In Greek and Parthian times it was called Orchoë [...]" (*ibid*. 133); and

3) "[...]in its latest days, under the Greeks and Parthians, it was to Uruk that there resorted all those who went out in search of the wisdom of the Chaldeans, of their astronomy, and of a decadent astrology" (*ibid*. 145).

The Greek name for the city gives a further etymology or even comparative and very scholarly dimension to the famed Beowulfian *hapax legomenon: orc-neas* ('carrion-creatures') which is usually assumed to be a compound, the first part of which is based on Latin *Orcus*, 'the underworld, realm of death'.[37] Further, it does not invalidate another (possibly related) etymology for the Old English word which argues that it "translates and may be a loan adoption of Old Irish *Goborchind*, 'horse heads'." (Wiersma 1961: 332) There is a further link with

---

36 The loose association, of Biblical Nimrod, Gilgamesh the king of Uruk, and Sauron in Tolkien's writing, has been noted by various critics. Compare also footnote 14.

37 See Ryan (1966: 52-53), reprinted Ryan (2009: 206).

the far north-west in the ancient name for the Orkney Islands, which means, according to Pytheas the Greek, *Orcades* "the islands at the edge of the world" and so to the approaches to death's realm.

Cultural Overview

As will be clear by now, this investigation was prompted by two Tolkien-inspired ideas: the first concept being that he had used the names *Uruk(-hai)*,[38] *Erech*[39] and *orc*, with a form of linkage between the first and last, and with the second as having some ancient and even numinous association, and the second aperçu being the realization that many race designatory words, such as *shark* or *barbarian*, have come to have perjorative semantic sense, whereas they meant, respectively, merely 'easterner' or 'bearded man' and so on, by extension, 'someone recognizably unlike us'.

Of course, the *Uruk* name may be held to have long been remembered because of

1) the awe felt by the Indo-European and other migrating peoples at the sight of the great walled city with on the eastern side the vast ziggurat and precinct dedicated to the goddess Inanna;

2) the reconstructions of the centre by many rulers down to Cyrus of Persia in the 6th century; and

3) the various notions of its magic which may be held to have moved west and north at a later date.

As William Irwin Thompson said so well in his survey of the origins of (European) culture, *The Time Falling Bodies Take to Light* (1981):

In humanity's "rise to civilization," the human race had been split into the civilized and the barbarian, and the pattern of barbarians against the city had been set. (1981: 207)

---

38 This last is an ancient suffix in various languages, as in the Gothic preterite of strong verbs, and may well have been used as an enclitic.

39 No attempt has been made here to link the story in the Gilgamesh fragment about how the Goddess Inanna, the Queen of Heaven, transplanted sacred trees to her holy garden in her main sanctuary in Erech. However, this must suggest Galadriel and her wondrous skills of healing and of restoration.

And linked with this, we may note that, as Robert M. Adams put it,[40] in his 'The Origins of Cities' concerned with the agricultural revolution in Mesopotamia following upon the earlier use of tools,

> [t]he rise of cities, the second great "revolution" in human culture, was pre-eminently a social process, an expression more of changes in man's interaction with his fellows than [...] with his environment. For this reason it marks not only a turning but also a branching point in the history of the human species. (1960: 3)

After the emergence of the Mesopotamian hill-villages by 5500 B.C., there was a period of stabilization for 1500 years or more, and then a sharp increase in tempo

> culminating in the Sumerian city-state with tens of thousands of inhabitants, elaborate religious, political and military establishments, stratified social classes, advanced technology and wide-extending trading contacts.[41] (*ibid.* 4)

The references to the towns like Uruk in the myths and epics are at best vague and allegorical. And archaeology's potential contribution is still limited, apart from the evidence of the sheer size of centres and surrounding fortifications. For Uruk itself extended over 1500 acres and contained possibly 50,000 people, which was contributing to a considerable increase in warfare.[42] Further, as W.I. Thompson would observe of the lasting impact which this culture made:

> But even in its death Sumerian civilization would take hold of the imagination of the ancient world. (1981: 207)

This phase had lasted for an entire Platonic month from 4000 to 2000 B.C.

But soon the highly mobile warrior societies of the Indo-Europeans passed through Asia Minor, the Greek people being established in Macedonia by 1900, the Hittites had settled in Anatolia by 1850, and other tribes were pressing forward with their patriarchal societies, highly effective for leadership in war. It is thus argued that the various names and words subjected to linguistic

---

40 In *Scientific American*, September 1960, pagination from the separately issued version.
41 See also Samuel Noah Kramer, 'The Sumerians', *Scientific American*, October 1957. It may even be held that this trade outreach is represented by the trafficking in tobacco between the Shire and the East in Tolkien's *The Lord of the Rings*. The same text certainly makes abundantly clear the East's burgeoning military establishment.
42 See V. Gordon Childe, *What Happened in History* (1946).

scrutiny above contain memories of those startling social contacts of the earliest Indo-European migratory period.

And so back to Tolkien's Remarkable Linguistic Intuitions and Perceptions

As the above etymological clusters make clear, although the writing down of names and words associated with the memory of Uruk would not take place until two or even three thousand years later, yet the pervasive and consistent idea which they embody is one of a terrible fear associated with death, whereas the original senses were designatory alone. While dictionaries of etymology have been necessarily cautious to assert in the face of fragmentary evidence, that the Tolkien-pondered 'Uruk' names, subtly embedded in his speculative history of an older Europe called *The Lord of the Rings*, suggested a deep concern for and an investigation of a possible or likely primary thread in the vast tapestry, fragments of surviving thought from the pre-history of Europe.

For his speculations on this and on other great cultural themes, he had chosen to concentrate his deductions in the languages of racial groups in immediate contact over limited periods and so to leave us his plausible conclusions embedded in his subtle – and apparently fictional – linguistic forms. However, we have access to some peculiarly interesting early lines of his thoughts on the unrecorded pre-history of the 'Middle East' and the later Europe. For, in 1924 Tolkien had contributed a survey review essay entitled 'Philology: General Works' to the *Year's Work in English Studies*, Vol. V,[43] in which he spoke of the shocks applied to Indo-European philology by the discovery of Tokharish and Hittite, and then he went on to refer to the fact that:

> [...] the pre-history of Europe and nearer Asia looms dark in the background, an intricate web, whose tangle we may now guess at, but hardly hope to unravel. All this we ought to take account of [...]. If our present linguistic conceptions are true, there is an endless chain of development between that far-off shadowy 'Indo-European' – that phantom which becomes more and more elusive, and more alluring, with the passage of years – and the language that we speak to-day. (27-28)

---

43 It was not published in the event until 1926.

By his keen insights into vestigiary language, and his imagined possible proto-history of certain key words, Tolkien has linked some of the perjorative nomenclature and lexis of European countries over many centuries to show, at least in later times, a xenophobic dislike of those who were other than of the comfortably familiar nation. That not all the links can be proved by unambiguous context passages is unimportant to the speculative philologist who saw his task as hoping "to unravel [part of] an intricate web," and travelling along certain surviving threads, to

> those times [...] when they were still a wandering people

before

> they had begun to settle down [...] in the west-lands [...] (*RotK* 385).

T.A. Shippey's contribution to the Memorial Volume, *J.R.R. Tolkien: Scholar and Story-Teller* was entitled 'Creation from Philology in *The Lord of the Rings*' (1979a: 286-316). While that perception is a valid one, it must also be added that there is no sharp line between its subject's creative writing and his formal scholarship and, perhaps more significantly, the 'fiction' enables the curious modern scholar to have access to Tolkien's own vast store of cultural speculation and not merely 'linguistic aesthetic'. Shippey is right to stress that, all too often, Tolkien "had read the dictionary's definitions and found them wanting" (*ibid*. 288), and so, again and again, his own "ancient knowledge begins to turn into new creation" (*ibid*. 293). For Shippey, the musing on orc arose from the Beowulfian crux, *orc-neas* –

> „Orc," then, he seems to imply, is not an English word but might have been if it had happened to survive (*ibid*. 294).

But its 'restoration' to English lexis (*O.E.D. Supplement* 1982: 100-01) and the presence of its linguistic pre-forms in Tolkien's text bestows most generously on the modern scholar of onomastics and of etymology the master word-smith's further thoughts on a vast cluster of forms, all originally designatory names, from that thought area, otherwise a

> [...] dark mystery of ancient Western Europe [...] come[s], some 5,000 years ago, from the Sumerian. (Tolkien 1926: 39-40)

Appendix

It will be noted that there has been no inclusion of the name Orc, from the poetry of William Blake (1757-1827). In his *The First Book of Urizen* (1794) and *Vala, or The Four Zoas* (1795-1804), Blake had described the conflict between Urizen, a cold god, working through snow, ice, and cold plagues, and Orc, an uprising spirit of energy which cannot find humanized form, but is associated with fire and lightning. Typical lines from the latter text are:

> Loud sounds the war-song round red Orc in his fury,
> > (Night VII, First Version, l. 142);
> He saw Orc, a Serpent form, augmenting times on times
> In the fierce battle;
> > (Night VIII, ll. 58-9);

and

> > > The folding
> Serpent of Orc began to consume in the fierce raving fire;
> > (Night IX, ll. 20-21).

While various American literary critics have attempted to link this name with Tolkien's orcs, the association is no more than a literary one and does not assist clearly with either etymology or semantics.

Oath-Swearing, the Stone of Erech and the Near East of the Ancient World

O ne of the most poignant passages in *The Lord of the Rings* occurs in the fifth book, in the account of 'The Passing of the Grey Company', when Aragorn and his men ride the Paths of the Dead to invoke the help of the undead, long ago faithless to his ancestor, Isildur.[1] As Aragorn explains the ancient events: "the oath that they broke was to fight against Sauron, and they must fight therefore, if they are to fulfil it [...] when Sauron returned and grew in might again, Isildur summoned the Men of the Mountains to fulfil their oath, and they would not" (*RotK* 35). When this happened, Isildur had laid his curse upon their leader and the oath-breakers:[2] "Thou shalt be the last King. [...] this curse I lay upon thee and thy folk: to rest never until your oath is fulfilled. For this war will last through years uncounted, and you shall be summoned once again ere the end" (*RotK* 55).

As the modern reader ponders upon this passage, he is most likely to recall first the (Germanic) abomination of oathbreaking and then the context in which it appears so memorably in Old English literature, viz. in *Beowulf*. These lines from early in the epic (81b-85b), referring as they do obscurely to the episode of later enmity between Ingeld and his wife, Freawaru, occur there as a contrast with the present proper use of Heorot hall for splendid hospitality and for the rewarding of loyal service. The passage may be translated thus:

> The hall towered high, lofty and wide-gabled, – it awaited the hostile surges of malignant fire. Nor was the time yet near at hand that cruel hatred between son-in-law and father-in-law should arise, because of a deadly deed of violence.[3]

This essay first appeared in *Inklings-Jahrbuch 4* (1986: 107-21) and I am grateful to its editors for the permission to reprint it.

1 Most of the background details of the making of their oaths and their subsquent breaking are given in this chapter of *The Return of the King*. The Isildur link with Erech is also stated in *The Silmarillion* (291).

2 Tolkien's use of the word *again* in *The Silmarillion* (83) is shown as a 'later example' use in Vol. III (*Supplement* 1982: 4) of the *Supplement to the Oxford English Dictionary* – "For so sworn, good or evil, an oath may not be broken, and it shall pursue oathkeeper and oathbreaker to the world's end." Compare also the form of oath of fealty sworn by Peregrin to Denethor: "I will not [...] fail to reward that which is given: fealty with love, valour with honour, oath-breaking with vengeance" (*RotK* 28).

3 As in the revised J.R. Clark Hall translation (Hall and Wrenn 1950: 24), to which Tolkien contributed

Thus there is here, as Wrenn in his notes to the translation observes, "a kind of tragic irony in this anticipation of the ruin of Heorot at the time of describing its glories." It will be noted that the compound 'oath-swearers' (84b) is, conventionally in this context, translated as 'son-in-law and father-in-law', since at the time of the marriage these were the powerful persons making a solemn pledge, here of loyalty and support. In the Old English epic, the matter of this tragic family enmity and feud is again referred to in lines 2024-69. Like the tragedy of Finn and Hengest, the Ingeld tale[4] is concerned with the supreme necessity of vengeance for a slain leader to be taken by his loyal followers, as well as with the tragedy of using princesses to patch-up temporary peace between warring nations. Clearly the link[5] with Tolkien's creative work is important, but his use of the motif focuses on the culturally antecedent archetypal situation of warriors of the *comitatus* having to obey and follow their lord, a stock situation in ancient Germanic society.

When we return to the fictional Middle-earth context, it is to notice the focus of both the ancient oath and its plot's contemporary restatement of loyalty to be made at the same numinous place of original pledging: "For at Erech there stands yet a black stone that was brought, it is said, from Númenor by Isildur; and it was set upon a Hill, and upon it the King of the Mountains swore allegiance to him in the beginning of the realm of Gondor" (*RotK* 55). Because of this being the place of oath, Isildur's descendant, Aragorn, must lead the Sleepless Dead back to that same spot: "And the terror of the Sleepless Dead lies about the Hill of Erech and all places where that people lingered. But that way I must go, since there are none living to help me" (*ibid.*). The mortals enter through the Dark Door and so come beneath the Haunted Mountain, passing on followed by the Sleepless to the ancient Erech Hill in Morthond Vale (*ibid.* 62) in Lamedon. The Stone of Erech had been set atop Erech as a symbol of Gondor and its kinship with ancient Númenor, from whence it had

---

'Prefatory Remarks' and C.L. Wrenn 'Notes'. The quotation is from Wrenn's note, p. 283. See also the Frederick Klaeber text, *Beowulf and the Fight at Finnsburg* (1936: 130).

4 This is discussed by C.L. Wrenn in his edition of *Beowulf* (1953: 74), in both the 'Commentary' and in the 'Introduction'.

5 Tolkien's full lecture notes on *Beowulf* have not been published, but one assumes their general similarity to those of his successor in that chair of Anglo-Saxon, C.L. Wrenn, as does A.J. Bliss in his (posthumous) edition (1982: 5-6) of Tolkien's *Finn and Hengest: The Fragment and the Episode*.

been brought in 3320, Second Age, by Isildur. To it Aragon and all his followers must come before the end of day (*ibid.*).

As they approach this hill, south of the mountains, it is stressed that the hilltop is ever a place of fear, and then its pedigree is given: "For upon the top stood a black stone round as a great globe, the height of a man, though its half was buried in the ground. Unearthly it looked, as though it had fallen from the sky, as some believed; but those who remembered still the lore of Westernesse told that it had been brought out of the ruin of Númenor and there set by Isildur at his landing" (*ibid.*). Rumour had long held it to be "a trysting-place of the Shadow-Men [...] in times of fear" (*ibid.* 63). And so it is right that they should come here[6] as the first stage of the ritual discharging of their ancient guilt – "[...] Aragorn dismounted, and standing by the Stone he cried in a great voice: 'Oathbreakers, why have ye come?' And a voice was heard out of the night that answered him, as if from far away: 'To fulfil our oath and have peace.' Then Aragorn said: 'The hour is come at last. Now I go [...] and ye shall come after me.[7] And when all this land is clean of the servants of Sauron, I will hold the oath fulfilled, and ye shall have peace and depart for ever [...]'" (*ibid.*).

Now while this last speech cannot but seem echoic of the apocryphal Harrowing of Hell,[8] the most interesting analogue is brought to our perception by the historical name Erech, and by the description of the Black Stone itself. But first, let us consider the name Erech, that of an ancient city of Mesopotamia, mentioned in the Table of Nations (*Genesis* 10:10), as one of the possessions of Nimrod. It is also named in the Sumerian King list as the seat of the Second Dynasty after the Flood. While the site was investigated well over a century ago by W.K. Loftus (1857), the continuing series of excavations probed the records and material culture of Mesopotamia, at the beginning of history. It was from these levels beneath the Great Temple, and dating from the 4th millenium B.C., that the most ancient inscriptions so far known were taken.

---

6 Compare the sign of Ragnarøk's coming in the *Vǫluspá* and in Snorri's *Gylfaginning*, chapter 51, when the dwarves come to stand outside the cliff face.

7 This is one of the many loose equivalences of Aragorn's speech to the words of John the Baptist in Scripture, and on this analogy or pattern, the Christ-figure is, of course, Frodo.

8 Derived from the so-called *Gospel of Nicodemus* and treated of in both Old and Middle English. When glossing the texts for K. Sisam's *Fourteenth Century Verse and Prose* (1921), Tolkien had given the necessary contextual meanings of the harder words of the miracle play 'The Harrowing of Hell'.

One of the inscriptions which was translated early on in the investigations is
included in a reader which was edited by A.H. Sayce, then deputy professor of
Comparative Philology at Oxford, but to hold the Chair of Assyriology from
1890 to 1919. It is entitled 'An Erechite's Lament'[9] by its translator, Theo. G.
Pinches who describes it as "a kind of penitential psalm written in the Sumerian
dialect [...] which I have entitled 'The Erechite's lament over the desolation
of his father-land' [...] (and) might well have been chanted by the sorrowing
Erechites [after the carrying away of the statue of the goddess]" (Sayce 1988:
84).[10] Pinches observed of the decipherable parts of the broken tablet:[11] "What
remains of the obverse refers to the devastation wrought by an enemy in the
city of Erech, and the subject is continued on the reverse which ends in a kind
of litany." (*ibid.*) Parts of it are then rendered thus (*ibid.* 85): "How long my
Lady, shall the strong enemy hold thy Sanctuary? There is want in Erech, thy
principal city; [...] He has kindled and poured out fire [...]. My Lady, sorely
am I fettered by misfortune; My Lady, thou hast surrounded me, and brought
me to grief. The mighty enemy has smitten me down like a single reed [...]. I
mourn day and night like the fields."[12]

Bearing in mind that Sayce was the author of two standard philology texts used
by Tolkien the student – *The Principles of Comparative Philology* (1874; fourth
edition, 1892) and *Introduction to the Science of Language* (2 Volumes, 1880,
etc.) – and that there are many other evidences of familiarities with the earlier
professor's work in the Tolkien *opera*, there seems no possibility of this passage
not being known to the younger scholar. Thus, if the original name, Erech, is
associated culturally with a poem of lament such as this, then the conclusions
are twofold – firstly, that this is an early Sumerian, and so non Indo-European,
source for the Tolkienian incident; and secondly, that the ancient nature of both
stone and original disloyalty are underscored by this further fictional expansion of the incident as a valid race-memory of both Aragorn's family and of the

---

9   The only reference to this in Tolkien scholarship runs thus: "The stone of Erech may have been
    suggested by the existence of a Sumerian city of that name" (Noel 1977: 32).
10 The goddess is probably Naná, rather than Ishtar.
11 He provided a drawing on the reverse of the fragment, accompanied with a transcription and
    translation in the *Babylonian and Oriental Record*, December 1886 (see Pinches 1886).
12 Pinches observes that a possibly better translation is "Like the *marshland*, day and night I groan."
    Compare Tolkien's 'Dead Marshes' in *TT*.

people of Morthond Vale. And so a prehistoric myth of non-Indo-Europeans has been made available to us through Tolkien's art.

The other matter of teasing complexity is the pedigree of the Stone[13] itself, the two salient details (given in *RotK* 62) being its look of a meteorite, but the fact that the old lore had argued that it had come from the wrack of Númenor. Now the only stone of renowned legend which fits both of these attributes is the Ka'ba at Mecca, referred to thus by E. Sidney Hartland: "[Primitive] Veneration of boulders and standing stones [...] In many cases probably the boulder was the object of worship which has been forgotten, and the tale is the method of accounting for the awe and fear in which it has been held. Many stones to which worship has been accorded are, there can be little doubt, aerolites.[14] Such, e. g. is the famous Ka'bah at Mecca" (*E.R.E.* XI: 865).[15]

G.R. Barton observes: "The ritual uses of stones [...] arose from the fact that [...] stones that have fallen from heaven are considered sacred. Such a stone existed at ancient Ephesus, and is mentioned in *Acts* 19:35. It is probable that the 'black stone' in the Ka'ba at Mecca is of this nature, and it has been conjectured that the Ark of Jahweh, carried from place to place by the Israelites in the wilderness, originally contained such a stone" (*ibid.* 876).

In the modern world, the Ka'ba is the small shrine located near the centre of the Great Mosque at Mecca and is considered by Muslims everywhere to be the most sacred place on earth. It is the focus of the five daily prayers and is the cherished object of the pilgrimage ordained by command of God in the Koran. The Ka'ba itself is cube-shaped, the dimensions being 40 by 35 by 50 feet. Its interior contains nothing but the three pillars supporting the roof. During most of the year the Ka'ba is covered by an enormous cloth of black brocade which is renewed annually. In the eastern corner is the Black Stone (*al-hajar al-aswad*), whose now broken pieces are surrounded by a ring of stone. According to popular legend, this stone, which was given to Adam[16] on his fall

---

13 A convenient article on 'Stones' in religion and early culture is to be found in the *E.R.E*, vol. XI (Hastings 1920; repr. 1974: 864-77). This standard reference work was often cited by Tolkien in lectures. (Personal knowledge.)

14 I.e. meteorites.

15 Ka'ba is an Anglicized spelling; more recent scholarship prefers 'Ka'aba'.

16 See the Ka'ba article in the *Encyclopædia Britannica* by Charles J. Adams (1968a: 178) as well as Donaldson (1953: 27); Lane (1908) and Nicholson (1907, reprinted 1966).

from Paradise, was originally white but has become black by absorbing the sins of countless thousands of pilgrims who have kissed and touched it.

While the early history of the Ka'ba is not well known, the following facts are clear: it was revered as a sacred sanctuary in the pagan period before the rise of Islam; Abraham and Ishmael (*Koran* 2:127) are said to have raised the foundations of the Ka'ba; and although disregarded by Mohammed early in his prophetic ministry, the sanctuary was cleansed when he took Mecca in 630.[17] With the conquest of Mecca, the Ka'ba was restored to the functions for which it had been consecrated many thousand of years before[18] by the Patriarch Abraham; once impiousness was cleansed the Prophet had forgiven his enemies; in later Muslim legend, it was said that the Black Stone had been brought in the first place to Abraham by the angel Gabriel from a sacred mountain (called Abú Qubais on the eastern side of Mecca), where it was said to have been since the 'Deluge'.

Another aspect of the hoary sanctity of the Ka'ba stone is one well brought out by D.B. MacDonald, namely the likely influence of the 'aesthetic-ecstatic life of Islam' upon the Roman Church and upon Aquinas in particular:

> The (Mecca) pilgrimage ceremonial [...] affects the pilgrim. It is, then, [...] with Roman [...] Christendom that Islam must be compared as to its emotional life [...] and supernatural faith. And for this theological likeness there is good ground. Almost certainly, Thomas Aquinas was deeply influenced [...] by [these] views; and he, in his turn, has moulded the Roman theology. (1909: 218-19)[19]

One assumes that this cultural fact was well known to Tolkien, and so the breaking of the oaths sworn on one of the most sacred objects, believed to date back to before [God's] flood, would have aroused in him personally the form of distress that it did in later Muslim society, as well as in (apocryphal) Old Testament story.

---

17 Khalifatul Masih II (1949: 278).
18 Compare the original setting of the Stone of Númenor on the hill of Erech by Isildur at the time of the founding of Gondor, and then the summoning of the mountain-people a full age afterwards in order to fulfil their vow.
19 The text comprised the Haskell Lectures on Comparative Religion delivered to the University of Chicago in 1906. There was a facsimile of the original 1909 edition issued by Khayats, Beirut in 1965. See also Lasater (1974) for other religious and cultural influences of the Arabs on Western European thought.

The problem of scanty evidence as to early (Arab) Semitic idols, altars and sacrifices is discussed by Theodore Noldeke, and he observes that "our information dates, for the most part, from the close of the heathen period, but [...] mythology, not to mention religious dogma, could scarcely be said to exist. Even as to the fundamental question of the relation in which Deity stood to the sacred stones [...] and other objects of worship, no definite belief seems to have prevailed" (*E.R.E.* I, 1908: 665ff).[20] His conclusion is that Arab and Semite alike "probably imagined that the block of stone which served as a fetish (after the primeval Semitic fashion so clearly portrayed in the Old Testament) was pervaded by a divine power" (*ibid.*). It is such potent cultural and Christian proto-history as this which glosses most profoundly the need for Aragorn to bring back both the men of the Mountains and the undead to the place of their own and their forefathers' earlier apostasy.

Thus it is that we find Tolkien, as was his wont, drawing upon multiple cultural associations to make his potent artistic impact. His various signposts to the past serve once again to explore (ancient) religion on the verge of monotheism and to give resonant meaning to what otherwise might seem mere folklore and idolatrous custom.

While it may be argued that it is not necessary to have this biblical type background teased out for its analogies, nuances and its 'illusion of historicity',[21] there can be no doubt that this place of oaths – loosely associated as it thus becomes with ancient Sumeria, – suggests the dawn of (historic) time of the Indo-European peoples, prior to their driving to the west and north. Also, its emphasis on the guilty consciences of the 'un-dead' not merely adumbrates the Christian 'Harrowing of Hell' by Christ himself, but also underscores one of Tolkien's great themes, that one's word should be one's bond.[22]

Although only the 'Erechite's Lament' and Ka'ba have been teased out here as Near Eastern analogues to or models for Tolkien's actual text, it is very clear that the older and more central and eastern regions of Middle-earth equate

---

20 The encyclopedia was long regarded as an essential background reference work by the Oxford School of English.
21 Phrase used by Tolkien (*Letters* 143).
22 Compare, for example, his 1941 comments on marriage (*Letters* 51) and the other quotations given in footnote 2.

in many associations with the early proto-history of the Indo-Europeans and their possible subconscious memories of their own ancient past, significantly, in the actual biblical lands.

While many parts of *The Lord of the Rings* were written *ab initio* in the years after 1937, sections like this concerned with Isildur clearly reflect much of the then unpublished, but much earlier written history of Númenor (*Silmarillion, UT*): for instance the story of the slaughter of the outnumbered Dúnedain (*UT* 272) and of the actual death of their lord – "the night-eyed Orcs that lurked there on the watch [...] loosed their poisoned arrows [...] and [...] Isildur [...] pierced through heart and throat [...] fell back into the water" (*ibid.* 275). Now although the focus in all texts is, seemingly, on the tragedy of Isildur's death, rather than on the sworn-allies who were not fulfilling their pledge, it is actual 'external' history,[23] that helps to fill out for us the ancient guilt of the Men of Erech – a guilt which has its origin in some tragedy of the ancient unwritten history of Sumeria.

As long ago as 1924, Tolkien the scholar had reflected on the then state of larger philological studies, noting "the search for new directions of advance" (*YWES V* 26) and stressing the need for more research, for, as he put it, somewhat enigmatically, "the pre-history of Europe and nearer Asia looms dark in the background, an intricate web, whose tangle we may now [only] guess at" (*ibid.* 27); and, later, he notes with approval G. Ipsen's work on the contact between "the ancient East and the Indo-Europeans" (*ibid.* 39). Then he refers to the "antiquity of the Near East" and how such careful, if speculative, philology, will illumine "the tantalizing glimpses and guesses that lie behind sure history [for these] have always an allurement, and they do not lack it here" (*ibid.*).

As this exploratory study has endeavoured to illustrate, the artist's disclaimers about 'external history' must be treated with some scepticism, for the young philologist[24] was, of course, in his story of the Stone of Erech, and the matter of oath-breaking, exploring the proto-history of the people of Erech, originally

---

23 'External history' is Tolkien's own term for 'real' names and events. See *Letters* 383 a passage actually quoted and discussed by Christopher Tolkien, *BLT II* 329.
24 All the stories of Middle-earth may, in a general sense, be seen as 'speculative philology' or explorations and ponderings as to the 'lost legends' of the Indo-European background.

Uruk, as outlined in the surviving Sumerian stories of Gilgamesh and of his times.

He was also quietly speculating about the Judaeo-Christian lore which became part of the cult of the famed Black Stone of the Ka'ba, and so showing us its ancient origins in the Old Testament by reference to its surviving the wrack of flood. The inclusion of the associations of the oath-breaking (as in the Old English epic, *Beowulf*) set up a further tension, or, rather, illustrated the recurring pattern of fallible man's inability to keep his binding pledges. Thus, the whole becomes a classic illustration of the Tolkenian use of the mediaeval story-telling device, *inventio*, or the combining of a selection of known ingredients – or at least familiar to him – to produce new artistic tensions and fresh literary insights. And it is this use of motifs from Western European man's ultimate cultural recollections which, in true Jungian fashion, so rouses the imagination and haunts the memories of all his readers, now enfranchised anew into the enjoyment of real or adumbrated stories from the dawn of the history of western man.

For the sake of clarity, the above survey has focussed specifically on the 'Lament' from Erech, as published (*v. supra*) in 1888 in *Records of the Past*. The full sub-title of those volumes was 'English Translations of the Assyrian and Egyptian Monuments published under the sanction of the Society of Biblical Archaeology'.[25] The original series of twelve volumes, edited by S. Birch,[25] appeared from 1873 to 1881. The 'new series', edited by A.H. Sayce in six volumes, was issued from 1888 to 1892, at which date Sayce observed: "The curiosity excited by the first attempts at the decipherment of the Egyptian and Assyrian texts appears now to be satisfied" (Sayce 1892: v), adding that "the public seems to prefer books about [...] the [ancient] Oriental World" (*ibid.*). Yet it may now be appropriate to list, *seriatim*, some of the other Erech(-ite) or numinous stone passages that are there accorded in translation and/or commentary.

The seventh volume (1876) of the original series contains an account (1876: 133-50) of 'The Eleventh Tablet of the Izdubar Legends – The Chaldean Account

---

25 Sayce contributed many introductions and decipherments of inscriptions to both series, as well as general editorial work.

of the Deluge', by George Smith, the Assyriologist, who identifies Izdubar with the Nimrod[26] of *Genesis* (*ibid.* 133). The following details may be excerpted:

1) Izdubar conquered a tyrant who ruled over the country (*ibid.*);

2) he was pious like his ancestor who was said to have been taken into the "company of the gods" (*ibid.*);

3) the forebear said that "the Lord of Hades [...] will destroy the sinner and life" (Col. I, 17, 22);

4) "the whole of mankind turned to corruption" (Col. III, 25);

5) "Izdubar [after the wrath] collected great stones" (Col. V, 52);

6) the men of Izdubar, built a city at Erech, taking the (deluge?) stones more than 400 miles (1876: 148; Column VI 3); and

7) "they piled up the great stones [...] 7. If a man in his heart take [...]8. [he] may bring them to Erech [...] 26. [...] they made the ascent, they came to the midst of Erech."

In volume XI (1878) there are included two related items – (a) reference by J. Halévy, when introducing various 'Assyrian fragments', to an 'Assyrian Elegy on the Destruction of Erech' (160 ff.); (b) discussion by Dr. Christian Ginsburg of 'The Moabite Stone' (*ibid.* 163 ff.), then in the Louvre. This last, a black basalt stone,[27] found in 1868 by the Rev. F. Klein, a German missionary working with the Church Missionary Society, is usually dated to c. 830 B.C. It commemorates the revolt of Mesha, King of Moab, against Israel (see *II Kings* 3:4 ff.), and indicates that Mesha threw off a heavy yoke of humiliation and honoured his god, Chemosh, by building a high place at Quarhoh. Thus, both entries add further background to the association with biblical times and with numinous stones.

The second volume (1889) of the New Series also contains material on 'The Moabite Stone' (1889: 194-203), this time contributed by Dr. A. Neubauer, while the fourth volume (1890) has a long chapter (1890: 36-79) by the Rev. Dr. Scheil on the Inscriptions of Shalmaneser II ('On the Black Obelisk',[28] etc.). This last stone, now long housed in the British Museum, is dated to c. 842 B.C. It is one of the 'external' (i.e. non-biblical) sources for Hebrew history

---

26 Nimrod was an early hero who lived in Babylonia, where his kingdom included Babylon, Erech and Akkad (*Genesis* 10:8-10; *Micah* 5:6). An equation with Tolkien's Isildur is possible on several heads.
27 Compare the initial quotations about the Stone of Erech from *RotK* and *Silmarillion*.
28 See Peake's *A Commentary on the Bible* (1919: 246, 307).

and contains the name of Jehu as a king paying tribute to Shalmaneser, and also reference to Elisha (cp. *II Kings* 9:1-27).

The last volume, VI in the New Series, and alike edited by A.H. Sayce, contains a "new story of the Creation from Sumerian Babylonia [...] discovered and edited by Theo Pinches" (1892: xix). This 'Non-Semitic' version[29] of the Creation is on a tablet found at Sippara in 1881-82 and refers on the obverse to the time before Creation when: "(2) [...] a tree had not been created [...] (7) Erech had not been built, Ê-ana[30] had not been constructed; (8) The Abyss had not been made (10) The whole of the lands, the sea also (20) Merodach made mankind (34) [He caused the plant to be brought forth], he made the tree. (40) [He build the city Erech, he built Ê-a]na the temple." As Pinches observes, contrasting this with other ancient Babylonian inscriptions on the same theme, "the principal thing [...] was not merely the formation of men and animals, but rather the founding of the first seats[31] of civilization in Babylonia, and [...] the assertion of their divine origin" (*ibid.* 111-12).

Clearly, the passage is remarkable for its anticipation of approaching monotheism, as well as for its ending with "the description of the building of those cities which, at the beginning, are said not to have existed, and gives the honour of their origination to Merodach, the principal god worshipped by the Babylonians" (*ibid.* 114). Some have even argued that the related city of Eridu was a form of earthly Eden.

*   *   *

It but remains to stress the oath's force in the constitutional origins of English law, coming from the Germanic cultural heritage and well established by the tenth century. As Jolliffe observes of the Anglo-Saxon court: "As the basis of its system it has established a conception of far-reaching importance, that of the 'lawful man', the man not only credible upon oath, but whose oath has in itself the decisive effect of proof [...] Such men, irrespective of wealth or influence, are

---

29 Earlier published in *Academy* (29. Nov. 1890: 508-09) and in the *Journal of the Royal Asiatic Society* 23.3 (1891: 393-408).
30 The name of the chief temple at Erech.
31 The others are Niffer, E-kura and Eridu.

'oath-worthy'.[32] But in the act of swearing they achieve something more than credulity, and their oath as it is spoken takes power – over them and over their cause which is other than their own. It is in ritual form" (1937: 8-9).[33]

*   *   *

As the entries from the *Oxford Dictionary Supplement* of 1982 make so very clear, Tolkien's prose has given new lexical and speech life to both 'oathbreaker' and 'oathkeeper'. Yet, this literary currency is not merely Old English common law, but comes also from pre-biblical legends which have been shown to go back to ages close to Creation and to the Deluge and its aftermath.

Thus it is that we may find a close association between the events of Tolkien's First and Second Ages and the biblical Divine Creation, the Deluge, and the earliest human fallibility in an area which can only be identified with the biblical lands. Again it may be said that the purposes of his new and echoic mythology are to glorify Christian story and to lead modern men by the 'illusion of historicity' to a deeper understanding of God's purposes both in the history of Middle-earth and in the 'external history' of our own world.

---

32 Edward I, Statute 3 (as in Jolliffe 1937): "Men who are notorious false swearers [...] shall never again be oathworthy, but only ordeal-worthy."

33 It has not been practical to discuss the many subtle nuances in Tolkien's work to the vampiric references in *The Lord of the Rings*, but many such promising comparative passages occur in Gregory A. Waller's *The Living and the Dead* (1986). This largely filmic or visual account is subtitled: *From Stoker's Dracula to Romero's Dawn of the Dead*. See also the revised version of 2010.

Saruman, 'Sharkey' and Suruman: Analogous Figures of Eastern Ingenuity and Cunning

W hile Saruman is one of the flawed great figures of Tolkien's Third Age, being the Chief of the order of Istari (Wizards), and is known also as *Curunír*,[1] the 'Man-of-Skill', most scholarly references to his name and to his origins are in agreement that his name is Germanic,[2] and related to the classical Old English adjective *searu*, 'wise, cunning'. Now while there is much Old English word formation and association in *The Lord of The Rings*, notably in reference to the Rohirrim, it should be noted that Saruman does not belong to that culture but had been sent to Middle-earth from Valinor early in the Third Age (ca. 1000).

Another clue to his name's meaning or origin is the fact that his adherents, both men and orcs of Isengard, call him 'Sharkey', from the Orkish, *sharkû*, 'old man'.[3] As Saruman himself comments upon his nickname –

> So you have heard the name, have you? All my people used to call me that in Isengard, I believe. A sign of affection,[4] possibly. (*RotK* 298)

It may be shown that his alternative form of nomenclature gives the clue to his non-Germanic, and, rather, Middle-eastern origin in both name and conception.

Firstly, let us notice the fact that a name and personality, both similar to Saruman occur in the 'Annals of Sargon', translated by Dr. Julius Oppert in a

---

This essay was originally printed in *Mythlore* 43 (1985: 43-44, 57) and is reproduced here with the kind permission of that journal's editors.

1 See *RotK* (365).

2 In fact, the Old English dialect, Old Mercian, according to Shippey (1982: 128), similarly Noel (1980: 28), derives the name from OE *searu*, 'craft, device' + *man* 'man'.

3 See *RotK* (298), where the etymology is given as a footnote. Tolkien expanded on this in his 'Guide to the Names in the *Lord of the Rings*' (1975a: 153-201), observing:

> This is supposed to be a nickname modified to fit the Common Speech (in the English text anglicized), based on orkish *sharkû* 'old man'. (*ibid.* 173)

4 This sense may well be the Western colloquial derogatory meaning, as it has been in English for more than 300 years.

seventh, Assyrian volume in the *Records of the Past: Being English Translations of the Assyrian and Egyptian Monuments* (1876: 21-56).[5] There occurs, as a referance to a monarch necessarily supressed (because of disloyalty?), the following passage

> they brought me [...] the (boxes?) containing the treasures of the palace of [...] Suruman [...] consisting in [...] the products of [...] brilliant ore, [...] crowns [...] in iron, [...] white lead [...] white marble [...] the land, [...] the great mountain of copper, one after one, he worked them [...]. (Oppert 1876: 39)

Thus a Suruman had been a vassal to the great king of Assyria, and had been possessed of great skills in metal work as well as considerable greed.

The other feature which demands attention is Tolkien's unexpected footnote, with a scholarly etymology, for *Sharkey*. This last is fascinating since it is the clue to take us away from the *saru – searu* Germanic word. The noun 'shark', first used in English of the 'large voracious seafish' in the sixteenth century is not given an etymology by C.T. Onions, who observed that it is:

> Said to have been so named by sailors of Capt[ain] John Hawkins's expedition, who brought home a specimen which was exhibited in London in 1569. (1966: 817)

In this explanation, Onions was following the earlier entry in the S-volume of the *Oxford English Dictionary*.

Yet other shark etymologies may be cited. W.W. Skeat, in his *A Concise Etymological Dictionary of the English Language* (1882: 479) argued that the fish name "comes from the Tudor verb, *to shark* (to prowl); [...] probably from the North F[rench] (Picard) *cherquier*, equivalent to the O[ld] F[rench] *cercher* (E[nglish] *search*)" and he compares Italian *cercare del pane*, 'to shift for how to live'. He also noted the usage, – following Dr. Johnson – of the noun *shark* as

1) 'a greedy fellow'; and
2) 'a greedy fish'.

---

5 These volumes were issued by the Society of Biblical Archaeology, of which the Oxford Professor of Comparative Philology, A.H. Sayce, was president. Tolkien's writings indicate familiarity with Sayce's *The Principles of Comparative Philology* (1892a) and also with many other of his works on the ancient Near East. The seventh volume was edited by Samuel Birch.

Ernest Weekley in his *An Etymological Dictionary of Modern English* (1921: 1328-29) argued that the earlier sense was, indeed, 'a greedy parasite', and that

> the word comes, per[haps] via Du[tch], from Ger[man] *schurk(e)*, 'a shark, sharper, rook, rake, rogue' [...], whence also *shirk* [...], It[alian] *scrocco*, as in *mangiare a scrocco*, "to feede a scotfree at another mans charge". (*ibid.*)

While Weekley notes the *Oxford English Dictionary*'s 1569 quotation, he also finds Spanish, and Florentine analogies and reflects that

> [t]his word may easily have been current among seamen before being recorded, and the quot[ation]s [of the word as intransive verb] suggest a naut[ical] nickname [...]. (*ibid.*)

Since this work was the major etymological dictionary for English published during Tolkien's earlier academic career, it is difficult to reject this last remark as being unfamiliar to him.

Thus we have the suggestion of a nickname for a ruthless predator of persons, as having a nautical background and as being current by ca. 1600 amongst sailors off Sierra Leone, in the Lowlands, and in the Mediterranean. At this point, we must turn to another noun of more obvious Eastern origin, namely: *Saracen*, the name of the nomadic peoples of the Syro-Arabic desert. Following the same dictionaries we find for it:

> a borrowing in the 13th century from Arabic, via French; perhaps from Arabic *sharqi*, 'eastern', *sharq*, 'sunrise, east', compare *sirocco*; (Onions 1966: 788)

> Lat. *saracenus*, a Saracen; lit. 'one of the eastern people.'; Arab. *sharqíy*, oriental, eastern; sunny [...] Cf. Arab. *sharq*, the east, the rising sun; id. From Arab. root *sharaqa*, it rose. (Skeat 1882: 525)

> much as Skeat, and noting that the names, *Anatolia*, *Easterling* have similar sense, initially of 'easterner'. (Weekley 1921: 1277)

Finally, it may be appropriate to recall that *sheikh*, the title of address to an Arab leader,[6] is from Arabic *shaikh*, literally 'an old man' from *shakha*, 'to grow old'.

The conclusions to be drawn from these interrelating background materials are several, and it is believed that most if not all are relevant to Tolkien:

---

6 See, for example, Weekley (1921: 1333).

1) that the Tolienian *saru*-link with Old English is simplistic, if not a non-sense;

2) that a similarly named leader in ancient Assyria, Suruman, had amassed great wealth and wrought brilliantly in metals and stone and had had to be subjugated when he challenged his lord;

3) that Tolkien told us (in *The Return of the King* and in his 'Guide to the Names in *The Lord of the Rings*') that in the East, Saruman was 'Sharkey', which name meant 'old man';

4) that Modern English *shark* (of uncertain origin) seems to have been first a noun, of marine usage, with the sense of 'prowler, predator'; and to have been used in the Mediterranean and possibly of Moorish pirates;

5) that its original senses when borrowed into Italian may well have been 'from the east', and so related to the Italian borrowing, *sirocco* or *scirocco*, 'a hot desert wind', from Arabic *sharq*, 'east', from *sharaqa*, 'to rise – of the sun';

6) that the related word *Saracen*[7] was to be found in English in the thirteenth century, and one may postulate even then an English Crusader colloquialism, *sharkey*, meaning 'the Arab (old man)';

7) that the sense 'ruthless old man' was current at a vernacular level[8] for centuries before its modern London or seamen's nickname for males with the surname Ward.

The whole makes for a feast of etymological speculation and it may be argued that Tolkien's character fits and adds to earlier musings of lexicographers.

What is certain is that it is not possible to ignore Tolkien's clues as to the name Sharkey and to his antecedents:

> less well documented is the story of [his] arising. For many years he wandered in the East of Middle-earth, acquiring arcane knowledge[9] and learning many new skills [...] and so trained himself for eventual dominance. (Tyler 1976: 420)

For the truth is, of course, that the earlier history of (the east of) Middle-earth relates very closely in many linguistic details to that of the Middle-east from pre-Biblical times to the Middle Ages and beyond. Even as the strong orcs, the Uruk-hai, have a tribal anthroponym going back to the ancient Sumerian

---

7   Other (semantically neutral) borrowings on this root include: *sarcenet, sarsnet* (a thin silk); *sarsen*, (earlier *Saracen's stone*), etc. Thus, there is further evidence of the common translation of Arabic *sh-* to English *s-*.

8   See Dunkling (1983: 99) where the association is linked with "a pirate so named." A Sharkey pirate also appeared in a story by A. Conan Doyle.

9   Perhaps a hint of Arabic science and medicine which was at its height as early as the ninth century A.D.

city name Uruk, or the Nazgûl, a name which echoes the Arabic *ghul* (a grave-robbing, corpse-eating, spirit), or – (a *jeu d'esprit*) – Rosie Cotton, a name[10] based on two borrowings from Arabic, – so Saruman or Sharkey has a name fitting the various translations accorded to Arabic a century or so ago. He also enshrines some of Tolkien's most interesting speculations in racial and perjorative semantics.

---

10 See Skeat (1891: 419-21).

    Rose, albeit already occuring in Anglo-Saxon, comes from an eastern source, is from either Armenian or Arabic origin. It was also a favourite word for the author of the *Ancrene Wisse*. *Cotton*, on the other hand, was certainly of Arabic origin, coming to England via Spain.

    Among J.R.R. Tolkien's former students in the 1960s, the discussion went along the lines that Rosie Cotton sounded charming and old-fashioned, especially if one took *Cotton* as a dative case of 'place', 'at/from the cottages'.

Túrin, Turanian and Ural-Altaic Philology

I n his biography of J.R.R. Tolkien, Humphrey Carpenter draws attention to his subject's schoolboy interest in Finnish language[1] and literature being one maintained into mature years and duly resulting in his invented language, Quenya, described as:

> based [...] on a fairly limited number of word-stems [...] [and] derived, as any 'real' language would have been, from a more primitive language supposedly spoken in an earlier age [...] (1977: 94)

Carpenter goes on then to observe that

> often in the heat of writing [Tolkien] would construct a name that sounded appropriate to the character without paying more than cursory attention to its linguistic origins. (*ibid.*)

Túrin and Turambar

It is the purpose of the present note that an early and highly significant name of this apparently invented sort[2] was *Túrin* or *Turambar*, one which is to be found widely in the 1916-1917 fragments, later edited by his son Christopher as *The Book of Lost Tales*, Part I, (1984) and Part II (1985). Further, these same names may be seen as a compliment to an exciting world of earlier and speculative thought about proto-history. It is also postulated that these *Tur-/Túr-* names

---

A somewhat shorter version of my paper was published in *Quettar* 22.3 (1985). *Quettar*, the British journal, which was described by its Editorial Committee as being concerned with Quenya, or 'High-Elven', and was long – from 1980 to 1995 – the Edinburgh-based bulletin of the Linguistic Fellowship of the United Kingdom's Tolkien Society; and this publication would, ultimately, run to some 49 issues. It was stated by its Editorial Committee that the core concern for the publication was with the languages invented by J.R.R.Tolkien, as well as an interest in Finnish Welsh, Old English and other, 'real world' languages. See also the 'Index' to issues 1-48, as compiled by Antony Appleyard, and available on the internet at www.quettar.org/qindex.txt.

1 From the portion of the work sub-titled 'The Making of a Mythology' (*ibid.* 87).
2 Compare also the similarity between the mansion, Ilmarin (*FotR* and elsewhere) with the name of the smith, Ilmarinen, in the Finnish *Kalevala*, as noted by Ruth S. Noel in her study, *The Mythology of Middle-Earth* (1977: 32).

have their origin in an eponym especially famous in Oxford, and more generally, in the scholarship of early comparative philology as to the Indo-European
peoples' background, especially before those races and peoples had moved
towards the west, and finally to the lands where they would remain and be
recorded in both inscriptions and ever more nuanced texts.

The cluster of names is complex and so it may suffice if the briefest list of
relevant entries is quoted from Ruth S. Noel's *The Language of Tolkien's Middle-
Earth* (1980):[3]

> *Turamath, S[indarin]* 'Master of Doom'. Sindarin form of Túrin's title *Turambar*.
> *tur* = master, *amarth* = doom (*S[ilmarillion]* 355);

> *Turambar, Q[uenya]* 'Master of Doom'. A title of Turin, *tur* = master, *ambar*
> = doom (*S[ilmarillion]* 217);

> *Turambar*, 'Master of Doom'.[4] The eighth king of Gondor ([*RotK*] 318);

> *Turgon*, 'Master Commander'. The Elven King of Gondolin, father of Idril
> Celebrindal. *tur* = master, *gon* from *kano* = commander. ([*FotR*] 284)

and

> Túrin 'Master'. A great hero and Elf-friend of the First Age. *tur* = master.
> ([*FotR*] 284)

Other similar names such as *Turondo* of Part I of *The Book of Lost Tales* (115,
132 etc.) may be added to Noel's list.

---

3 This book is sub-titled 'A complete guide to all fourteen of the languages Tolkien invented'. Parts of
   it had appeared in 1965 and 1974. The page references of the lexical items are to the more accesible
   editions as used by Noel and not necessarily to the ones used in this volume of essays.
   The -mb- consonant cluster is much referred to in the linguistic antecedents of Latin, as by J. Wight
   Duff, and other similar historians of the nuances and recollections to be found in the earliest Latin
   lexis, fragments, as in the collections made by A. Ernout (b. 1879), the author of *Recueil de textes latins
   archaïques* (1916), a seminal work for so much of Tolkien's teaching of etymology.
4 Rendered as 'lord of the world' by Jim Allan in *An Introduction to Elvish* (1978: 41).

The Place of Max Müller in Furthering this Suggested Proto-Etymology

Now the (sub-conscious) source of this name group does not lie in either ortho-dox or its user's speculative etymology but, rather, in the thought of that grand populizer of the new and exciting 'science' of comparative philology, Professor Max Müller (1823-1900), who had first used the term *Turanian* in his lectures at the Taylorian Institute for Modern Languages, Oxford in the session 1851-1852. The fuller study of the concept was published in 1853 as his essay on the Turanian languages (Müller 1854). Tolkien himself refers to Müller with a mixture of exasperation and affection at many points in his printed critical writing (e.g. in *TL* 22, 67), and also to the older professor's classic study of the creation of language in general – and of the rise of Indo-European languages in particular – entitled *Lectures on the Science of Language* (1861-1863) in two volumes.[5] This work was still regularly recommended and set as a textbook when Tolkien worked on comparative philology – and for *The Oxford English Dictionary* – at the end of World War I.

Müller who had popularized the term *Aryan*[6] for the Indo-European group of languages (from the Sanskrit word *arya*, 'noble, of a good family') had dis-tinguished from them and from the Semitic group, a third covering much of the Middle East, and various areas elsewhere. His seminal thought behind the groups from the centre of the Euro-Asian land mass may be cited –

> I can only state that the etymological signification of Arya, seems to be 'one who ploughs or tills,' and that it is connected with the root of *arare* [Latin for 'to plough']. The Aryans would seem to have chosen this name for themselves as opposed to the nomadic races, *the Turanians*, whose original name *Tura* implies the swiftness of the horseman. (1873: 276-77)

Earlier he had described 'the Turanian' group of peoples and inferred speech communitites as comprising

---

5 Both had many reprints. Quotations are from the seventh edition (1873) of Vol. I.
6 See especially Müller (1873: 274ff).

the dialects of the nomad races scattered over Central and Northern Asia, the Tungusic, Mongolic, Turkic, Samoyedic, and Finnic,[7] all radii from one common centre of speech (*ibid.* 35);

and its agglutinative structure as characterized by the feature that

whatever the number of prefixes and suffixes, the root must always stand out in full relief, and must never be allowed to suffer by its contact with derivative elements.[8] (*ibid.* 315)

In yet another passage, when discussing the relative unity of the Persians, Medes and others at the time of Strabo, he adds

we may well understand [...] that they should have claimed for themselves one common name, in opposition to the hostile tribes of Turan. (*ibid.* 279);

and that the Turanians were specifically

described in the later epic poems of India as cursed and deprived (*ibid.* 282).

Of course, the most fascinating comments relate to the inter-relations between Turanians and Aryans, attested by Scythian names mentioned by such Greek writers as Ptolemy (*ibid.*) – and also to the way in which

this Turanian family comprises in reality all languages spoken in Asia and Europa, and not included under the Aryan and Semitic families [...] (*ibid.* 333).

The Northern division of the Turanian family, sometimes called the *Ural-Altaic* or *Ugro-Tataric*, is divided into five classes, the Tungusic, Mongolic, Turkic, Finnic, and Samoyedic (*ibid.* 334). Of the cultural nuances of the group Müller postulated their nomadic nature,[9] that among them

no such [binding or forming] nucleus of a political, social or literary character has ever been formed (*ibid.* 335);

and had, in poetic fashion, added that

---

7 He also has a footnote, "names in -*ic* are names of classes as distinct from the names of single languages." The tables (*ibid.* 451 and 452) show some 51 languages in the Northern Division belonging to the five language groups mentioned above, and some 65 in another, Southern Division.
8 Tolkien's invented language, Quenya, was modelled on this same linguistic principle. See also Müller (1873: 331ff).
9 See Müller (1854: 285) and also Rau (1974).

[their] empires were no sooner founded than they were scattered again,[10] like the sand-clouds of the desert; no laws, no songs, no stories outlived the age of authors (*ibid.*);

while, unlike theirs, all surviving legends must be 'distinct' (*ibid.* 337). There then follow various speculations as to the echoes of their cultural contacts with the Mongols and with the Osmanli of Constantinople (*ibid.* 345ff), as attested by

languages like Finnish and Turkish approaching more and more to an Aryan type. (*ibid.* 384)

While Müller's main concerns were with the clearly 'agglutinative' nature of these languages (i.e. with the grammatical additions to the root part of the word – the which was and would still be clearly visible), his comments – as in the 1853 essay – contain many related speculations about the movements of and/or the contacts between and possible protohistory of the several proximate peoples, especially those at the Western end of the vast group. In particular there is much about "the wear and tear of speech [i.e. the grammar and lexis] in its own continuous working" (*ibid.* 387) at the time of juxtaposition of "the Turanian,[11] Semitic,[12] and Aryan branches" (*ibid.*).

Small wonder, then, that Tolkien had the name of an eponymous or mythic 'Turan' already clearly shaped in his imaginative collection of possible names. Further plausible legends behind or before the Finnish proto-text, the *Kalevala* must have surely suggested or even demanded some form of (fictional) reconstruction of these highly suggestive contacts.

A.H. Sayce,[13] (1845-1933), long the deputy professor of Comparative Philology and also working under Müller at Oxford from 1876 to 1890, is, at least in his

---

10 While much of this is poetic, rhetorical, and clearly exaggerated, if not untrue, the generalizations well fitted the pro-Indo-European bias of the mid-Victorian period. More significantly, there are many ideas here for the creation and the characteristics of the 'northern' settings of most of *The Silmarillion*.
11 Elsewhere, as in his 1868 Rede Lecture, *On the Stratification of Language* (published text, 1868: 8), he uses the more standard term Ural-Altaic.
12 Later conservative scholarship wrongly queried Semitic influence on European languages. Excellent philologists like Tolkien or Szemerényi challenged this (see, for example, Szemerényi 1962: 19).
13 His scholarship on Sumerian Erech may be shown to have influenced Tolkien's Stone of Erech and the notion of the oath-breaking of the Sleepless Men ('The Passing of the Grey Company') in *TT* (see also essay 2 – 'Oath-Swearing, the Stone of Erech and the Near East of the Ancient World of this volume).

earlier writings,[14] another scholar who had much to say on the theme – and one which would have been equally intriguing to the young Tolkien – in his *The Principles of Comparative Philology* (1874).[15] Early on in that work, Sayce, on philological grounds, had narrowed the sense of the core name thus:

> The term *Turanian* must be confined to those Ugro-Altaic languages which, as it seems to me, have been proved [...] to be related to one another (extending from Finland on one side to Manchuria on the other). Under the Ugrian dialects are classed Finnish, Lapp, Mordvinian [...] etc.; while the Altaic comprise the three great sub-classes of Turkish-Tartar, Mongolian, and Tungusian. (1874: 21)

Sayce's Turanian interests include: numerals (*ibid.* 22); Akkadian (i.e. ancient Semitic) *erc*, a city,[16] as a borrowing from Turanian (*ibid.* 207); the consonant similarities between Finnish and Assyrian (*ibid.* 247), etc. Of peculiar fascination is 'Appendix I' (*ibid.* 389ff.), entitled 'The route followed by the Western Aryans in their Migration into Europe'. This contains many intriguing and linguistically plausible speculations:

> 1) did the speakers of this primitive European language move [...] through Armenia[17] [...] or through [...] the steppes of Tartary and across the Ural range? (*ibid.* 392);

or the illustration long ago

> 2) that the ancestors of the Finns must have come from a southern Asiatic home, the name Suomi being "strangely like Sumir" (*ibid.*);

while

> 3) [t]he legends of the creation, the flood, the giants, and the monsters contained in the Epic of the half-savage, Voguls, resemble those of ancient Chaldea.[18] (*ibid.*)

Perhaps it only remains to stress that Sayce, even more than Müller, had seen the force of such probing language studies or 'comparative philology' as, surely,

---

14 In his *Introduction to the Science of Language* (1880: vol. II, 189), he prefers the term Ural-Altaic to Turanian.
15 The book was used by Tolkien as both student and teacher. The references are to the Fourth (enlarged) Edition, 1892.
16 Compare Tolkien's use of this base in names.
17 This is echoed by Tolkien discussing the movement of the Indo-European peoples along "the Armenian highlands" (*YWES V* 39).
18 See Adam (1874).

very concerned with ethnology and mythology, and so arouse for them both – and one particular follower – their preoccupation with

> the road by which our Aryan forefathers entered Europe (*ibid.* 389);

for

> [w]hen Comparative Philology first sets them before our view [...] [t]hey were herdsmen and cultivators [...] (*ibid.*)

Perforce the Indo-Europeans, like the Turanians who settled in Europe, and especially the Finno-Ugrians, had acquired various characteristics of language and legendary experience of their antecedents from their time of contact with the Sumerians and other Semitic peoples in southern Mesopotamia.

Recalling the Earliest Struggles and Wars from the Dawn of Memory

Further, the pre-biblical legends of creation and of wars against monsters of great menace were an inheritance for 'speculative mythology' that could not be resisted by the young scholar Tolkien. Small wonder, then, that Finno-Ugrian materials are referred to in his earliest surviving stories as published in *The Book of Lost Tales*, in *The Silmarillion*, and, perhaps most significantly, in the three apparently 'general' – but widely ranging – philological essays[19] of his early academic career. Indeed, it is there that he unashamedly declares his own fascination with

> the pre-history of Europe and nearer Asia [...] an intricate web, whose tangle we may now guess at [...] [for] Germanic and Indo-European philology are part of the history of English (*YWES V* 27-9).

Perhaps even more significantly, the notion of Turanians had persisted on and into the acceptable Georgian scholarship that was part of the mental climate of the young academic's intellectual life. Thus, in writing in 1921 on the Central

---

19 See *YWES IV* 20-37, *YWES V* 26-65 and *YWES VI* 32-66. These are variously referred to in Ryan (2009: 75-79, and elsewhere).

Asiatic Turks, the Oxford trained ethnologist Marya Antonia Czaplicka,[20] a comparativist well known to William Craigie, had – in the *Encyclopædia of Religion and Ethics* – referred to "their Turanian conquerors" (Hastings 1921: 479).

Postscript

The contention at the core of this shorter paper of mine, as offered to *Quettar* nearly thirty years ago, is that there was a vast field for both imaginative and intuitive story-making limned out or Tolkien by his English philology heroes and that the challenge[21] so eagerly accepted is summed up in that then selected and made so creatively into the Tolkienian legend-generative name, that of Túrin.

---

20 An anthropologist of Northern Europe and a member of Somerville College, she was a staunch Roman Catholic of Polish extraction, and someone whose grave is not far from Tolkien's own in Oxford.
21 Summed up as "the tantalizing glimpses and guesses that lie behind sure history" (*YWES V* 39).

Gollum and the Golem: A Neglected Tolkienian Association with Jewish Thought

> Another involved but linguistically suggestive etymology is Gollum's original name Smeagol, and that of the brother he murdered (in Cain and Abel fashion), Deagol. (Ryan 1969: 136)

> *golem*. Also Golem [from Hebrew, *gōlem*, 'shapeless mass']. In Jewish legend, a human figure made of clay, etc., and supernaturally brought to life; in extended use, an automaton, a robot. (*O.E.D. Supplement* 1972: 1258)

> The Hebrew word golem occurs once in the Old Testament (Psalm 139.16) where it means a human being not yet fully formed, an embryo. (Cavendish 1983a: 1135)

> Gollum possessed a dark, antisocial ego and a compensating prosocial shadow. (O'Neill 1979: 63)

Although the word *golem* does not appear in English literature until 1897 when it was used by Henry Iliowizi in the story, 'The Baal-Shem and His Golem', in his *In the Pale: Stories and Legends of the Russian Jews*, to refer to a human agency, likened to a bolt of lightning "which killed the people and destroyed the building" (1897: 171), such a creature had already occurred in print in the late Jewish Legend, as re-told by Jacob Grimm in 1808 in his *Zeitung für Einsiedler* [i.e. *Journal for Hermits*] (56). There the golem is a figure, akin to a human being, created artificially by magic from clay or mud, and brought to life when the miraculous name of God was pronounced over it. The golem is dumb, but it can understand orders – some versions of the legend accord it the power of speech – and it may be used for menial tasks, but it is never to be allowed to leave the service of its master.

This essay was originally printed in *Orana* 18.3 (1982: 100-103) and is here reproduced with the kind permission of its editors.

In the oldest extant code of Jewish law, the *Talmud* (third to fourth centuries), the word is used: once for Adam's body during the first hours of its existence but before it was fully endowed with life and consciousness; and elsewhere to denote an uncultured, boorish man. It then occurred in the *Book of Yesirah* (or Creation), c. A.D. 500, which, despite its short length, is one of the most difficult works to understand in all Jewish literature. That book, which shows strong Hellenistic and Gnostic influence,[1] is based on a magical picture of the world, and has enshrined in it a notion of the metaphysical principles of the universe and the stages of its creation as being bound up with various numbers and letters. These ideas are connected with the Golem doctrine, that is, with the notion according to which living creatures can be produced from lifeless matter by the proper recitation of the creative letter combinations.

In the circle of Jewish mystics of the twelfth and thirteenth centuries, these conceptions gave rise to a mystical rite of creating a golem, by taking earth from virgin soil and shaping it into a golem, and of bringing it to life by walking round it and using the appropriate combinations of letters and mystical 'names of God'. By the act of walking in the opposite direction and reciting the magic formulae in reverse order, the golem would again become lifeless.

Norbert Wiener in his 1964 *God and Golem, Inc.*, a work subtitled *A Comment on Certain Points where Cybernetics Impinges on Religion*, continued an investigation begun in his earlier *The Human Use of Human Beings* (1950) into the general area of knowledge, power and worship, as well as into the control and the evaluation of human purposes, noting that:

> In Jewish legend, *Golem* is an embryo Adam, shapeless and not fully created, hence an automaton. (*O.E.D. Supplement* 1972: 1258)

He also refers[2] to Rabbi Loew of Prague

> who claimed that his incantations blew breath of life into the Golem of clay [...]. (Wiener 1964: 49)

---

1 See Scholem (1960: 209-59). The book had an English translation in 1965.
2 His book is cited in the *Supplement to the Oxford English Dictionary* Vol. 1 (1972: 1258). This volume was compiled by Tolkien's former doctoral student, R.W. Burchfield. It is understood that the editor had discussed this entry with Tolkien.

This last association – according to R.J. Zwi Werblowsky – marks the transition of the concept from an essentially mystic-symbolic ritual to a subject for popular folklore and legend and which then made the golem

> an actual creature serving his master and fulfilling menial and other tasks laid upon him. Legends of this kind were fairly widespread among German Jews after the 15th century and came also to be known among non-Jews; *Goethe's Sorcerer's Apprentice* is indebted to the golem legend. (Cavendish 1983a: 1136)

Wiener's reference to the Rabbi of Prague brings in the best known golem legend, one which seems to date – though it has no historical foundation – from the end of the 18th century and which is connected with the history of the ghetto and old synagogue of the Bohemian capital city. In the more developed versions, the Golem serves both Rabbi Judah Loew and the Jews of Prague by discovering various plots against them and by preventing their execution.

A series of novels and folklore type treatises concerned with developing the legend have been popular in the last hundred years, including:

> 1) the mystic-occultist novel *Der Golem* (1915) by Gustav Meyrink (translated into English by Madge Pemberton in 1928);
> 2) the Yiddish drama *Der Golem* by H. Leivick (1921); or
> 3) Abraham Rothberg's *The Sword of the Golem* (1970).

The last work is dedicated

> [t]o all who have searched the past of the Golem and questioned his meaning; but most of all to the great Leivick, who breathed new life into the Golem's clay. (v)

A more recent work is Alfred Bester's poignant exploration of Golem's perception of humanity in his *Golem 100* (1980). It is the contention of the present writer that the list may well include the name of J.R.R. Tolkien for his creation of Gollum in *The Hobbit* and, particularly, in *The Lord of the Rings*.

*   *   *

All readers of Tolkien's 'On Fairy Stories' (1947) will be aware of his interest in the creative process[3] and in the unselfish and selfish creation of art and of life.

---

3 See, for example, my own 'Folktale, Fairy Tale, and the Creation of a Story', an essay published in several versions over the years, last in *Tolkien's View* (2009: 153-77).

This notion of a hierarchy of peoples between the 'free' and the 'slaves' is well discussed by Paul Kocher,[4] who discerns vestiges of a 'Chain of Being' with "life (discerned) in terms of the doctrine of Creation and Fall" (1973: 83), illustrated by Tolkien's distinction between the human and the subhuman:

> Other creatures are like other realms with which Man has broken off relations, and sees now only from the outside at a distance. (2001: 66f)

Clearly, in very many ways, this Tolkienian notion of lesser beings who also serve is implicit in the later notions of both the golem, and the Gollum of *The Lord of the Rings*.

As Werblowsky stresses (Cavendish 1983a: 1136), the golem acquires enormous strength, the ability to ferret out secrets, and the power to prevent (vicious) plots – all more or less true of Tolkien's Gollum.

If we examine closely the Rothberg novel as an extended late study of the Golem, various interesting details emerge –

> "Golem (is) a creature that God sent to protect us" (1970: 17);
> "a Golem with whom (the Rabbi) would defend Jews against their adversaries" (*ibid*. 13);
> "a golem – an incomplete creation deprived of the light of God within him" (*ibid*. 20);
> that Golem "shall die for the Jews"[5] (*ibid*. 39);
> "who kills Cain shall become Cain" (*ibid*. 74); and
> "He is a golem. A golem is neither murdered nor mourned." (*ibid*. 220).

The work also quotes, through the mouth of the fanatical Dominican monk, Thaddeus, the curse upon all Jews enunciated by Pope Innocent III:

> The Jews, like Cain, are doomed to wander the earth as fugitives and vagabonds, and their faces shall be covered with shame. (*ibid*. 116)

Tolkien was particularly interested in the legend of the Wandering Jew, vestiges of which he found in the old man in Chaucer's 'Pardoner's Tale';[6] the essential innocence of the Jewish people of whom in 1938 he wrote to his possible German

---

4 See, particularly, pp. 82-83 of his *Master of Middle-earth* (1973).
5 It is notable how many times the hobbits are enjoined to pity Gollum and to spare him and in the end his death in sin proves necessary to the world's salvation just as Christ's is as the remover of all sins.
6 Personal knowledge from Oxford lectures in 1955.

publishers, "I can only reply that I regret that I appear to have *no* ancestors of that gifted people" (Carpenter 1981b: 37); and in the central European origins of a paternal forbear.

He was also a scholar of Hebrew and was one of the "principal collaborators in translation and literary revision" of *The Jerusalem Bible* (Jones 1968: ii). For all these reasons, it would seem that there is more than enough probability of his knowledge of this legend which had received such sensitive humanizing in the last century or so.

The only actual etymology given the name Gollum is repeated by Robert Foster in 1978 –

> He was called Gollum because of the disgusting noise he made in his throat
> – after he found the Ring. (168)

But we need not accept merely this simplistic jest and seeming onomatopoeia. If one muses over the later associations of the golem in legend, it is clear that various writers have tried to explore the subhuman creature's yearning to be something more than a programmed primaeval being – Rothberg, for example, suggests very subtly that the creature's desire to love and be loved by a woman and to be treated as a son. In *The Lord of the Rings* it is Sam who particularly misunderstands Gollum's sincere desire to be a good person and to escape the control of the Ring as some kind of slinking and fawning,[7] which is very far from the true case.

While no exact equations are possible or desirable between these Jewish legends and Tolkien's great fictional construct, it would seem that some of the following equivalences can only assist our understanding of the associative richness of the sub-creation:

> Gollum's elemental nature and essentially rudimentary emotions = the largely unformed and elemental golem;
> Hobbits of earlier centuries (Gollum is perhaps 589 at the time of his death) = the Jewish race;
> Gollum = The Wandering Jew/the Golem;

---

7 See Foster (1978: 167).

Gollum's desire to escape Sauron's cruel service = the golem's desire to escape his terrible destiny of sacrifice for his ungrateful and manipulative master and the latter's people;

Gollum's position as 'outsider' = the Golem's inability to find acceptance amongst the people whom he serves reluctantly;

Gollum is a ferreter out of secrets = the golem's similar ability;

Gollum's destiny was to save his people = the golem's role in all late legends;

Gollum shall be returned to the basic elements of his being in the furnace of the Circle of Doom = the Golem is 'unmagicked' into clay by his human creator.

Although the list of these parallel associations might be extended in various details, the more significant aspect is the loose equivalence between the two and the way in which acceptance of the general identification enables the reader to make quite subtle variations between the two Gollum identities. Certainly the Tolkien equation, like the exploration of the psyche of the Golem by Rothberg (in whose work he is also known as Joseph) assists our understanding of the essential ambivalence of the primitive 'servant figure' and in particular of his two 'masters', Frodo and Sauron, the first of whom he loves and is anxious to serve, the second of whom he fears and knows that he can never escape.

And so, in Summary

This legend and equivalence, if accepted, enable his readers to further explore Tolkien's thoughts about the Jewish race, and in particular, the seeming divinely cursed archetypal wanderer of all mediaeval and later European legend. It also assists peculiarly our understanding of the great commandment of Middle-Earth, the need for pity. Yet, the most poignant implication of the link may well be the need for Christian (Catholic) man to love his alter ego, the Jew of the oldest race of all.

Part B

Romano-British Lydney and its Remarkable Importance for Tolkien's Œuvre

The Lydney Archaeological Site and Tolkien's Portrayal of the King as Healer

> Doing research on the creative writings of
> Tolkien, are you? Then do not neglect Lydney,
> that is most important. [Nora Chadwick,[1] the
> Dark Ages and Celtic scholar, to the present
> writer, in the Cambridge University Library,
> in March, 1965]
>
> His [Aragorn's] power over sickness [...] is taken
> by all as a divine gift, which can belong only to
> a sovereign. (Paul Kocher 1973: 157)

It is noticeable that, to date, no critic has commented on the fact that the character of Aragorn as King is, in one particular, quite unlike the usual (non-Christian) Dark Age monarch – someone necessarily a warrior, a lawgiver if he should be a wise man, and occasionally with a priestly function – but never someone endowed with the power of a sensitive and compassionate healer.

It is the purpose of this relatively short paper to draw attention to a remarkable, and arguably deeply influential, experience associated with Tolkien's younger adult life and reflecting his strong Christian faith; and it is also a case of a conjunction of circumstances which may well have drawn his reflections to ponder on the survival in Mercia of one renowned place of healing and of much public resort to it, in an earlier phase in the history of 'England', and in a time of disorder, of the eclipse of ruling hierarchies, and of much social unrest. The actual geographical setting for this set of associations and experiences is one just inside England as one approaches from Wales in the north, and it is

---

This essay first appeared in the Australian journal, *The Ring-Bearer* 7.1 (1990: 26-36) under the title 'Tolkien's Use of the Lydney Archaeological Site in his Portrayal of the King as Healer' and is here reprinted with the kind permission of its editors. It has been somewhat expanded and revised for this publication, particularly in view of the later publications of the *Victoria County History for Gloucestershire*, especially as in Vol. IV (1988), Vol. V (1996), and Vol. XII (2010). It may also be read in connection with the essay 'Dwarf's Hill and the 'Dwarf's Chapel'...' on pp. 121-27 of this present volume of essays.

1 Initial contact with her had been made by me during the 'Golden Age in Northumbria' seminar in the University of Durham, in the summer of 1958, when she had discussed and interpreted various apparent Roman survivals in that area and at various Roman excavations along the Wall.

at the southern edge of the ancient Forest of Dean, to the immediate west of the wide Severn estuary, and so it "is by nature a part of the Welsh foothills" (Hawkes 1982: 45).[2]

In an enlightened move towards the clearer establishment of the likely significance of the historical landscape, the then Lord Bledisloe in 1927 had offered for re-excavation a hilltop site on his estate which, with its waist-high walls in one area, was known locally as the 'Dwarf's Chapel'.[3] Thus it was that Mortimer Wheeler and his wife, throughout the summers of 1928 and 1929, were invited to – and then did – direct an archaeological operation at Lydney, on a spur 200 feet above the banks of the Severn, a site last dug into in 1805. The result of these early nineteenth century investigations had still left many gaps in the knowledge of exactly what had happened at a place known to have been occupied since pre-Roman times. It was then, in 1927, felt by both the owner of the land and by the Society of Antiquaries that a proper scientific excavation might produce a more complete picture of its past.

In particular, it was hoped to discover the possible or likely reason for the long survival of this ancient Celtic place of so much recourse under the Roman rule. And so, for two summers, the Wheelers worked painstakingly to lay bare the story of the Lydney settlement, thereby discerning from the evidence:

the outline of the pre-Roman village;

the infiltration of Roman customs;

the cutting of a Roman iron-mine inside the settlement's bounds;

the developement of the site as a place of pilgrimage towards the end of the Roman occupation (of Britain); and

the fact that the place then had built on it a shrine to a mysterious god, soon to be known as 'Nodens'.

The whole site, of some five acres extent, was probably established in – or shortly before – the first century B.C.[4] After discussion of the early occupation by Celtic

---

2 See the map on p. 14 of the present volume.
3 The north east of the eminence was also known as Dwarf's Hill in the eighteenth century. That aspect of the place, and the old iron mine, as influences for Tolkien's *The Hobbit* were earlier discussed by me in my note, 'Dwarf's Hill, Lydney Park, Gloucestershire' in the *Book of Mazarbul* 7 (1986: 12-14), reprinted here in this volume on pp. 121-27.
4 The general details are taken from Wheeler and Wheeler, *Report on the Excavation of the Prehistoric, Roman and Post-Roman Site in Lydney Park, Gloucestershire* (1932). Specific references are given as in the Report and the page numbers there are then shown.

peoples, and then "during the second and third century A.D., occupied by a Romano-British population" (1932: 1), the summary continues:

> Soon after A.D. 364-7[5] a temple, dedicated to the otherwise unknown deity Nodens, was built within the earthwork, and with the temple, which was of unusual plan, were associated a guest-house, baths and other structures, indicating that the cult was an important centre of pilgrimage. About the end of the fourth century, the buildings were surrounded by a precinct wall; but later, they fell into decay and the final phase of occupation, coinciding probably with the fifth and sixth centuries, is represented by a reinforcement of the prehistoric earthwork. (*ibid.*)

Among the many assistants and scholarly collaborators in the excavation there were two close friends and trained classicists, R.G. Collingwood (M.A., F.S.A.), and Professor J.R.R. Tolkien, both of the University of Oxford.

Robin Collingwood (1889-1943), Romano-British archaeologist, philosopher and only slightly older friend of Tolkien's – and another Fellow of Pembroke College in Oxford – had visited the site and helped in the initial dating of its pottery finds, of the brooches and of parts of the inscriptions found there (*ibid.* 100ff.) Tolkien, then called in as a suitable philologist and inscriptions consultant, had duly "presented a detailed report upon the name of the Lydney god, Nodens" (*ibid.* 3).[6] As the various progressive datings made clear, it was not until the last half-century of Roman rule in Britain that stone buildings of a Roman type[7] were first erected on the Lydney promontory. They are five in number and may be described briefly (*ibid.* 22ff):

1) the most southerly, a temple the dominant structure, dedicated to the otherwise god, Nodens or Nudens; and this building with seven projecting Bays or 'chapels';

2) a long narrow building, styled by Wheeler the 'abaton';

3) to the north-east, a large building "consisting of four ranges of rooms opening upon a central courtyard, and including a great hall in the southern range [...] 'the guest-house' [...];"

4) to the westward a large and elaborate public bathhouse; and

5) a small square water tank to the north.

---

5   Dated by coins found there in great numbers.
6   This note is listed in his 'Bibliography' by Humphrey Carpenter, in his *J.R.R. Tolkien: A Biography* (1977), but the archaeological work is not discussed at all.
7   Earlier structures were of timber and largely associated with the peasant population's somewhat rudimentary essays at iron mining.

The Wheeler report gives considerable space (*ibid*. 42-57) to an analysis of the 'guest-house' and to its relationship with the baths, the former covering "nearly half an acre of ground [...] with an open central courtyard, roughly square" (*ibid*. 44),[8] a possible upper level (*ibid*. 45), with much wall decoration (*ibid*. 46). Further, it was not like the normal country residence[9] as found in various (often Celtic) parts of the Empire in the west. The 'Long Building', contemporary with the 'guest-house', is one conjectured to have

> contained a number of small shops for the traffiking of wares – small votive offerings and the like – to visitors to the shrine. (*ibid*. 51)

The Wheelers also drew attention to the elaborate mosaic pavements[10] in the building, and then they referred to various valid parallels to the shrine at Epidaurus, where the temple of Asklepios was the greatest centre of the healing cult, and the long building or 'baton', adjacent to the temple there, was deemed to be a

> private house of incubation to which patients, after due preparation, repaired for the holy sleep in which the god of healing was expected to bring them helpful counsel. (*ibid*.)

Wheeler also explores the notion of holy sleep, as discussed by Pausanias in his *Description of Greece* (book ii, chapter 27) and argues (1932: 51-2) that there is a pattern in the ancient Indo-European medical places – at Epidaurus, at Kos and at Athens[11]

> [the juxtaposition of such buildings being] a recurrent feature of some of the principal classical shrines of healing, and we may provisionally regard the Lydney building as a member of the series [...] for the purpose of that temple-sleep through which the healing god and his priesthood were wont to work. (ibid. 52)

---

8   Wheeler also noted the tree roots (an original planting, – or a later intrusion?).
9   The reader is referred to the then recent and definitive account of this style of building, namely, R.G. Collingwood, *The Archaeology of Roman Britain* (1930).
10 For the Lydney parallel to Tolkien's 'Numenorean' titles, see J.S. Ryan, 'Ancient Mosaics from out the West: Some Romano-British 'Traditional' Motifs' in *Minas Tirith Evening Star* 15.3 (1986d: 13-17), with one map and three illustrations, re-edited in this volume on pp. 129-35.
11 Mortimer Wheeler then (on p. 52) refers the reader to a [then] authoritative work on the whole subject, which is: Hamilton, Mary, *Incubation or the Cure of Disease in Pagan Temples and Christian Churches* (1906). There is much parallelism between this comparative work and Tolkien's own and later fictional notion as in the epic's 'The Houses of Healing'.

The God Nodens and Tolkien's Interpretation of the Name

In his own remarks (*ibid.* 132-37) in the official report, Tolkien was at some pains to emphasize the limited validity of any philological interpretation of the name itself, for, as Wheeler had then stressed,

> [...] by the end of the fourth century A.D., many of the older cults had assumed or begun to assume a new guise; and even were it possible to define with certainty the original significance of the name, it would still be quite unwarrantable to infer that that significance had any real bearing upon the nature of the cult in A.D. 370. (*ibid.* 39)

Tolkien's own appendix, although a complex essay in comparative philology, contains certain very clear details:

> 1. the name 'Nodens' (in three inscriptions and, perhaps, also in a mosaic (*ibid.* 132) is the phonetic equivalent of the Irish Nuada; one of the bearers of that name[12] was the king of the possessors of Ireland before the Milesians;
>
> 2. the name is Celtic and probably Goidelic (*ibid.* 40, 133-35);
>
> 3. the name is akin to the Germanic stem *neut*, which, in its oldest sense, meant 'to catch', 'entrap'[13] and so 'acquire', thus suggesting that the name 'Nodens' may originally have been given to a divine 'trapper' or god of hunting and, possibly, even of fishing.

He concludes with a reference to "the ancient fame of the magic hand of Nodens the Catcher" (*ibid.* 137).

The Evidence of the Cult-Objects

The main text of Wheeler's report notes the above points and then draws our attention to the cult-objects found on the site: figures of dogs, wrought both in stone and brass; an oculist's stamp (*ibid.* 41); more than 320 pins, both of bronze and of pine (*ibid.* 41-2); and various sea-motifs. The conclusion then drawn is that the cult is a complex one, having come about by the probable 'coalescence' of a number of different elements.

---

12 *Nuada Argat-lam*, 'of the Silver Hand'.
13 Tolkien (*ibid.* 136) also draws attention to the 'fisherman' sense to Gothic *outa* and its use in *The Gothic Gospels*, as in the *Gospel of St. Mark* 12.13. Gothic was studied by Tolkien when a pupil to Joseph Wright, even as he would, as professor, regularly urge his Course I students to do the like. For *St. Mark* was long the prime text for all Oxford students of Gothic.

Collingwood's Further Thoughts on the Site

Interestingly, Collingwood had been asked for a revision of his earlier travelling and pocket-sized book, entitled *Roman Britain*[14] towards the end of 1931, this appearing in his revised edition of this work, the 'Preface' to which is dated January 1932. The third section of it is focussed on temples in the Roman Empire, with some discussion of the official temple of Claudius at Colchester, and the temple of Sul at Bath, he then moving to a discussion of the ordinary Romano-British temple, square, and built to a Romano-Celtic standard, this being one variously growing up in "the Celtic provinces under Roman rule and under the influence of Roman architectural ideas" (137).

Collingwood had then inserted into the text, a summary of the very recent analysis of the several scholars' Lydney experience:

> The most interesting Temple in Britain, however, is of a different type again. This is the temple of Nodens [...] built [...] late in the fourth century, perhaps in the pagan revival that took place under Julian the Apostate. The sudden development of this remote hilltop [...] into an important religious centre [...] suggests that [...] a primitive cult had long been carried on by an un-Romanized peasantry [...]. (*ibid.* 137/39)

and had then gone on to observe that

> The temple of Nodens is a basilica, with a central nave and aisles at each side, and in each aisle are two side-chapels. Beside the temple stood a large court-yard house, doubtless an inn for the accomodation of visitors to the shrine; there was also a fine suite of baths, and behind the temple was a row of what may have been shops. The whole settlement was clearly a place of pilgrimage, and gives a vivid picture of the last phase of pagan religion in Roman Britain. (*ibid.* 139)

Writing in the same year in a related text,[15] prepared for presentation that August (of 1932) to the International Congress of Prehistoric and Protohistoric Sciences in London, and entitled *The Personality of Britain, Its Influence on Inhabitant*

---

14 Other publications by Robin Collingwood published in the aftermath of his Lydney experiences include: *The Archaeology of Roman Britain* (1930); and *Roman Britain and the English Settlements* (1937).

15 Issued as a separate monograph and published in Cardiff by the National Museum of Wales. The quotation is from the Fourth Edition, 1952 impression. Wheeler is referred to variously, as in the Lydney sections (82, 88).

and Invader in Prehistoric and Early Historic Times, the distinguished Cyril Fox had referred to his own work as

> a convenient summary of a variety of influences, internal and external, which helped to mould the successive cultures of the Highland Zone[16] [...] and [a survey of] the relations of the Zone [...] to the rest of Britain, to Ireland, and to Western Europe generally. (1952: iii)

And so to 'The Houses of Healing' in *The Return of the King*[17]

Tolkien's major references in the trilogy to the healing of the sick occur in Chapter VIII of Book V, and in Chapter V of Book VI, in the last volume of *The Lord of the Rings*. The special chambers themselves are first referred to as "fair houses set apart for the care of those who were grievously sick" (*RotK* 131) and the place is associated with 'light' (*ibid*. 132) and good care ("there they were tended well", *ibid*. 136).

> For though all love was in these latter days fallen from its fullness of old, the leechcraft of Gondor was still wise [...]. (*ibid*.)

Soon after this, Ioreth quotes the old proverb: "'*The hands of the king are the hands of a healer*. And so the rightful king could ever be known'"(*ibid*. 138); and then her speech is repeated by Gandalf (*ibid*. 139), to justify in formal fashion Aragorn's entrance therein and then his therapeutic – almost sacramental – use of the medicinal herb, kingsfoil (*ibid*. 140). Thus there are duly treated by him Faramir,[18] Éowyn, Merry, and then all those "in peril through hurt or wound, or who lay under the Black Shadow" (*ibid*. 147).

Again, after the field of Cormallen, Aragorn has the appropriate task of healing the many hurt (*ibid*. 235) and we are again taken to the Houses of Healing, where the wise Warden tells how the army now has

---

16 Including hill forts and settlements like Lydney.
17 This 'Gondor' association gives it connections with the Western Sea, rather than locating it on the larger ('European'?) landmass.
18 This cure is also wrought, at least in part, by Bergil's faith.

[...] the new captain out of the north [as] [...] their chief. A great lord is that, and a healer; and it is a thing passing strange to me that the healing hand should also wield the sword. [O]nce it was so, if old tales be true. (*ibid*. 236)

As soon as she has been healed of her sickness and of her unnatural lust for battle, Éowyn, – as sister of the new king of the Rohirrim, Éomer – now puts aside her 'winter', and avers: "I will be a healer, and love all things that grow [...]" (*ibid*. 243).

Tolkien and Lydney

It is the contention of this short paper that the 'spirit of place' of the Lydney hill temple, in the territory of the Romano-Celtic Dobunni had worked subtly upon Tolkien to influence both his concept of Aragorn as healer and, so linked, the careful creation of his 'Houses of Healing'. While more recent Celtic studies[19] may have modified this interpretation of the Gloucestershire temple somewhat, it is not to be doubted that Tolkien was stirred very deeply by what Wheeler called "that lovely spot," and both a "forest sanctuary and a place of pilgrimage" (Dillon and Chadwick 1967: 140).[20] And it was seen by his friends, Wheeler and Collingwood, as a therapeutic place, perhaps Aesculapian in character, with its cells for the patients and guest-quarters for their families and visitors. As the many votive offerings make it clear, the native population frequented the ancient site in such numbers in the later fourth century that the cult had flourished on the re-occupied Iron Age site.

Arguably Tolkien's garrulous old healing woman, Ioreth,[21] is a subtle and significant creation, the purpose of which was to suggest the antiquity of the cult, and so of the legends that it had come from far away and much earlier in time. While the Lydney proximity to the Severn estuary is not paralleled precisely in Tolkien's story, soon after his second period of healing, Aragorn

---

19 E.g. see Anne Ross, *Pagan Celtic Britain*, where Nodens is equated with Mars and Silvanus (1967: 191, 198, 201), and the healing and fertility aspect of the Cult is stressed (*ibid*. 207).

20 This is, of course, the same Mrs Chadwick and the widow of H.M.Chadwick of *The Growth of Literature* fame who had been insightful and directional in her immediate response to the present writer's to probe this matter when researching Tolkien's texts as published to that date, i.e. 1965.

21 Some have likened her to Juliet's Nurse in Shakespeare's *Romeo and Juliet*, a valid comment, since Tolkien liked to utilise 'Warwickshire'–style (Shakespearean) figures in his several folk portraits as often associated with 'the Shire'.

quotes the old Numenorean words that Elendil spoke when he had come up out of the Sea –

"Out of the Great Sea to Middle-earth I am come." (*RotK* 245)

In the following line, Aragorn proclaims: "In this place will I abide, and my heirs, unto the ending of the world." In this sentence one hears echoes of both Jesus Christ's founding of His Church and of Peter as Head of the Established Church. There is even a suggestion or echo of William Blake's hymn,

And did those feet in ancient time
Walk upon England's mountain's green. (*Milton*, 'Preface', ll. 1-2)

It is this Christ-like dimension of Aragorn that removes this healing kingship from that of mediaeval kings, with their ability to cure the king's evil, and makes it more akin to the power of the sacramental touch of Christ to heal the believer, as it is told to us in the *New Testament*: as with the healing of the leper, *Matthew* 8.1-4 (and we may compare from elsewhere in the Gospels, such passages as: *St. Mark* 1.40-45; *Luke* 5.12-16; or the healing of the son of the King's Officer, *John* 4.46-54).

While we cannot now verify in any proximate fashion the rich and speculative talk of Collingwood and Tolkien in Pembroke College on the actual or the possible cults in Roman Britain, or whether it was specifically of the god or priest-healer, it would seem that the spirit of Lydney, of its long abiding faith in healing, and of its ancient associations with the sea and the oldest Goidelic kings had fired Tolkien's mind. The survival there of the belief held by humble folk through many centuries and troubled times could not but have moved him deeply, and his original 1932 note contains for Lydney the significant and powerful link with Christ as a 'fisher of men'.

Even more poignant would have been the fact of the site remaining inhabited after the end of Roman rule and its attempted later protection by various out-works (Wheeler 1932: 57ff.). The 1932 excavation report is filled with details that either parallel the Middle-earth texts or are similar to Tolkien's formal scholarly writings[22] on Roman Britain – none more so than the fact that a Celt

---

22 See, amongst other places, J.S. Ryan, 'Mid-century Perceptions of the Ancient Celtic Peoples of 'England'', in *Seven* 9 (1988: 57-65), reproduced in *Tolkien's View: Windows into his World* (2009: 189-198).

on the Governor's staff acted as clerk of works for the enlarged temple of circa 367 A.D., as Wheeler reports.

Conclusion

The significance of Lydney for Tolkien's developing thought is not a matter of speculation, since his own appendix to the official report on the excavation more than validates our intuition that he would have been fascinated by this example of an ancient Celtic faith, one persisting and growing even stronger in times of turbulence and impending social chaos. He would have been further stimulated by the excited remarks made about his own linguistic probings concerning Lydney by Christopher F.C. Hawkes.[23]

> The change that befell [the site] in the years 364-7 is positively theatrical. (1932: 489);

> [...] the religious implications of the whole are admirably set forth and illustrated. (*ibid*. 489);

and

> The whole study makes a refreshing start on what should be a most vital approach to the rediscovery of our Dark Ages. (*ibid*. 490)

The Spirit of Place at Lydney

It is, in short, the contention of this paper – much in the way that Pausanias had treated of the Jordan, Corinth and Crete – so had Lydney's 'spirit of place' communicated itself dramatically to Wheeler, Collingwood, as well as to Tolkien and Hawkes. The last named had put his finger on the very likely then-conceived fictional exploration by Tolkien of a pre-Christian religious culture, of which only alluring traces had, thus far, been discovered. He had thus had the intuition and inspiration to ponder on the healing god, a likely precursor of Christ, and so to muse as to what manner of mortal man might serve as his chief attendant. For it cannot be denied that this context and place

---

23 Hawkes, an Oxford archaeologist of considerable promise, would duly become Professor of European Archaeology there in 1946.

constitute a most potent source for the developing characterization of his war-rior-king-healer, Aragorn.[24]

The many echoes of John the Baptist in the Aragorn portrait and of other Biblical figures are separate from the healing theme. Tolkien's changing of the style of the hypothesized Dark Age king is a remarkable concept on its own, but less so when we have identified the spirit of Lydney and so understood how the unknown priest-celebrant of that healing cult would contribute to the portrait of Aragorn. Thus, the Biblical echoes then become a natural possible dimen-sion to the thoughts of a larger society on the brink of Christian certitude, and already insightful in matters of the spirit by the possible or likely presence there of a form of Mithratic belief. Perhaps it had been indeed brought thither by the legionaries who had served there long before the coming of Christianity to Canterbury in the person of St Augustine, with his monks, in 597 A.D.

Appendix

The site is discussed illumatingly by Roger J.A. Wilson, on pp. 130-32, in his *A Guide to the Roman Remains in Britain* (1980). He dates the part collapse of the shrine to "some time between 367 and 375, with the consequent collapse of the temple" (*ibid.* 131). He also refers to the side-chapels and their likely use for "some temple-rite, perhaps healing" (*ibid.*) even as he summarizes the attempts to mine iron ore there in the third century as "in many parts of the Forest of Dean" (*ibid.* 132).

---

24 This may be deemed to be reflecting on the intimations of Divine Healing in the Old Testament, as in *Numbers* 19.21, *Isaiah* 53.4-6; or *Ezekiel* 47.1-12, with its reference to the water flowing from under the Temple and to the healing power of this River of Life.

The Mines of Mendip and of Moria, with some Reflections on *The Lair of the White Worm*

His close scholarly associations with the Lydney (Gloucestershire) excavations of R.M. (later Sir Mortimer) Wheeler in the period 1929-32 gave J.R.R. Tolkien his knowledge of the Roman and Romano-Celtic mining at that place,[1] and it can be shown how that excavation, and the subsequent *Report*[2] on it gave some shape and detail to both the narrative account and to the various drawings by Tolkien of Bilbo's experiences in Smaug's Lair in *The Hobbit*. To date there has been no specific analogue or plausible source cited in Tolkien scholarship for the rich and detailed accounts of the actual Mines of Moria in *The Lord of the Rings*, especially as they are described in such detail in its Book Two, in Chapters IV and V.

There is, however, just such a comprehensive and intriguing possible source book, which came into the hands of various of Tolkien's friends such as R.G. Collingwood,[3] philosopher and archaeologist, in the year 1930. It is the Oxford publication, *The Mines of Mendip*, by J.W. Gough, who elaborated particularly on the earlier Roman period work of Professor F.J. Haverfield in *The Victoria History of the Counties of England, Somerset, vol 1*. The latter's scholarship as to various Roman inscriptions[4] found on fibulae, metal pigs, lead weights, etc. is conveniently summarized for the Roman mining (*VCH Somerset 1* 1906: 27 ff.). It is also possible to use the readable 1930 volume as a guide to the prolific and romantic literature as to the caves and underground mines of East Somerset, from the Roman period on, their decline and then concerns about certain later periods of renewed activity, followed by further eclipse.

This essay was first published as 'The Mines of Mendip and of Moria' in *Mythlore* 63 (1990: 25-27, 64) and is here reproduced, with a much extended Appendix, with the kind permission of its editors.

1 On this matter please see 'Dwarf's Hill and the 'Dwarf's Chapel' ...' on pp. 121-27 of this present volume.

2 R.M. Wheeler's excavation report on Lydney was published in 1932 by the Society of Antiquaries. It contained an appendix by J.R.R. Tolkien on the significance of a Latin inscription found on the site.

3 It was Collingwood who drew Tolkien into the Lydney 'dig' as a helper in interpreting the Nodens inscription.

4 Compare the inscription of Balin's death in *FotR* (333).

A particularly attractive aspect to the work of Gough is his indication of the
wealth of the written material about Roman, and later, mining of the cave type
– largely in the West Country – as in (sequentially):

> Pliny, *Naturalis Historia*;
>
> *Letters and Papers, Domestic and Foreign, of the Reign of Henry VIII*;
>
> Toulmin Smith (ed.), *The Itinerary of John Leland in or about the Years 1536-1543*;
>
> Georgius Agricola, *De Re Metallica* (Froben, Basel 1556);
>
> Sir J. Pettus, *Fodinae Regales* (1670);
>
> Sir J. Pettus, *Fleta Minor, The Laws of Art and Nature in Knowing ... Metals; and Essays on Metalic Words* (1683).

Even more intriguing items from Gough's very considerable 'Bibliography'
(1930: 258-64) are:

> Browne's book (a manuscript held at the Bishop's Registry in Wells, Somerset, describing "the mining customs, laws, and orders");
>
> E.A. Baker and H.E. Balch, *The Netherworld of Mendip* (1907);
>
> F.A. Knight (the cultural historian), *The Heart of Mendip* (1915);
>
> H.E. Balch, *The Caves of Mendip* (1926);

or, related,

> A.K. Hamilton Jenkin, *The Cornish Miner* (1927).

There is noted, too, the long series of exciting local articles by the Rev. Preb.
H.M. Scarth, e.g.:

> 'Some Account of the Investigation of Barrows on the Line of the Roman Road between Old Sarum and the Port at the Mouth of the River Axe, Supposed to be the 'Ad Axium' of Ravennas',[5] in *The Archeological Journal* 16 (1859: 146-57);
>
> 'Notes on the Roads, Camps, and Mining Operations of the Romans on the Mendip Hills', in *Journal of the British Archaeological Association* 31 (1875: 129-42);
>
> 'On the Roman Occupation of the West of England, Particularly the Country of Somerset', in *The Archeological Journal* 36 (1879: 321-36); etc.

---

5 As survey maps show, a Roman road ran along the spire of the Mendip Hills, some of it being the
base of the modern B3134 road. It has been thought to have some link with the mines of the Roman
period. See Gough (1930: 46).

Thus it is clear that the mining in and under the Mendip Hills has had a very long course, despite the seemingly serious setbacks to it due to war, political upheaval and various other causes.

There follows now an early modern map (also reproduced by Gough) of the imagined perimeter villages around the mines and caves.

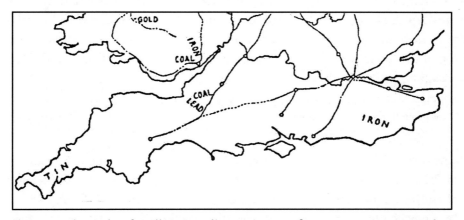

This is to the style of Collingwood's 1936 map of Roman mines in southern Britain. The word 'lead' locates neatly the spine of the Mendip Hills.

The Mendip Region and Tolkien's Dwarf City of Moria

Very familiar, if not echoic, to careful readers of the text of Tolkien will be such 'Introductory' remarks by Gough as:

> The 'netherworld of Mendip', as is well known, is traversed in all directions by the ramifications of innumerable natural caverns [...], and into these the miners delving underground must often have struck. [...] Several of the most famous Mendip caves have owed their discovery to the work of the miners. [...]
>
> Instances are also recorded of vast caverns having been discovered by the miners, but subsequently lost sight of altogether [such as] the great Banwell cave [...] and [...] a prodigious cavern in Sandford Hill, the identity of which has been [...] elusive. (1930: 9)

Even more intriguing for us is his, Gough's, quotation from J. Rutter's text, *Delineations of the North Western Division of the County of Somerset, and of its Antediluvian Bone Caverns: with a Geological Sketch of the District*, as to exploration in 1770 of an enormous cave called 'the Gulf' on the northern Mendip escarpment:

> 80 fathoms, or 480 feet, below the plane of Sandford Hill; they also affirm, they have let down a man, with a line 240 feet deep, without his being able to discover top, sides or bottom. (Rutter 1829: 109)

Another hill cave, in the complex, and one which cannot but remind us of the deep in which the Balrog had been confined so long, is that called Lamb's Lair, the entrance to which lies near the Wells road, a few yards beyond the top of the hill above West Harptree.[6] Gough paraphrases J. Beaumont's 1681 account of the caves thus:

> The ground thereabouts has been the scene of mining operations for ages, and it was about the middle of the seventeenth century that miners working there struck into a cave whose dimensions were far beyond the ordinary. (1930: 10)

The intrepid antiquarian himself found the Cavern to be "about 60 Fathom in the circumference, above 20 Fathom in height" (*ibid.*); yet it was lost sight of and was not entered for nearly two centuries (i.e. between 1681 and 1873). In the later Victorian period it was possible to climb down and view the cave – "and for a few years its beauties became widely renowned" (*ibid.* 12). There was, however, no legend of a monster lurking therein.[7]

Paul Kocher, in his *Master of Middle-earth: The Achievement of J.R.R. Tolkien*, observes, of Gimli's response to earlier dwarves' smithy work and excavations:

> Caught up above his usual dour self, Gimli proceeds to give a superbly lyrical picture of the echoing domes and chambers underground, the glint of polished walls [and] marble columns [...] 'springing from [...] [the] floors [...]'. (1973: 105-6)

This is, of course, a more wonderful account than any recorder of the 'beauties' in certain of the larger Mendip caves.

Another parallel to Tolkien's text occurs in the matter of the actual pollution of the water by (orcish?) mining, smelting, etc. As the members of the Fellowship

---

6 This is about 4-5 miles from the possible 'entrance' in the west under Sandford Hill and could well be said to be near the line of the imagined thoroughfare through the mines, if one were passing from the 'top' of the range to the 'bottom' (or southern end).

7 One may well imagine that in the creation of the Balrog there comes in some measure from Bram Stoker's *The Lair of the White Worm* (2008: 38-40). See the Appendix to this essay.

approach the western gate to the way under the Misty Mountains, they discover a new feature, "[...] a dark still lake. Neither sky nor sunset were reflected on its sullen surface" (*FotR* 314). This may be seen to parallel the mid-nineteenth century Mendip water pollution:

> It is said that the river Axe in the levels below the hills was so much affected that the stock in the neighbourhood through which the river ran became liable to diseases of the lungs. Fish certainly suffered, and people at Cheddar complained of the way in which their stream [...] was made to run "in a semi-muddy state, objectionable to the sight" [...] utterly destructive of all the fish [...]. (Gough 1930: 14)

The Loose Historical Equivalents of Tolkien's Dwarves

While any exact British regional equation cannot now be made for the Tolkienian dwarves' multifarious activities or for the fictional history of their achievement and warring in Moria, it is clear that their lifestyle owes more than a little to the Cornish,[8] and their complex activities parallel in many ways the rise and later eclipse of Roman mining in southwestern Britain. As Pliny reported in the thirty-fourth book of his *Naturalis Historia* (Chapter 49), Britain would, and did, become the chief source of lead in the Roman Empire, and the deposits would also yield silver,[9] much as in the First Age mining did in Moria. And much as there were lesser (lead) mines used by the Romans in Flint, Wirksworth in Derbyshire, and Shelve Hill in Shropshire, with the great centre at Mendip, so there were dwarf-cities at Erebor and others at Nogrod and Belegost, with the great city at Moria, it being called by the dwarves themselves *Khazad-dûm*.

Some notion of the believed legendary complexity of the vast Moria mines is gained by the fact that they ran far under the Misty Mountains, occupying the area under Caradhras and the two other peaks.[10] That this fact is to be set against the (imagined) sprawl of the Somerset mines is clear from the 17th century map below from Gough.

---

8   Tolkien's early enthusiasm for Cornwall is discussed by H. Carpenter in the official biography (1977: 70-71, 73, 160).
9   It is, perhaps, the argentiferous aspect of the ore that gave Tolkien the idea of the prized metal, *mithril*, also called "Moria-silver, or true silver" (*FotR* 331).
10 See Tyler (1976: 314).

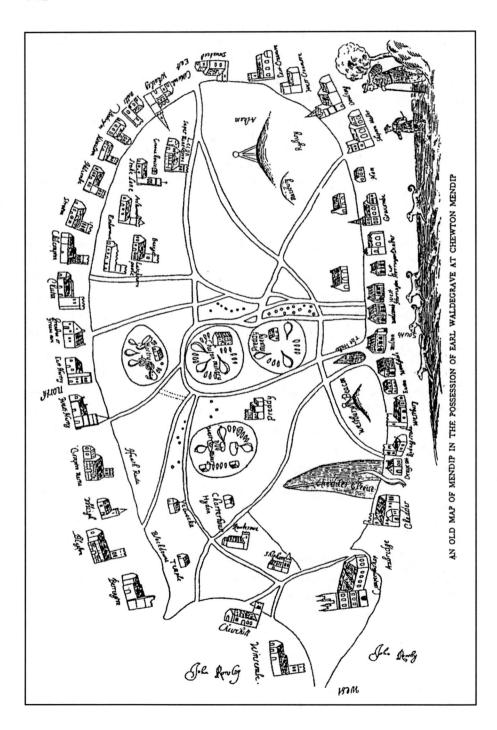

AN OLD MAP OF MENDIP IN THE POSSESSION OF EARL WALDEGRAVE AT CHEWTON MENDIP

Any scrutiny of Somerset topographic maps will show the Mendips to run from the north west near Sandford Hill to the south east, near Shepton Mallet, for some 25 to 30 miles.[11]

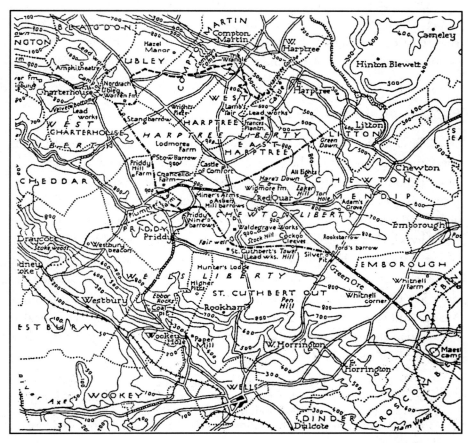

The Mendip Mining District, showing the boundaries of the Liberties of the Lords Royal, Based upon the Ordnance Survey Map, with the sanction of the Controller of H.M. Stationary Office. While Sandford lies off the map to the west, the main caverns lay under the 'Harptree Liberty' in the upper centre of this map.

---

11 In *FotR*, Gandalf observes that: "It cannot be less that forty miles" (323).

And Hopeless Historical Last Stands of (Later) Mendip Men

As much as the dwarves were to be decimated under orcish attacks (*FotR* 333-36), so the fiercely independent Mendip men fought valiantly in the hopeless struggle at Sedgemoor in 1685, and again more than a century later, at the time of the French invasion at Fishguard in 1797. Yet, despite their terrible sufferings, they remained, as Gough observes, "notorious not only for the vigour and independence but for the violence and turbulence of their manners" (1930: 17).

Conclusion on the Mendip Link

It will be clear from these legendary Somerset vignettes and anecdotes regarding the Mines of Mendip that there was here available for Tolkien a splendid model of ancient mining in England – an industry which had waxed and waned and, if one cares to note, had been marked by the subsequent discovery of its early associated treasure hoards.[12] And as Gough observes "we do not even know the name by which [the Romans] called their settlement" (1930: 47).[13] The mystery of the mines and their former glories have haunted all who have speculated about 'the netherworld of Mendip', and it is now postulated that Tolkien had done just the same thing in his confident and forceful account of the realm of Moria. And who is to say that Tolkien was not fired by some archaeological or antiquarian survey essay like that of Gough, with his challenging farewell to the enigma of the great Roman workings?

> When all is told, we know practically nothing of the origins of the industry; under the Romans we catch some glimpses of it, but they are dim and fragmentary [...] and years before Honorius withdrew the legions from Britain in 410 complete darkness has once more descended and blotted it out from our sight. (*ibid.*)

---

12 H.M. Scarth wrote on the coins found at East Harptree in 1883, while H. St. George Gray published his report on those on Sandford Hill in 1925/26.
13 See *RotK* 415; and *FotR* 331, where we are told by Gandalf: "The Dwarves have a name which they do not tell."

Appendix – Bram Stoker's *The Lair of the White Worm*

In an Ancient (Roman?) Mine

In another essay we have already referred to Tolkien's interest in the ancient Roman mining in the West Country – notably that associated with Lydney in Gloucestershire. There is a further analogue to the underground, one only partly fictional, in a novel of his young manhood.

For this theme, in a closely parallel form, is also to be found teased out in another underground context, a literary one to be sure, namely Bram Stoker's *The Lair of the White Worm*.[14] The fascinating story is associated with a legend of Mercia, and with a part of that kingdom with Roman associations. It is believed to have been written between March and July 1911 (Murray 2004: 253ff, 262) and the original edition of the novel was published in London in 1911, with six dramatically coloured plates by Pamela Colman Smith, a member of the Golden Dawn and the creator of the designs for the classic Rider-Waite deck of Tarot cards.[15]

The plot begins with a classic inheritance situation, one in which the key informant is

> Sir Nathaniel de Salis [...] devoted to history, and [...] President of the Mercian Archaeological Society [...] he has a special knowledge of the Peak and its caverns, and knows all the old legends of [...] prehistoric times. (Stoker 2008: 9)

The great house of the cavern legend in question is Castra Regis in the Peak District and it is one with a strange pedigree from "old Mercia" (*ibid.*), being near the Peak and its caverns and associated with the very same "old legends of the days when prehistoric times were vital" (*ibid.*). The major local family is one deemed to be a "race [...] cold, selfish, dominant, reckless [...] of the early Roman type" (*ibid.* 12f), while the neighbourhood itself is one of ancient

---

14 All references are taken from the 2008 Penguin Red Classics edition of the original from 1911.
15 The book received very positive reviews and it moved into paperback in 1925, again in 1945 and 1961, as well as later. Additionally it became a film in 1988, the director being Ken Russell, and the cast including Hugh Grant. For close discussion of the novel see Paul Murray, *From the Shadow of Dracula: a Life of Bram Stoker* (2004). Main references to *The Lair of the White Worm* are on pp. 254-64.

traditions and superstitions, such as those associated with an original nunnery "founded by Queen Bertha, but brutally done away with by King Penda, the reactionary to Paganism after St Augustine" (*ibid*. 17).

The Haunting Past Myths

The setting is one of much legend from antiquity, and current events there cause the past's terrible legends to come alive as the narrator figure explains.

> Diana's Grove [...] has roots in the different epochs of our history [...]. We find that this particular place had another name [...] besides Diana's Grove. This was manifestly of Roman origin [...]. [The other] is more pregnant of adventure and romance than the Roman name. In Mercian tongue it was 'The Lair of the White Worm.' (*ibid*. 35f)

The meaning of the place-name, near the Mercy (i.e. Mercia) farm, and the legend behind it are then likened to both the 'Worm Well' of Lambton Castle and to the 'Laidly Worm of Spindleston Heugh' near Bamborough.

> In both these legends the 'worm' was a monster of vast size and power [...]. [In] England [...] the streams were deep and slow, and there were holes of abysmal depth, where any kind and size of antediluvian monster could find a habitat [...] mud-holes a hundred or more feet deep. Who can tell us when the age of the monsters which flourished in slime came to an end? [...] There must have been [...] places and conditions which made for greater longevity, greater size, greater strength than was usual. (*ibid*. 36f)

and

> The lair of such a monster [...] would not have been disturbed for hundreds – or thousands – of years. (*ibid*. 38)

It is worth noting that the Somerset Mendips could well be deemed at the south-west extremity of the ancient kingdom of Mercia. All of this is explained to a brave young descendant, Adam, welcomed 'home' from Australia by Sir Nathaniel and another antiquarian, the young man's uncle, Richard Salton.

After a detour to some tale in the Terai of Upper India, where a giant snake of one hundred feet in length was seen, the two antiquarians come to a possible source for persisting primaeval monsters –

"Just imagine such a monster anywhere in this country, and at once we could get a sort of idea of the 'worms,' which possibly did frequent the great morasses which spread round the mouths of any of the great European rivers." (*ibid.* 37)

Another motif that reminds us of Tolkien – this time of Gollum on the brink of doom before Sauron's great pits – is found in the struggle between Adam/Frodo and Oolanga/Gollum, as "clutching at each other, they tottered on the very brink" (*ibid.* 124). And the whole convulsion at the Worm's hole finally leaves "a round fissure seemingly leading down into the very bowels of the earth" (*ibid.* 231).

As the troubled myths continue, we also obtain, variously, a set of details applicable to both Smaug of *The Hobbit* and to the Balrog of *The Lord of the Rings*, among them an explanatory reference to the Anglo-Saxon *wyrm*, meaning a dragon or snake, to the Gothic *waurms*, 'a serpent', the Icelandic *ormur* and the German *wurm*.

From an Ancient River to the Persisting Vast Caverns

The connection of the theme of the cavern's denizen with the Diana's Grove is expanded later in the novel, when the owner of the house, the bizarre Lady Arabella March is, unexpectedly, attacked by a mongoose – a sure sign of her incarnate evil. The antiquarians deduce from this that the Lady March, of Diana's Grove, has had her body taken over by the primaeval force of the legendary White Worm as her departing soul was leaving her body after a severe illness. In his summary reflection on this theme, Paul Murray, Stoker's biographer has commented:

Stoker probably derived the concept of this vast, underground-dwelling worm from Wirt Sikes who wrote in *British Goblins; Welsh Folk-lore, Fairy Mythology, Legends and Traditions* of a dragon or demon [...] which guarded underground treasure vaults in Wales. It was supposed to be a creature of vast size whose breath destroyed two districts, and it lay out of sight in a cave near a river (2004: 263).

And in the Stoker text itself – and later – the two elderly wise men are made to ponder on the greater purposes behind the universe, far beyond the White Worm:

We may get into moral entanglements; before we know it we may be in the midst of a bedrock struggle between good and evil. [...] At the same time, we must remember that 'good' and 'evil' are terms so wide as to take in the whole scheme of creation and all that is implied by them and by their mutual action and reaction. (Stoker 2008: 56)

Something Reminiscent of Sauron's Ring

Interestingly the Stoker plot also features an ancient numinous object that will finally destroy the White Worm. It is a lump of loadstone, almost certainly from the goddess, Bes,[16] "an Ægyptian idol cut out of Loadstone and found among the *Mummies*" (*ibid.* 86). The further motif of a treacherous woman turning a princess into a great worm living in a cave is reflected on thus by Stoker's biographer –

> The subject had a powerful attraction for Stoker's contemporaries, the pre-Raphaelites especially. It inspired Swinburne, and the artist, Walter Crane, exhibited an oil painting of the Laidley Worm at the Grosvenor Gallery in 1881 (Murray 2004: 263).

And a Model for Gollum?

Another figure in the plot is the African servant to the proud Caswell –

> Oolanga [...] hideously ugly, with the animal instincts developed as in the lowest brutes; cruel wanting in all the mental and moral faculties – in fact, so brutal as to be hardly human." (Stoker 2008: 26)

While he is not to be discussed now in any detail, many of Oolonga's actions and betrayals must suggest close parallels to Gollum in his relationship to Shelob, and in his terror of Sauron. Yet another fascinating motif is the plague of huge numbers of (migratory?) birds.

Thus it is to be noted that Stoker's tale is both an analogue to parts of the Balrog incident, as well as offering the possibility of the Pre-Raphaelites inspiring Tolkien's imagination.

---

16 Pleasingly Stoker had linked this object to "Sir Thomas Brown's *Popular Errors*, a book of the seventeenth century" (2008: 86).

Ancient World to Early Mediaeval

The very recent scholarship of the end of Roman Britain – as from Robin Fleming – contains much evidence of the re-use of most ancient monuments as with "and in Wales and the Peak District Bronze Age funerary monuments were selected for burials during the Roman period" (2010: 94) and of the habit of nobles claiming "some sort of kinship with the original builders of mounds and to assert that families of the recent dead had tilled nearby fields since time immemorial" (*ibid.*). Similarly, Fleming points out that "small towns lay at the centre of exchange networks [for] the Romano-British countryside" (*ibid.* 14), even as some were re-organizing both the land use and the pattern of society.

Clearly, Lydney was a place of this great cultural change, one where the Roman and the compassionate Christian worlds could be seen in the moment of transition.

Relevant Bibliography of Fourth Century Change

Knight, Jeremy K., 1999, *The End of Antiquity: Archaeology, Society and Religion, AD 235-700*, Stroud, Gloucestershire et al.: Tempus.

Collins, Rob and James Gerrard (eds.), 2004, *Debating Late Antiquity in Britain, AD 300-700*, BAR: British Series, Oxford: Archaeopress, especially pp. 77-87 and 103-11.

Dwarf's Hill and the 'Dwarf's Chapel' ... the Matter of the Ancient Mining There and the Ideas for Further Story that that Fabled Activity might well have Engendered

> On Dwarf's Hill, Lydney Park,[1] Gloucestershire
> (Between the Forest of Dean and the River Severn)
>
> When the estate was purchased [...] in 1723, all this part was overgrown with bushes, but there were walls remaining about three feet above the ground, particularly in a part called the Dwarf's Chapel [...]. (Bathurst, 1879: 3)

In the summers of 1928 and 1929, R.E.M. (later Sir Mortimer) Wheeler, an already renowned British archaeologist, had led the excavation of a 'promontory fort', or small embanked hill-town, once an Iron Age hill fort, some five acres in extent, established at Lydney, on the western side of the Severn valley in Gloucestershire, in or just before the first century B.C., and located close to one of the principal Roman roads into south-west Wales, to the legionary fortress at Caerleon. The hilltop place was re-occupied in the second and third centuries A.D. by a Romano-British population, one engaged to some extent in iron-mining.

An economic expansion occurred after 367 A.D., when a considerable cult pilgrimage thither much increased and the buildings were surrounded by a precinct wall. The complex itself is rectangular, measuring 72m by 54m, with its north-west end divided into three chambers, some 6.3 metres deep. The

---

This note is an expansion of an earlier and shorter one published in *The Book of Mazarbul* 7 in 1986 (12-14). The two illustrations now on pp. 122 and 124 were originally published as Plate VIII to R.E.M and T.V. Wheeler's *Report on the Excavation of the Prehistoric, Roman and Post-Roman Site in Lydney Park, Gloucestershire* and are reproduced here by the kind permission of the report's publishers, The Society of Antiquaries of London. We are not concerned now with the further excavations there by John Casey in 1980 and 1981.

1 Lydney was also – and this is of some romantic historical significance – the home of Sir William Wintour, Admiral of the Fleet of Queen Elizabeth I in 1588, while it was also from here that the timbers were taken, from the Forest of Dean, for the so many of the great ships built to oppose the Spanish Armada.

imposing classical style temple has been interpreted as an *incubatio* or dormitory for sick pilgrims to sleep – compare the 'Houses of Healing' in Book Five of *The Lord of the Rings* – and so to experience a vision of divine presence in their dreams. It has been argued by various scholars that the site was probably chosen because it offered a clear view of the massive bore up the River Severn, a tidal wave of impressive dimensions, and of a linked and even mystical significance. However, later, the fine buildings fell into decay.

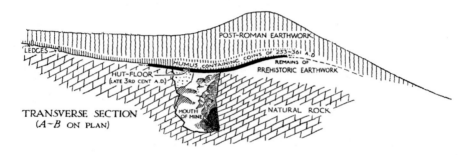

Plate VIII: Iron Mine – Transverse Section A-B of Plan on p. 146 (from Wheeler & Wheeler 1932)

The first serious excavations, those of 1805, had exposed the buildings and uncovered many votive artefacts including a curse tablet and a famous votive figurine of a dog. The 1928 discovery there of an earlier iron-mine, with many of the pick-marks of the miners well preserved, was nationally unique in its explicit dating by coinage found there to the Roman period and even earlier.

Assisting Mortimer Wheeler in the whole 1928-29 investigation were: the brilliant Robin G. Collingwood, as much a Roman archaeologist as an Oxford philosopher – for he held both the chair of Romano-British Archaeology at that time, as well as that of Metaphysics; and, for work on the interpreting of the inscriptions, the latter's friend at Pembroke College, a little-known and very youthful professor of Anglo-Saxon, one J.R.R Tolkien.[2] In the event the latter provided for the scholarly

---

2 Since perhaps the end of the twentieth century, much has been made of the Tolkien link by the tourism industry, as can be seen in this recent entry (2012) on Lydney Park from *Wikipedia*:

There is a legend that after about 20 years of the Romans leaving, the local people forgot the Romans had settled there and began to believe the ruins were the home to dwarves, hobgoblins and little people. The site was excavated by Sir Mortimer Wheeler in the 1920s.

record a special appendix on one of the inscriptions, i.e. 'The Name 'Nodens'', in the *Report on the Excavation of the Prehistoric, Roman and Post-Roman Site in Lydney Park, Gloucestershire* (Wheeler and Wheeler, 1932: 132-37).

It is the contention of this brief note that the site's history had a remarkable influence on the mind of the young academic, already, if largely privately, something of a national myth-maker and a re-fashioner of legend as a (still domestic) story-teller, for *The Hobbit* was soon to be in an embryonic form in the tales which Tolkien was telling his children. At Lydney he could not but have been vastly stimulated by the place, its history, and the speculations of his scholar companions.

The Aura of the Lydney Site

Some of the more dwarvish aspects of the wondrous mental adventures available there for the writer may be tabulated:

1) personal contact with an ancient site formerly known as *Dwarf's Hill* (*ibid.* 1, 3);

2) a folk memory (of mining there) preserved for more than 1200 years in the names *Dwarf's Hill* and *Dwarf's Chapel* (*ibid.* 1);

3) the fort there, presumably occupied by at least several forces and at different times, and one presumably built for the defence of a settlement of Early Iron Age culture;

4) its floor with mosaics being found to seal the adit of an iron-mine;

5) an outer fortification or protective wall, with a horn-work at the north-east corner;

6) an ancient mine that could be entered by a [side] tunnel-shaft;

7) a number of treasure-hoards (largely coin), these found high up on and to the northern end of the site;

8) later repairs to the inner slope of the bank (*ibid.* 5); and

9) the decay of the settlement and its reversion to barbarism, and to a final abandonment.

The author of *The Lord of the Rings* novel, J. R. R. Tolkien, was part of the excavation team and he is said to have been influenced by such folk tales which he used to develop his stories of Middle-earth. He wrote a report, *The Name 'Nodens'*, following the excavation.

This link has also been increasingly broadcast by the B.B.C. (British Broadcasting Corporation), as can be seen in the following weblink: http://www.bbc.co.uk/gloucestershire/films/tolkien.shtml.

While there are other and various possible influences of the Lydney site on the mind and art of the soon-to-be famed mythographer for England, it cannot be doubted that the 'dwarvish' or excavation and mining ventures at that place would have had considerable impact on the mind of a young man, someone

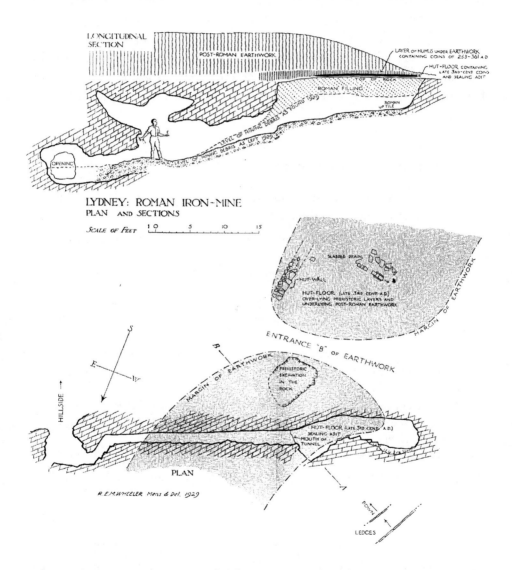

Plate VIII: Iron Mine – Longitudinal Section and Plan (from Wheeler & Wheeler 1932)

who was still to some extent under the influence of his earlier and long exposure to the classical and the Scandinavian languages.[3]

Nor is it an undue stretch of the imagination to see in the appended sketch of the cross section of the iron-mine a quite remarkable resemblance to parts of the Tolkien painting related to Bilbo's dangerous adventure in *The Hobbit*, illustrated by the sketch captioned 'Conversation with Smaug'. Similarly, items 1, 2, 4, 5, 6, 7, 8 and 9 of the list above are all true of the setting to the fabled dwarvish place, the Kingdom under the Mountain (even as many of them are also echoed later in the highly atmospheric account of the Mines of Moria).

The excavation itself was a remarkable English instance of the coming together in a mutually supportive and creative fashion of a region's legends, history and archaeology – quite apart from the (tradition and) practice of an earlier and special religious worship in the temple atop the hill. While dwarves had not, of course, mined there, the toponym, *Dwarf's Hill*, indicated a stubborn retention of a memory of a persistent[4] mining activity there from some 1600 to 1700 years before. And the fabled presence of some 'treasure' in the form of votive artifacts – including a curse tablet and a famous votive figurine of a dog – had been found there in 1805, and that tale was one of the romantic reasons for the digging 123 years later.

The approaches to the mine from above and from the side must have intrigued Tolkien, and probably suggested the very shape of a treasure chamber – as would quite soon be published in *The Hobbit*, a legend-packed heroic tale which was already in embryonic form in his own family's developing cycle of story. Pleasingly, too, this chamber of and for treasure was uniquely English in its form – and of old Wessex in its location, for all its generic similarity to the Maeshowe in Orkney, or to the dragon's lair of the Old English epic poem, *Beowulf*. Here at Lydney there were already so many elements for story, not least that of a

---

3 See particularly the essay, 'Trolls and Other Themes – William Craigie's Significant Folkloric Influence on the Style of J.R.R. Tolkien's *The Hobbit*', in J.S.Ryan, *Tolkien's View* (2009: 33-46).
4 It is also the case that the general location is not so far from the almost gnome-like and mythical underground mining associated with the west of Devon and the east of the County of Cornwall, and so in areas where the Tolkien family had often holidayed and would do so again.

precursor in the *one* Dwarf – perhaps the king of those who had laboured there and led an investigation for some vein of precious substance or metal.

The curse tablet has been translated thus:

> 'To the god Nodens. Silvianus has lost a ring; he hereby gives half of it (i.e. half of its value) to Nodens. Among those who are called Senicianius, do not allow health until he brings it to the temple of Nodens.' (*ibid*. 100)

This and other inscriptions enabled Tolkien – and his several successors and co-interpreters of the inscriptions, the votive offerings there, or the thousands of coins, and individual bronze letters – the latter items presumably attached to wooden boards to make an inscription, a prayer to the gods, or to record the fulfilment of a vow – to investigate some of the details or patterns of religious practice at the sanctuary. It was presided over by its *Mars Nodens*, a deity of Roman and Celtic parentage. This same deity is so named on two other metal plaques as *M(ars) Nodons* and *Nudens*. The name is Celtic and its etymology may suggest a possible association with catching or trapping (see the full *Report*).

And a Romantic and Timeless Wood

Of equal interest to readers in the twenty-first century is the fact that the Forest of Dean region has long been a place of myth and magic, even a source for some of the ideas in the Harry Potter books. In this respect it is also very much one of Britain's Nameless Woods, persistingly alluring, timeless and enigmatic, as has already been discussed in the 'Prequel' to the present collection of essays.

Further Reading – I Archaeology

Wheeler, R.E.M. and T.V. Wheeler, 1932, *Report on the Excavation of the Prehistoric, Roman and Post-Roman Site in Lydney Park, Gloucestershire*, London: Printed at the University Press by John Johnson for The Society of Antiquaries [Tolkien's appendix is on pp. 132-37].

Hawkes, Christopher, 1932, 'Reviews', In *Antiquity: A Quarterly Review of Archaeology* 6.24 (December 1932), 488-90.

Clark, Ronald, 1960, *Sir Mortimer Wheeler*, New York: Roy Publishers [see pp. 55-57].

Hawkes, Jacquetta, 1982, *Mortimer Wheeler: Adventurer in Archaeology*, London: Weidenfeld and Nicolson [see pp. 145-49].

Further Reading – II Cultural Surveys

Nicholls, Henry George, 1858, *The Forest of Dean; An Historical and Descriptive Account, Derived from Personal Observation, and other Sources, Public, Private, Legendary, and Local*, London: John Murray.

Walters, Brian, 1992, *The Archaeology and History of Ancient Dean and the Wye Valley*, Cheltenham: Thornhill Press.

VICTORIA COUNTY HISTORY, *A* HISTORY OF THE COUNTY OF GLOUCESTERSHIRE, 1996, Vol. V, ed. by N.M. Herbert: Oxford, Oxford University Press

VICTORIA COUNTY HISTORY, *A* HISTORY OF THE COUNTY OF GLOUCESTERSHIRE, 2010, Vol. XII, ed. by A.R.J. Jurica, Woodbridge et al.: Boydell & Brewer.

The Lydney ironworks are discussed in vol. XII (2010: 154). In vol. V (1996) there are chapters on mining in the Forest of Dean (326ff), as well as on ironworks (*ibid.* 339-44).

Ancient Mosaic Tiles from out the West: some Romano-British 'Traditional' Motifs

> Few can be aware that he was a practising draughtsman, and water-colourist, over a long period. (Garlick 1976: 5)
>
> Back cover to the English edition of *The Silmarillion* (1977) has the coloured emblem motifs of Fingolfin, Eärendil, Idril Celebrindal, Elwë and Fëanor, all of which are water-coloured squares in diamond position with curvilinear motifs, except the third, which is larger and circular.

While admirers of the mythic writings of the late J.R.R. Tolkien will be familiar with his vivid pictures to illustrate his stories, as with the subtle drawings of trees which, according to Baillie Tolkien, show "deep attention to the details of their many shapes in nature " (1976: 7), few perhaps have given much thought to the water-colour emblematic devices such as those associated with *The Silmarillion* itself and *The Silmarillion Calendar* of 1978. They might have seemed no more than exquisite doodlings of the sort recalled by his family as being added to the newsprint page by their father while he was completing the crosswords in *The Times*. Yet, whether or not his readers see the curvilinear motifs and emblematic designs as vaguely suggestive of (ancient lost) Númenorean art, they can be shown to have their origin, at least partly, in a remarkable phase of the young professor's academic career.

*   *   *

In the summer of 1928 and 1929, R.E.M (later Sir Mortimer) Wheeler led the excavation of a 'promontory fort' or small embanked hilltown, now in Lydney Park, Gloucestershire, established there in or just before the first century B.C.

This essay, which contains drawings on the site of Lydney as well as on its mosaic floors, first published in Bathurst (1879), was originally printed in *Minas Tirith Evening-Star* 15.3 (1986: 13-17). It is reproduced with the kind permission of that journal's editors.

The then neglected place was re-occupied in the second and third centuries A.D. by a Romano-British population engaged to some extent in iron-mining.

Late in the fourth century there occured an economic expansion there and the building of a temple or basilica for the worship of the god Nodens. The events may well have been part of the pagan revival that took place under Julian the Apostate.

> The sudden development of this remote hilltop, on a spur of the Forest of Dean that overlooks the Severn Valley,[1] into an important religious centre, suggests that Lydney must have been one of the places in which a primitive cult had long been carried on by an un-Romanized peasantry in such a manner as to leave no trace for the archaeologist to find. The temple of Nodens [...] has beside [it] a large courtyard house, doubtless an inn for the accomodation of visitors [and] a fine suite of baths. (Collingwood 1932: 139)

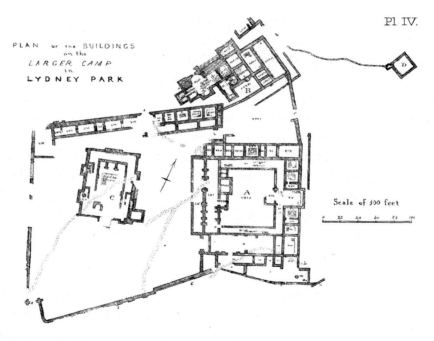

The Temple of Nodens at Lydney on the left with the guest house to the right and the baths above (from Bathurst 1879: Plate IV)

---

1 I.e. faces to the west. Compare a number of similarly situated pagan places around Reykjavík, in the south-west of Iceland.

It is the name, 'Nodens', and the mention of Collingwood who worked on the inscriptions (Wheeler and Wheeler 1932: 3) which are the link with Tolkien. Robin Collingwood, as much a Roman archaeologist as an Oxford philosopher, was a friend at Pembroke College in the later 1920s to the newly-arrived young professor of Anglo-Saxon, J.R.R. Tolkien. He knew of the latter's etymological ability and training as a classicist and had him advise the excavators on the possible etymology and so the significance of the inscription, *Nodens*, the name of the deity worshipped there. This Tolkien did, observing *inter alia* that

> [...] it is a fairly old 'northern' word; if not a common Indo-European word, one early adapted to a thoroughly Indo-European form of speech [...]. (*ibid.* 136)

The Floor Mosaic

The site had been purchased by the Bathurst family in 1723, and sporadic digging occured there until 1805, when the Right Hon. Charles Bathurst carried out systematic excavations and discovered a series of Roman buildings. The record which he made was published by his son, the Rev. W.H. Bathurst in 1879, with additional notes by C.W. King as *Roman Antiquities at Lydney Park, Gloucestershire.* There are in all a series of ten mosaic pavements of which fragments or records[2] survive, none being earlier than A.D. 367. Some of the culturally significant points maybe listed:

> As dated mosaics, they stand at present almost alone in Britain (Wheeler and Wheeler 1932: 65);
>
> [they] consist in every case of a border made up of Old Red Sandstone cubes [...] (*ibid.*);

and the inner decorative pannel is

> made up of small cubes [...] of red (brick), white (pale, slightly pinkish [...]), blue [...], or greenish blue colours [...]. (*ibid.*)

The designs are in six main patterns:

> 1) a frieze of sea-monsters and fish, with circular framed panels;
> 2) simple interlace patterns;

---

2 Described and analysed by Wheeler in his report (1932: 65-67).

3) geometric patterns, in room XVIII of the guest-house, a central panel containing four 'lotus-leaves', with chequered border work (see Plate XVI) and in Room L of the Long Building (see Plate VII);

4) circular panels in pastel;

5) a chequer-bordered panel including a representation of a two-handled urn; and

6) three pavements, one of which (XXA) was formerly corridor XI in the guest-house inner verandah (see Plate XIV). [3]

Plate XVI: Mosaic-floor from the guest-house with four 'lotus-leaves'

Plate VII: Mosaic-floor in Room L of the Long Building

---

3 The illustrations in this essay are from Bathurst (1879).

Plate XIV: Corridor XI in the guest-house inner verandah

In his comments on this last motif, Wheeler (1932: 66-67) noted that it also occurred in the English-Welsh border area[4] and that

> from the end of the fourth century to the twelfth century, the pattern had a wide vogue throughout southern and western Europe [...]. (*ibid.* 67)

He pondered on the origins of the craftsmen using it, and whether it might not be a compromise between 'the British' and 'the foreign'. These remarks, coupled with Tolkien's speculations about Baltic religious perceptions (*ibid.* 136), and as to

> [w]hether the god was called 'the snarer' or the 'catcher' or the 'hunter' in some sinister sense [...] (*ibid.* 137),

---

4 This was a traditional cultural area, preserving older values and much loved by Tolkien. See his paper on that culture at a later period in *Essays and Studies by Members of the English Association* (1929) and variously in the annotations to his edition (with E.V. Gordon) of *Sir Gawain and the Green Knight* (1925).

are all vastly intriguing and suggest very forcibly the complex neo-pagan cult praticised at the place. It is certainly the case that, as Collingwood said more generally in print in the same year:

> The whole settlement was clearly a place of pilgrimage, and gives a vivid picture of the last phase of pagan religion in Roman Britain. (1932: 139)

*   *   *

In 1965, Mrs N.K. Chadwick of the University of Cambridge first drew attention of the present writer to the importance of Lydney for understanding Tolkien's work. Her own writing of that time stressed that Lydney was

a forest sanctuary;

a therapeutic temple of Aesculapian type;

a place of ample baths; and that

the religion [...] was essentially a nature religion. (Dillon and Chadwick 1967: 140)

These remarks accord well with Tolkien's own abiding interest[5] in the paved Roman floor at Fawler in North Oxfordshire and the large bath-house preserved at the Roman villa at Chedworth, a little to the north. Of even more interest are the other 1967 comments by Anne Ross in her *Pagan Celtic Britain* that the cult was concerned with healing,[6] occultist matters, the sun, water and the divine hunter, *Silvanus* (230).

Conclusion

Now while this note meanders a little, it does so with the purpose of stressing the young Tolkien's contact with ancient cults, the more complex symbolism of which is to be found in the Lydney mosaic designs excavated in the southern part of Old Mercia, and in the official commentary upon which he had a considerable and formative influence. The essential rightness of his perceptions is

---

5 Personal knowledge and supported by Tolkien's remarks made in lectures and seminars, 1954-57, about the place name Fawler in North Oxfordshire. Henry Alexander already drew conclusions from the place name that there must have been a coloured "tesselated pavement" in the Roman villa there (1912: 104), as was duly discovered by Antiquarians later. All these scholars were referring to the half-line *attertanum fah* in *Beowulf*.

6 Compare the role of Aragorn as healer in *The Return of the King*.

attested by the works of Dillon and Chadwick, Ross and, earlier, of his friend Thomas F. O'Rahilly.[7]

The cultural point is that the tile designs associated with old Númenor, through *The Silmarillion*, have a basis in proto-British archaeology and religion and are no mere beautiful doodling. The same (watered) colours are used as those item-ized by R.E.M. Wheeler for the site at Lydney – "red [...], white (pale, slightly pinkish [...]), blue [...], or greenish blue colours [...]" (1932: 65). Lacking the browns and vivid greens of his nature painting, his tiles accord very well with those excavated at the temple of Nodens in 1928-29. Thus, as is usually the case, the smallest item of Tolkien's artistic creation is capable of linking his Middle-earth and its past history with England's own history and legendary (religious) past.

Appendix

Plate V: A corner of the mosaic in room XXXV of the Lydney bath-building (late fourth century).

---

7 See his *Early Irish History and Mythology* (1957), especially pp. 321, 527, etc. Tolkien attended O'Rahilly's Indo-European and later period lectures in Oxford in 1956.

Part C

The North and West Germanic Tradition and Christianity

Frothi, Frodo – and Dodo and Odo

> *frōd (adj.) 'old, wise'*
>
> A chiefly poetic word, regrettably without de-
> scendants, which means old and wise at once.
> (Barney 1977: 79)

While there have been many vague etymological guesses at place and personal names in the writings of J.R.R. Tolkien, few, if any, have presumed to probe the etymology or linguistic associations of Frodo, although many names such as Gandalf, Balrog, Shelob and the like have fairly obvious Germanic cognates. It is also noticeable that Tolkien's own 'Guide to the Names in *The Lord of the Rings*' published in 1975 by Jared Lobdell, in the collection he edited entitled *A Tolkien Compass*, is, in fact, largely concerned with the place names of Middle-earth and not with those of his own animate creations which he deliberately left for his readers' speculation and musing.

J.B. Bessinger in his *A Short Dictionary of Anglo-Saxon Poetry* (1960: 23) indicated the occurrence of some 80 instances of the adjective *frōd* meaning 'wise', 'experienced', 'old'. The Barney Glossary (1977: 79) indicates that *frōd* is the 220th commonest word in Old English poetry, where it occurs some 21 times. It also mentions a cognate in Gothic, *fraþi*, 'understanding', and Old English compounds in *in-*, *un-*(*frōd*). Henry Sweet's *The Student's Dictionary of Anglo-Saxon* (1896: 68) notes that it may be used with and followed by a genitive, *frōd fēores*, 'wise of life', or found in the verb *frōdian*, 'to be wise'.

More assistance is given in the Bosworth-Toller first volume, *An Anglo-Saxon Dictionary* (1898: 339) and in that work's *Supplement* (1921: 269). Putting these two entries together, the following associations and actual usages may now be given for the adjective:

This essay appeared first in *Orana* 16.2 (1980: 35-38). It has been modified in several details, has several Gloucestershire references added, and is here reprinted with the kind permission of that journal's editors.

1) Senses

(a) 'wise', 'prudent', 'sage', 'skilful', variously glossing Latin *sapiens, prudens, sciens, peritus.*

It appears in the *Exeter Book,* the *Gnomic Verses, Beowulf, Exodus* and *Elene.* In one example the phrase *se frōda,* 'the sage', is used for Isaiah. A half-line which occurs several times is *þurh frōd gewit* – 'through wise mind'. There are two occurrences of this half-line;

frōdra and godra gumena, 'of wise and good men'; others of

frōde men, 'prudent men', while *fricge mec frōdum wordum,* 'question me in prudent words' recurs, as does *hy bēoþ ferþe þy frōdran,* 'they will be the wiser in mind'.

(b) *frōd* may also render 'skilled in (a subject)', as in *fyrngidda frōd,* 'skilled in ancient songs', which occurs in *Elene.*

(c) it may also be used of judicious discourse or counsel, e. g.:

frōde geþeahte – 'with wise counsel';

frōde lare – 'with wise teaching';

frōdum wordum – 'with wise words'.

2) (as wisdom and experience belong to old age, hence –) 'advanced in years', 'aged', 'old', 'ancient, with the now lost qualities of an earlier age', glossing such Latin terms as *aetate provectus, senex, vetus, priscus.*

Some examples of this are:

wintrum frōd, 'advanced in [burdensome] years', (which occurs more than 15 times);

frōd cyn, 'the ancient race';

se frōda Constantinus, 'the aged Constantine';

haefde frōd haele nigon hund wintra and hundseofontig (in *Genesis*), 'the man was 970';

frōd cyning, har hilderinc occurs in *Beowulf,* with the meaning 'the old king, the grey battle-warrior'; a poetic line of significance is *Draca sceal on hlaewe frōd,* 'the dragon must needs become old on the mound'; while *The Phoenix* produces the line *Fugol frōd, geealdad, wintrum gebysgad,* 'the aged bird, very old, harassed with the years'.

A statue is said (in *Andreas*) to be *frōd fyrngeweorc,* 'an ancient work of great age', while in *Elene, frōd fyrngewritu,* 'old and ancient writing(s)' is used of the Old Testament.

3) *frōde* (adv.) means 'wisely', 'prudently'.

4) *frōd-ness* (n) 'wisdom' occurs, as does its opposite, *un-frōdness.*

5) the verb *frōdian,* glosses Latin *sapere* and means 'to be wise' or 'prudent'.

6) There are also certain cognates to the word:

Old Saxon *frōd*	Icelandic *frōðr*, 'learned'
Old Frisian *frod*	German (dialect) *frod, vrood*;
M.H. German *vruot*, 'healthy, brave';	Frisian *froed*
O.H. German *fruot, frot*	Dutch *vroed*
Gothic *frōþs*, 'prudent'	

Despite this cluster, most of the critics who essay cultural notes on the personal names of the three-volume epic avoid any speculation on the associations behind the form *Frodo*. Even the by then retired Germanic linguist, Paul Kocher, in his *Master of Middle-earth* (1973) does not probe this name. Yet there are a number of passages around the North and West Germanic languages and culture of the Dark Ages and later which assist us to identify various significant persons associated with this root name for and meaning 'old/wise'.

Thus, in his discussion of the treaty of Wedmore (886 A.D.) between the Dane Guthrum and Alfred, R.H. Hodgkin in his *A History of the Anglo-Saxons*, volume 2 (1935: 580) refers to the ancient Danish agreements, reported by Saxo Grammaticus, as to amounts paid for manslaughter.

> Alfred's agreement [...] was better than the law ascribed by tradition to Frodi,[1] a King of the Danes, the law which demanded that the death of a Dane at the hands of a foreigner must be redressed by the death of two foreigners.

It is the reference to Saxo Grammaticus which takes us to the various ancient myths long associated with this name. Thus the index to Oliver Elton's translation (1894: 424f) of *The First Nine Books of the Danish History of Saxo Grammaticus* refers to several kings of the name, viz.:

Frode I, (Frotho), King of Denmark, son of Hadding;

Frode II, (Frotho Vegetus), King of Denmark, the Vigorous (known in Iceland as *Hinn froekni*);

Frode III, (Frotho), King of Denmark, son of Fridleif;

Frode IV, (Frotho), King of Denmark, son of Fridleif;

Frode V, (Frotho), King of Denmark, son of Ingild; and

Frode VI, (Frotho), King of Denmark, son of Kanute I.

---

1 This was probably King Frode III – see the index to O. Elton's translation of Saxo Grammaticus' *Danish History* (Elton and Powell 1894: 424) and the specific references to his laws (*ibid.* xi-xliv, 187-89, and 192-94).

The total (and ominous) significance of the name *Frode/Fróda* is seen in L.M. Hollander's translation from the Danish of Axel Olrik's *The Heroic Legends of Denmark* (1919: 478), where Peace-Frothi occurs in the genealogy of Scyld (also in *Beowulf*), while Frothi the Peaceful is found in the line from Dan to Ingiald, as "the incarnation of the realm's (Denmark's) peace and good fortune in remotest antiquity." As Olrik (1919: 478) concludes

> To be more precise, Peace-Frothi and Frothi the Peaceful really are the same personage, whilst Scyld is the eponymous ancestor of the Scyldings, and Dan, in the same manner, of the Danes and Denmark.

Yet other genealogies suggest a form of association – if not etymological link – between *frōd* – ('old') and *friþ* – ('peace'), as in the compound *friþo-webbe* or 'weaver of peace' used in the epic, *Beowulf*, of the foreign (i.e. non-Danish) Queen Wealhtheow. She is 'balanced' in Old English by the figure only found in Anglo-Saxon tradition, the treacherous counsellor Unferþ (or 'unpeace', i.e. 'breaker of peace'), the literary antecedent of Tolkien's malicious Wormtongue of the second volume of the epic.

Olrik (1919: 444) also suggests that King Frothi of the many ancient Danish legends, who appears as fighter, law-giver, and mythic ancestor, is but a form of

> the great ancestral figure of Ingvi, or, when considered as a divinity, of Frey, the god of fertility; and he lives again in the King Frothi of the Frothi Peace. This heroic figure appearing in so many shapes conceals a bit of nature symbolism: he is the lord of light and of warmth who comes to the land every spring, who drives off and defeats the trolls of the evil powers of nature, teaches men agriculture, shipbuilding, royal power and battle; but himself finally succumbs to the trolls and dies in autumn. Amid the lamentations of the people his body is sent away over the sea in order to return newborn next spring.

The thought of a *Fróðafriðr*, 'Peace of King Frothi', lived on through Northern antiquity and occurred in two places; first at the beginning of the Scylding line, – in the person of Scyld who is referred to in the opening of the epic, *Beowulf*, – and also as a mythical monarch, Frothi, where he is distinguished by his wealth, more especially by the gold he gains by grinding it out of his mill. The other occurrence is found later in the line, and this ruler is a stern administrator of justice, with a vast realm.

But the legends will not tolerate two kings Frothi as ruler of the 'Frothi Peace', so the traditions tend to give preference to one, and to eliminate the other. The Icelandic versions favoured the first, attributing all achievement to him and relegating the other king to ordinary human rank. The Norway legends, preserved by Saxo, decide for the second, making the first a mere sea-king. Clearly each set of legends is right to only have one king of the Golden Age who cannot be one who comes and goes. The Icelanders put the Frothi Peace in the very earliest times when the gods still walked the earth, the Danish historian set it sometime later.

The features of Frothi's reign may now be given. It is a time of a golden mill or quern, and of a golden ring which was placed on the open highway without anyone daring to lay hands on it, and of a violent death for the King who allowed this to happen, that punishment to be caused by a cow or stag. The gold mill is the oldest story, one which epitomises his entire being and his fate, his wealth and his tragic end, the oldest source for which is the *Biarkamal* (about 900 A.D.). The (related?) kenning, 'the flour of Frothi', occurs for gold in Egil Skallagrimsson's writing (c. 950 A.D.) and elsewhere.

The 'Quern Story' or, as it is named in ancient times, the 'Song of Grotti', is one of the most famous Eddic poems. Grotti is the name of the quern, and the song of 24 verses is sung by two giant maidens who must turn the mill of wealth for King Frothi. The general conception of a wishing-mill is here seen expanded into an elaborate poem where:

1) the quern is so large that slaves of unusual strength are needed to turn it;

2) man has chained the forces of untamed nature for this purpose, and their rebellion against his greed causes the death of the owner and the destruction of the beneficient mill;

3) this rebellion is seen in the moment when King Frothi, in unnatural rapacity, tries to extend their labours far beyond the space of a human day's work;

4) his palace and power are destroyed by the sudden arrival of an army of enemies, created presumably by the curse of the maidens; and

5) the curse radiates out to become the tragedy of the entire ancient dynasty of the Scyldings.

The root of the story is that of one Frothi who had a pair of millstones of great size which gave whatever he who ground commanded – usually gold. As this was done at sea, the ships sank and where the waters rushed in through the eye of the millstone, the sea grew salt.

This event is associated in the Edda Manuscripts with the Pentland Firth, between Scotland and the Orkney Islands, the tale originating, probably, among the Scandinavian inhabitants of the islands, where, in 1895, the linguist Dr. Jakob Jakobsen could still collect fragments of the story.

Even later the giant maidens, Menia and Fenia, were being invoked on Fair Isle, in the form of 'Grotti Finnie and Lucky Minnie' to frighten naughty children. The last part of the story, 'How the sea grew salt', is a different motif and similar to one told all around the North Sea, in the Faroes, in Normandy, and elsewhere. The Quern Song itself represents the stage of the myth which has passed the primitive and, significantly, has moved close to the heroic, to the heroic flaw and the consequent Nemesis.

At the beginning of the second book of Saxo's history, there is an extensive story of a King Frothi,[2] who, desirous of gold, kills a dragon as it issues from its lair on an island. One detail in this story has to do with the Frothi Peace: the ground gold which Frothi strews on his food. The dragon fight, which as an act of an ancestor-king is identical with that in *Beowulf*, is really subordinate to many viking adventures, but it is the core of the legends of the Danish sea-kings, the Scyldings, and it harmonises with the stories of that dynasty as told in relation to Hrolf Kraki and, later, of the hero Beowulf.

While these many Scandinavian and Scottish stories blur and become confusing, particularly in their inter-relationship, there is no doubt that we have two original stories, sometimes confusingly linked – those of Frothi the rich and greedy, and of Frothi the wise ruler of a country where total peace and the rule of law prevail.

In 1732 Samuel and Nathaniel Buck, the English engravers, published a fine landscape plate entitled *The North West View of Tewkesbury Abby, in the Country*

---

2 In Elton (1894: 45ff) a countryman has told Frode how to slay the dragon. "There is a place under his lowest belly whither thou mayst plunge the blade" – a motif to be used by Tolkien, in chapter 21 'Of Túrin Turambar' of the 'Quenta Silmarillion' (*Silmarillion*) where Túrin plunges his sword into the dragon Glaurung's belly and in *The Hobbit*, in the form of the vulnerable spot on Smaug's belly.

of Gloucester. Beneath the sketch there run six long lines of description, the first part of which is as follows:

> Tewksbury Abby, was at first a little Monastery, built by two Dukes of Mercia, Odo and Dodo; for a few Benedictine Monks and dedicated to the Virgin Mary, about the year 715. / About the Year 800, Brichtric a King of the West Saxons was buried here. Robert Fitz-Hamon An: 1102 built it and made great Endowments, advancing it to an Abby and / reducing Cranburn Abby in Dorsetshire to be a Priory and to be a Cell to it.

And the *Victoria County History* for Gloucestershire

This scholarly material evidence of the names Odo and Dodo is neatly confirmed from the various volumes on Gloucestershire in *The Victoria History of the Counties of England*, commonly known as the *Victoria County History* – all published long after Tolkien's use of the name Frodo, viz.: in

Vol. VI (1965) – Dodo (fl. *c.* 715), 217, 226;

Vol. VII (1981) – Dodo (fl. 1066), 123;

Vol. VIII (1968) – Dodo, 154, and Odo, 154; and

Vol. XI (1976) – Odo, 237, with a reference to an 'Odo after the Conquest'.

It will be convenient to take them in the sequence.

Vol. VI refers to one Dodo (fl. c. 715) at two places. On p. 217 we are told that the Manor of Lower Lemington "may have been included in the grant of Stanway and other land to Tewkesbury Abbey by Dodo *c.* 715," and on p. 226 that "the manor of Stanway with its members was said to be part of the original endowment of Tewkesbury Abbey by Dodo *c.* 715." [This last was attested by transcripts in the Bristol and Gloucestershire Archaeological Society Library.] It is also discussed in its management until the dissolution, when it passed into private hands, the Tracy family.

Vol. VII (123) refers to a Dodo, fl. 1066 in discussion of Brightwell's Barrow Hundred, viz.:

> Eight hides of land in Quenington, held as 3 manors by Aluuold and two men called Dodo in 1066, passed to Walter de Lacy [...].

Vol. VIII (154) refers to both Dodo and Odo thus [in the Borough of Tewkesbury]: "The 8th-century Oddo and Dodo are unsubstantiated."

The last of these fugitive references occurs in Vol. XI (237) in relation to the Longtree Hundred, viz.:

> An estate of 3 hides and 3 yardlands at Hazleton was held by Elnoc in 1066. After the Conquest the manor was granted to Odo, bishop of Bayeux, from whom it was held by his vassal Roger for a rent of £16.

There is also a transference of demesne titles to St George's Chapel in Oxford Castle, as noted in the Domesday Book (Rec. Comm.), i, 168.

Whether or no we choose to assume that Tolkien was aware of the documents attesting the Gloucestershire/Mercian use of the names of the several 'Dukes of Mercia', it is a pleasing and euphonic association and one which accords well with Tolkien's lifelong interest in Mercia, its pre-Conquest history, its fine religious texts for the nurture of enclosed ladies of rank, as well as with his admiration for the Gawain poet.

Inevitably, too, one is reminded of the words of Tolkien's on the twelfth century prose style from the same area:

> There is an English older than Dan Michel's and richer, as regular in spelling as Orm's [...] one that has never fallen back into 'lewdness', and has contrived in troublous times to maintain the air of a gentleman, if a country gentleman. It has traditions and some acquaintance with books and the pen, but it is also in close touch with a good living speech – a soil somewhere in England. (Ancrene Wisse, 106)

There had also been an Odo prominent in the ninth century – Odo, count of Paris, from 888 A.D. the king of the Western Franks, and some one whom King Alfred, when a boy, had met on his visit to the Frankish court in 856. His father, Count Robert the Strong, had been killed soon afterwards by that Haesten who was to persecute Alfred in the early 890s.

Clearly 'Dukes of Mercia' would be a pleasing euphonic association to Tolkien for his later heroic and very different leader figure from such a western location.

And so a Form of Accumulative Associations for the Reader

While none of these legendary and noble associations or allusions equate completely with Tolkien's plain hobbit hero of *The Lord of the Rings*, there is ample comparative and figurative material here for our aesthetic, onomastic and etymological satisfaction.

In the etymology of the Old English adjective, we have linked the twin concepts of 'age' and 'wisdom', even as the Scandinavian legends combine two other more assertive concepts, those of 'wealth' and of 'peace'. Odo and Dodo were mythical names long associated with the area of the Cotswolds, and West Midlands, Tolkien's 'Shire' of both *The Hobbit* and *The Lord of the Rings*. Thus his Frodo is an obvious personal name to occur in these parts of Middle-earth.

Further, he is a new kind of leader, one whose importance comes from suffering and from the willing acceptance of intolerable burdens. And like King Frothi he receives a wound which necessitates his passing across the sea – this time to the mythical Far West.

Perhaps we might conclude with an indirect, yet aesthetically satisfying answer to Stephen Barney's quiet regret which was quoted at the outset. There *is* a survival of that ancient poetic word, *frōd*, even though it occurs in a personal name, whose specific etymology and cultural associations are left deliberately obscured in the writings of his creator. Yet it cannot but give the reader of the vast corpus of tales of Middle-earth an enormous satisfaction that his hobbit hero has a name which contains so many echoes of mighty Scandinavian legends of heroism.

Indeed, it shows by example the moral wisdom of someone whose central wish is to serve, and who is generous in his enjoyment of the world of Middle-earth, and yet willing to leave it before his time, and so himself quite free from the terrible and destructive greed of so many of his apparent namesakes. For his character is different, being humble and so deeply moral in his readiness to assume burdens of a weight that the mighty of Middle-earth would hesitate to assume, lest they then be overwhelmed and suffer the inevitable denuding of their human spirit.

The Knee and the Old English *Gifstol*[1] as Sacral Symbols of Protection and of Forgiveness

> Presently out of the darkness Gollum came
> crawling on all fours, like an erring dog called
> to heel [...] He came close to Frodo, almost
> nose to nose, and sniffed at him.
> (*TT* 296)

The passage just quoted occurs in the harrowing account of Frodo and Sam journeying agonizingly slowly towards Mordor, immediately prior to Gollum's being seized by Faramir's men. Frodo, travelling east to attempt to destroy the One Ring, and now using its power, had forced Gollum to come to him, in order that he, Frodo, could save the pitiful creature from danger to him there by the Forbidden Pool, putting himself at risk from the eye and avenging forces of Sauron, the Dark Lord.

Analysed closely for its rich and complex motif-content, it is clear that the passage quoted contains certain highly significant themes:

the mesmeric influence of Frodo (and of the Ring) as 'masters' over Gollum;

the humility and even desperate supplication of Frodo by Gollum at that climacteric moment in their journey into the void;

the fear of the Ring Bearer, and yet sense of sanctuary felt towards Frodo by the terrified Gollum, when he is near the kindly hobbit; and

the abasement of posture which Gollum chooses to adopt in approaching Frodo.

All these qualities are important in themselves and the more so in that they are found a little later in the better known sequence of events immediately prior to the hobbits' unwitting approach[2] to the Great Spider, to Shelob's terrifying Lair. The further passage may be cited in shortened form:

This essay was first printed in *Minas Tirith Evening-Star* 16.3 (1987: 7-11). It is reproduced with the permission of that journal, and the text has been somewhat expanded and revised for this publication.

1 This is the Old English word meaning literally 'gift-seat', and one often used of the 'throne' of a king, or even that of God.

2 At the end of Chapter VIII, 'The Stairs of Cirith Ungol'.

A strange expression passed over his lean hungry face. The gleam faded from his eyes, and they went dim and grey, old and tired. A spasm of pain seemed to twist him, and he turned away [...] shaking his head, as if engaged in some interior debate. Then he came back, and [...] slowly putting out a trembling hand, very cautiously he touched Frodo's knee – but almost the touch was a caress. (*TT* 324)

Then there follows in quick succession: Sam's awakening; his immediate feeling of alarm that Gollum was "pawing at master;" Gollum's withdrawal; and the author's sadly omniscient remark that "[the] fleeting moment had passed beyond recall." Clearly there had been a possibility of some form of confession or abasement and humility in – and so of forgiveness for – the oldest and most tired of all the hobbit race.

The Sinner and the Moment to Seek Forgiveness

Both in life[3] and in reported talk to friends, Tolkien had said that he found this sequence the most painful to recall from the many dramatic contexts in all of his own creative writing. His repeated comment thus allows us to focus on it with certainty as to its importance in one of the richest and most meaningful context passages in all of *The Lord of the Rings*. The main layers of implicit meaning may now be tabulated, given brief explanation, and then assessed for their full cultural implication and impact. The several associations are as follows:

1) The passages must be linked by the widely-read reader with a famed sequence in the Old English poem, *The Wanderer* (ll. 25a-29a), an elegy uttered by one solitary member of a warrior company who had formerly known happiness with his (now dead) lord in the latter's hall:

   I sought gloomily the hall of a [new] treasure-giver – who might take thought of me – or comfort me, left without friends, treat me with kindness.

   and continuing a little later (ll. 41a, ff.):

   It seems to him [such a wanderer] in his mind that he [again] clasps and kisses his lord and lays hands and head on his knee, as when formerly in ancient days he benefited from the gift-seat.

2) There is another similar passage about a gift throne, a famed problem context in *Beowulf* (ll. 168-69) which may or may not have been moved from another

---

3 This was observed by Tolkien to the present writer many years ago.

place in the poem, as both Tolkien and his long-time Oxford assistant Charles L. Wrenn[4] believed and said in print. Their interpretation may be translated[5] thus:

> He [Grendel] could not approach the throne, nor receive a gift because of the Lord; He did not take thought of him. (Hall and Wrenn 1940: 28)

Thus the passage does not mean that Grendel could not approach Hrothgar's 'gift-seat' but, rather, that Cain could not approach God because of his crime, nor could Grendel. As Wrenn translates the preceding lines on Grendel and his forebears, the brood of Cain:

> On Cain's kindred did the everlasting Lord avenge the murder, for that he had slain Abel; he had no joy of that feud, but the Creator drove him far from mankind for that misdeed. (*ibid.* 24-25)

3) The *Beowulf* lines (168-69) – whether they are applied to Grendel alone, to Cain[6] (but are misplaced in our text), or whether, on more mature reflection, Tolkien held that they were perhaps only about Grendel (but to be applied back to Cain by analogy) – are one of the *cruces* (i. e. most famous sense and manuscript problems of the text or allusions) in *Beowulf*. And Tolkien had to discuss them many times in class during his tenure of the Anglo-Saxon chair (1925-45). That they have intrigued all readers of the epic is evident from the vast early scholarship of the couplet and the context, an investigation of the implicit[7] which continues to this very day.

4) There is a related issue – the sacral nature of the seat and formal presence of a monarch – a matter given compact treatment by William A. Chaney in his 'Grendel and the *Gifstol*: A Legal View of Monsters' (1962) and set in a larger context in his later and profound book, *The Cult of Kingship in Anglo-Saxon England: The transition from Paganism to Christianity* (1970). As he quoted from another's scholarly article of 1944, and a piece relevant to our modern text by Tolkien:

> [...] the high-seat (*gifstōl*) of Hrothgar he [Grendel] could not touch because, as a symbol of semi-divine royalty, it was sacrosanct [...]The pagan beliefs here briefly touched by the poem had their origin in the basic concepts of Germanic kingship [...]. (Estrich 1944: 384)

---

4 Tolkien was talking about *Beowulf* having "suffered later unauthentic retouching" (*MCE* 39) and referred in a footnote to ll. 168-69 without going into further detail (*MCE* 47) and left it to Wrenn – who succeeded him in the Anglo-Saxon Chair – to point to the likely position after l. 110 in his 1953 edition of *Beowulf* (68-69 and 188-89).
5 It is Wrenn's 'diplomatic' translation that is given here.
6 A more recent exhaustive exploration of this famous matter/theme is to be found in *Cain and Beowulf: A Study in Secular Allegory* (1982) by David Williams.
7 See the bibliography to the Williams book, and also Ruth Mellinkoff, in *Anglo-Saxon England*, Vol. 8 (1980a) and Vol. 9 (1980b), and continuing in that standard series of annual overviews and bibliographies of the best research in the field of the Old English period.

Whether or no Tolkien was himself familiar with or had access to this American standard article of 1944, it is clear that originally a legal taboo surrounded a pagan king and his throne, and this attitude was one which was transformed fairly easily into a notion of the royal seat being a sacrosanct place in Christian thought.

5) The knee of the monarch or leader as he sat in authority could be, and often was, regarded as a sacred object[8] – such a context full of significance as occurred in Snorri Sturluson's *Life of Haukon the Good*, when the youthful king-to-be of Norway is placed on the knee of King Æthelstan in England, to ensure that the boy would be protected by the English monarch. A like veneration had long existed for a king's hands.[9]

6) Frodo is perceived by Gollum as a king or great leader of hobbits – of which race Gollum was an aged member of an earlier time of the race. This rank and potency was accorded Frodo – either for his moral stature, because of his bearing the One Ring, or because of his compassionate refusal to pass judgement on Gollum. We know that, much like Cain after his slaying of Abel, Gollum (Smeagol) as murderer still feels a need to beg for an easing of his terrible burden and a formal forgiveness from a lord or magnanimous one of his own kind for his slaying of Deagol so long ago.[10] (This is the ancient Indo-European view of the monarch as healer, forgiver, and so the bestower of Grace.)

7) In this situation there are also overtones of the archetypal approach in order to betray – as of Judas's doubts before his betrayal of Christ and his falsity in bestowing a kiss – an act of signal to the Roman soldiers, and of betrayal of His Master – for Gollum has not yet finally decided on his course of action, and given his companions over into the charge of their enemies, Shelob and Sauron.

Obvious Closeness to the Sacrament of Confession

Just as the passages in both the Old English *Wanderer* and *Beowulf* focus on the exile or outcast, and on his desperate need for:

a lord to cherish him;

his and every warrior's need to receive gifts from his lord as the protector of his life and in every sense his worldly lord;

---

8 See Chaney (1970: 116).
9 See Bede's *Ecclesiastical History*, III, 6, of the hands of King Oswald. Tolkien had taught their lives in Norse classes. The king as healer – 'the King's touch' – was long an aspect of popular medical history in English folklore.
10 *The Fellowship of the Ring* (62).

   [...] he caught Deagol by the throat and strangled him, because the gold looked so bright and beautiful. Then he put the ring on his finger.

permission to approach the lord's seat and/or his sitting person as some form of amelioration or forgiveness for sin or crime committed; and

forgiveness for the murderous crimes so long ago that drove him originally so tragically far from his kind,

so the exile situation and concomitant state of a lack of forgiveness or the opportunity to supplicate for this may be seen to operate in the tragic loneliness of Cain, Judas, and Grendel, and, now, of Gollum. The *Beowulf* poet has also told us that terrible progeny would come from such criminal 'monsters' as Cain and Grendel –

Thence all evil broods were born, ogres and elves[11] and evil spirits – the giants also, who long time fought with God, for which he gave them their reward. (ll. 110-114)

The Cain-Grendel kind – like Gollum – were guilty of brother-murder,[12] much as Judas was. Yet Gollum and Judas 'murdered' for material reward, for the One Ring or for thirty pieces of silver. Under point 1 above, the translation was that of Wrenn, but another version is possible, that of R.K. Gordon:

He might not approach the throne, the precious thing, for fear of the Lord, nor did he know his purpose. (1926: 6)[13]

Thus the original's *maððum* is taken in opposite to *gif-stol* and given the more orthodox translation of 'precious' rather than Wrenn's choice of 'a gift' for the word. It is the older translation as used by Oxford students from 1926, and for generations after, which allows us to see likely linked sets of cultural associations for Tolkien:

1) King/gift-seat/precious and its owner/Grendel;

2) lord/knee/gift/exile (e. g. in *The Wanderer*); and

3) Frodo-'Master'/the One Ring/Gollum.

---

11 These are the equivalents of the 'black elves' or goblins.

12 Interestingly Tolkien is himself recorded in *The University of Oxford Gazette* as having taken part in Faculty of English seminars on the ancient Germanic origins of the Shakespearean play, *Hamlet*, the Danish originals of which were called, 'Brother-murder', and always focussed on the murderous crime of the Claudius-figure who slew his brother to obtain his queen.

13 This was for many years the definitive translation of the epic, and it so served alike during both Tolkien's early training, and for his earlier teaching career.
Compare the similar account, in the Old English *Juliana*, of the devils in hell:

The thanes in that dark dwelling, the flock of retainers in that deep pit, had no reason to look expectantly to the overlord for the appointed treasures, or that they would receive upon the beer-bench rings and embossed gold in the wine-hall. (ll. 683a, ff)

It now becomes clear that Gollum, by approaching the knees of the dozing Frodo in the manner described, is, at once, attempting several actions:

worshipping 'the Precious':

seeking forgiveness from a later 'lord of the hobbits' for his murder long ago of one of their number;

trembling on the brink of explaining that (his desire for) the One Ring was forcing him, Gollum, to some form of betrayal or worse;

acting out a tragic and madly jealous impulse to murder those others[14] enjoying the sacral 'throne'; and

coming at last to the place of (Germanic) sanctuary beside the knees and hand of one's lord.

Conclusions on Tolkien's Treatment of Forgiveness

Thus it is possible to argue – both here and more generally – that there is no clear line of division – present or intended – as between Tolkien's teaching of older texts, their scholarship and the (more heroic of his) creative writings. As in so many passages, it is the text of *The Lord of the Rings* which contains his further musings on the words, concepts and situations of such classic 'set' texts as *Beowulf* or *Sir Gawain and the Green Knight*. In this instance, it may be claimed, there is created an interlace or cluster of passages, each of which sheds light on the others, as well as the way in which Tolkien played them off each other:

Cain's shame at his killing Abel;

his exile for that crime;

Grendel's exile and yearning for forgiveness;

the divinity that surrounds a (Germanic) king;[15]

the parallels between Gollum and Judas;

the tragedy of Judas's self-damnation;

the yearning of the Judas/Gollum/Grendel figure for human forgiveness;

---

14 I. e. Gollum's desire to murder Sam, even as Grendel devours a sleeping Geat warrior guard, protecting the royal person in Hrothgar's hall (*Beowulf* ll. 738-45).

15 Tolkien has participated in various Faculty of English more literary symposia on texts well outside his statutory duties, several times shedding a different perspective on the sources of Shakespeare's play, *Hamlet*, and variously discussing the Danish legends behind Shakespeare's play.

the indissolubility of social and religious function; and

the 'peace'[16] which the king/lord/master/the Lord can bring to all his/His true followers and to all who seek his forgiveness.

Sanctuary according to Old English Law

As early as the earliest known legal code, the laws of Ine of Wessex (688-726 A.D.), one could obtain legal sanctuary in England by fleeing to a church, and later laws stressed the like sanctuary beside the king's person and the need for there to be inviolate peace at that equally sacred place. Thus Sam's attempt to restrain Gollum from approach to the exhausted and resting Frodo is capable – at one level – of being deemed, not a protective, but an immoral and outrageous act.[17]

The *Beowulf* poet, writing in the eighth century (as Tolkien believed) of earlier pagan days, was fascinated by the linked concepts of:

royal person/sacred place/exile seeking forgiveness/legal sanctuary;

the religious 'crime' of preventing such sanctuary; and

the 'preciousness' of the place of Divine forgiveness as exercised by and through one's human lord.

And so Sam's misunderstanding adds a further complexity to this issue of the clash between the wordly, sacramental and Divine aspects of Forgiveness and Absolution.

All these themes and the many others adumbrated above Tolkien has been able to focus in one of the most culturally rich, spiritually significant and personally tragic moments in the presentation of sin and the desperate urge to seek forgiveness in all the chronicles of his own and of our lives in the kingdoms of Middle-earth.

---

16 Compare the 'peace' associated with 'Frodo' in the ancient legends, and assuredly, in the character of this name in Tolkien's most beloved writings (treated in Essay 10 of the present volume, see pp. 139-47).

17 See, for example, Æthelberht 2-3, in *The Laws of the Earliest English Kings*, ed. F.L. Attenborough (1922: 5).

Appendix: Recent Research on the Relationship between Cain, Grendel and Gollum.

In 2008, Brent Nelson of the University of Texas, Brownsville published a closely related article to the above argument, his piece entitled 'Cain-Leviathan typology in Gollum and Grendel', it appearing in *Extrapolation* 49.3 (466-485). In that essay, much is made of the Leviathan of romance, as elaborated by Northrop Frye, and of the Old Testament account of the fall of Cain. As Nelson points out in his closely referenced survey, Tolkien's "most enduring influence as a critic is his defense of the monster's central place in *Beowulf*" (466), and also that Gandalf does something similar, in the reflective account of Gollum's origins, this indicating very clearly the close link of Gollum with Grendel, as in the creature's delight in the epic in diving into deep pools, tunneling under hills and through the back of caves, and the like, all of which evokes traditional associations with Leviathan, 'the abhorred other'. Nimrod, too, is not far from this set of images.

Nelson draws his readers attention to Grendel's role as a breaker down of social order, much as the Beowulfian dragon's was. Much of this seems to link with the considerable Old Testament typology in *Beowulf*, with Grendel always presented in the worst possible way, totally antithetic to the fellowship and order of Heorot's hall. All of this is opposed to the socio-spiritual order of Heorot – a link to both the Old Testament's Ham and Cain, and to the latter's unwillingness to participate in the rituals of the covenant. And Gollum occupies a similar place, both socially and scenically, to that of Grendel. For water is a dominant theme in the accounts of both these creatures, and when Gollum re-appears in *The Lord of the Rings*, he clearly prefers pools, swamps, and fens, and so is able to guide Frodo and Sam "through the marshes, through the mists, nice thick mists" (*TT* 233). All of this mass of archetypal story is concerned with the theme of temptation, the struggle of the characters to fight the Ring – one analogous to and directly reflecting the temptation of those in the *Bible*. See *Matthew* 4 and *Matthew* 6, or, earlier in *Genesis* 3:6.[18]

---

18 See also the related articles by Kathleen E. Gilligan, of Rutgers University, New Jersey (2011). An earlier essay is Jeffrey L. Morrow's 'J. R. R. Tolkien as a Christian for our Times', *Evangelical Review of Theology* 29, 2 (2005: 164-77).

King Alfred's Developing Concept of 'Wisdom' and its Relevance to Tolkien's Grand Moral Philosophy

> [...] I wish I had never seen the Ring! Why did it come to me? Why was I chosen?'
>
> 'Such questions cannot be answered,' said Gandalf. 'You may be sure that it was [...] not for power or wisdom, at any rate. But you have been chosen [...]. (*FotR* 70)
>
> Yes, you have grown very much. You are wise [...]. (*RotK* 299)

T he first cited passage is one of the twenty to be found in *The Lord of the Rings*[1] giving an early context to the writer's extended exploration of the meanings of and glosses on the proper noun *wisdom*. The second comes very late in the epic. Its famous words, some of the last uttered by Saruman-become-Sharkey, tell the reader of the great change which his many adventures and experiences have wrought in Frodo. Both the contexts serve to give us a focus on a particular aspect of Tolkien's moral purpose in all his writings about Middle-earth, the investigation of the historical meanings and nuances to the words *wise* and *wisdom*. It is the purpose of this note to show how this great theme, particularly treated in Old English by King Alfred's vernacular prose, is one which was a part of Tolkien's early studies and teaching, and how it may assist our perception of their creator's development of his two most significant human characters, Frodo and Aragorn, as well as being at the heart of Tolkien's metaphysics.

In his early work in Old English, and particularly in the period 1913-15, J.R.R. Tolkien had studied in the closest detail and read all the texts of the classic

---

This essay first appeared as 'King Alfred's Developing Concept of Wisdom and its Relevance to Tolkien's Moral Philosophy' in two separate parts in *Minas Tirith Evening-Star* 22.4 (Winter 1993: 3-7) and 23.1 (Spring 1994: 3-5) and is here re-published with the kind permission of its publishers.

1 Location, frequency, etc. can best be verified from Richard E. Blackwelder's *A Tolkien Thesaurus* (1990). This analysis of the epic shows the above-mentioned 20 uses of *wisdom*, 26 of *wise* (adjective), and 18 related usages, giving a total of 64 uses of this root.

anthology volume, H. Sweet's *Anglo-Saxon Reader* (1876),[2] including Alfred's preface to his own[3] West Saxon version of the *Cura Pastoralis* ('Pastoral Care') by Gregory the Great (540-604 A.D.). The *Cura*, a handbook on the priestly office, was a much loved work in Alfred's day, not least because of Gregory's interest in England and from his actual sending of Augustine to convert the English in 597 A.D. The translation of this Latin work is probably the earliest one by Alfred and the 'Preface' by the king is notable for some nine references in its short text to *wisdom* and to *wise men*, both of which preserves have tragically fallen away. The address given at the outset to each bishop[4] stresses the following points:

> "what [numbers of] wise men there formerly were throughout England" (101);[5]
>
> how they "prospered both with war and with wisdom" (*ibid.*); and
>
> how the present recipient should "apply the wisdom which God has given" (*ibid.* 102); and
>
> how "we have lost both the wealth and the wisdom" (*ibid.*) in this country.

Shippey on the Semantic Nuances Implicit

In this 'Preface', *wisdom* is a practical matter and it is juxtaposed with education as the necessary qualities, if England is to regain some measure of its former (moral) strength.

One of the clearest modern scholars on the 'Preface' is Professor T.A. Shippey who has discerned[6] some five sequential phases in the text's glances at what was then more recent 'English' history:

---

2 Tolkien studied from the eighth edition (1894) and taught from the ninth (1922). References are to D. Whitelock's 15th edition (1967), for page and line numbers.

3 The authorship is not in question nowadays, although it was occasionally queried earlier in the century.

4 The (surviving) copies were sent to various dioceses, the relevant bishop being greeted in the opening words.

5 These paraphrases follow the 'Preface' in the classic translation of Tolkien's student days, i.e. Cook and Tinker's *Select Translations from Old English Prose* (1908: 101-04).

6 See his 'Wealth and Wisdom in King Alfred's Preface to the Old English *Pastoral Care*' (1979b: 346-55). In his *Road to Middle-earth*, Shippey also observes (1982: 108) that Tolkien "knew well [...] King Alfred the Great's personal translation of Boethius into Old English."

1) "a time of material and spiritual prosperity with both wealth and wisdom";

2) 855-65 A.D., a period of wealth and no wisdom;[7]

3) 871 A.D. and after, a period of "neither wealth nor wisdom", as the Danish attacks demoralized men;

4) "now" – a time with a lingering trace of 'wisdom' – or 'yearning for knowledge'; and

5) the future, a time when Alfred and his bishops will strive for the wisdom that will be their and the country's true prosperity. (1979b: 352)

While scholars have disputed about the exact meaning here of Alfred's first recorded reflections on *wisdom*, it would seem to follow the general purposes of Gregory, who was also deeply concerned with the well-ordered society and the psychological well-being of the ruler. The emphasis is on practical *wisdom* and it seems to refer to the king's ability to make society work, and to maintain good order. This text puts the emphasis on temporal things and never on ideals or on the spiritual dimension to the life of mortals.

An Anticipation

A conventional chronology[8] of Alfred's prose works (all in West Saxon) is:

1) *Handboc*, a commonplace book, carried about with him, but lost in the Old English period;

2) the translation of the *Pastoral Care* of Pope Gregory, with his 'Preface' "which is obviously meant as an introduction to all his works" (Wardale 1935: 242);

3) his translation of *The Compendious History of the World* by Orosius, the textbook of the day on geography and history;

4) the translation from the Latin of Bede's *Ecclesiastical History of the English People*;

5) the translation of the *Consolation of Philosophy* by Boethius; and

6) part of the *Soliloquies* of St. Augustine.

---

7 That of Alfred's youth, he being born in 848 A.D.

8 Readers may consult the more detailed account given by Tolkien's assistant of the time, E.E. Wardale (see the 'Appendix' to this essay), in her *Chapters on Old English Literature* (1935: 239-60). There is no doubt at all that this work accords at most points with the views of the then professor of 'Anglo-Saxon', Tolkien himself. (The language is, of course, Old English, but Anglo-Saxon, the older comprehensive term, is carried on from various traditional usages.)

While these translations are fairly close to the originals, all of them contain Alfredian enlargements or explanations, most of which both helped his contemporary readers and, one might add, assist ourselves as we seek for some light on the purposes working within the historic model king as concerned translator-educator.

In his additions to the fifth text, King Alfred referred particularly to both *wisdom* and *kingship*, substituting the English word *wisdom* for Latin *philosophia*. Whether Boethius was a Christian or not,[9] his philosophy is essentially pagan, referring to Aristotle and Plato and not to Christ. But Alfred's version is much more positive[10] and concerned with the 'kingly' qualities shown by Boethius, comforted in prison, and suggesting that like comfort could come to the 'beleaguered' kingdom. While the Boethius text is concerned with Roman disasters, the Alfredian emphasis is positive, as is indicated by running titles such as these given by Cook and Tinker to the sections which they translated thus:

3. Of True Riches

5. Of Wordly Power

6. A King's Ideal

7. The Emptiness of Fame

8. The Unspeakable Power of God; or

12. The Nature of the Deity (1908: 116-131)

Alfredian Emphases

In further illustrations of Alfred's cast of thought, there may be cited some of his important additions[11] to the *Consolation of Philosophy*:

> [in the former age of this world men] *cared not for luxury* [...] *Men of evil will were not yet seen* [...] (*ibid.* 119-20);

---

9 Because of his suffering, patience, and acquiescence to the 'Divine Will', he is usually reckoned as a Christian.

10 An interesting parallel between the Boethius text and Tolkien's epic is the fact that the Roman had attempted to rid his people of a tyrant, the King-Emperor, Theodoric, who did not use his 'kingly power' in a correct way. Alfred stresses in his first chapter that he was attracted to the contrast between the Christian Boethius and the heretic – i.e. of Arian and not of Catholic denomination – Theodoric.

11 Taken from Cook and Tinker (1908), where all these Alfredian interpolations are italicized.

[*wisdom* sang of worldly power] *ye remember not nor understand the heavenly power* [...] (*ibid.* 120);

[if your worldly power] came to the worst of men, [...] *as recently it did to this same Theodoric, and formerly to the Emperor Nero,* [...] [will he not] *destroy and lay waste*[12] *all the regions which are subject to him or anywhere near, just* [...] *as the burning brimstone consumes the mount which we call Ætna,*[13] [...] *or* like unto the great flood *which was of yore in the days of Noah?* (120-21); and

Because power is never good unless he is good who has it [...].[14] *Hence it is that no one by reason of his authority attains to virtue and excellence, but by reason of his virtue and excellence attains to authority and power. No man is better for his power, but because of his virtue he is good, if he is good* [...]. *Learn therefore wisdom, and when ye have learned, do not despise it. For verily I say unto you that ye may thereby attain to power, though ye do not desire it. Ye have no need to be anxious for power* [...]. *If ye are wise and good, it will follow you* [...]. (121)

In the sixth extract selected by Cook and Tinker and entitled 'A King's Ideal', Philosophy, the comforter of Boethius, is now become Wisdom, while Boethius as speaker is now become *Mod*, which might well be translated as 'mind' or 'heart'. Many of Alfred's remarks through the changed character, wisdom, are definite statements reinforcing his notion of true kingship. Thus we have here (in extract 6) an expansion of the ideal situation:

[A king] *ought to have men for prayer, men for war, and men for labor* [...]. *For every kind of skill and power quickly grows old* [...] *if it is devoid of wisdom; because no one can manifest any skill without wisdom* [...]. (1908: 122)

Mind, often sorrowful and uncomforted, is reproved by Reason or Wisdom, who points out that power it not necessarily a good thing, and fame is of no value. Rather must a man seek happiness within himself.

In the latter part of the book, considerable space is given to the question of the presence of evil in the world, Boethius asking why folly and wickedness reign all over middle earth and wisdom has no honour. To this Wisdom replies that, from the heavens, it is clear that the good always have power since Divine

---

12 This passage suggests Tolkien's Sauron as being modeled on Theodoric and Nero. Tolkien, the undergraduate, had studied W.J. Sedgefield's edition of Alfred's version (1899) and his translation (1900), as well as H.F. Stewart's *Boethius: An Essay* (1891).
13 Cp. Mt. Doom. One is also reminded, perforce, of the almost Biblical flood which destroyed Númenor.
14 This is in the Latin, but the following section is Alfred's gloss.

Providence rules, Providence being "the Divine Reason". Indeed, the original additions reveal a depth of Alfred's pondering upon the manifold moral issues, as well as the political, which pressed upon him. Preeminent amongst these reflections are the original materials in chapters XVII, 'On [Earthly] Kingcraft', and XLII, 'On the Nature of God', the first being concerned with the dynamics of an agricultural (Christian) society,[15] where king and people all practice their craft and are concerned that they leave after them their memory in good deeds. Wisdom had been deeply concerned about Free Will, then expanding on a king's need of true friends, not serfs, and of people who would love to serve[16] him, rather than obey obsequiously.

The famous chapter 42 is a splendid expansion on the nature of God,[17] or how best we may try to understand Him; for "*to Him all is present* [...] *He knows all* [...] *He always wills the good* [...] He is ever watching [...]." (Cook and Tinker 1908: 130). The interpolated defining passage concludes:

> *His greatness no man can measure; yet this is not to be understood corporally, but spiritually, like wisdom and righteousness, which He Himself is.* (*ibid.*)

Alfred on St. Augustine

The last of the important Alfredian translations chronologically is his version of St. Augustine's[18] *Soliloquies*. His first two books are based upon the unfinished Latin text, the third book being almost totally an original text. Throughout there is stress on *wisdom*, the preface urging a journey to the 'forest of wisdom' as a way to God, even as the beginning of Book One calls God 'the ruler, father of truth and wisdom'. The Latin *sapientia* is translated as *wisdom* and is linked to various concepts – good roads, the fairest trees,[19] worldly travel, the learn-

---

15 This is applicable to both Anglo-Saxon England at peace and also to Tolkien's Shire before the troubles come.

16 This ideal is very applicable to the service obtained by Aragorn or Faramir, as opposed to Sauron or Saruman.

17 This is also translated by the American, Margaret Williams, in her *Word-Hoard*, a work owing much to "the helpful guidance of Professor J.R.R. Tolkien" (1946: vii).

18 This is, of course, the Latin Father, 354-430 A.D.

19 One feels that Tolkien must have been deeply moved by the early simile of the teacher/author, Alfred, being like a woodcutter choosing trees in a wood: "I chose the fairest trees, as far as I might carry them away [...] in every tree I saw something of which I had need at home." (Wardale 1935: 259)

ing obtained from books and good government, as well as the quality which binds man to God. This last shows Alfred's final perception of *wisdom* in the *Soliloquies* as an interior virtue connected with the Christian life and with a proper attitude to God. He has left behind the earlier view that *wisdom* is a worldly virtue and turned to the concept that it is only a part of man's soul, necessary to prepare him for the life after death. Indeed, as a modern scholarly work, has it,

> [...] Alfred's version of the *Soliloquies* is a free rendering of the original; in effect, Augustine's work serves as a point of departure for Alfred's reflections on the human soul, its immortality and its knowledge of God after death. (Keynes and Lapidge 1983: 138)

And so to Instances of Wisdom in the Tolkien Canon

While one cannot treat in brief compass all the contextual nuances of Tolkien's many *wise/wisdom* passages, it is very clear that two forms of *wisdom* are being explored – those essential in a (potential) ruler, and those needful for a very ordinary person first living and, finally, passing from his mortal life – in this case, Frodo himself. The wisdom of the (potential) ruler, or of 'Big People' is presented in various encounters of humanlike rationality, these occurring *seriatim*:

1) "For the very wise cannot see all ends" (*FotR* 69) – Gandalf conceeding to Frodo the limitations of his kind and order;

2) "like some wise king of ancient legend" (*FotR* 239) – Frodo's folkloric perception of Gandalf's dignity at Elrond's;

3) "You are wise and fearless and fair, Lady Galadriel" (*FotR* 380) – Frodo's remark to Galadriel;

4) "[he] became [...] a mighty king, benevolent and wise" (*FotR* 414) – Frodo's first reaction to Boromir's talk of the way to combat Sauron;

5) "[as a] tall heir of kings, wise with many winters" (*TT* 119) – Eowyn's first perception of Aragorn;

6) "[...] wisest of counselors, most welcome of wanderers" (*TT* 129) – Theoden's address to Gandalf;

7) "[...] as being of loftier mould [...]: reverend and wise [...]" (*TT* 187) – the retainers' thoughts on Saruman and Gandalf; or

8) "[...] Faramir [...], a man less self-regarding, both sterner and wiser [...]" (*TT* 274) – Frodo's response to Faramir, as opposed to Boromir; etc.

These passages and others like them serve to establish *wisdom* as a characteristic kingly quality in Gandalf, Galadriel, Aragorn, Faramir and others, but, from its absence, to indicate flawed character in such figures as Saruman, Boromir and those like them. Yet others again have this proper responsibility in their spheres, such as Gandalf saying of Barliman – "He is wise enough, on his own ground" (*FotR* 233).

Further aspects of *wisdom* are those manifested by the brave and humble of Middle-earth, like the hobbits and other innocents. Thus Aragorn perceived the Rohirrim as "[...] wise but unlearned, writing no books but singing many songs [...]" (*TT* 33), while the cautious Faramir tells Frodo: "Wise man trusts not to chance-meeting on the road [...]" (*TT* 267), and Imrahil found Aragorn's words to be "wise" (*RotK* 137). And it was Ioreth, the "wise-woman of Gondor" (*RotK* 139) who uttered the famous words on kingly healing ministration:

> The hands of the king are the hands of a healer, and so shall the rightful king be known. (ibid.)

Yet, as with the seemingly lesser operation to destroy the Ring of Power, a quieter form of moral action is centered on the little people of the hobbits. While their *wisdom* can be prudence – compare Sam's 'wiser' thought to "[...] save the waybread[20] of the Elves [...]" (*TT* 260) – it was the faithful Sam who reflected that "[...] Mr. Frodo was the wisest person in the world [...]" (*TT* 248). It is this quotation which is morally midway between the other two on Frodo's *wisdom* at the head of this essay. Significantly it occurs in the context of Frodo's exercise of pity towards Smeagol-Gollum, even as the last is used in like situation of Frodo's behaviour to Saruman-become-Sharkey.

Tolkien's Thought Links with Boethius and with King Alfred

While many interpreters of Tolkien have seen very clearly that the moral and religious systems of Middle-earth owe much to Boethian notions of Providence, of the World-Order and of human Free-will, in the face of the One's Foreknowledge, there does not seem to have appeared to date any attempt to link Tolkien's prose

---

20 The context may be read as the thought of the Deacon reserving the Eucharist in the office of Holy Mass.

use of *wise* and *wisdom* with the like philosophical and Christian usages which
are the core of the prose instruction and philosophy of King Alfred. It would
be complex to trace all these themes and to relate them to Alfred's thought,
yet there is evidence enough for like Tolkien context notes on

> Gandalf's practice of wisdom – seen by the false or his enemies as 'folly' (*FotR*
> 414);
>
> Glorfindel's wisdom (*FotR* 239);
>
> Saruman's fading wisdom (*FotR* 280 and *TT* 165);
>
> Denethor's mocking of wisdom (e.g. *RotK* 88); or
>
> Gandalf's understanding of the "wisdom and mercy" (*RotK* 261) available to
> Sharkey from King Aragorn.

Indeed, it is the last passage which makes it clear that at the end of the Third
Age and the beginning of the Fourth Age (our age), *wisdom*, as socially practiced
by both King Aragorn and the hobbit Frodo are much the same, consisting
of extending pity and mercy to all our fellows, however much they may have
hurt us. The more private moral and religious quest of mortals is not spelt out
as specifically, although the *occasions of wisdom*, carefully analyzed, will lead
us along the way of such understanding.

And so the reader is exhorted to turn again to King Alfred's prose, so carefully
crafted for the healing of his nation, both treating of earthly kingship and for
directing every man's religious quest. The *Pastoral Care* had been concerned
with *wisdom* in a well-ordered society; the Boethius text had largely been reflective on wisdom and kingship; and the new material added to St. Augustine's
Soliloquies turned to human wisdom as the individual's way to God. 'Justice' in
social dealings is replaced by the exercise of pity and awed humility as we near
our own individual experience of the love and spiritual Justice of God.

Conclusion

It is now posited that the various Alfredian senses for the words *wise* and *wisdom*
are to be found in similar senses in Tolkien's most polished creative prose, his
great epic designed to explore the moral behaviour of all men.

Appendix: The Significance of E.E. Wardale for Tolkienian Semantic Nuances

Edith Elizabeth Wardale (1863-1943) was a remarkable scholar of Old and Middle English who had a brilliant student career in Oxford, before completing a Ph.D. in the philology of Notker's psalter. She had been supported by Joseph Wright for a first teaching post in Old English in 1891, and was the first woman examiner in English, being so appointed in 1925, in effect then becoming Tolkien's close assistant after Craigie's departure to the United States of America. Her textbooks proved very popular – *An Old English Grammar* (1922) and *An Introduction to Middle English* (1937).

An essay on E.E. Wardale in the *Oxford Dictionary of National Biography* (Philipps 2004: 367) describes finely her fresh focus as a scholar and the power of her teaching Old English during Tolkien's occupation of that discipline's chair, citing her words of 1921 in defence of Old English:

> English literature was visibly based upon Old English though enormously modified by the influences that have come in since Anglo-Saxon literature gave the English outlook on life, and this has at all times been the same.

Quite certainly Tolkien learned much from her fine study of Old English literature as well as giving her much opportunity for continuing lecturing to both men and women students from 1925 until her retirement.

Uncouth Innocence –
some Links Between Chrétien de Troyes,
Wolfram von Eschenbach and J.R.R. Tolkien

> The main theme – of *The Lord of the Rings* – is
> the ineluctable conversion of hobbit into hero.
> (Lewis 1955: 1373)
>
> The hobbits have the universal appeal of little
> things – they are self-indulgent, childlike, but
> self-sufficient. Their power lies in an unexpected
> ability to withstand evil. (Noel 1977: 59)
>
> No other mediaeval author, indeed, perhaps no
> author before the nineteenth century, has shown
> such keen and sympathetic insight into the
> mind of a child [as Wolfram von Eschenbach].
> (Mustard and Passage 1961: 9)

It is a commonplace of Tolkien criticism that it should be observed of the hobbits that they possess 'a Parzival-like innocence'. It is also noted from time to time that there are in the Tolkien canon various parallels to older German continental literature[1] as opposed to Old English (West Germanic) or to Old Norse (North Germanic) influences. Both types of passing remarks are not further expanded upon, because of the looseness of association of the content of the two forms of story. The following paragraphs are intended to probe the 'Parzival' link with Tolkien, an important literary nexus, not least because of the central place which this writer's invented race of hobbits comes to assume in the affairs of Middle-earth.

This essay appeared in very similar form in *Mythlore* 11.2 (1984: 8-13) and in *Inklings-Jahrbuch 2* (1984: 25-41) and I am grateful to the editors for permission to reprint.

1   See, for example references to the Nibelungs in Edmund Fuller's 'The Lord of the Hobbits' in *Books with Men Behind Them* (1962), reprinted in N.D. Isaacs and Rose Zimbardo, *Tolkien and the Critics* (1968).

Perceval

Perceval is an important hero in Arthurian romance and the Grail winner in
the oldest extant account of the Quest for the Holy Grail, *Le Conte del Graal*
or *Roman de Perceval*, written between 1179 and 1191 by Chrétien de Troyes.
He is not mentioned as one of Arthur's knights in Geoffrey of Monmouth's
Historia regum Britanniae, or in Wace's poetic version of it, although the name
Peredur, which in medieval Welsh literature is equated with Perceval, is to be
found in an early Welsh poem *Y Gododdin* ('The Gododdin', after the name[2]
of the tribe and the country which furnish its theme).

Perceval first appears as one of Arthur's knights in a list of names at the opening
of *Erec*, the 12th century romance by Chrétien de Troyes, and he is promoted
to the position of the hero in Chrétien's last unfinished romance, *Le Conte del
Graal*.[3] Here his chief characteristic is an awkward and blundering naïveté, a
variant of the theme of the 'Great Fool'. This maladroitness – usually perceived
sooner than his moral goodness – remains throughout all Arthurian romance,
although he is later seen to be the most perfect knight in search of the Holy
Grail. In this survey, the emphasis will be largely upon the two most important
Perceval stories, the French and the German, both by knights of lower status
who, like Tolkien also, saw that moral qualities rather than courtly prestige
were the true determinants of the religious seeking (finally associated with the
talismanic Grail).

Though the various questions of Chrétien's originality of plot and detail are
hotly debated, it is possible to show that he drew largely on traditional materials
which came to him indirectly from minstrels and which ultimately went back

---

2 The oldest literature of Wales belongs not to Wales itself but to districts which today form part of
   southern Scotland and northern England. Gododdin was the name of the inland country between
   the rivers now called Forth and Tyne, and that was also the name of the tribe which inhabited it.
   No attempt is made here to explore the various associations and loose links between 'Gododdin' and
   'Gondolin'.

3 Very famous early studies in this area were the two volumes by Jessie L. Weston, *The Legend of Sir
   Perceval, Studies upon its Origin, Development and Position in the Arthurian Cycle* (1906). The volumes
   were reprinted by AMS as a single work in 1972. Some of her theories are now outdated, although they
   would have been taken very seriously in the earlier career of Tolkien. A more standard work is that
   edited by R.S. Loomis, *Arthurian Literature in the Middle Ages* (1959). Professor Loomis of Columbia
   University was a fairly regular visitor to the English Faculty at Oxford in the years after the Second
   World War, e.g. in 1955, and Tolkien talked of him and his excited and intense Celtic enthusiasms to
   the present writer on several occasions.

to Welsh[4] and even to Irish story patterns. For, if we may anticipate, Perceval's riding on horseback into Arthur's hall and his reception there bear a marked resemblance to Kilhwch's arrival in the same court as described in the Welsh *Mabinogion*. [Similar abrupt features occur in the Middle English poem *Sir Gawain and the Green Knight*.]Scholars have also pointed out that the early history of Perceval presents a marked parallelism to the Irish stories of the boyhood of Cúchulainn and Finn.

In Chrétien's poem, since his father and brothers have been killed in the pursuit of chivalry, the boy is brought up by his mother in a lonely forest in isolation from the world and in complete ignorance of the order of knighthood, let alone its true ideals. Thus, at the opening of the poem, he is on his way to see his mother's farm labourers[5] who are harrowing her oats with twelve oxen and six harrows. There is a charming and even idyllic tone to this account –

> It was in the season when trees bloom, bushes put forth leaves, meadows turn green, birds sing sweetly in their language at dawn, and all things are aflame with joy – he entered the forest, and at once his heart rejoiced at the sweet season, and at hearing the warbling of the birds. All these things pleased him, and, filled with the sweetness of the calm weather, he took the bridle from his horse and let him graze the fresh, greening grass.[6]

Then he meets some knights by chance and plies them with naïve questions, after hearing their noisy approach and assuming them firstly to be devils –

> Are they angels?
>
> Is one of them God Himself? (He adores the Lord.)[7]
>
> What is that which you hold (of a lance)?
>
> What is this and what is it for (of a shield)?
>
> Can one be born with armour on him?

He then determines to become a knight and seems not to hear the remarks[8] about himself.

---

4 For a succinct statement of Welsh influence on Chrétien, and on the latter's general influence on later Welsh romances, see Parry (1955: 86-87).

5 More is made of this simple environment in the modern recension, Richard Monaco's *Parsival or a Knight's Tale* (1977). The publishers, Messrs. Macmillan (Monaco 1977: 1) liken this recension to *The Lord of the Rings*, because it is "about the quest for innocence and the struggle against evil."

6 These lines are taken from the summarized story in Loomis (1957: 9).

7 In the Loomis summary, Perceval says to the Lord: "I have never known a Knight, nor have I seen one – but you are more beautiful than God" (1957: 11).

8 There are here obvious parallels to the comments of the court when the Green Knight arrives at Arthur's palace in *Sir Gawain and the Green Knight*, ll.232ff.

Lord:	He knows nothing of manners, so God help me, for he never answers properly any question I ask, but instead he asks the name of everything he sees and what it is good for.[9]
Knight:	Sir, be assured that the Welsh are all by nature more stupid than beasts at pasture, and this one too is like a beast. It is a foolish man who stops to deal with him unless he wishes to trifle away his time. (Loomis 1957: 12)

His further ignorance is manifested as he journeys, by his strange treatment of a maiden whom he meets, by his forcible taking of her ring, by his ravenous eating of venison pasties and by his indifference to information proffered him as to the political situation ahead. When he reaches Arthur's court, at a castle beside the sea near Carlisle, he rides into the hall, fails to recognize the king, and when the latter sits silent, Perceval "turned the head of his horse, but like an idiot, he had brought him so close to the King that the horse knocked the cap off his head onto the table" (*ibid.* 23).

Finally, the king, aroused from his introspection, welcomes the young man and promises him knighthood. Despite his being mocked by the seneschal, Sir Kay, Perceval has a great destiny prophesied for him by both a fool and a damsel at the concert. "Young sir, if you live long enough, I believe in my heart that in all the world there will not be, nor will there be acknowledged, a better knight than you" (*ibid.* 25). He visits the Grail Castle where he is received by the Fisher King and sees a damsel holding a *graal*[10] which gives forth light. It is only after leaving the Grail Castle that he learns of the disastrous consequences of his silence.[11]

He sets out to find the Grail and in the rest of the romance this quest for the mysterious vessel is associated with Perceval's education in chivalry. Although he has a lady, his chivalry is not inspired by human love, but is given a more spiritual foundation and is associated rather with the teachings of the Church.

---

9   There is an echo of this in the hobbit habit of collecting numerous *mathoms* or discarded objects for their possible later usefulness.

10 Defined soon after Chrétien as *scutella lata et [...] profunda*, 'a wide and [...] deep dish', like the Welsh festal platter.

11 Caused by his too literal heeding of the knightly instruction that chattering was sinful – *"Qui trop parole péché fait."*

Chrétien did not complete the romance, but, had he done so, Perceval would almost certainly have returned to the Grail Castle and broken the spell.

Parzival

Various other works[12] appear to be based upon this poem, although there remains uncertainty as to their exact relationship to it. The next and for us most important of these is the *Parzival*,[13] composed, probably between 1200 and 1216, by the knight of the petty Bavarian nobility, Wolfram von Eschenbach, and it is of a very different character to other works treating the same topic. It is deemed to be one of the greatest works of the Middle Ages, both for its high purpose and moral tone and for its poetic quality. It is cast in short rhyming couplets, more than 12,000 in all, divided into 30-line sections by modern editors who also separate the text into sixteen books. Books I to II and XIII to XVI do not derive from Chrétien but from other romance sources. It is also clear that there is much material either invented or at least completely transformed by Wolfram. Seventeen complete manuscripts and more than sixty surviving fragmentary ones attest its considerable popularity.

In his hands, it is a tale of spiritual education and growth, being largely concerned with other-wordly values and leading from the empirical and temporal (as espoused by Gawain, Arthur's nephew, in Books VIII to XIII) to the ideal and to the divine. It is also an allegory of man's life on earth, from his innocent happiness as a child in God, through enticement by the world,[14] – more than four years spent by Parzival ignoring God, – and his final contrition, forgiveness, and return to all spiritual values. Many of the involved details of personal relationships and steps towards self-knowledge are dependent on early hints, and the organizational qualities displayed in the text are remarkable, and another similarity to *The Lord of the Rings*.

---

12 E.g. the Welsh *Peredur* in the *Mabinogion*, and the 14th century Middle English rhymed romance, *Sir Perceval of Galles*. Perceval is also present in the Vulgate-cycle *Quest* and in Malory's Le *Morte D'Arthur*, in both of which he preserves that quality of childlike innocence to be found in Chrétien's *Perceval*.
13 Translations into English are those by E.M. Zeydel in 1951 and by H.M. Mustard and C.E. Passage in 1961. There is also one in the Penguin Classics series by A.T. Hatto (1980a).
14 Much as the greater world of Middle-earth lures various adventurous or curious hobbits out of the Shire.

Parzival is not only a model of chivalry but also an Everyman who learns to overcome his weaknesses and faults and he is not confined within the inhibiting codes of martial prowess and knightly good form, but is ever embarrassingly humble.[15] Thus the process of acquiring even the minimal social skills is seen to be both extremely difficult and spiritually painful. As in Chrétien, Parzival goes into the world in the garb of a fool, his mother's device to cause him to be laughed out of his knightly ambitions. He is literal minded and unbeliev-ably willing to follow the advice of an 'old grey man', one of whose precepts is against asking too many questions. He is also unaware of his own name until told of his identity – a symbolic way of presenting the process of initial and very limited self-knowledge.

Chrétien, Wolfram and Tolkien

While the *Parzival* is a difficult poem, the approach of scholars to occupy them-selves rather with problems of language and of style has diverted attention from the profundity of the work itself. Of the sixteen books into which Wolfram's work is divided, Books III to XIII correspond to Chrétien's narrative, and two signal additions affect Parzival, namely

> 1) a conclusion which gave the Mediaeval German poem coherence as a significant and artistically valid whole; and

> 2) a vast expansion of the scene[16] of Parzival's visit to the hermit (whom Wolfram calls Trevrizent).

Thus although we may not doubt that Chrétien's intentions were any other than didactic and entertaining, Wolfram's tone is deeply religious and often the "atmosphere is charged with liturgical associations" (Walshe 1962: 161). The two heroes are respectively secular and amorous on the one hand, and immature and burdened by guilt on the other, yet able to avoid the mortal sin of *zwîvel (desperatio)* – that despair of God's grace which makes salvation impossible. Then, too, the *Parzival* "is a combination of the religious epic and the romance

---

15 Such behaviour is true of both Bilbo and of Frodo. Peregrin Took or Pippin found it vastly more
    difficult to refrain from asking questions, and so, being extremely curious by nature, he looked into a
    palantír and was thus seen and questioned by Sauron.
16 300 lines in Chrétien become 2100 in the German poem.

of adventure, which are fused into a higher synthesis by the white-hot magic of Wolfram's genius" (*ibid.* 164).

If a comparison is to be reached about these several romantic texts, it could be phrased in various ways. Jessie L. Weston long ago compared Chrétien to Tennyson and Wolfram to Browning in her *The Legend of Sir Perceval* (1906). There is merit in this analogy, if only because the French writer is concerned with mood, while the German – and the English modern – is concerned with 'positive romanticism', and with the phenomenology of hope.

While the 'parallels' or analogous motifs as between Tolkien and Wolfram are not so obvious as are such sources for Tolkien as Old Norse dwarf name lists, or the various echoes of Othin in the appearance of Gandalf the Grey, these parallels operate at a much deeper level. And it must be stressed that the parallelism is not all between Parzival and Frodo. Thus the passionate devotion to his wife by Parzival is to be equated rather with Aragorn's service for Arwen. The fact that God is lord of the little birds, as his mother tells Parzival, is more an attitude of Radagast's. And the renunciation of God by Parzival is not found in that form in *The Lord of the Rings*, although Saruman loses Valinor forever.

Rather is one's conclusion that the tone and central philosophies of Wolfram and of Tolkien have much in common. The core of Wolfram's 'court epic' is the long discourse by Trevrizent, the burden of which is that compassion[17] is the heart of the spiritually good life, and pride, thinking or unthinking, is the greatest sin. While this great moral flaw does not afflict the hobbits, they observe it working in others, as in poor Boromir, or in the distraught Denethor. And much as Cundrie the Loathly Damsel tells Parzival that he will be the Lord of the Grail, so Saruman wonders at the strength and power of forgiveness which Frodo acquires before the end. Since the role of a king is to cure, and Parzival does that for the Fisher King, it is only right that similar healing of the sick, and so of the land, should fall to Aragorn who is a 'King who had been lost'.

---

17 Compare Tolkien's continual stress on pity, as in the remarks about Faramir: "He read the hearts of men [...] but what he read moved him sooner to pity than to scorn" (*RotK* 337).

While Chrétien was concerned with the wonders and rituals of the Grail,[18] Wolfram turned his attention to the fact that Parzival had failed to be moved by his host Anfortas's suffering to show the sympathy, which would have cured him (315, 26 – 316, 3). Thus Parzival's shyness and lack of feeling for others, that is, a lack of *triuwe* or *caritas*, is to be explained as an excessive concern for oneself and with outer form (*zuht*), at the expense of inner feeling. After he had been denounced by Cundrie, Parzival was determined not to rest until he had made good his failure (329, 25-30). Although these great sins are scarcely appropriate for hobbits generally – since they seem largely unfallen – one may argue that Tolkien has explored very thoroughly in the leaders of the Rohirrim, of Gondor, of Orthanc, and of the Rangers, the moral issues of shame, injustice, disgrace, despair, apathy, and in the last group persistence in the attempt to recover what was lost, their refusal to accept discouragement, the practice of courage and the true meaning of chivalry.

Although Chrétien de Troyes is a vehicle for the story, and so an intermediary in the cultural relation, it is clear that many details of the gaucherie of the hobbits can be equated more closely with Wolfram's text. But in the separate central relationships of *The Return of the King*, Tolkien has underscored what may also be seen to be Wolfram's central tenets: "Warm human relationships and the love of man and woman join with knightly perfection and the spiritual maturity of the love of God to achieve a sane and happy balance of the claims of this world and the next" (de Houghton 1971: 2143).

The great difference in the modern text from Chrétien is the democratic and yet truly Christian concept that sheer moral goodness has little to do with rank and even those of the most noble rank must respect total sacrifice, magnanimity, humility and compassion of the sort which Frodo attains to. Also, by an artistic decision of the highest order, the various inherited attitudes were transferred – gauche wonder to Sam, continual chatter to Merry, and foolish and dangerous questioning to Pippin, while spontaneous generosity was made the characteristic of all normal hobbits.

---

18 The Inklings were brought into consideration of the Grail through Charles Williams's work. His novel, *War in Heaven* (1930 and, in a new edition, 1947) is on this theme, as are many of his Taliessin poems which can be found in *The Arthurian poems of Charles Williams* (1982). C.S. Lewis' reaction to them were published in *Arthurian Torso* (Williams 1952).

The significance of Chrétien's work for the study of Tolkien is that it was a known text and mediaeval model as an extended treatment of the theme of the naïve or ill-made knight, the artistic effect of which was to provide many occasions of ironic juxtaposition of conflicting values. Clearly the German treatment by Wolfram is closer to the Tolkien recension and it affords us more matters for fruitful comparison. Yet the whole mediaeval treatment of the Perceval/Parzival theme is one which is a general source for the various aspects of Tolkien's hobbit character, both collective and individual.

Areas of Close Parallelism between Wolfram and Tolkien

Both texts have many parallels of structure and of symbol: the quest adventure; the many renunciations by the central figure; the loneliness of the path to be followed (cp. Tolkien's 'Keep to the path'); the evocation of the mood of the forest; the background of nature used as a means of emphasizing the mood of the hero; the feeling that he is continually guided towards his goal; the concept of a dedicated group – the Grail servers in *Parzival*, and the Fellowship of the Ring in the modern text; the range of places visited and personalities met – individuals in the earlier text, strange new races and orders of being in the later; the intermingling of the worldly and the spiritual aspects of human existence; the stress on love and marriage – as opposed to the courtly in Chrétien and generally in the middle ages; the affirmation of the goodness and meaningfulness of life in this world; the seeming eastern direction of the hero's quest; the mode of immediate reporting of battle pieces; the western rural region from whence the action springs.

Other important aspects of structure include the use of contrast between events in the seeming foreground and the significance of those out of the reader's gaze, and the strong sense of place. Peculiarly similar are the long sequences when the struggling central figure disappears from our view – although he is there in the background, be he Parzival or Frodo,[19] and our attention is almost more on him because of that absence. Wolfram's balance between the Grail characters and those of the Arthurian circle reminds us of the Fellowship, versus Mordor,

---

19 See C.S. Lewis (1955: 1373-74).

in Tolkien's work. And it is also the case that the central positive symbols of the two texts are not unrelated – the Graal in the one, with its guardians who are both knights and monks – and in the other, the renunciation of power and the practice of service and of pity.

Both texts have similar elaborately worked-out geographical backgrounds, so that maps could easily be produced from the data supplied (although, in the case of Tolkien, the maps were provided by the maker himself). Consider the following: "Not the least puzzling factor in *Parzival* is its geography, which confronts the reader at every step with an astonishing mixture of known or unknown names. 'Where in the world are we?' one may well ask" (Mustard and Passage 1961: xlv). For here are what may loosely be called: the Orient; echoes of Africa; the Spanish language territory; the Welsh; and the allegorical. The total landscape seems to be bisected by the River Plimizoel, on one side of which extend diversified lands which may be designated loosely as Arthur's, while on the other side lie those under the control of the Graal. Thus the one side corresponds loosely to Mordor, the other to the moral forces of Tolkien's western parts of Middle-earth.

Then there are parallels of literary mode. Both works are romances (one verse, the other prose), both of which are underpined by a religious epic tone, and concerned with a naïve young hero who is tardily wise, but aided by an innate stability of character and generosity and compassion towards others. Both in the *Parzival* and in *The Lord of the Rings* we are presented with the workings of chance or divine providence, and in both the ultimate success of the protagonist is to be seen as a single act of grace, dependent though it is on a process of maturation by both errors and earlier choices. Also, in the course of the long and agonizing questing, there are moments of fair reception (at the Round Table in Book VI, or at Elrond's and in Lothlórien).

Tolkien, in the best mediaeval manner, made many 'appeals to authority', particularly to the Red Book of Westmarch. There is little doubt that this is an elaborate cover for his own inventions. It is possible to argue that the appeals to source by Wolfram – to the Provencal Kyot or his investigations into Toledo – are deliberately tantalizing, and used by Wolfram as some cover to excuse his flights of fancy. And finally, at the very end, Wolfram refers to his use of "Master Chrétien de Troyes" and of Kyot "who sent us the true Story" – "From Provence to German lands the true story has been sent to us, and the final conclusion of these adventures." All of this elaborate 'appeal to source authority' cannot but remind us of Tolkien's citations of the Red Book and of similar Shire records as his authentication of genealogy, chronology, and the like. Both writers make much of the 'correctness' or 'preciseness' of source quotation,[20] as a proof of their care as transmitters of the true story.

Other parallels and analogues need much more teasing out than space here would warrant, but an actual example will prove illustrative. The name of Wolfram's Grail castle, Munsalvaetsche, may be interpreted in various ways, just as *mons silvaticus* could be interpreted as 'wooded hill' or as 'thoughts of salvation' – both concepts may be held to be contained in Tolkien's Mundburg which looks like the Old English for 'thought fortress', but could be translated a 'sheltering hill'.

Further details of similarity might well relate to the time analysis of *The Lord of the Rings* and of *Parzival*.[21] Yet others are metaphysical and theological. Thus the crushing burden of error and responsibility upon Parzival cannot but remind us of the terrible weight of the Ring upon Frodo, particularly in his last struggle up Mount Doom. While despair and grace are not formally used in the Tolkien text in the way in which they are in Wolfram's poem, there is little doubt that both states are continually investigated in *The Lord of the Rings*, despair being particularly manifested by Boromir and Saruman, whereas grace – be it Gandalf's help, or the allowed practice of hope – recurs continually for so many other characters.

There are many details of the evil side of Parzival's world that parallel those in Frodo's. Certain aspects of Clinschor, the maimed adversary of Arthur, must suggest the similar lack of wholeness in Sauron, while the former's knights who are black shapes of fear are a very potent source for Tolkien's Nine Black Riders. Clinschor himself is a magician, and owner of the Castle of Wonders. "For the shame done to his body he never again bore good will towards anyone,

---

20 For Kyot, see particularly Sacker (1963: 112ff), and Mustard and Passage (1961: xxii-xxv).
21 See, for example, 'The Time Analysis of the Poem', in Mustard and Passage (1961: l-liii).

man or woman, and when he can rob them of any joy, especially those who are honoured and respected, that does his heart good" (658, 1-8). The source of Clinschor's power is magic, to which he turned after his disgrace. As Sacker puts it, referring to 658, 26-30: "In him is embodied that aspect of diabolic activity which presents a direct threat to Arthurian society. Without the aid of God, neither man nor spirit can prevail against him" (Sacker 1963: 142). This passage makes it abundantly clear that his power is that of fear, and so he becomes a supernatural adversary against whom all are powerless without God's help. And there are many other parallels between the metaphysics of the two fictional worlds which could be teased out like the comments on Munsalvaetsche or on Clinschor, and their similarity to Tolkien's on Gandalf or on Sauron.

If we may return to the initial premises of this article, it should now be clear that there is much in the *Parzival* story – both in its own text, and in its rebuttal of the values enshrined in Chrétien's work – which make it a most fruitful source and analogue for further interpretation of the vast prose romance created by J.R.R. Tolkien. Both the German and the English writers are concerned to challenge the worlds of chivalry and of social honour by their stress on simple things, on human weakness and on (personal) faults. Much of the greatness of both Parzival and of Frodo lies in their frailty and in their continually overcoming faults. Yet they attain their objectives, not within the codes of martial prowess like Gawain or Boromir, but by mastery of themselves and by the operation of divine grace. Both go out humbly in symbolic realization of the spiritual inadequacy of mere force of arms and of martial panoply.

As with Parzival, so with all the hobbits who leave the Shire, their simplicity shows how unsatisfactory is the martial code of Rohan or of Gondor on its own. Unskilled though they are in matters of chivalry and formal courtesy, their modesty, loyalty and kindliness cause wonder and win them respect among the great ones of Middle-earth. And in both works, it is one of the greatest achievements of their authors that it is not at all clear how the protagonist is to achieve his objective, so that the reader participates very intimately in the agonisingly slow development of the hero, since information is presented fragmentarily to him, just as it is presented to Parzival or to Frodo.

Both texts are concerned with the operation of 'chance' which is divine providence. Both heroes seek only to serve, from which acts comes all true strength. Both experience single moments of grace which transcend the forms of penitence expressed in dialogue with their aged advisers. The staying of his hand when raised by Frodo against Gollum cannot but remind us of the moment when Parzival was saved from the sin of killing his half-brother by the direct intervention of God (744, 10-16). Both central figures are accorded God's grace, although that terminology is not used formally by Tolkien but rather such phrases as 'the gift of the One to the many'.

Both works have metaphysical cores concerned with: absolution; compassion; sorrow for evil (or contrition); religious education; suffering as part of the divine order; the practice of reverential wonder; continual testing by situations demanding choice; exploration of essential innocence; the hidden working of divine purpose; and the many divergent grades of existence encountered[22] (as creation seeks perfection in many divergent ways).

Yet the true centre of each is the exploration of the relationship between grace and free will, and there is a sense in which both seekers win salvation in defiance of the seeming conditions. Then, too, both works are concerned with the paradox that only those who do not seek it are accorded the greatest spiritual privilege – total service of the Grail or of the One. And both works are concerned with a world of work where not merely grace, but in part a degree of conscious endeavour must effect the outcome of a simple man's quest. As one of the most helpful *Parzival* critics puts it: "One may say that pre-destination (*erben*), free-will (*erstrîten*) and grace (*benennen*) all play a part in Parzival's success. The story at different times emphasises the necessity of being the right person in the first place, the impossibility of succeeding in spite of God, and the glory of persisting no matter what the cost" (Sacker 1963: 170).

---

22 This Thomist concept is usually termed 'gradualism'. Cp. St. Thomas Aquinas, "Oportuit ad hoc, quod in creaturis esset perfecta Dei imitatio, quod diversi gradus in creaturis invenirentur." See J.F. Poag's thesis (1961) which later became his book, *Wolfram von Eschenbach* (1972). And note variously, D.H. Green, as in his *Irony in the Medieval Romance* (1979) or his essay 'Irony and the Medieval Romance' (1970).

Clearly not only the theme of innocence but also the greater metaphysical construction of Tolkien's world are illuminated at many points by careful consideration of Wolfram's greatest work.

It will also be of interest that both Wolfram and Tolkien both received dubious initial critical responses to their work, because of problems of genre and tone. Thus Wolfram was attacked by contemporary critics in a manner not unfamiliar from such onslaughts as those by Edmund Wilson on Tolkien. So the 13th century poet scornfully refers to his enemy without even naming him, comparing him to a swindler who claims to make gold from worthless objects to impress children (*Willehalm*, 237, 11-14). The rebuttal by Wolfram indicates that he was much concerned to stress the differences of his own work from his contemporaries. Thus he stressed in *Parzival* the quest for innocence and the struggle against evil, while in his *Willehalm* he gave us an unusually humane crusading epic. His deep spiritual meaning accorded with traditional themes and genres, making him a moral radical and an advocate, not of the usual ideal of ascetic celibacy and retirement from the world, but of marriage and the fulfillment of duty.

An Insightful Analogue

This somewhat eclectic survey of the *Parzival* romance is intended to do little more than introduce readers of Tolkien's work to the most luminous of its spiritual antecedents, and to suggest that, whether one accepts a specific or indirect influence or no, there is here a world of vast illumination for Tolkien's conception of modern heroism, as well as of his explanation of the spiritual strength of innocence, however seemingly uncouth or naïve this may appear at first sight.

While this account may be held to have departed somewhat from the concept of the career of Perceval/Parzival as a source for the moral character of hobbits in general, and of Frodo in particular, it will be seen that it is not merely the growth of awareness and responsibility in a rustic personality that Tolkien may be seen to owe to this source. Apart from possible origins for Sauron, for Middle-earth's geography, and for many details of the plot, *Parzival* stands firmly beside *The Lord of the Rings* by reason of its similar presentation of the most important aspects of human existence, worldly and spiritual, and it is, similarly, set against a great panorama of wars, battles and of the eclipse of nations. Loyalties, human endeavour and the operation of compassion are opposed to the cruelty and suffering of life. For both writers affirm continually the inherent unity between man's temporal condition and his (necessary) quest or the lack of it.

The parallels between the two writers are endless – stress on kinship; highly individual style; brilliant architectonic skill, binding together the wide-ranging action by a series of memorable links and associations; heroic acts of renunciation in women; the deepest mystical feelings for nature; and the stress on the need for innate and fundamental stability of character.

To Edify Good Men

If this paper is successful in arousing a desire in readers of Tolkien's works to explore this remarkable mediaeval work, it will have achieved its purpose. For it will soon be obvious that, for elevated purpose, moral tone and power of inspiration, Wolfram's corpus, like Tolkien's, was written for the edification of good men, setting before them an example of the most meaningful spiritual humility and of the attaining of real honour in the world of men, a true personal salvation as the consequence of one's acts of service and of substitution for others.

Lore of Dwarves –
in Jacob Grimm and Thomas Keightley

T he short note in *The Book of Mazarbul 1*, entitled 'Song of the Sybil' (Murphy 1984: 18-19) draws attention to the Icelandic poem as a source for the dwarf names in *The Hobbit*. That had been known for some time, but a better known Norse passage had been cited –

> The dwarf company of *The Hobbit* are nearly all found in the *Gylfaginning* catalogue. (Ryan 1966: 51)[1]

It was also observed there, in passing, that "for much of the detail in the depiction of the dwarves,[2] the author has had to go far beyond the few extant [Norse] references to that people" (*ibid.*). The purpose of this note is to suggest that many of the details about these (named) dwarves come from two standard texts during Tolkien's early academic career:

> 1) Grimm, Jacob, 1880, *Teutonic Mythology*, translated by J. Stallybrass; and
>
> 2) Keightley, Thomas, 1850, *The Fairy Mythology*, reissued in 1878 as *The World Guide to Gnomes, Fairies, Elves and other Little People* and reprinted in facsimile in 1968.

The more accessible second work draws largely on the first, and will be cited for ease of reference. The essential point to note is that our and Tolkien's perception of dwarves is a composite one, drawing on characteristics from various parts of Northern Europe. Old Norse provided the names above, although there was a suggestion of an important history behind Thráin, Thorin and Thrór (an epic past to be fleshed out imaginatively in the later tales of Moria).

It is convenient to follow the regional material in Keightley, who initially treats of Scandinavia. From this section (1968: 94 ff.) we may note that

---

This essay was originally printed in *The Book of Mazarbul 7* (1986: 7-10) and is here reproduced with the kind permission of its editors.

1 In the reprint of the essay in Ryan (2009), this is found on p. 205.
2 I will use the plural spelling 'dwarves' in this essay when referring to Tolkien's creatures, while maintaining standard spelling 'dwarfs' when dealing with traditional folklore and mythology.

dwarfs and trolls became synonymous[3] there being largely believed in by the peasants (*ibid.* 94);

pointing out that as at Ebeltoft, red was their hood colour (compare Balin) (*ibid.* 96);

underscoring

their ancient dignity (*ibid.* 96); and

their love of feasting. (*ibid.* 130)

Next, Keightley treats of the Northern Islands referring to:

a 17th century Icelandic belief that "this people are the creatures of God" (*ibid.* 157);

Finnus Johannaeus's belief that they are our "half-kin"[4] (*ibid.* 159);

and that Icelandic dwarfs, as in *Njal's Saga*, wore red clothes (*ibid.* 161);

while Orkney dwarfs,[5] according to Brand, in 1703, "were frequently seen in armour" (*ibid.* 171), etc.

Of particular significance is the chapter on the dwarfs of the Baltic island of Rügen (*ibid.* 174-205), from which the following details are of interest:

they dress in white, brown or black (compare Oin in brown, Gloin in white), the white being 'beautiful', 'innocent', 'still', 'quiet', crafting the finest work "of too delicate a texture for mortal eyes to discern" (*ibid.* 174); and

thirteen is a legendary number for a dwarf company (*ibid.* 177), etc.

The dwarfs of Germany have always been respected, more recently being seen as the most Christian (*ibid.* 206), but earlier they had been depicted the most benevolent, as in the *Heldenbuch*. In this last there appears the Dwarf-king, Laurin, a magnificent and heroic figure who yet stoops to treachery (*ibid.* 207); only to lose his hill treasure and be abased spiritually (compare Thorin). Another dwarf leader yearns for a lost kingdom, and we are reminded of the theory that, in Germany, they were

[...] a people subdued between the fifth and tenth centuries by a nation of greater power [...]. The vanquished fled [...], and concealed themselves [...] (*ibid.* 213)

---

3 A debasement which Tolkien would, progressively, redress.

4 Another source for halflings?

5 In 1972 – according to Bartholomew's *Gazetteer of the British Isles* (231) – the only surviving Dwarf-names for all these lands are at Hoy Island, Orkney – namely Dwarfie Hammers (rocks) and Dwarfie Stone.

They (now) have "no proper communication with mankind" (*ibid.* 217). Another ambiguous but fascinating passage links them to dragons –

> God [gave] the Dwarfs skill and wisdom. Therefore they built handsome hollow hills [...]. God created [...] the great dragons (*würm*) that the Dwarfs might thereby be more secure. (*ibid.* 215)

This is then followed by an even more intriguing reference to the preface to old editions of Hero-tales as to how, after further oppression of the dwarfs

> God then created the heroes [...] and they then came to the aid of the Dwarfs. (*ibid.* 215-16)

Clearly this raises the question as to what is best for the Dwarfs – craftsmanship and quiet, presumably, rather than lust for empire and contempt for all else.

Many of these references are extraordinarily close to story-motifs in *The Hobbit*, as are:

> the Dwarf-hill (*ibid.* 221);
> the 'Journey of Dwarfs over the Mountain' (*ibid.* 223);
> the dwarf exodus to the east (*ibid.* 224);
> or their association with barrels (*ibid.* 227).

The Swiss tales are very similar, but one is crucially similar to Tolkien: 'The Dwarf in Search of Lodging' (*ibid.* 278-79):

> [...] a Dwarf came travelling through a little village [...] knocking [...] for admission [unsuccessfully, until at a little house he] tapped modestly [...] and [was then] offered [...] the little that the house afforded. (*ibid.* 278)

This motif would seem to have been marvellously expanded in the various increasing demands on Bilbo's hospitality.

*   *   *

In short, these somewhat disparate folkloristic materials, as collected up and commented on by Keightley, indicate for the speculative reader such otherwise inadequately recorded motifs as:

> 1) the forgotten but essential humanity of the dwarfs;
> 2) an heroic past largely forgotten and largely unknown to other races in the smaller race's period of eclipse;

3) (God's) gifts of skill accorded to the dwarves;

4) a (divine form of) protection now largely lost by the race, presumably because of moral flaw or sin;

5) the notion of a hero coming to the aid of the dwarfs, who, however, retain their human freewill to choose power and materialism (i.e. *draconitas*) and so to bring about their individual and racial damnation.

Thus the Grimm-collected and Keightley presented material on this race of the 'little people' already contains for *The Hobbit* the elements of a race's talents, materialism and fatal fall. Even more interesting is Tolkien's later focus on the individual, Gimli, who by friendship for a foe (Legolas) and admiration for the wise (Galadriel) was able to escape the hereditary doom of his race.

Sadly no such alternative was available for Fili and Kili, doomed, by the (Germanic) blood – and *comitatus* bonds – to fall beside their power and destiny crazed kinsman, Thorin.

Warg, Wearg, Earg and Werewolf – a Note on a Speculative Tolkienian Etymology

> The word vargr [...] had a double significance [...]. It signified a wolf, and also a godless man. (Baring-Gould 1865: 48)

> *wearg* (-h), -es. m. (of human beings) a villain, felon, scoundrel, animal. II (of other creatures) a monster, malignant being, evil spirit. (Bosworth and Toller 1898: 1177)

> *Wargs* – In the Third Age of Sun in Rhovanion, there lived an evil breed of Wolves that made an alliance with the mountain Orcs. These Wolves were named Wargs and often when they set off for war they went with the Orcs [...] In the [battles of] the War of the Ring, the Wargs were devastated and [...] the histories of Middle-earth speak no more of these creatures. (Day 1979: 236)

Most readers of Tolkien's *The Hobbit* and of *The Lord of the Rings*, will remember the *wargs*,[1] the wolf-creatures which pursue Gandalf, Bilbo and the Dwarves in chapter VI of the former – and which are led by "a great grey wolf" (*Hobbit* 112), fear fire, fight and plunder with the Goblins (i.e. Orcs), and which are routed in the climatic Battle of the Five Armies (*ibid*. 112, 114, 295). They will also recall the Warg chase of the members of the Fellowship (*ibid*. 310-12) when the Wargs have come west of the Mountains, led by "a great dark wolf-shape", the "'Hound of Sauron'" (*ibid*. 311). In the former text Gandalf feared the Wargs, but in the chapter 'A Journey in the Dark', he is powerful enough to rout the "great host of Wargs [which] had gathered silently and was now attacking them from every side at once" (*ibid*. 312). In his gloss

---

This essay was originally published as two separate items, as 'Warg, Wearg, Earg and Werewolf – A Note on a Speculative Tolkien Mythology' in *Mallorn* 23 (1986: 25-29) which makes up the main argument, and as 'Warg and Oath and their Ancient Legal Word Field, Including 'rope' and 'choking'' in *Quettar* 29 (1987: 6-8) which has been added as an Appendix. Both items are here reproduced with the kind permission of their editors.

1 "[...] the wild Wargs (for so the evil wolves over the Edge of the Wild were named [...]) (*Hobbit* 112).

on these creatures Robert Foster observed of the Wargs of *The Lord of the Rings* that "they [...] do not seem to have been true Wargs, in that they were west of the Misty Mountains and were not real" (1978: 415) – a view born out in that Gandalf is able to combat them relatively easily.

It is the contention of this note that Tolkien was indulging himself with this word and concept in both etymological speculation and in restoring to the living English language a pattern of meanings long forgotten. As T.A. Shippey was to point out much later, in 1982, in his *The Road to Middle-earth* – "'Wargs' are a linguistic cross between Old Norse *vargr* and Old English *wearh*, two words showing a shift of meaning from 'wolf' to 'human outlaw'" (50). This is both true and simplistically confusing in that the thought associations are also blended to some extent with the concept 'werewolf', on which form the following entry is excerpted from C.T. Onions' *The Oxford Dictionary of English Etymology*:

> **werewolf** [...], **werwolf** [...] person transformed or capable of transforming himself into a wolf. Late O[ld] E[nglish] *werewulf* (once) = L[ow] G[erman] werwulf; [...] cf. W[est] F[riesian] *waerūl*, [...], Sw[edish] varulf, the latter perh[aps] repr[esenting] O[ld] N[orse] **varulfr*, whence O[ld] N[orth] F[rench] *garwall* (Marie de France²), later *garoul* (in mod[ern] F[rench] *loup-garou*). The first el[ement] is doubtful, but it has been identified with O[ld] E[nglish] *wer* (= L[atin] *vir*) man. After the M[iddle] E[nglish] period [the word was] chiefly Sc[andinavian] until its revival through folklore studies [in the nineteenth century]. (1966: 1000).

As the last point makes clear, there was considerable academic interest in such human shape-changing in folklore studies in Europe in the later nineteenth century, as it was realised that notions of similar metamorphosis in classical mythology were paralleled widely in medieval, and, not infrequently, in later records of many of the Indo-European peoples. The depiction of wolves alongside the hunters was done in many cave-paintings of more than 50,000 years ago. A number of further such wisdoms were published under the item ANIMALS in vol. 1 of Hastings' *E.R.E.*, as in the following:

---

2 See specifically her 13th century lai *The Were-Wolf* (*Bisclaveret*), translated into English in Vol. 4 of *Arthurian Romances Unrepresented in Malory's Morte d'Arthur* (Weston 1901: 81-94). The work was reproduced in facsimile by AMS in 1970. The title word, *bisclaveret*, is held to come from *bleiz* ('wolf') + *garou*. The story itself is found in other literary versions, such as the 14th century *Roman de Renart* by the clerk of Troyes.

In Europe the wolf was especially associated by the Greeks with Apollo [...].

Probably the wolf was originally worshipped or received offerings, as was the case among the Letts [...] in process of time the cult was associated with that of Apollo, and it was supposed that he received his title from having exterminated wolves [...].[3]

In Delphi [in the temple of Apollo] was a bronze image of a wolf; this was explained as commemorating the finding of a treasure with the aid of a wolf. Like Romulus and Remus, many children of Apollo by human mothers were said to have been suckled by [gentle] wolves. (1908: 531)

As the last dangerous animal to survive in many parts of Europe, the wolf has given its name to the group of beliefs based on the idea of the temporary or permanent transformation of living men into wolves[4] or other animals (see LYCANTHROPY). (*ibid*. 532).

Yet these beliefs had, to a large extent, passed from English, though, as Baring-Gould explained:

English folk-lore is singularly barren of were-wolf stories, the reason being that wolves had been extirpated from England under the Anglo-Saxon Kings, and therefore ceased to be objects of dread to the people. The traditional belief in were-wolfism must, however, have remained long in the popular mind, though at present it has disappeared, for the word occurs in old ballads and romances. Thus in Kempion –

O was it war-wolf in the wood?
   or was it mermaid in the sea?
Or was it man, or vile woman,
   My ain true love, that mis-shaped thee? (1865: 100)

Clearly, as with other such literary losses of folk-concept, Tolkien was concerned, to some degree, to re-animate the lost thought by showing the various meanings in his story constructs.

Related to this were-wolf notion is that of the link between the concepts of 'wolf' and 'outlaw', as referred to above by both the Bosworth and Toller dictionary (1898) and, more recently, by T.A. Shippey (1982). As Baring-Gould put it in

---

3 The Warg attacks and their repulsion by Gandalf may be held to be a witty recollection of the epithets used by Homer of Apollo (*Iliad*, iv: 101, 119) which may be glossed as either "twilight-born" or "wolf-born" (Hastings 1921: 531).

4 For myths and folk-tales of the wolf, see De Gubernatis, vol. II (1872: 142-49). S. Baring-Gould presents many like legends in his overview study (1865).

1865, "*Vargr* had double significance [in Norse] [...]. It signified a wolf, and also a godless man. This *vargr* is the English *were*,[5] in the word were-wolf [...]" (48). He had also noted, a few lines above, that the Norse *vargr* may be seen as *u-argr*, 'restless', the second element being a cognate of Old English *earg*. This last adjective is listed in classical Old English by Bosworth and Toller (1898: 233) as having two main senses –

1) inert, weak, timid, cowardly;

2) evil, wretched, vile.

The first sense is illustrated excellently by the Beowulfian half-line (l. 2541b) comment on Beowulf's approach to the dragon:

ne bið swylc earges sið!
(Such is not the way of the coward!).

While Tolkien is not primarily concerned with the link between *warg* and *earg*, the *warg* cowardice is stressed in the contexts under discussion, and so there is left floating the possible etymological link which modern scholarship prefers not to stress, despite Baring-Gould's suggestion (1865: 48).

The actual word-form *warg* is an interesting one, since it is older[6] than those occurring in written Old English, where the word shows the sound-change, breaking, and is spelt *wearg*. There are, however, various early forms extant which show Tolkien's lexical source, such as:

1) Gothic *vargs*, a 'fiend';

2) Pluquet in his *Contes Populaires* (1834)which tells that the ancient Norman laws said of criminals condemned to outlawry for various offences: "Wargus esto!" "Be an outlaw!";

3) The *Lex Ripuaria*, tit. 87: " 'Wargus sit, hoc est expulsus.' " [i.e. "Let a man be a warg, (then) he is driven out."]; or

4) The *Salic Law*,[7] tit. 57, which orders: " 'Si quis corpus jam sepultum ef-foderit, aut expoliaverit, *wargus* sit.' 'If any one shall have dug up or despoiled an already buried corpse, let him be a warg.' "

---

5 This identification is not certain – see the quotation above from C.T. Onions.

6 See my earlier essay 'German Mythology applied – The extension of the Literary Folk Memory' in *Folklore* 77.1 (Spring 1966: 45-59), especially pp. 53-54, as reprinted in Ryan (2009: 199-213), here especially on p. 207.

7 Quoted by Baring-Gould (1865: 48). There is some possibility of confusion with vampires here.

In his own elaboration on these forms, their semantics and sense implications, Baring-Gould notes from Palgrave's *The Rise and Progress of the English Commonwealth* (1832) that, among the Anglo-Saxons, an outlaw "was said to have the head of a wolf", and he then concludes:

> If then the term *vargr* was applied at one time to a wolf, at another to an outlaw who lived the life of a wild beast, away from the haunts of men – 'he shall be driven away as a wolf, and chased so far as men chase wolves farthest,' was the legal form of sentence – it is certainly no matter of wonder that stories of out-laws should have become surrounded with mythical accounts of their transformation into wolves. (1865: 49)

While the linguistic speculation by Tolkien is perhaps most clear in his earlier references to *wargs*, the notion of were-wolf was probably present initially in his thought as in the account of Sauron's wolves on the Guarded Plain in *The Silmarillion*. These creatures are there variously referred to as 'wolves' and 'werewolves', and their mightiest and strongest is a wolf form of Sauron himself, who, when seized by Huan, shifts his shape from wolf to serpent and then back to his usual body, finally flying away in the form of a vampire dripping blood (*Silmarillion* 175). As we have been told a little earlier, Sauron had made various strongholds of evil, such as "the fair isle of Tol Sirion [which] became accursed and it was called Tol-in-Gaurhoth, the Isle of Werewolves" (*ibid*. 156). As the Appendix on elements in proper names tells us, in this name the constituent *gaur* means 'werewolf' and comes from the root *ngwaw-*, 'howl' (*ibid*. 359).[8]

In a similar note, in *Unfinished Tales*, the *Gaurwaith* are defined thus: "The outlaw-band on the western borders of Doriath that Túrin joined, and of which he became the captain [...] [The name being] [t]ranslated Wolf-men" (440).

The note points to two text passages, the first of which – in a section entitled 'Túrin among the Outlaws' – gives an excellent gloss on the concept of out-laws:

> [...] all that region lay under the fear of Orcs, and of outlaws. For in that time of ruin houseless and desperate Men went astray: remnants of battle and defeat and lands laid waste; and some were Men driven into the wild for evil deeds.

---

8 The then editor of *Mallorn*, Jenny Curtis, added the following commentary to this: "It seems to have escaped the eye of Mr. Ryan that the two words *gaur* and *warg* may be cognate in the mind of the author, the second being the Westron translation of the first and, indeed, a metathesis of it: *gaur* → *gawr* → *warg*, and I wished to emphasise this point since it furthers Mr. Ryan's theory."

Tolkien continues:

> They hunted and gathered such food as they could; but in winter when hunger
> drove them they were to be feared as wolves, and Gaurwaith,[9] the Wolf-men,
> they were called by those who still defended their homes. [...] They were hated
> scarce less than Orcs, for there were among them outcasts hard of heart, bear-
> ing a grudge against their own kind.

Although it is not at all obvious from the passage in *The Hobbit* where there
is "a great grey wolf" as leader, or that in *The Fellowship of the Ring* with 'the
Hound of Sauron', in the van, the section in *The Silmarillion* certainly shows
that Sauron (or 'the Necromancer') was leading the wolf-outlaw pack in all
cases, and that the notion of (temporary) shape changing is implied in most, if
not all, the references to outlaws/wolves/were-wolves throughout the canon.

Shape-Changing

The ancient notion of actual shape-changing is, however, more thoroughly
explored in another place – in the character of Beorn in *The Hobbit*. In discussing this problem of enigmatic humans in Tolkien, Shippey observes of Túrin
in *The Silmarillion*:

> [H]e is only half a man. This idea Tolkien clearly took from Norse sources,
> for instance from the famous *Saga of Egill Skallagrimsson*. In that saga Egill's
> grandfather is Kveld-Ulfr ('Evening-Wolf'), not entirely human, 'a great shape-
> changer', very like Beorn in *The Hobbit*. (1982: 198)

Earlier he had noted that Beorn "is a were-bear, who changes shape, or 'skin'
as Gandalf calls it, every night" (*ibid.* 62).

This last is in accord with general nineteenth century theory of lycanthropy,
as in Professor J.A. McCulloch's definition:[10]

> 1) It may indicate merely a form of madness in which the patient imagines
> that he is an animal, especially a wolf, and acts as such. [...];

---

9 One assumes a recollection of a root *Gaur-, which might be postulated to lie behind the ONFr
   garwall (see Onions, above). Norman *guar-wolf* is also cited in various etymological dictionaries as an
   occuring form. A. Brachet's *Etymological Dictionary of the French Language* derives Modern French
   garou from Old French *garoul*, from Medieval Latin *gerulphus*, a word of Scandinavian origin (1882:
   179).
10 In his article on 'Lycanthropy'.

2) It indicates the popular belief that on occasion a human being can actually transform himself, or be transformed, into a wolf or some other animal. In this form he slays and eats men. [...] (Hastings 1915: 206)

As McCulloch and others[11] stressed, while the superstition is practically world-wide and the wolf transformation has been the most usual one in all parts of Europe and in North Asia from early times, in the Northern parts of Europe, the bear form is also general. For example Boniface, Archbishop of Mayence, in the 8th century mentions the belief (in *Sermo* XV).

The change was caused by a man himself – e.g., by donning a wolf-skin (*Ulfhamr*, hence the name 'skin-changer') or a wolf-girdle. In such cases the man was a wolf or bear by night, and a man by day, at night howling and devouring like the actual animal. Such persons were said to be *eigi einhamr*, 'not of one form'. In later times the Scandinavians thought that Finns, Lapps or Russians had the power of changing others to wolves or to bears at will.[12] McCulloch also suggested the point of linked thought and association:

The belief was apparently much mingled with and probably influenced by the fact that wild warriors and outlaws – *e.g.* the *berserkr* – wore wolf-skins or bear-skins over their armour or clad themselves in these, while they were often victims of ungovernable passion and acted as if they were animals. (Hastings 1915: 208)

Many Scandinavian instances of this are to be found in classical Norse literature, e.g.:

the account of Sigmund and Sinfjötli donning skins and becoming wolves (*Vǫlsunga-Saga*, chapters 5-8);

Björn (in *Hrólfs saga kraka*) being transformed into a bear[13] by his stepmother, who shook a wolfskin glove at him. He lived as a bear and killed many of his father's sheep, but by night he always became a man;

the statement by the hag, Ljot, in the *Vatnsdæla Saga* that she could have turned Thorsteinn and Jokull into boars[14] (ch. xxvi); or

the account of Thorarinn becoming a boar when pursued and afraid (*Eyrbyggja saga*, ch. xviii).

---

11 E.g. Robert Eisler, *Man into Wolf* (1949), Enid Starkie, *Petrus Borel the Lycanthrope: his Life and Times* (1954), Ian Woodward, *The Werewolf Delusion* (1979).
12 See Grimm (1888: 1097), Dasent (1859: lx-lxiv) or Vigfusson and Powell (1883: 425).
13 Compare Scott (1839: 354).
14 The expression *verða at gjalti* 'to become a boar' is often met with in the sagas.

The Complex of Fable and Horrific Motif

Of this mix of fable and romance relative to such transformation into wild beasts, Baring-Gould well observed:

> among the Scandinavian nations there existed a form of madness or posses-
> sion under the influence of which men acted as though they were changed
> into wild and savage brutes, howling, foaming at the mouth, ravening for
> blood and slaughter, ready to commit any art of atrocity, and as irresponsible
> for their actions as the wolves and bears, in whose skins they often equipped
> themselves. (1865: 51)

Beorn's Mythic and Cultural Pedigree

The Beorn of *The Hobbit* in the late Third Age was the chieftain of the clan of Northern Men whose traditional duty was to maintain the safety of the trade routes from Eriador to Mirkwood. As presented in Chapter VII ('Queer Lodgings'), he is someone of appalling anger (126), "a skin-changer" (*ibid.*), perhaps "descended from the great and ancient bears" (127),[15] normally very inhospitable (136), indifferent to gold and silver (137-8),[16] at night like "some great animal" (139), but who "loves his animals as his children" (147).

Thus while Beorn conforms to all the usual *berserkr* qualities, Tolkien has made him a distant blood relative[17] of the Edain of the First Age and the *Quenta Silmarillion* relates how some of that stock were skin-changers, the greatest of whom was Beren. Further, as Gandalf makes clear, Beorn comes from ancient stock and "is under no enchantment but his own"[18] (127). Yet some of the traditional ruthless violence is allowed by Tolkien to his creation:

> "What did you do with the goblin and the Warg?" asked Bilbo suddenly.

---

15 Presumably also the lord of all the bears which came to dance at night (141).
16 This suggests that he came from a time before the lust for wealth and possessions inspired malice
   among the dwellers of Middle-earth.
17 This background is neatly summarised by Day (1979: 30-31).
18 This ancient strenght and his various marvellous deeds liken him to Bombadil in *The Lord of the
   Rings.*

"Come and see!" said Beorn, and they followed round the house. A goblin's head was stuck outside the gate and a warg-skin was nailed[19] to a tree just beyond. Beorn was a fierce enemy. (143)[20]

Any careful reading of the Baring-Gould[21] study of werewolves will indicate Tolkien's close indebtedness to this collection which he follows very closely for its chapters I-IV, and VIII, i.e. the period prior to the Middle Ages. He is also in sympathy with the earlier parts of chapter X, 'Mythological Origin of the Were-Wolf Myth', particularly those concerned with metempsychosis or sympathy (and communication) between men and beasts.

While he could not, as Christian, have subscribed to the ancient's belief in a soul-endowed animal world, yet transformation into beasts was a part of Greek mythology, while in Scandinavian mythology Odin changed himself into the shape of an eagle, and Loki into that of a salmon. As Baring-Gould puts it of such transformations and communicating –

> [t]he line of demarcation between this and the translation of a beast's soul into a man, or a man's soul into a beast's (metempsychosis) is very narrow.

> The doctrine of metempsychosis is founded on the consciousness of gradation between beasts and men [...]. [...] in the myth of metempsychosis, we trace the yearnings and gropings of the soul after the source whence its own consciousness was derived [...] (1865: 153-4)

At many points in *The Hobbit* there is much such communication between various orders of rationality, a possibility which has largely passed by the time of Frodo's quest. Thus, in the earlier text, Bilbo understands the dragon, the great spiders, and the eagles; Gandalf can follow the speech of the Wargs;[22] both thrushes and ravens speak to the Dwarves; and Beorn has the ability to talk to his animals, ponies and dogs. This primitive sympathy for the state of

---

19 This is very similar to the nailing of Grendel's claw to the gable of Heorot in *Beowulf* (11.833-36).

20 In the original publication of the essay we find another commentary here by the editor of the day, Jenny Curtis, pointing to the importance of Beorn's nature as a shape-changer when considering the particular hatred he bears for the Wargs.

21 Tolkien referred with approval to his own studies in the field of folklore in various lectures and seminars attended by the present writer in the years 1954-1957. Tolkien was also aware of – and commented on – the many Oxford lectures in the area of French lycanthropy by Dr. Enid Starkie, some of which were later included in her book on *Petrus Borel*.

22 This must remind us inevitably of Montague Summers, in his *The Werewolf*, discussing: "certain fantastic beings known [in Normandy] as *lupins* or *lubins*. They pass the night chattering together and twattling in an unknown tongue" (quoted by Douglas Hill in his article on 'Werewolves' in Cavendish's *Man, Myth and Magic*, vol. 11, (1983b: 3012))

animals is something which Tolkien allowed himself in the sphere of myth, as opposed to the more history-like mould of the latter Third Age in *The Lord of the Rings*. What were perhaps mythological stories, if found early in *The Simarillion*, have gradually deteriorated into attitudes alien to superstition, blood-thirstiness, cruelty and even cannibalism by the later times of *The Lord of the Rings*. Perhaps naturally, fables and fears are seen for what they are in the face of morality and theology at the end of the Third Age.

In a similar antiquarian vein, Tolkien allowed himself the inclusion – in skeletal form, at least – of the vampire concept. While both werewolf and vampire have a liking for human flesh and blood, there is a marked difference in them. Whereas the former is a living person assuming animal form, the latter is a resuscitated corpse which rises from the grave to prey on the living. Despite his use of the vampire idea, Tolkien seems not to be influenced by post-medieval Balkans (and especially Rumanian) story, but, rather, to be drawing on his classical knowledge of such antecendent beings as the blood-consuming ghosts in the *Odyssey*, in Ovid, and elsewhere. There may also be echoes of the demonic Lilith of ancient Hebrew legend, who had many vampire traits, or of the Roman *lamia* which enticed men sexually[23] and then feasted on their blood.

The brief Tolkienian account of the phenomenon occurs in *The Silmarillion* in the account of Thuringwethil, a creature of monstrous evil and perhaps one of the corrupted Maiar, described thus as

> [...] the bat-fell of Thuringwethil. She was the messenger of Sauron, and was wont to fly in vampire's form to Angband; and her great fingered wings were barbed at each joint's end with an iron claw. (178)

Typically she is the companion of "the ghastly wolf-hame[24] of Draugluin" (178), whose name and description imply some form of obscene misgenation.[25]

---

23 Compare "he saw upon his flank a bat-like creature clinging with creased wings" (*Silmarillion* 179).
24 The second element may well be connected with the dialect verb *hame*, 'to have sexual intercourse with', from Old English *hǣman*, 'concubere, coire, nubere' (see Wright 1903: 39).
25 Jenny Curtis added a third commentary here on a further study on vampires by Michael Burgess, published in *Amon Hen* 75 (1985: 15-16), prompted in his turn by another essay by Professor J.S. Ryan in an earlier issue of the same journal (1985: 10-11).

Tolkien's Final Views on Vampirism

While Tolkien's thoughts about ancient vampirism are suitably enigmatic, the same cannot be said about his views on the related phenomena of male cruelty, outlawry and preying in cannibalistic fashion on other humans. As with his other such investigations of ancient Indo-European and Germanic thought, the clue is as always in the words used and in what is said in his stories about these seemingly strange and fabled forms of being. While he would not have accepted that he was conducting 'an anthropological interpretation of sadism, masochism and lycanthropy',[26] there is no doubt that Tolkien has tried to trace the idea of the were-wolf back to (Germanic) pre-history. If he does not quite see its origin as Eisler does, in primeval clash of cultures between peaceable vegetarian early man and the brutal, fur-wearing carnivorous creature that he was forced to become, yet his stories do inculcate similar probing thought about

> the stern autonomy of ancient figures like Beorn;
>
> the nature of the cowardice and aggression of outlaws (OE *earg/wearg*);
>
> the ancient and vindictive laws which made solitary men *wargs*; and
>
> the revulsion felt by even the most elemental of men, like Túrin or Beren, in the presence of the obscene, mindlessly malevolent and the grotesque travesties of humanity created by Sauron.

As on many other occasions,[27] Tolkien has extended the folk-memory by exploring and reanimating old words for too long lost to the English-speaking peoples, so that, like our forebears we 'recover' the freshness of words and in so doing make for ourselves "a discovery in the inner world of consciousness" (Barfield 1926: 72).

---

26 The subtitle of Robert Eisler's *Man into Wolf* (1949).

27 See, for example, Ryan, 'German Mythology Applied' – already mentioned under footnote 6, or his 'Before Puck – the Púkel-men and the *puca*' (1983d: 5-10), reprinted in Ryan (2009: 223-33).

Appendix – Warg and Oath and Their Ancient Legal Word Field, including 'Rope' and 'Choking' – and the Celtic, Gothic and Further East Associations

In his *The Tolkien Companion*, J.E.A. Tyler provides us with a composite text-based definition of Wargs:

> A Northern Mannish name for wolves, but more properly applied to the evil werewolves which appeared in Middle-earth during the Third Age[28] and remained to plague the wilderness ever after. Unlike real wolves, the Wargs were phantasms [...]. (1976: 509)

In an essay in *Folklore*, entitled 'German Mythology Applied',[29] the present writer had observed of them (**warg* being a possible earlier form of *wearg*):

> Old English literature uses the word 'wearg' of human beings, as meaning 'villain, felon, criminal'; of other creatures as meaning 'monster, malignant being, evil-spirit'. [...] By [Tolkien's] playing on both senses the reader is given the impression of shape-changers, outlaws, becoming bestial and so preying on humans and animals alike, yet able still to plot with evil-doers [...]. (Ryan 2009: 207)

While both these descriptions are of assistance in aiding our perception of the seemingly Tolkien-created race of *wargs*, they are much extended by the taut scholarship of Heinrich Wagner of Queen's University, Belfast, in his 1971 publication, *Studies in the Origins of the Celts and of Early Celtic Civilization*. In the first five pages of this text, in a discussion of Old English *fír*, 'oath', Wagner draws together a number of quotations from Old Norse, Old Irish, Gothic, Middle Latin, Hittite and Sanskrit. While Wagner's purpose is to explore various interrelations between Celtic and non-Celtic languages by virtue of their vocabulary, it is possible to excerpt the varius clusters of forms and concepts which are relevant to the philological (i.e. creative mythological) thought of J.R.R. Tolkien.

---

28 This would accord with the notion of man falling from an original state of grace. Compare the Old English glossing of *wearg* as *deofol* (Bosworth-Toller 1898: 1177).
29 The essay has been republished as part of Ryan 2009 (199-213) from which the quotation is taken.

1) In the Eddic poem, 'Sigrdrífumál', the man who swears falsely an oath (*eið*), "will have terrible ropes put upon him" and he is called *vargr*, 'the wolf (i.e. breaker) of vows'. This is likened to the Irish ordeal of truth where the rope or 'collar of truth' [30] around the neck tightened for a lie, but was loose for the truth. There is also an etymological link between Old Norse *símar*, 'ropes' and Old Irish and Welsh words for 'magic' – compare Old Icelandic *seiðr*, 'magic'.

2) The words for 'oath, truth' are linked[31] or borrowed in a number of Western European languages: O. Engl. *áð*; O. Norse *eiðr*; Gothic *aiþ-s*; O. Irish *ōeth*; etc. Wagner adds the detail: "In Norse tradition *Vár* is the goddess who [...] listens to the oaths of men [...], wherefore these agreements are called *várar*; she also punishes those who break them" (*ibid.* 3). (She is called the ninth goddess in Snorri's *Gylfaginning*, ch. XXXV.)

3) The *vargr* (i.e. the breaker of vows) of 'Sigrdrífumál' is, it is stressed, a kenning for 'wolf', and is an outlaw who is to be hunted down. As is explained by Peter Andreas Munch: "one who desecrated [hallowed ground] was denominated *vargr i véum* (a miscreant in the sanctuary) and declared an outlaw" (1926: 268).
Many Western European medieval words are related to this: Gothic *wargiþa*, 'damnation', compare OE *wiergþo*, Middle Latin *wargida*, etc. It is postulated that these words originally meant 'neck-fetter' and were connected with Middle High German and Modern German *würgen*, 'to choke'. E. Partridge linked these words with the Modern English verbs 'to wring' and 'to worry' (1958: 812). Since it also occurs in Hittite, Wagner argues that the notion of "the wolf as a symbol for the outlaw must be an old oriental idea" (1971: 4).

4) Wagner follows H. Lüders and H. Peterson in linking Varuna, the god of oath in India, with a root **wer*, 'to bind, to put in fetters' (1971: 5).

*   *   *

Now while this account is necessarily skeletal, its present importance lies in the various illuminations which the postulated – and very plausible – 'word-field' has for Tolkien's Middle-earth:

1) Many etymologies in Indo-European languages make it clear that Tolkien's name, *warg*, in medieval times implied some form of oath-breaking, particularly in the mode of the heroic Old Norse poetry. While this does not occur in *The Lord of the Rings*, it is a plausible further dimension to the surviving ancient texts of Middle-earth.

2) The choking of the criminal, e.g. by hanging on the gallows (much as occurs at l. 2446 of *Beowulf*) – is not found in our texts, but we do have the exquisite pain which the seemingly loose elf-rope causes to Gollum's foot (*TT* 224) – an indication of his deceit and misrepresentations to Frodo as to his purpose.

---

30 Its owner was Morann, the famous judge, who believed in the true God before the coming of St Patrick.
31 This has long been known – e.g. see Holthausen (1934: 8).

3) In Middle-earth the most significant form of sin is oath-breaking,[32] very much as it was the case in the Old English and Old Norse aristocratic and heroic society. The immediate consequence of this sacrilege was banishment or outlawry. Sabine Baring-Gould in his *Book of Were-Wolves* has it thus:

> Pluquet in his *Contes Populaires* tells us that the ancient Norman laws said of the criminals condemned to outlawry for certain offences, *Wargus esto*: be an outlaw! In like manner the Lex Ripuaria,[33] tit. 87, has "Wargus sit, hoc est expulsus." ["Let a man be a warg, (then) he is driven out."] (1865: 48)

*   *   *

There is another fascinating 'English' analogue to the texts already cited, namely the text held in the Taylorian and elsewhere in the Oxford of Tolkien's student days. This is Elliott O'Donnell's *Werewolves*, a fascinating collection of beliefs held in Europe early in the twentieth century. Notably it refers to the belief in a werewolf in the Doone Valley, Exmoor. This passage is said to be "the spirit of one of those werewolves referred to by Gervase of Tilbury and Richard Verstegan – werewolves who were still earthbound owing to their incorrigible ferocity" (1969: 280).

Summary and Overview

The consequences of this linguistic and folkloric collocation may be elaborated further, but enough has been said to indicate that:

> 1) Tolkien's fantasies are indeed philological, i.e. they are concerned to tease out and illustrate by *exemplum* ('appropriate story') lost or half-forgotten senses to words that survive today.
>
> 2) They illustrate the movement, across the whole Indo-European cluster of countries and of languages, of thought enshrined in lexical form, i.e. words, whose roots prove their common source and identity or early borrowing.
>
> 3) The most serious of his writings are in no sense 'A Secret Vice' of made-up language, but, rather, highly unorthodox and imaginative explorations of the meanings of words, extending the senses found in medieval texts.

---

32 Compare *The Silmarillion* (83): "For so sworn, good or evil, an oath may not be broken, and it shall pursue oathkeeper and oathbreaker to the world's end."

33 I.e. the law-collection of the Ripuarian Franks, the Franks living in the Lower Rhine area in the 7th century.

While most of the individual points of Wagner's essay have been known for many years, his contribution is the identification, as highly likely, of

> an archaic legal "Wort-feld" (word-field) in the light of which etymologies of the words in question could emerge. (1971: 4)

It would also seem that many of the sense-links had occurred to Tolkien the philologist as is evidenced by the writings of Tolkien the storyteller.

The Number Fifteen, Heroic Ventures and Two Horrible Songs

> Fifteen birds in five firtrees,
> their feathers were fanned in a fiery breeze!
> (*Hobbit* 117)

W hile it is a relative commonplace of Tolkien criticism to link Bilbo Baggins in many aspects of his adventures with the Old English epic hero, Beowulf, perhaps few have seen a peculiar piece of ancient numerology which also enforces the link – the highly significant number, 'fifteen'. In the poem, Beowulf, the hero, resolves to come from amongst his own people, the Geats, to assist Hrothgar, the Danish king who has been suffering from the depredations of Grendel. Thus, at the head of fourteen men (*XVna sum, Beowulf,* 1.207b), he sets out to right these wrongs. As the whole passage may be translated:[1]

> He bade make ready for himself a good ship [...] said he would seek the warrior-king, the noted prince [...] Wise men did not blame him for that expedition [...] The hero had chosen warriors from the people of the Geats, from the boldest he could find; with fourteen men he went to the ship [...] he himself led the way to the shore.

Bilbo, in much less heroic mould, is also with fourteen heroic companions, on his mission to recover a large hereditary treasure, although he seems at this stage very far from the assertive leader of Thorin, the twelve other dwarves, and the but occasionally present Gandalf.

The mocking chant cited by the head of this note is that of the evil goblins when they have set fire to the firtrees in which the members of the band have taken refuge from the pursuing goblins, and the fleet wargs. The pain[2] already being felt is described through Bilbo's experience:

This essay was originally printed in *Minas Tirith Evening-Star* 24.4 (1995: 10-11) and is here reproduced with some clarifications with the kind permission of its editors.

1 Summarized from ll.198-209 in J.R. Clark Hall's (revised) translation of *Beowulf and the Finnesburg Fragment* (Hall and Wrenn 1940: 29-30).

2 The passage, for all its minimal detail, must remind us of the burning of Njal in *Njáls Saga*, or of the night raids on Icelandic homesteads such as occur in *Hrafnkels Saga*.

Smoke was in [his] eyes, he could feel the heat of the flames; and through the
reek he could see the goblins dancing [...] could hear the goblins beginning
a horrible song:

Fifteen birds in five firtrees, [...]
(*Hobbit* 116-17)

Various almost magical uses of the number fifteen occur in older Germanic
literature, particularly since the fifteenth day is half-way through the phases of
the moon (see OE *leechdoms* as in Cockayne 1865: 146f, 338f). It is also used
in Old Icelandic, as in the 'Sagas of the Norse Kings', to indicate a ritually
significant number. as in *fimmtan-sessa*, 'a [Viking] ship with fifteen seats'.

As stressed already, the goblin song is, rightly, described as 'horrible', and it
savours of a gleeful gloating over the inevitable fate of one's victims. It is also
echoic of a much more recent ghastly song, one eternally on the lips of Long
John Silver in Robert Louis Stevenson's *Treasure Island* (1883), and a continual
theme in that work, where it is sung most memorably in the second chapter:

[...] I remember [...] that filthy, heavy, bleared scarecrow of a pirate of ours [...]
Suddenly he [...] began to pipe up his eternal song:–

"Fifteen men on the dead man's chest –
Yo-ho-ho, and a bottle of rum!
Drink and the devil had done for the rest –
Yo-ho-ho, and a bottle of rum!" (*ibid.* 7)

On the very first page it was called "that old sea song" (*ibid.* 2), and next "his
eternal song" (*ibid.* 7): then repeated again and again by the green parrot Captain
Flint, till it became a "wearisome refrain" (*ibid.* 225). Yet it is terrifying to the
old sailors on the island, as Jim Hawkins recalls:

I have never seen men more dreadfully affected than the pirates. The colour
went from their six faces like enchantment; some leaped to their feet, some
clawed hold of others; Morgan grovelled on the ground. (*ibid.* 268)

And in the last chapter Jim reflects on the few men who came back from the
ill-fated quest of the 'Hispaniola', musing to himself:

"Drink and the devil had done for the rest," with a vengeance; although, to be
sure, we were not quite in so bad a case as that other ship they sang about:

"With one man of her crew alive,
What put to sea with seventy-five." (*ibid.* 291)

In 1934 Vincent Starrett was writing about the real location of *Treasure Island* in his reflective piece, 'The Dead Man's Chest, A Stevensonian Research' and Tolkien may well have known of this reappraising essay. But a much more subtle possible influence of Stevenson's is the one suggested here, in an earlier quest for an accursed treasure.

Robert Giddings and Elizabeth Holland in their *J.R.R. Tolkien: The Shores of Middle-Earth* (1981) have shown very persuasively the echoes in *The Lord of the Rings* of some of the most familiar texts of then modern romance – Buchan's *The Thirty-Nine Steps* (1915), Haggard's *King Solomon's Mines* (1885), R.D. Blackmore's *Lorna Doone* (1869), and James Hilton's *Lost Horizon* (1933). They do not mention R.L. Stevenson, but it is difficult to dismiss the possibility of like influences in the case of the goblins' chant. As the Clark Hall translation[3] has it, as Grendel advanced on Heorot, "from the eyes there came a horrible light" (*leoht unfaeger*, l. 727b). He does devour one sleeping Geat, but God saves the others from a like fate. A similar divine intervention or grace operates here, in the form of the rescue by the eagles, to save Bilbo and his fourteen companions.

Whether this is no more than a pleasing coincidence, or a deliberate use by Tolkien of the potent Germanic number fifteen, there is no doubt that two 'horrible' songs have much in common in their settings. Equally pleasingly to the moralistic reader, both are reminders of the trains of death awaiting all who seek treasure hoards already steeped in blood. But Bilbo's company is as yet not required to pay with many lives for their presumptuous questing. That would come after the dwarves have attained the treasure and fought in heroic frenzy to retain it.

---

3 Its revised phraseology was attributed to Tolkien in Oxford in the 1950s. The pair, Wrenn and Tolkien, had clarified it, with the royalties to go to Clark Hall's estate.

Fear and Revulsion in "the cold, hard lands"

At the beginning of Book IV, in Tolkien's *The Two Towers*, the hobbits Frodo and Sam, on "the third evening since they had fled from the Company" (*TT* 209), are discovered climbing and labouring on heroically among the barren slopes and jagged stones of the Emyn Muil, and trying, finally, to descend a tall cliff.

This they do eventually by an act of quiet faith, after a terrifying moment of blackness, great wind and "a high shrill shriek" above them, probably from a Ringwraith passing overhead. That they have been in great psychic and spiritual danger is indicated by the remarkable language used of the risk, "the skirts of the storm were lifting [...] and the main battle had passed" (*TT* 215). What saved Frodo from despair was trust in "the silken-grey rope made by the folk of Lorien" (*TT* 214), and for Sam, too, "the rope seemed to give him confidence." The grace accorded the new owners of the elven rope is further attested when Sam's almost subconscious invocation, "Galadriel," causes the knot to loosen and the rope to come down by itself. A touch of the rope and respect for it seems sympathetically to bring out the stars and the moon to "cheer the heart."

Some time later, when they have apprehended their pursuer, Gollum, they tie him up with the same cord, only to find that its touch really tortures the poor creature.

'It hurts us, it hurts us,' hissed Gollum.
'It freezes, it bites! Elves twisted it, curse them!' (*TT* 224)

Now, while the passage is peculiarly memorable, it is not one commented on by critics in any detail. This is regrettable since there are several fascinating elements of old religion and superstition working in it.

This essay first appeared in *Minas Tirith Evening Star* 18.1 (1989: 18-19) and I am grateful to the editors for permission to reprint it.

Firstly, the valid hobbit fear of a terror above them draws on the pagan Germanic motif of the Valkyries as malign death-dealing figures in the sky,[1] one repeated frequently in Middle English as in the concept of the Wild Hunt, most famously perhaps for its appearance in the romance, *Sir Orfeo*,[2] but still encountered in American and Australian folk ballads. Secondly, the rope is made (for us) to be felt to be a religious object, belief in which ensures physical safety and moral salvation. It is a preventative of danger for the trusting, but an instrument of torture for the obscene and blasphemous, as is Gollum's attitude to the elves as 'fierce' and cruel. The third interesting aspect of the events is that both Frodo and Sam (*TT* 217) use the ancient Shire word, *ninnyhammer*, to rouse themselves to commonsense and action. It is, of course, the general dialect word for "simpleton" or "a stupid or weak-minded person,"[3] but it is used also dialectically, as in Tolkien, to suggest the person who fails to practice patience, courage and common-sense. Thus it is a rallying-cry to calm, stoic control and quiet hope when under duress.

But perhaps the most interesting aspect of the whole chapter is the anguish experienced by Gollum at the touch of the rope, and later, at the taste of waybread (*TT* 229, 260). These owe their origin to late medieval conceptions of damnation and to renaissance fears of witchcraft. In the documents of the Inquisition it was stated that a suspect devil, in the guise of a Jew might be detected thus:

> On the day of the Passover you watch him [...] Tempt him, offer him bread and see whether he puts the bread in his mouth. See whether he will touch the bread. Press the bread into his hand and see whether he drops it the way you would drop a hot coal.[4]

The good and bad aspects of a cord may be summed up in the symbolic strength of the cleric's girdle, or, by an obscene inversion, of the monstrous red cord[5] of

---

1 A point made publicly by Tolkien in his lectures on the Old English *Exodus* in Michaelmas Term, 1956.
2 Glossed by Tolkien as early as 1921 in his 'Vocabulary' to accompany K. Sisam's reader, *Fourteenth Century Verse and Prose*.
3 See Wright, *EDD*, vol. IV (1903: 275-76).
4 The quotation is taken for convenience from the short biographical novel, *Torquemada* by Howard Fast (1966: 119). Thomas de Torquemada was Prior of Segovia who in 1483 was named Grand Inquisitor of all Spain by King Ferdinand and charged with the sacred duty of purging the land of heretics.
5 Encountered particularly in accounts of witchcraft in Scotland in the sixteenth and seventeenth centuries.

the Maiden or Inquisitress-Murderer of a disloyal witch deemed to have lapsed from the coven.

Thus it is that a prose passage of haunting poignancy gains in power from the subtle uses of images with potent associations within Christianity, although such a monotheistic and compassionate religion is, of course, adumbrated rather than suggested specifically in the world of Tolkien's creative writing.

Addendum

Ninnyhammer, as Wright recorded (*loc. cit.*), had considerable usage in Yorkshire as in "Wha yo stupid ninny hammer", cited from Barnsley, 1859.

This robust language is a register used amongst the wandering hobbits to arouse each other to more chearful attitudes.

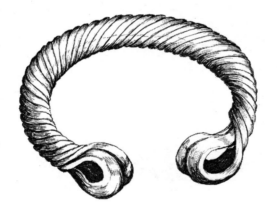

The Origin and Cultural Associations of the Place Name *Wetwang*

> 'As you go down the water,' [Celeborn] said, 'you will [...] come to a barren country. There the river flows [...] until at last after many leagues it [...] casts its arms about the steep shores of the isle [of Tol Brandir], and falls then [...] down into the Nindalf, the Wetwang as it is called in your tongue. [...] There the Entwash flows in by many mouths from the Forest of Fangorn in the west. (*FotR* 389)

> Celeborn's 'Wetwang' is also a place in Yorkshire [...]. (Shippey 1982: 78)

> [Hugh Smith] graduated from Leeds in 1924, was appointed Vaughan Fellow in the University, and proceeded to his doctorate [in place-names] in 1926. (Brown 1968: 177)

In the first volume of his Middle-earth epic, *The Lord of the Rings*, the late Professor Tolkien first refers to these marshes to the east of the Anduin, caused by the merging of the Anduin and Entwash rivers and by the subsequent division of the Anduin into many rivers.[1] Although the region is not referred to again, it has an actual English name of complex etymological association, and serves to illustrate the richness of associations of one of the seemingly minor place-names of the created fantasy world of Middle-earth, as well as being a clue to Tolkien's literary use of details of the Yorkshire landscape, not least because of his friendship with his former pupil when at the University of Leeds, one Albert Hugh Smith.

Despite the late professor Eilert Ekwall's views, the actual etymology of *Wetwang* may be more complex than that recorded in his *Concise Oxford Dictionary of English Place-Names*, viz.:

This essay was originally printed as 'The Origin of the Name *Wetwang*' in *Amon Hen* 63 (1983: 10-13) and is here reproduced with the kind permission of its editors.

1 See the endpaper map to *FotR*. See Map 35 in Strachey (1981:79). This fine detail would seem to indicate the relative dryness of the area.

Wetwang. Yorkshire East Riding (*Wetwangham*, Domesday Book, *Wete Wang* 1114, *Wetewanghe* 1145-56, [...] *Wetewonge* 1190 [...]). Probably 'wet field'. Old English *wang* means 'plain, field'. (1951: 486)

Indeed, there can be no doubt that the word *wang* and this name are forms that must have afforded much early speculation to Tolkien as well as to his friends E.V. Gordon[2] and A.H. Smith who were, like him, associated with the Department of English at the University of Leeds in the 1920s.

Hugh Smith (1903-67), later for many years Reader[3] and then Quain Professor of English Language at University College, London, was a Yorkshireman of humble origin[4] and of apparently insatiable (linguistic) curiosity[5] and extraordinary distinction. Much later, he was described by his friend and colleague Arthur Brown (1968: 180-81) as "a convinced and unrepentant linguist and medievalist" and as the contributor to the merry *Songs for the Philologists* (1936: 25) of the following lines:

> Though critics jibber in their holes
> Of style and form and metre,
> Yet literature (the little moles!)
> They miss her when [they] meet her.
> This is my faith, I do maintain, while
>   songs by men are sung, sir!
> They only earn the English name who learn
>   the English tongue, sir!

He had been able to go to the university in Leeds in 1921 early in the reader-ship there of J.R.R. Tolkien, been taught by him throughout his undergraduate studies and been appointed to his research fellowship by the same scholar. Smith's lifelong research into English place-names[6] began in these years and he published his *The Place-Names of the North Riding of Yorkshire* in 1928. The work contains in its 'Preface' the author's expression of "deep gratitude to my

---

2 Collaborator with Tolkien in editing *Sir Gawain and the Green Knight* (1925).
3 He was also associated with Tolkien in the privately printed booklet, *Songs for the Philologists* (1936).
4 His father was a butler and he had first worked as a booking clerk when he left school.
5 He admitted to the present writer in a private conversation in London in March 1966 that he had been a model for Tolkien for various hobbit antiquarian characteristics.
6 In addition to producing many volumes in this general area, he was the Director of the English Place Name Society from 1951 until his death.

old teacher and friend Professor E.V. Gordon" (1928: vii), and an acknowledge-
ment of his indebtedness to

> Professor J.R.R. Tolkien, MA., for encouragement and valuable help in con-
> nexion with the philological problems which arose. (*ibid.* ix)

J.R.R. Tolkien's own association with Yorkshire had begun with his military stay
and training in a camp near Hornsea and then in a Harrogate sanatorium. Later
still, he was at "an army signalling school in the North-East" (Carpenter 1977:
95).[7] As Carpenter also records, at the end of that year the young lieutenant, his
bride and infant son lived near Roos, "a village north of the Humber estuary"
(*ibid.* 97). The strange name Roos is derived from the Old Welsh word, *ros*, 'a
moor, a heath', itself a borrowing into English, and surviving in the English
dialectal forms, *ross* 'march', and *rossland* 'moorland' (Smith 1956b: 87). In
this conjunction, it may be relevant to quote Christopher Tolkien's etymology
from the 'Appendix' to *The Silmarillion*:

> *ros* 'foam, spindrift, spray' in *Celebros, Elros, Rauros*; also in *Cair Andros*, an
> island in the river Anduin. (363)

Thus it may be seen legitimate to postulate that the period 1916-18 was one for
some familiarization for Tolkien with the distinctive Yorkshire landscape and
with its various more unusual place name elements. As Carpenter (1977) also
recalls, a small wood near Roos, where Tolkien and his young wife wandered,
engendered:

> the story [of Beren and Luthien] that was to be the centre of *The Silmarillion*.
> (97)

It is indeed probable that he saw more of rural Yorkshire during these military
and medical alarums than he did during his later period as Reader and Professor
at the University of Leeds.

*   *   *

---

7 It was perhaps this period when he attended his troops' cutting up of a poached deer from the Pennine
   Uplands – an event excitedly referred to in a lecture in Oxford on *Sir Gawain and the Green Knight* in
   Hilary Term, 1955 (the present writer was in the student body then present).

If we may return briefly to the career of Hugh Smith, it becomes clear that, like Tolkien's tutor Joseph Wright, another Yorkshireman and editor of *The English Dialect Dictionary*,[8] Smith's academic career was equally based on his own detailed knowledge of Yorkshire language[9] and landscape – as the volumes on the North Riding (1928), East Riding (1937), on place-name elements (2 volumes, 1956) and on the West Riding (8 volumes, 1961 to 1963) make abundantly clear.

While Tolkien has been mentioned as having assisted with the 1928 North Riding volume, it was the 1937 survey[10] which would have appealed to him more. Not only had it subsumed a draft study on the same topic by Tolkien's friend E.V. Gordon (1937: vii), but it expanded on various names of interest to the now Oxford professor. Thus, under the Holderness Wapentake, Roos is discussed at some length, with the further comment on inter-relationship between the races:

> It is possible that the word *ros* was taken over from British into the common word-stock of the Anglo-Saxons, much in the same way as were *foss* [...], *cumb*,[11] *carr*, and *cors* [...]. (*ibid*. 56)

Under the Buckrose Wapentake, there is discussion (*ibid*. 128-29) of the Domesday Book place-name, *Wetwang*, some 27 miles to the north west of Roos. As Smith points out

> *wang* as the second element in place-names is almost certainly of Scand[inavian] origin [...] a loan-word from OScand. *vangr* 'field' [...]. (*ibid*. 128)

Although he concedes that the first element might be OE *wæt* 'wet', it is almost certainly

> derived from the OScand. legal term *vætt-vangr* (*véttvangr*) 'field of summons for the trial of an action'. This explanation, with a detailed account of the topography of the place, was also put forward by E.M. Cole, *Saga-book of the Viking Society*, iv, 102. (*ibid*. 129)

---

8 First published in the years 1898-1905 in six volumes and reprinted in 1981.
9 He observed to the present writer in London in the summer of 1965 that he had been a dialect speaker by birth and had had to 'launder' his speech to advance his own academic career.
10 Its full title was *The Place-Names of the East Riding of Yorkshire and York*.
11 This, for example, translates into the language of the Rohirrim, as in Deeping Coomb, the valley below the Hornburg, or *carr* into the element *carag* ('fang') in *The Silmarillion*.

Because of the refusal of Ekwall to accept this explanation, first in 1936, and in later editions of his dictionary, Hugh Smith felt impelled to repeat his etymology in the terse entry in the second part of his *Elements* (1956b: 229):

> *vaett-vangr* ON, 'a field for the trial of a legal action', cannot formally be distinguished from OE *se weta wang* 'wet meadow' (v. wēt), but the topography is decisive in [...] Wetwang YE 128 (ON *vaetti* 'witness, evidence', *vangr*, cf. *Sagabook* iv, 102, 106)

As Smith notes, the element *vangr* from Old Norse can mean 'a garden, an in-field', and he quotes the Cumberland place-name *Whangs*. Since the site in Tolkien's fantasy world is not discussed, apart from Celeborn's description above as "a wide region of sluggish fen" (*FotR* 389), it is possible to argue that Tolkien did not 'come down' on any etymology. He may well have recalled Joseph Wright's dialectal entry

> **WONG**, sb. Yks. Not. Lin. Lei. Nhp. e.An. Also in forms **wang** Yks. Nrf. Suf.; **wung** Nhp. [...]
>
> 1. A field; a meadow; low-lying land, often marshy [...] [e.g.] 'The Wong,' a large field near Belvoir Castle. [...] I know five or six fields so named; they are all meadow, with a small rill of water rising in them, *N. & Q.* (1856) [...]
>
> 2. An unenclosed division of an unenclosed parish [...]
>
> 3. A measure of land. n.Lin.1 [1. OE *wang*, a plain, mead, field, place (Hall).)] (1905: 535)

Perhaps we may conclude that Tolkien's use of the old Yorkshire name, *Wetwang*, has a nice complex of motives

> 1) a glance back to his own animated discussion of the 'wet' words – 'Wash-Wavy',[12] in *YWES IV* (1924: 20-37);
>
> 2) a recollection of his own army and courtship and early marriage times of residence in the East Riding of Yorkshire; and
>
> 3) a sly refusal to take sides in the dispute[13] over Wetwang between his old pupil, Hugh Smith, and the encyclopedic Eilert Ekwall, as to whether the *Wetwang* was really 'wet'.

*   *   *

---

12 See particularly Ryan (1981: 11-12), republished as pp. 75-76 in Ryan (2009).

13 Compare his own guying of the blunderbuss definition in the *O.E.D.* in Farmer Giles of Ham, so wittily teased out by Paul Kocher in his *Master of Middle-earth* (1973: 181).

Even if this musing has raised more issues than it has resolved, it will have achieved its purpose if readers understand the Yorkshire topographic dimension to Tolkien's (linguistic) world and realise that a particularly interesting, if largely unexplored, research field is to be found in the publications of the master's old pupil, Hugh Smith, the doyen of English place-name scholars and the man who built into that discipline of applied etymology the need to scrutinize with the utmost care that most illuminating and exciting dimension to North Country toponymy, the surviving landscape.

Appendix

Hugh Smith's long-time home in Gloucestershire gave him an abiding love of that county's terrain, resulting in his late and meticulous EPNS publications, *The Place-Names of Gloucestershire* (1964-65), 4 volumes.

Part D

Twentieth Century Oxford & England

The Wild Wood – Place of Danger, Place of Protest

> Wild or Wyld, Berkshire (first recorded 1183); Monkton Wyld, Dorset (first recorded 1186). Apparently from Old English *wil*, 'trick'; used of some mechanical contrivance or trap. (Ekwall 1951: 494)

> *wilder, wild-deor,* Old English, 'a wild beast, a deer', as place-name element, e.g. in Wilders Moor, Lancashire. (Smith 1956: 266)

> *bewilder* (vb), confuse. From *be + wilder,* 'lose one's way, cause to lose one's way'. (Onions 1966: 92); perhaps a back formation from *wilderness,* an uncultivated tract of land O.E. *wild(d)eornes,* from *wild(d)eor,* 'wild beast'. (*ibid.* 1006)

There has long been a tradition in the Earlier (i.e. Old) English and other Germanic peoples' languages and thought of 'the wild' as a place of danger – one apparently dating from well before the Christian era – and of the likely presence there of the manifestations of evil in a dualistic universe; and in Britain, since the conversion of the Angles and Saxons, the notion has been widespread that it was a place of unhallowed, unconsecrated land, where the powers of darkness were given free reign. Thus, to use a familiar example, it was in the 'wild' – and so well away from the (Christian and thus protective) aura of their village – that the Three Rioters, central in Chaucer's *The Pardoner's Tale,* in their search for the Black Death, found under a tree the pile of gold, the lust for which unleashed murder in each of their hearts. Thus, in a drunken quest of retribution for the deaths of so many of their acquaintances by the Black Death, one now quite forgotten, they actually killed each other

This text first appeared in briefer form in the earlier period Australian literary periodical, *Orana: Journal of School and Children's Librarianship* 19.3 (August 1983: 133-40). It has been somewhat developed and further expanded in the text as presented here.

in their greed for the pile of gold through Death's unexpected and shrewdly psychological stratagem.

For perhaps the last thousand years, then, the English-speaking peoples have had a complex and largely fearful folklore about dark (forest) regions, regarding them as untamed places of ancient power, whose physical manifestations are dangerous if not actively malevolent. This mindset is well defined by the comparative scholar, Richard Cavendish, towards the beginning of his classic if summary article, 'Wildwood':[1]

> The uncanny quality of woods is part of the lore of childhood. In the forest you are far from home, from fireside warmth and kindliness and the settled accustomed order of things. In the forest you are lost. (1983b: 3024)

He continues

> Groves and woods have many symbolic connotations and are by no means always places of evil [...]. They may be a place of retreat from the [...] noisy human world to the peace of Nature [...]. (*ibid.*)

Yet, however it is regarded, the forest of legend and of folklore does tend to be strange and eerie, the realm of Nature there is still untamed by man, and giving the sense of immense antiquity and, to some degree, of the malign.

In the Middle Ages, the wild forest – particularly in Arthurian legend[2] – was associated with both enchantments and wonders and, very often, with encounters with supernatural beings, as in Malory's *Le Morte D'Arthur*, or in the anonymous 14th century romance, *Sir Gawain and the Green Knight*. The hero of that alliterative verse romance is forced to travel through "the Wilderness of the Wirral" (1. 701) on the borders of Cheshire and Lancashire, finally reaching "a wondrously wild wood" (1. 741) of ancient trees in which he finds the deceptively gracious host and the welcoming Castle of the Green Knight.

---

1 This article was first published on pp. 3029-32 of part 108 of the series of fascicles, *Man, Myth and Magic*, issued in 1972. The quote references are made to the 1983-edition.
2 Compare the Questing Beast in the modern children's book *The Once and Future King* (1958) by T.H. White, or the strange encounters in the more recent *Parsival or a Knight's Tale* (1977), by Richard Monaco.

Whether we choose to identify this latter wood with the Inglewood Forest in Cumberland,[3] or with the Forest of Bowland in Eastern Lancashire[4] – and then running into Yorkshire –, it is known that both these great forests of the uplands of the more northern Pennines of Britain date from periods of milder climate in the early Bronze Age, before the arrival of the Romans. The Bowland Forest would also seem to be suggested by the quirkish 'B.B.' in his two stories[5] of the gnomes of ancient times, *The Forest of Boland Light Railway* (1955) and *The Wizard of Boland* (1959). There is also a presumptive case for the ancient forest of the Ents in J.R.R. Tolkien's *The Lord of the Rings* – Fangorn, on the eastern side of the Misty Mountains – itself being deemed to have been inspired in various ways by the Forest of Bowland. For, as a young soldier, Tolkien had visited it during Army manœuvres quite early in the First World War. The most obvious evidence of this link is the discussion by A.H. Smith[6] in his very early study of English regional toponymy, *The Place-Names of the East Riding of Yorkshire* (1937: 128) under the heading for the Buckrose Wapentake of the Wetwang[7] Parish names of Fimber, Bowlands, and Wetwang.

*   *   *

The actual human residents of the Wild Woods tended to fall into various types, of

> 1) the wild men of the woods, variously called 'woodhouses' and 'woses';
>
> 2) unearthly woodmen who guarded the forest and its creatures, most familiar to general readers from the Tolkien creation of Tom Bombadil, in the *The Lord of the Rings* and elsewhere; and

---

3 See N. Davis (p.98) in his revised 1967 second edition of J.R.R. Tolkien and E.V. Gordon (eds.), *Sir Gawain and the Green Knight*.

4 This area, also known as the Bowland Fells, is an area of barren gritstone fells, deep valleys and peat moorland, being long famed for its upland bird populations. The name 'forest' is used in its traditional sense of 'a royal hunting ground', and much of the land still belongs to the British Crown as part of the Duchy of Lancaster. In the past boar, deer, wolves, wild cats and game roamed the forest.

5 See my article on his work in *Orana* 19.1 (February 1983: 11-24). 'B.B.' was the pseudonym of Denys Watkins-Pitchford (1905-1990), a much loved nature-writer and long also a highly productive artist illustrator, especially of his own books. Something of a hermit as a child, he became a pen and ink craftsman in training at fifteen, subsequently studying both in Northampton and Paris. The vast majority of his writings, fictional or otherwise, were concerned with life, animal and human, and largely in the southern parts of England.

6 Interestingly Hugh Smith had been Tolkien's student at the University of Leeds soon after World War I, and was a co-contributor to – and, in effect, the printer of – in group collection, *Songs for the Philologists* (1936), a private publication celebrating their mildly roistering good fellowship.

7 This same name is to be translated from the Old English as 'wet / moist plain or low lying ground'.

3) the outlaw figure, who, for whatever reason, was outside both society and its laws,[8] – a type rendered immortal by the manifold legends of Robin Hood.

We may again quote Richard Cavendish for a succinct sketch of the English outlaw of the Middle Ages –

> The forests of mediaeval England sheltered thieves, vagabonds, fugitives from justice, men who had been turned off their land, rebels and misfits of all sorts. The poor, themselves suffering in a hard, rigidly stratified society, romanticized them and credited them with superhuman abilities [thus] [t]here grew up the picture of the merry outlaw in the greenwood [...]. (1983b: 3029)

Perhaps predictably, the wild and often entirely honourable outlaw figure had lasted much longer in Scottish folk literature, ballads[9] and the like, although the more rugged and bare terrain largely precluded his being linked with forests, save in the legends of the Central Highlands associated with the ancient Rothiemurchus pine forest.[10]

A Memorable Resurgence of this Wild Wood Theme in the Writing of Kenneth Grahame

For the reader of children's books from England over the last hundred years, the term, 'Wild Wood', is inevitably associated with Kenneth Grahame's *The Wind in the Willows* (1908). Long an official of the Bank of England, Grahame (1859-1936) loved to escape from his desk in London[11] and to wander for hours along the Thames Valley or across the rolling open landscape of Berkshire and Oxfordshire. An experienced writer of essays for the London magazines, he showed in them his keen eye for the ways of nature and of the countryside. Of course, this strange yearning of the same writer for the mysterious (southern) English style of neighbouring woods had appeared much earlier than in *The Wind in the Willows*, as in his essay, 'The Finding of the Princess', in his *The*

---

8   Compare in nineteenth century Australia the convict 'bolter' and the earlier phase of bushranging. See particularly pp. 214-216 in *The Australian Encyclopædia*, Vol 2 (1958 edition and reprints).
9   Something of and apparent in this general background contributes to the initial characterization of Aragorn in J.R.R.Tolkien's *The Lord of the Rings*.
10 See H.M. Steven and A. Carlisle (1959).
11 Grahame had moved permanently from London to Cookham Dene in the lower Thames Valley in 1906, and his timeless masterpiece was to be penned there very quickly over the following year or so.

Golden Age, first published by The Bodley Head in 1895. From there we may quote from the section, 'The Finding of the Princess',[12]

> I scrambled through the hedge, [...] and struck into the silence of the copse.

> If the lane had been deserted, this was loneliness become personal. Here mystery lurked and peeped; here brambles caught and held you with a purpose of their own and saplings whipped the face with human spite. The copse, too, proved vaster in extent, more direfully drawn out, than one would have ever guessed from its frontage [...] and I was really glad when the wood opened and sloped down to a streamlet brawling forth into the sunlight [...] The excitement of the thing was becoming thrilling [...]. (42)

And Grahame would never more evocatively catch this thrill than in the account, in the third chapter of the classic book, *The Wind in the Willows*, of how the Mole sets off by himself one winter's day to 'explore'

> the Wild Wood, which lay before him low and threatening, like a black reef in some still southern sea. (1968: 58)

Once inside it, he becomes increasingly uneasy, being harassed by evil faces (*ibid.*), whistling (*ibid.* 59), a pattering sound (*ibid.* 60), and, finally, he is only too aware of

> that dread thing which other little dwellers in field and hedgerow had encountered here, and known as their darkest moment – that thing which the Rat had vainly tried to shield him from – the Terror of the Wild Wood! (*ibid.*)

A few moments later Rat himself, arriving armed for the rescue, explains in part:

> I did my best to keep you from it. We river-bankers, we hardly ever come here by ourselves. If we have to come [...] we understand [...] passwords, and signs. (*ibid.* 62)

He also stresses the need for "sayings which have power and effect,"[13] "and dodges and tricks" – verbal precautions suggesting what in the adult world would be a prayer for salvation – the which are soon seen to be necessary since the wood now has "quite a changed aspect" (*ibid.*).

---

12 The excerpts are taken from the version with illustrations by Ernest H. Shepherd, and first published in 1928. Soon after this cited passage, the excited narrator is made to imagine pirates, contrivances and a gun-boat.

13 The implicit Christian and healing aspect of the language is supported later by the benign encounter with Pan in Chapter VII, this entitled 'The Piper at the Gates of Dawn'.

When, after their time with Badger, the two animals look back at the Wild Wood, they see it more clearly as

> Rocks and brambles and tree-roots [...] confusedly heaped and tangled [...][14] the whole mass [...] dense, menacing, compact, grimly set in vast white surroundings [...] Nature in the rough. (*ibid.* 83)

It is only towards the end of the tale, after Toad's return from prison, that the Wild Wood animals' behaviour is discussed explicitly and the necessary actions of retribution against their brutal arrogance are reported by the Rat:

> [...] the Wild Wood animals said hard things, and served you right, and it was high time this sort of thing was stopped [...] They argued from history [...]. They said that no criminal laws had ever been known to prevail against cheek and plausibility [...]. (*ibid.* 186-87)

Thus, they had cynically occupied Toad Hall, befouled the house and had been wasting its stored provisions

> and they're telling the tradespeople and everybody that they've come to stay for good. (*ibid.* 188)

After the necessary cleansing of the Hall in the climactic twelfth chapter;[15] one mischievously, delightfully and (mock-)heroically styled 'The Return of Ulysses', the events of upheaval in the social order of the River Bankers are called, "civil war"[16] (*ibid.* 217) and then "risings" and "invasions". Thus, when the friends chanced to walk finally in that direction they noted that

> the Wild Wood (was) now successfully tamed so far as they were concerned; and it was pleasing to see how respectfully they were greeted by the inhabitants [...]. (*ibid.* 218)

*   *   *

---

14 This is a very similar description to both the earlier *Sir Gawain and the Green Knight* passage and to the account of the Forest of Fangorn in *The Lord of the Rings*.

15 The epic structure in twelve books is modelled – cunningly and amusingly – on Homer's *Odyssey*, even as Mole is, in part, modelled on Telemachus, Toad on aspects of Ulysses, and the stoats and weasels on the suitors who occupied Ulysses' hall in Ithaca during his twenty year absence at the siege of Troy and on after that, during his later trials and wanderings.

16 These references are obviously echoic of the English Civil War of the mid-seventeenth century, and a time peculiarly echoic of the Cavalier dragoon presences to the north of Oxford, on Otmoor in the nearer north, and even in Merton College where Court persons lived for a time. There are some echoes of [the Battle of] Otmoor and in adjacent places, several involving cavalier mounted excursions, in Tolkien's *Smith of Wootton Major* (1967b).

In his deeply insightful biography, *Kenneth Grahame, 1859-1932: A Study of his Life, Work and Times* (1959), Peter Green has showed how, in the larger story and elsewhere, Grahame had divided the world of the Thames Valley into symbolic zones - the River, the Wild Wood, and the Wide World (240-241), having all his life

> fought with nostalgic doggedness to preserve his faith in a pre-industrial, agricultural, essentially aristocratic society. (*ibid.* 242)

And so he had thus created in *The Wind in the Willows* a "sub-conscious defence against" "approaching peril"; "a fantasy in which country gentlemen finally triumphed over the unprincipled radical canaille" (*ibid.* 243).

In short, the lawless terrorizing of the local inhabitants by those from the Wild Wood was to be understood as a projection of Grahame's own fears of social change from the western sprawling of London and the desecration of the beautiful Thames Valley landscape.

Whether we accept Green's developed psychoanalysis or not, it is clear that Grahame's classic work belongs to several literary genres –

> mock-heroic;
>
> charming fantasy raised to the level of myth (of the childhood faith in the promise and wonder of life);
>
> sensitive response to nature;
>
> beast fable;
>
> and some form of satire – in this case the nineteenth century's social and political milieu in England at its end.

The last aspect of the book the writer denied in a letter of 10 October 1908 to the admiring Theodore Roosevelt –

> Its qualities, if any, are mostly negative – i.e. – no problems, no sex, no second meaning – it is only an expression of the very simplest joys of life as lived by the simplest beings [...]. (Chalmers 1933: 138)

This denial Peter Green, much later, rebutted with some vehemence –

> this is so flagrantly untrue that one's curiosity is at once aroused. (1959: 274)

Even if we reject or elect to modify Peter Green's apparent obsession with the author's subconscious as revealed in this classic tale of the end of Victorian England, it is clear that there is in Grahame's text a continual structure of wise beast and foolish beast, and a similar exposure of human folly and excess – be it in Mole, Toad or the creatures of the Wild Wood. The latter are, however, different, being presented as destroyers of social order and so requiring to be put down very firmly. And even the 'nonsense' passages of the text may be seen to have ironic social point – much like the greatest intended punishment being for 'cheek', with the least for theft.

In the book of Grahame's as a whole, there are many complex political attitudes, not least towards the new and London-exiting inhabitants of the nearer regions of the Thames Valley country. And we may well agree with Green that

> Toad [...] stands for a figure [...] becoming increasingly prevalent [...] the landed *rentier* squandering his capital on riotous pleasures. [...] In this sense the 'Adventures of Toad' constitute a social object-lesson (*ibid*. 245),

if it is not the case that

> the Wild Wooders, stoats, weasels, and the rest are clearly identified in Grahame's mind with the stunted, malevolent proletariat of contemporary upper-middle-class caricature. (*ibid*. 246)

And yet the wise Badger, – another possibly Homeric figure as Grahame conceived him – with his memory of the far past recalls or affects to recall the ancient city[17] there long before the Wild Wood (1968: 81), and how its original residents had all passed away. Indeed, before he rallies his friends, to displace the usurpers, he seems to approve the democratic and eminently practical aspects of the Wild Wooders' style, rough but honest –

> Animals arrived, liked the look of the place [...] spread, and flourished. They didn't bother themselves about the past – they never do; they're too busy [...]

---

17 If the general Tolkien interests and the influences of his reading and scholarly interests are to be accepted, Badger may well have contributed some elements to the similarly long-memoried Tom Bombadil, again the eldest of the society of the place. Both in view of Grahame's own classical background, and from the details of the description, this setting is clearly meant to be like one of the lost cities of Roman Britain, the nearest one for both writers being Silchester, on the Berkshire boundary, to the south of Reading. It had aroused enormous interest in the late Victorian period and was a place to savour on a visit of inspection while walking, for both Kenneth Grahame and – between the wars – for J.R.R. Tolkien.

And they don't bother about the future, either. [...] The Wild Wood is pretty well populated by now; with all the usual lot, good, bad, and indifferent [...] They're not so bad really; and we must all live and let live. (*ibid.* 82)

Clearly, too, Grahame's attitude to Toad is extremely ambivalent, since the writer seems to both deplore his waste and Bohemianism, while at the same time secretly admiring it. Images which are not ambiguous are: the terror of losing property; the condoning of (aggressive actions necessary in obtaining) independent means; the approval of a life of boating,[18] tramping around the countryside, eating enormous meals, and getting caught up in occasional adventures. But Green is right to stress that Toad is blamed for behaving badly, rather than for neglecting his duties as a landlord (Green 1959: 248).

Peter Green is also quoted – very significantly – by Peter Haining in his later reflective introduction to a set of the earliest Grahame essays, *Paths to the River Bank: The Origins of The Wind in the Willows*:

> There is the idealised river landscape with its peaceful Epicurean inhabitants; the menace, finally destroyed, of the Wild Wood; the conflict between a paternalistic society and the hubristic, Bohemian individual, as exemplified by Toad [...]

> [...] [i]n the pages which follow I have set out to show how [...] he had explored some of the paths which led to the river bank and thence along the open roads of the English countryside [...]. (Grahame and Haining 1983: 25)

The matter of the true nature of the enigmatic Wild Wood denizens might well have been left there, since the various additions to the theatre text by A.A. Milne in his *Toad of Toad Hall* (1929) were mainly for the entertainment of children, although they do include the stern warning remark of Alfred, the horse, to Rat on one of Toad's violent outbursts:

> Psychological – that was the word he wanted [...] psychological. (1952: 20)

---

18 This is very much like the behaviour near water of Smeagol and Deagol in Tolkien's writings, while the later qualities are akin to the behaviour of those hobbits who possessed the famed / infamous Took blood and so a passion for wandering in strange places.

However – And then, quite suddenly – the Grahame Story Continues on, to Become a Further Myth

Then, quite suddenly, after the classic story had attained its definitive place, in 1981, Andre Deutsch would issue a remarkable book, Jan Needle's *Wild Wood*, an ingenious narrative which is neither a parody of Kenneth Grahame's work, nor yet a satire on it, but rather an extension, providing some of the missing parts of an immortal story which may now be seen to have always needed this filling out of the pristine account of those enchanted places, the River Bank and the Wild Wood, and, perforce, the middle and upper reaches of the River Thames, – all so easy of access from Oxford.

At the end of this 'new' book, or adapted / recensionist text, its further moral purpose is revealed, for it is the motivation of the occupation of Toad (or Brotherhood) Hall, as the very long memory of an ancient and thoughtful ferret, Baxter, the narrator, reveals it, this being a strategy, one intriguingly furthering the text of 1908, whereby, as we are then told,

> a lot of the injustices of life between the River Bankers and the Wild Wooders was ironed out. Some of Toad's surplus wealth went to providing more and better jobs like, and he introduced pensions and so on, and stopped sacking people for pique or in slack times. (1981: 181)

The recorder himself reports it as he had it from his eccentric friend Willoughby who had actually met[19] Baxter Ferret and left his friend to tell, within his own added 'Prologue and Epilogue',

> the story of Brotherhood Hall – Toad Hall as it is more usually known – through the eyes of the Wild Wood. Or to be exact, the sharp and penetrating memory of that ancient and helpful ferret. (*ibid.* 7)

The modern driver of the vintage car, Willoughby, had felt that he had

> hit upon something of the utmost significance. A historical event of shattering implications (*ibid.* 6),

and, finally, discovered a collision of social groups,

---

19 Rather was it that he had knocked him down during a Brighton Veteran Car Run, while driving a 1907 Armstrong Hardcastle, the very model once – in Grahame's story – belonged to and was driven by Mr Toad. After Willoughby's own death, the recorder presents the tale-within-a-tale for the enlightenment of posterity.

what he chose to call the only serious attempt at a full-scale workers' revolution in this country since the Peasants' Revolt. (*ibid.* 184)

*   *   *

But all of this is to anticipate somewhat. *Wild Wood* itself is a strange text, one seemingly modelled on several differing sources:

1) Kenneth Grahame's classic;

2) the earlier style of the country or national surveys like those of William Cobbett,[20] or of Rider Haggard; and

3) the influence of the more general social criticisms, accusatory and explicit, in the works of such late reflective and socially conscious Victorians as W.E. Henley, Ruskin, Carlyle and William Morris.

The Wild Wooders themselves are now described by Baxter as: "all pretty thin and lean and fit, and we all tend to keep ourselves out of the public eye" (*ibid.* 8); and as those who gather at the village store or the tobacconist's (cf. p. 23), "having a yarn and a game of dominoes round his pot-bellied coke stove" (*ibid.* 44). What with their harsh mode of life, minimal subsistence and isolation from more prosperous society, conditions could indeed be very bleak. It is notable that the following is the ferret's response – with all its similarity to the Mole's much earlier cautionary fears –

The Wild Wood, when I finally entered it, seemed to have grown darker, bleaker, blacker than I could ever remember it. There was no animals about, no birds. Nothing edible grew, nothing but the tall, hard trees that soughed in the bitter wind, occasionally dropping great gouts of snow that crashed from high branches into what meagre undergrowth rose out of the drifts. (*ibid.* 83)

In opposition to this tragically enforced mode of subsistence now with every "hard and hungry winter" (*ibid.* 46), is the life-style of the aggressive River Bankers, traditionally savouring and maintaining "the old old friction" (*ibid.*) between them. The River Bank folk are remarkable for financial and social

---

20 As in *Rural Rides*, first published between 1822 and 1826 in the Political Register. See also the finely context-set and enlightening volume, *The Autobiography of William Cobbett*, ed. by William Reitzel (1967), a text first published in 1933.

superiority (cf. p. 26); and for their exploitation[21] of the rural folk, particularly in the servant role

> Here we all are, poor as church mice, living in cramped, overcrowded conditions [...] and there's the other lot and their huge houses, more money than sense, more bedrooms than bodies. It's disgusting. [...] All my *four* sisters – is in service. On the River Bank, every one. And they bring back pennies. Five o'clock in the morning they start, and work till they drop. [...] It's a scandal. (*ibid*. 29);

and for their cynical pride in their ability to inspire quite unmerited respect as 'the good folk' (*ibid*. 117).

As may be expected, the Needle recension – or the 'other side' of Grahame's story – is by no means a simple account of class confrontation. As the wise Baxter points out:

> Winter's a strange time, and hunger's a peculiar thing, if not a funny one. A wood is a big, dark, lonely, dangerous place and ours was more so than most, whence perhaps its name. The Wild Wood was all sorts of things to all sorts of animals. (*ibid*. 58)

Mole's own visit to the Wood had now seemed to its wretched residents to be an act of patronizing bravado[22] (cf. p. 58), particularly to the long-suffering stoats. But his reception there seemed to the more astute keeper of the peace, the Chief Weasel, as

> not to mince words, a disgusting display of rudeness, bad manners, hooligan- ism and oafishness directed at a harmless, reasonable, well-meaning animal. (*ibid*. 75)

As might have been anticipated, Badger is here presented as an enigmatic 'authority' figure whose actions are only too easily misinterpreted by the two small cold hedgehogs[23] being given a porridge breakfast. Baxter Ferret described him[24] thus much later to Cedric Willoughby:

---

21 This speech comes from Boddington Stoat, a moralist leader of the Wood's wretched people, whose character and mode of angered expression seems to have indebtedness to both the medieval reformist, William Langland and to George Orwell.

22 Compare the similar interpretation often/usually given to visits to Sherwood Forrest by the Sheriff of Nottingham and to those of various plump prelates in numerous Robin Hood stories.

23 The Needle account of them runs thus:

> "The hedgehog boys that live over oak clump; [...] Dad's a road-mender. They got bogged down in the snow on the way to school." (*ibid*.7)

24 Many of these remarks – which neatly tease out Grahame's text– could be applied equally to the character of Beorn in J.R.R. Tolkien's *The Hobbit*.

> "[...] Mr Badger was a strange enough old codger, who was not really a part of the Wild Wood set-up, despite living slap-dab in the middle of it. For a start he was a solitary sort of a bloke, almost a recluse. Then of course, he was big, and strong, and fierce. Truth to tell, he was more than a bit frightening to us smaller fry. Then too, he was pretty well-off, by our standards. [...] When he mixed at all, which wasn't often, it was with the River Bankers, not us; as being more in his class, so to speak." (*ibid*. 71-72)

Perhaps in keeping with this older order of society, he is the one to lay off various of Toad's staff at a time of crisis[25] and, later, to sack them all, thus precipitating

> a day of reckoning [...] When we've driven the River Bankers out, them poor animals what's been made homeless shall live there again. Only this time it'll be their hall, not Toad's. The servants shall rule. And the poor shall come in too [...]. (*ibid*. 129)

And a Possible Class War?

While this presentation of the extension to both *Wild Wood* and to the much earlier *The Wind in the Willows* as somehow symbolic, this form of class war greatly simplifies the text and omits many of the charming vignettes of the woodland folk in happier time, as well as the conflicting loyalties among the leaders of the wood as to how best to serve their people, even as it also underscores the reasons for the uprising against Mr. Toad's palatial abode. This action is described thus by one of its planners –

> "We've been doing a deed as should have been done years ago. We've been doing something for the good of all in the Wild Wood. [...] We've put an end to poverty and hunger, that's what we've been doing." (*ibid*. 140)

As with the River Bankers,[26] so is it with the Wild Wood folk, there is one enigmatic figure, the Chief Weasel, who seems to both object to the arrogant, on account of their vicious and criminal misuse of other animals' wealth (cf. p. 137) and to feel that injustice can best be "ironed out" (*ibid*. 181) by constructive dialogue with the enemy. His behaviour, like the text itself, is ambitious, witty, ingenious and socially both logical and respectful of the need for the old

---

25 Compare the remarks about Badger as presented in *The Wind in the Willows*.
26 As at the end of Chapter Twelve of *Wild Wood*.

order. Thus Jan Needle is no more of a revolutionary than had been Kenneth
Grahame himself.

Changing Responses

While the Wild Wood has long been a potent symbol in English literature, it
would seem that the Dark Age notion of pagan menace has been sequentially
overtaken, first by the mediaeval Greenwood; and, more recently, by various
fables about eccentric behaviour, as well as a concern for the preservation of the
pristine landscape; and then, finally, by the realm of the small animals (surely
an objective correlative of the abject poverty and obsequiousness forced upon
the hitherto free country folk in the wake of the Industrial Revolution).

As Cavendish well puts this evolving sequence of responses to 'the Wild',
thereby moving to the person forced to live there – at the end of his 'Wildwood'
survey:

> The [earlier] wild man [...] [was] a proud, heroic figure, admired because he is
> free of the chains and shackles of society. The same aura surrounds highway-
> men, and romantic wanderers [...], nomadic motor cyclists[27] [...] and hippies,
> but here the lure of the wildwood has turned into the longing for the open
> road. (1983b: 3029)[28]

It is, of course, the purpose of this present essay to give the background to the
contention – argued elsewhere in this book – that *The Wind in the Willows*,
in both its style and forest depictions has had an otherwise ignored influence
on the Woods to which Tolkien introduces us in *The Hobbit*, and so, perforce,
on the sequences of *The Lord of the Rings*, when the hobbit-adventurers first
leave the Shire.

---

27 This reference may well be a reflective reference to the peacetime motor cyclist (Aircraftsman Shaw),
   who killed himself on a Somerset road to avoid a collision with picnickers, and was really T.E.
   Lawrence, i.e. Colonel Lawrence of Arabia.
28 Compare Jeffrey Farnoll's classic novel of the road in the beloved Regency-period set text, *The Broad
   Highway* (1910).

A Coda – The Abiding Power of the Tales of the Wood and – Related to them – of the Road

It is, perhaps, not such a surprise that the beloved literature of English childhood, like the corpus of fairy tales itself – has retained the much more ancient moods of fear, menace and uncertainty of the forest and of journeying through it. The threat of the unknown is an eternal one, as is the accompanying wretchedness of outcasts and the sufferings of its denizens. As in all beast fables of those excluded from warmth, fellowship and hospitality, all of this persists as a jab to the social consciences of those who are infinitely better off.

And so it is not too much to put *The Wind in the Willows* somewhere alongside *Animal Farm*, much as Ned Hedges did, when he asked in his survey *The Fable and the Fabulous*[29] –

> Both use fable to some extent for the purposes of political satire. On the basis of their artistic revelation of the corruption in a specific political system, and their implicit recommendations for improvement of the system or correction of the corruption, which is the better of the two books? (1968: ii)

At least for older European folk tales and the perdurable fables of the southern English landscape – as for those works that appeal to all ages of readers – the persistently haunting associations of the (the wild) woodland would seem to be likely to remain potent archetypes, in fact much as Kenneth Grahame set them for us at the beginning of the twentieth century.

And so it was, perhaps, inevitable that the story-teller, J.R.R. Tolkien, a very late Victorian who would walk for so many years with his friends across the Berkshire Downs and along the reaches of the Middle Thames, would, like Grahame, savour – and seek to re-capture – all these moods and so much of the ambiguity of the ancient forests as well as the calm of their, or any adjacent and eternally murmuring waters.

Perhaps the most fitting conclusion to these reflections on the 'Wild Wood themes' – those of mystery, adventure and enchantment for late English Victorians and for all wanderlust-driven folk alike – as well as their innumerable kindred

---

29 This book published in 1968, is subtitled *The Use of Traditional Forms in Children's Literature.*

in other lands and in later times – is the section from a potent earlier essay, 'The Eternal Whither' by Grahame[30] that has been collected for *Paths to the River Bank*, a piece about a City clerk who chose to serve as a turnpike man in his annual holiday:

> There was [...] once an old cashier in some ancient City establishment, whose practice was to spend his yearly holiday in relieving some turnpike-man at his post, and performing all the duties appertaining thereunto. [...] [He] had discovered for himself an unique method of seeing Life at its best, the flowing, hurrying, travelling, marketing Life of the Highway [...]. He belonged, above all, to the scanty class of clear-seeing persons who know both what they are good for and what they really want. (Grahame and Haining 1983: 109-10)

The dark wood, the road, and the river are all to be seen as timeless symbols of human life and of man's activities, and they have functioned thus throughout so much of humanity's story,[31] having been so often set in unchanging landscapes of both natural beauty and of brutal menace.

The Greater Symbols for Tolkien and his Followers

The link between the two late Victorians, Kenneth Grahame and J.R.R. Tolkien has been ignored too long, and they form an engaging coda to the opening essay, one largely concerned with the concepts of the Nameless Wood that is in front of all humanity, and of The Path with all its dangers that all must seek and follow if they are to attain their Destinies.

---

30 The collection of 'important essays [lets us see] how they formed pathways to *The Wind in the Willows*' (1983: 25). The printed book cited does not give the actual dates or the specific print locations of these earlier essays.
31 Interestingly the fine Australian poet, Judith Wright, had written a like (political) fable of humanity, its corrupt practices and strivings, and of the patience of nature in the face of her country's earlier and its ongoing social history, *The River and the Road* (1966).

J.R.R. Tolkien, C.S. Lewis and Roy Campbell

> I do think you may be chasing after a fox that isn't there.
>
> (Lewis 1966: 287; for May 15, 1959, to Charles Moorman "who was proposing a literary inquiry into a group of writers.")

A Meeting in 1944

Humphrey Carpenter, in his survey of the Oxford Anglo-Catholic intellectuals and writers, *The Inklings* (1978: 191-92) refers to the South African poet Roy Campbell, who met Tolkien and Lewis on Monday, October 3, 1944, in Oxford at the 'Eagle and Child' public house. It is clear that the encounter, as reported then by Tolkien to his son Christopher, had two elements of interest to him:

> 1) A strange tall gaunt man half in khaki half in mufti with a large wide-awake hat, bright eyes and a hooked nose, sitting in the corner. The others had their backs to him, but I could see in his eye that he was taking an interest in the conversation [...] It was rather like Trotter [i.e., Strider] at the Prancing Pony, in fact v. like. (quoted by Carpenter from J.R.R. Tolkien's letter to his son, October 6, 1944; *Letters* 95); [and]

> 2) it was (perhaps) gratifying to find that this powerful poet and soldier desired in Oxford chiefly to see Lewis (and myself). We made an appointment for Thursday [...] night. (*ibid.*)

And thus it was that Roy Campbell (1902-57) became an occasional visitor to the Inklings' circle – a position he still held in 1949, according to the 'official' biography of C.S. Lewis (Green and Hooper 1974: 156).

This text, *C.S. Lewis, A Biography*, records of Lewis that "his favourite contemporary poets seem to have been Charles Williams, Roy Campbell and Kathleen Raine – perhaps he inclined to be over-partial to the poetry when he liked the

---

This essay first appeared in *Minas Tirith Evening Star, Appendix R2* (1979: 2-6) and I am grateful to the editors for permission to reprint.

poet" (*ibid.* 89); a point they amplify later in regard to the 'moderns' – "he was on friendly personal relations with W.H. Auden and T.S. Eliot towards the end of his life, and admired some of Roy Campbell's work" (*ibid.* 153). In the Tolkien-Lewis encounters reported by Carpenter (1978: 192), it is clear that the South African, while liked by Tolkien as a person, provoked violent reactions in Lewis who had declared fervently, "I loathed and loathe Roy Campbell's particular blend of Catholicism and Fascism, and told him so." (*ibid.*)

The value of this Campbell link is not so much that the South African was a visitor to the Inklings, as Carpenter confirms (*ibid.*) or even that C.S. Lewis had decided opinions about his work (which he subsequently modified), but that it gives us a clue that Tolkien would seem to have been familiar with Campbell's poetry, since the letter cited describes him thus –

> In a few seconds he was revealed as Roy Campbell (of *Flowering Rifle* and *Flaming Terrapin*). (*ibid.* 191)

Campbell's Student Days

Campbell had been in Oxford before, of course, as he explains in the account of his earlier life, *Light on a Dark Horse – An Autobiography, 1901-1935* (1969) wherein he describes the stormy South Atlantic, stressing one of his early loves in poetry –

> But it is only Camoes, the greatest of all South African poets who gives one in words a real sense of its awe and the grandeur of its stormy seas in that wonderful passage about Rounding the Cape. (174)

Sponsored by Sir Walter Raleigh and Sir Ernest Barker he was sent in 1918 to Merton (not to be Tolkien's home until 1945), and in his year there met in London all the Sitwells, Eliot and Wyndham Lewis, while his Oxford friendships included "Robert Graves, Edmund Blunden, L.A.G. Strong, [...] Richard Hughes, Louis Golding, Hugo Dyson [...] etc." (*ibid.* 184). He concludes, "With many of them I have enjoyed a long friendship" (*ibid.*).

One can well understand Campbell's liking for Dyson, an Inkling-to-be, whom Lewis was to describe thus in 1931:

He was a most fastidious bookman [...] but far from being a dilettante as anyone can be; a burly man, with the stamp of the war on him, which begins to be [...] a rarity, at least in civilian life. (Lewis 1966: 145)

Essentially, then, it may be noted that both Dyson and Campbell brought a physical strength, personal dynamism and experience of the world of action into the relatively calm backwaters of these Oxford scholars in the 1930s and, later, into the Inklings' meetings which sometimes needed some fresh catalyzing.

In the passage by Carpenter, mentioned at the outset it is suggested that the meeting on the evening of October 6, 1944 was one

> [...] which revealed a deep-seated difference between Lewis and Tolkien [...] Lewis believed in the democratic control of power while Tolkien did not [...] Lewis and Tolkien both feared the rise of Communism and the growing power of the Left; they also hated and feared the growth of Fascism in prewar Britain [...] But during the Spanish Civil War, Tolkien largely sympathized with Franco's cause in Spain [...] because he saw Franco as the defender of the Catholic Church against Communist persecution. (1978: 192)

While this may well be true, it underscores the essential problem with trying to come at Tolkien, either through Lewis, or through Carpenter, for that matter. *The Supplement to the Oxford English Dictionary* (1972: 196, col. c) records the former's remark on his friend

> No one ever influenced Tolkien – you might as well try to influence a bander-snatch. (Lewis 1966: 287)

But to Tolkien's Own Tastes and Preferences

Lewis himself always had much to say and publish – many would feel too much – and the list of his books and personality preferences is endless, but the same is far from true of John Ronald Tolkien. We are largely dependent for our knowledge of his fictional, critical and personal preferences on:

1) his biographers – the considerable remarks of both Lewis and Carpenter;

2) the encounters by such scholars as Walsh, Ready and Moorman (all Americans) with the great man;

3) the interviews which he granted but seldom to persons he barely knew, and who occasionally obtained a gem; or

4) the more persistent but sympathetic strangers like Clyde Kilby or Daniel Grotta-Kurska who record much, and obtain a surprising number of insightful details.

It would seem that there is still another source for us, apart from his fictional and scholarly writings, and that must be what he would call the 'folk memory', the common body of things known to those who knew him in another way again, his pupils, especially the research and senior students whom he made his friends. Many such memories held by the present writer have been published already – in his *Tolkien: Cult or Culture?* (1969), – and it is clear that more teasing out is needed for obtaining the significance of such 'encounters' as that of Tolkien and Campbell.

Tolkien and South Africans

Colonial students, particularly those from the Dominions, were often drawn into long conversations with Professor Tolkien. Thus, in the period 1954-56 he was particularly interested in the backgrounds of Rhodes Scholar/boxer, A.S.K. (Harry) Pittman, and footballer W.S. Getz, both South Africans in Merton. He was equally delighted with all scholars being men of action – as was made clear when he regretted that it was Emeritus Professor Nichol Smith (already in his eighties) and not he himself, who had gone out at 3:00 a.m. and cut from the outer wall of Fellows' Quad an offending but protected vine trunk. In one of the last lectures I heard from him as Merton Professor in 1957, he deplored the fact that when his men had 'poached' a deer, while on manoeuvres in Yorkshire during training, he had not been on hand to 'broach' the carcass, in the fashion described in *Sir Gawain and the Green Knight*. His remarks about persons known to him typically included those on: G.V. Smithers, a South African don in Merton; various academics who were Highlanders; Douglas Gray, a New Zealand lecturer in Pembroke; or the war and national service careers of various persons, particularly when they clashed with present appearances. Thus the extraordinary activities of Norman Davis (then at Glasgow, but to succeed him as Merton Professor) in the Balkans, especially in Yugoslavia with Tito's partisans, were a matter of particular delight.

His own interest in the Viking-like physique and personality are discussed by Ready (1968: 67-68) who stresses the attraction felt by the scholar towards two particular literary wild men. The first was Evan Llewellyn, of Cardiff, an Anglo-Saxonist and Sagaman, and someone whose vitality appealed to Tolkien. The second was the roistering South African Roy Campbell, whose gusto equally intrigued Tolkien.

The latter had already met Tolkien in the thirties, and his personality was often commented on by the author, according to his close friends, like Hugo Dyson, an atypical scholar in many ways.

It may be idle to speculate whether Tolkien had read widely in the poetry of Roy Campbell before he met him again in 1944. What is surely significant is that he delighted in his sudden reappearance, so like that of Strider at Bree, that he was amused at Lewis's discomfiture then (due to the latter's hostile reviewing of Campbell),[1] and that he recalled or deliberately quoted to his son certain works by the stranger.

> All of a sudden he butted in, in a strange unplaceable accent, taking up some point about Wordsworth. In a few seconds he was revealed as Roy Campbell (of *Flowering Rifle* and *Flaming Terrapin*). (1978: 191)

It is not surprising, either, that Tolkien seized on the early work *The Flaming Terrapin* (1924), a volume which had burst upon London and yet had some of the late Victorianism or Georgianism that Tolkien's own 'poetry' may be said to contain. It included such concepts as the noisy exposure of romantic fallacies of 'open spaces' even as it also celebrated the vigour and force of nature. The later work, *Flowering Rifle* (1939), was an exultation of force which Campbell regarded as his masterpiece and which strangely excited Tolkien, whose feelings toward it were ambivalent, although he referred to it on a number of later occasions.

The point of this note is to suggest that while Lewis and Carpenter are invaluable for the mass of Tolkienian detail which they have saved and recorded for

---

1 Lewis under the pseudonym of Nat Whilk had commented adversely on Campbell in the *Cherwell*, on 6 May 1939, in his 'To Mr. Roy Campbell'; later to be published as 'To the Author of *Flowering Rifle*' (1964: 65).

posterity, they do not always catch the nuances of Tolkien's expressions. The zany enthusiasms which many of his conversations revealed, and which were only partly modified by the decorum of the lecture situation, have still to be retrieved from the recollections of those who attended his lectures or were his personal pupils and friends over extended periods. We have much from those who met him under 'meeting' pressures, but all too little from the young and receptive, for whom he was keen to share his insights.

When in the Spring of 1957, he broke with the 'rule' of keeping off Old English in public lectures, and expatiated on the early poem *Exodus*, the 'class', which was largely fellows of the colleges included: Miss Griffiths, Miss Gradon, Alistair Campbell and Eric Dobson (both later Oxford professors), Bruce Mitchell and many others. They were not disappointed and a highlight was his suggestion that – in the mind of the *Exodus* poet – the Valkyries as demon women loomed over the Egyptians in their doomed attempt at crossing the Red Sea after the fleeing Israelites.

It is this form of *aperçu* which the master-pupil situation brought forth, since Tolkien's strange reserve and humility prevented him from testing his scholarly insights on either his colleagues or his many unfamiliar interlocutors. Thus the present writer still remembers Tolkien's bursts, while pacing the Merton rose garden, on such topics as: college farms in East Anglia; pigs and their personalities; garden summerhouses; Wulfstan the eleventh century homilist; the birds and beasts of battle, as a set piece in Germanic verse; the influence of Hegel on *The Hobbit*, etc.

Lewis was very right when he stressed the impossibility of influencing Tolkien directly. As he continued in his 1959 letter to Moorman:

> We listened to his work, but could affect it only by encouragement. He has only two reactions to criticism: either he begins the whole work over again from the beginning, or else takes no notice at all. (1966: 287)

Tolkien did, of course, alter things, but only very tardily, and never immediately on the prompting of anyone. Indeed one of the reasons for his dilatory attitude to publication was his reluctance to finalize his own views in the printed form – which accounts for the belated, posthumous appearance of his translations from Middle English originally intended for Sisam's *Fourteenth Century Verse and Prose*. He was, however, desperately keen to have his students publish work which was in large measure his. Examples of this, which are legion, would include (1) S.T.R.O. d'Ardenne's *Life and Passion of St. Julienne* (1936);[2] (2) Margaret Williams's *Word Hoard: Passage from Old English Literature* (1946); or (3) my own 'Othin in England', (1963: 460-80).[3]

*   *   *

It is helpful for us to have the Campbell-Tolkien encounters recalled, but not necessary for us to accept Carpenter's interpretation of them. In many ways an enigmatic man, Tolkien's responses, particularly at any depth, were very difficult to interpret. His enthusiasms, however, were the areas over which he pondered and then came to slow and very ent-like conclusions, and even ponfications. He liked many aspects of Roy Campbell, not least for their positive and masculine quality, and such views he adhered to, despite their moral illogicality. Above all he was warm and generous, exciting and excitable, if lacking in the expected views or decorum. The former want is indicated by Ready, as in "Tolkien is a bluff and hearty know-nothing when it comes to blacks [...]" (1968: 9), the latter by a former pupil J.I.M. Stewart (also known as the writer of detective stories Michael Innes), "He could turn a lecture room into a mead hall in which he was the bard and we were the feasting listening guests" (Norman 1967: 36).

The Classic Biography is still to Come

Perhaps it only remains to conclude that Carpenter's work is not the final biographic work on Tolkien, not least because of its coldness, and the many things which remain unsaid. The official biographer, a young man who never heard Tolkien in action, in his serious and reverential style, has missed much which still remains to be gathered. It is to be hoped that there will appear ere long some study which collects the offbeat unofficial Tolkien, not the man seen by his family or his peers, but the one who was very much a combination of Gandalf, Treebeard and Tom Bombadil to his eager if ingenuous hobbit students.

---

2 This was republished as *Þe liflade ant te passiun of Seinte Juliene* in Liège in 1936 and later by the Early English Text Society (1961).
3 This last essay has been republished in the meantime in my earlier collection of essays, *Tolkien's View: Windows into his World* by Walking Tree Publishers (2009).

Tolkien and Auden

O n 29th September 1973 there died in Vienna, while on a weekend visit, an Anglo-American poet, who was about to return to his cottage in Oxford, where he had once been a student and, later, Professor of Poetry (1956-61). In Oxford, some twenty-seven days earlier, there had also died one of that university's most eminent scholars. The first man was Wystan Hugh Auden (born in 1907); the second was John Ronald Reuel Tolkien (born in 1892), who had held two early English language and literature chairs[1] at Oxford from 1925 to 1959. The two were connected by a close friendship for many years. Even more significantly, Auden has perhaps been the most sensitive and relevant interpreter to date of the significance of his early teacher's best known fantasy story, *The Lord of the Rings* (1954-55). Their interest in Icelandic culture and early Germanic language and literature had brought the two together and it helped them continue their relationship over almost fifty years, the later parts of which saw the issuing of the younger man's brilliantly simple yet profound responses to his senior's literary achievement. While the one was a Thomist, the other became an "Anglo-Catholic though not too spiky" (Osborne 1979: 202), yet both saw individual salvation for modern man through his love for his fellows (*caritas*) and from his willingness to bear others' burdens ('substitution'[2]).

W.H. Auden was born in Yorkshire as the third son of a medical practitioner with strong antiquarian interests. Both of his parents were the children of Church of England vicars. His mother was a deeply committed High Anglican,[3] while his

---

This essay first appeared in the Australian journal *Quadrant* 295, Volume 37.4 (1993: 60-66) and is here reprinted with same slight emendations with the kind permission of its editors.

1 In a sense he had held three, since he gave all the Old Norse lectures for some 20 years while that position was left vacant.
2 Interestingly both had been assisted in their religious thoughts by Charles Williams, Auden before his return to Christianity in 1940-41, Tolkien during the Second World War when Williams was living in Oxford. Auden quotes numerous passages from Williams in his own *A Certain World: A Commonplace Book* (1970).
3 It was her death that year which caused his return to the Anglican communion in October 1940.

father, G.A. Auden, a distinguished scientist, had a sound knowledge of both classical and Icelandic literature, and also had many Shropshire antiquarians in his immediate family.[4] George Auden was long a prominent member of the Viking Club, a 'Society for Northern Research', addressing it on 22nd January 1909 on 'Scandinavian Antiquities found in York'. Auden senior had lived in York from 1899 to 1908 and had edited, in 1906, for the British Association for the Advancement of Science, the volume *Historical and Scientific Survey of York and District*, to which he contributed the section on prehistory and archaeology. Thus it is not surprising to find that he then

> told Wystan about [...] Thor, Loki, and the rest of the deities of Icelandic legend. Dr. Auden was particularly keen that his son should learn these tales, for not only was he deeply fond of Norse antiquities but he also believed that his own family name, Auden,[5] showed that he was himself of Icelandic descent [...] [and] [...] related to a certain Auden Sköhull, who is recorded as one of the first Norse settlers in Iceland in the ninth century. (Carpenter 1981a: 7)

Certainly the poet could say later of his early childhood, "With northern myths my little brain was laden" (*ibid.*).

Letters from Iceland

The Christian name, Wystan, was chosen by his father from his early familiarity with the parish church at Repton, dedicated to St Wystan, a Mercian prince[6] murdered in 849 A.D. Auden was always fascinated by his own early experience of northern landscapes, on which he based a private sacred world, and deeply moved by various northern 'Proper Names' which he found numinous and even sacred. His public school, Gresham's in Norfolk, turned his studies towards science, and he went up to Oxford in the autumn of 1925, as an exhibitioner in natural science, but he changed to English studies the following year. He then manifested an unfashionable interest in such texts as George Dasent's

---

4 Several of these are listed by Charles Osborne in his *W.H. Auden: The Life of a Poet* (1979: 9, footnote 2). Auden senior was also a Fellow of the Society of Antiquaries, London.
5 Scholars of etymology, however, trace the name back as a variant of *Alden, Aldwyn*, or even *Edwin*, and thence further back to *Healfdene* (see Carpenter 1981a: 7, footnote).
6 St Wystan is discussed in the *Little Guide to Shropshire* by the poet-to-be's uncle, the Rev J.E. Auden (1912), and by D.H. Farmer in his *The Oxford Dictionary of Saints* (1978); and referred to by Tolkien in his poem, 'For W.H.A. – in Modern and Old English', published in *Shenandoah* 18.2 (1967a), as now printed below.

translation of *Njáls Saga* and the various short poems in Old English which were part of the compulsory core English syllabus:

> [Anglo-Saxon] was my first introduction to the 'barbaric' poetry of the North, and I was immediately fascinated both by its metric and its rhetorical devices. (Carpenter 1981a: 55)

His philological tutor was C.L. Wrenn, but he was much more inspired by the young Professor of Anglo-Saxon, J.R.R. Tolkien, as he recalled in his own Inaugural Lecture, 'Making, Knowing and Judging', delivered before the University of Oxford on 11th June 1956:

> I do not remember a single word he said but at a certain point he recited, and magnificently, a long passage of *Beowulf.* I was spellbound. This poetry, I knew, was going to be my dish. I became willing, therefore, to work at Anglo-Saxon because, unless I did, I should never be able to read this poetry. I learned enough to read it, however sloppily, and Anglo-Saxon and Middle English poetry have been one of my strongest, most lasting influences. (1963: 41-42)[7]

Auden's early narrative and lyric verse contained many Germanic references, both to Old English poetry and to the saga-world, with its feuds, dark threats and laconic understatements. Icelandic feud, as found in *Gisli the Outlaw*[8] was a subject discussed between Auden and Isherwood, the latter early on referring to saga figures to be found in Auden's first play, *Paid on Both Sides* (1928).[9]

This verse play derives from various medieval sources, not least the sagas which, as he would observe in 1937, enshrined "only the gangster virtues" (119), qualities which Tolkien would suggest subtly in his Gondor-Haradrim feuds in his three volume epic. Further debts by Auden to Old English literature and evidence of a close study of R.K. Gordon's excellent translations in his popular *Anglo-Saxon Poetry* (1926) have been traced by John Fuller in his *A Reader's Guide to W.H. Auden* (1970). Fuller identifies many of the Old English echoes in the shorter poems of Auden's early and middle career. The Icelandic background to his poetry is further illustrated by the many echoes of the medieval culture to be found in his contributions to *Letters from Iceland* (1937).

---

7 The lecture was first published in 1956 by the Oxford University Press, and later reissued in *The Dyer's Hand and other Essays* (1963), to which references are made throughout this essay.
8 *Gisli's Saga* was lectured on by Tolkien, though not when Auden was in residence as a student. See Ryan (2002).
9 See Isherwood's 'Some Notes on Auden's Early Poetry' in *New Verse* (November 1937).

In the early 1950s, Auden had shown himself very much aware of Tolkien's interest in MacDonald, as was also the case with C.S. Lewis. Thus he would make passing remarks in book reviews and the like to the element of the subjective, i.e. fantastic, in the works of Tolkien.

Auden as a very Early Interpreter of *The Lord of the Rings*

On 31st October 1954 he contributed to the *New York Times* a review of the first volume of Tolkien's *The Lord of the Rings*, in which he stressed that it was an adventure story "various and exciting" with "unflagging" invention, and then praised in Tolkien "an amazing gift for naming and a wonderfully exact eye for description" (1954a: 37). His conclusion was:

> Lastly, if one is to take a tale of this kind seriously, one must feel that, however superficially unlike the world we live in its characters and events may be, it nevertheless holds up the mirror to the only nature we know, our own; in this, too, Mr Tolkien has succeeded superbly. (*ibid.*)

A matter of days later there appeared his much longer response to *The Fellowship of the Ring* in *Encounter* (1954b: 59-62), entitled 'A World Imaginary, but Real', which made the points of the American newspaper review, plus various significant others:

> that *The Hobbit* was "the best children's story written in the last fifty years" (*ibid.* 59);
>
> that *The Fellowship* is not a "normal Quest" since "the numinous object [the Ring] [...] must be destroyed" (*ibid.*);
>
> that the Hobbits "in their thinking and sensibility [...] resemble those arcadian villagers who so frequently populate British detective stories" (*ibid.*);
>
> that the Elves "are creatures of an unfallen world" (*ibid.*);
>
> that the nature of the work necessitated "scientific historical research" (*ibid.* 60);
>
> that the speech accorded the several "verbalising species [...] seems inevitable" (*ibid.*);
>
> that it is a "topographic" style much as "the traveller", Frodo, saw its landscapes "with his senses kept [...] sharp by fear" (*ibid.*);
>
> that in the situations "of elemental crisis" the choices were few (*ibid.*); and
>
> that the main characters were partly archetypal but their pasts, as with Aragorn's, are more those of the racial group "to which they belong" (*ibid.*).

He concluded that the text is "a heroic romance [...] wholly relevant to the realities of our concrete historical existence" (*ibid.*). In such a genre, evil ideas may be incarnate in evil beings, however disastrous a notion this is in history. The last point stressed is the ordinariness of the hero, only selected because "chance, or Providence, has chosen, and he must obey" (*ibid.* 61).

While he did not write on the epic story's second volume, *The Two Towers*, on its first appearance in America, Auden had produced an extended article on the third, *The Return of the King*, for the *New York Times*,[10] in which he stressed that the Quest of Frodo was fulfilled and "The Third Age is over." His opening referred prophetically to the current reception of *The Lord of the Rings*:

> I rarely remember a book about which I have had such violent arguments. Nobody seems to have had a moderate opinion: either, like myself, people find it a masterpiece of its genre or they cannot abide it, and among the hostile[11] there are some, I must confess, for whose literary judgment I have great respect. (Becker 1978: 41)

He expanded on the ideas of his *Encounter* article, and discussed the difference between the individual's subjective experiences and his more external and objective responses, stressing his own continuous practice of choice and perception of time itself as "an irreversible history of unique moments which are made by my decisions" (*ibid.* 45). He probed the journey image, arguing that both it and the conflict between Good and Evil were far from "clear-cut" in most lives or stories, then emphasising that Tolkien had succeeded "more completely than any previous writer in his use of the traditional properties," while at the same time satisfying "our sense of historical and social reality" with his imaginary world (*ibid.*). Auden then claimed that the peculiar achievement of Tolkien's Middle-earth was that the careful reader would know as much of its objective reality "as, outside his special field, he knows about the actual world" (*ibid.* 46). Its presentation of "intelligible law" was a remarkable quality in the epic, as was Good being made manifest in the story as love and freedom (*ibid.*).

---

10 On 22nd January 1956. All quotations are made from the more accessible text as printed later in Becker (1978: 44-48). Both are entitled: 'At the End of the Quest, Victory'.
11 Edmund Wilson would launch his devastating attack on the epic, 'Oo, Those Awful Orcs' in *Nation* 182 on 14th April 1956, p. 312, in which he criticised Auden for admiring and defending Tolkien and those who saw many parallels in the epic to the works of Malory and Spenser.

The *Apocalypse* of Holy Scripture and *Paradise Lost* had awkward and unconvincing battles, he stressed, due to the Deity being at once both a God of love and a God of absolute power. Auden then argued that, in the presentation of omniscience and divine purpose, Tolkien had succeeded where Milton failed. Evil, in the person of Sauron, is shown to be inferior in imagination, prone to worship power, filled with anger, and with a lust for cruelty. Such victory as is won is impermanent: "there was Morgoth before Sauron and no one knows what dread successor may afflict the world in ages to come" (*ibid.* 48). Thus, as Auden explains it very quietly, teleology and eschatology are supplied with total consistency in this world. He finally stresses that the demands made of the writer in such an epic are "enormous" and increase from situation to situation, "a challenge to which Mr. Tolkien has proved equal" (*ibid.*).

The Inaugural Lecture

Auden in his Inaugural Lecture as Professor of Poetry to the University of Oxford, referred to his early limited interest in "what is called Imaginative Literature," although he did mention "a private world of Sacred Objects" and pleasure derived from "a few stories like George MacDonald's *The Princess and the Goblin*" (1963: 34). He then expatiated on his deep respect for "the Proper Name of a Sacred Being," continuing:

> A Proper Name must not only refer, it must refer aptly and this aptness must be publicly recognizable [...] the most poetical of all scholastic disciplines is, surely, Philology,[12] the study of language in abstraction from its uses so that words become, as it were, little lyrics about themselves. (*ibid.* 34-35)

In short, he felt that he had been "enjoying the poetic use of language for a long time," and savouring anthologies free from "literary class-consciousness" which allowed for the enjoyment of counting-out rhymes and other humbler forms of poem. Germanic and folk rhymes spoke directly to the hearer.

His account of student days told of his hearing Tolkien reading *Beowulf* (*ibid.* 41-42), of his taste for Anglo-Saxon and Middle English poetry, for *Piers*

---

12 See also his stress on the importance of wooing and winning Dame Philology for his 'Writing', as in *The Dyer's Hand and other Essays* (1963: 22).

Plowman and W.G. Hoskins' *The Making of the English Landscape* (*ibid.* 44). The musing of Auden over the right qualities for a sound critic included as the first two of four *desiderata*, with the strongest approval for

1) long lists of proper names such as the Old Testament genealogies or the catalogue of ships in the *Iliad*; and
2) riddles and all other ways of not calling a spade a spade. (*ibid.* 47)

He is similarly personal in his insistence on the importance of knowing the critic's position for an understanding of his judgments and then the statement of his own essentially moral question as reader:

> What kind of guy inhabits this poem? What is his notion of the good life or the good place? His notion of the Evil One? What does he conceal from the reader? What does he conceal even from himself? (*ibid.* 51)

This is followed by a somewhat tongue-in-cheek self-reproof for the impact of (mythic?) reading on his own mind, *qua* poet:

> Many of the books which have been most important to him have not been works of poetry or criticism but books which have altered his way of looking at the world and himself and a lot of these, probably, are what an expert in their field would call 'unsound.' (*ibid.*)

The last part of the essay gives Auden's slight modifications of the terms 'Primary and Secondary Imagination', as used by Coleridge in the *Biographia Literaria*: "The Primary is only concerned with sacred beings and sacred events," these being of overwhelming importance and arousing awe, sacred events gaining in significance over sacred beings as one grows older. The Secondary Imagination is active and concerned with the beautiful and the ugly, is social and craves agreement. Thus it is that

> [t]he impulse to create a work of art is felt when, in certain persons, the passive awe provoked by sacred beings or events is transformed into a desire to express that awe in a rite of worship or homage [...]. (*ibid.* 57)

His argument is, then, that poetry is a verbal rite, concerned to name and to be formal, ritualistic, beautiful and above all "it must praise all it can for being and for happening" (*ibid.* 60).

*   *   *

In 1961 Auden produced his third review article 'The Quest Hero'[13] on *The Lord of the Rings*, expanding on that of 1956, even as it had extended the short (850 words) review of 1954. The tone of the essay makes it clear that he was concerned to elaborate his published responses, now discussing generally:

1) man's history-making propensities; and

2) his inheritance of city images and of roads reaching out to invisible destinations.

Against these there was

the persistent appeal of the [fairy story] Quest [...] due [...] to its validity as a symbolic description of our subjective personal experience of existence as historical. (1961: 82)

His concern then was to analyse[14] the typical Quest story, with its essential elements – (1) a precious Object; (2) a long journey; (3) a hero; (4) a Test/series of Tests; (5) the Guardians of the Object; and (6) the Helpers (*ibid.* 83) – stressing the contradictory forces in the self and the dualistic nature of the enterprise, with friends and enemies taking sides. He then turned to the non-epic Quest Hero, a being whose *arete* is concealed, seemingly not clever and weak in spirit, but magician-aided,[15]

the one whom everybody would judge as least likely to succeed, [who] turns out to be the hero when his manifest betters have failed. (*ibid.* 84)

Various atypical modern examples are analysed, each to be seen as a "literary mimesis of the subjective experience of becoming" (*ibid.* 85) and as comprising a starting out and a final achievement. The isolation of the Quest Hero means that

[...] the only sustained relationship which [he] can enjoy is with those who accompany him on his journey, (*ibid.* 86)

this being either the democratic or feudal association. Thus this necessary form for the tale is ill-adapted to subtle character portrayal.

---

13 It was first issued in the *Texas Quarterly* 4 (1961: 81-93) and then, in 1968, it appeared in two places, viz: (1) Isaacs and Zimbardo (1968: 40-46) and (2) Grebstein 1968: 370-81).

14 This is done in a Jungian fashion very similar to the text of C.G. Jung's *Modern Man in Search of a Soul* (1933), ch. 8.

15 While Gandalf is first seen as a master of fireworks, his appearances and interventions, which cannot be summoned up, are more akin to the operation of Grace.

The conclusion of the essay is focused on Tolkien's epic, its setting (imaginary yet concrete), its seven or more species endowed with speech and "a real history" (*ibid.* 87), its topographical sharpness, political variants, and moral climate – "the unstated presuppositions of the whole work are Christian" (*ibid.* 88). The Quest is now related to "the religious vocation that [...] comes from outside the self, generally to the self's terror and dismay" (*ibid.* 89), and to the operation of heroic conscience, so that Frodo is absolutely committed – "on him alone is any charge laid" (*ibid.* 90) – and to the fact that, as Gandalf explains, "Victory cannot be achieved by arms" (*ibid.*). In a new section entitled 'The Conflict of Good and Evil', Auden adds a powerful sketch of the limitations of Evil – its mistakes about human altruism, its inability to comprehend selfless motivation, its irrational cruelty and "unstable and untrustworthy" alliances (*ibid.* 91) and its unintended arousal in Frodo of the healing emotions of Pity and Mercy. Auden's last section 'The Fruits of Victory', is a stern rebuttal[16] of the simplistic formula, 'And so they lived happily ever after':

> Victory does not mean the restoration of the Earthly Paradise or the advent of the New Jerusalem. In our historical existence even the best solution involves loss as well as gain. (*ibid.* 92)

The poet's last words argue, then, that the epic is both primarily concerned with the subjective life of the individual person and yet more than just in its representation of "our experience of socio-historical realities" (*ibid.* 93).

And a Birthday Present for Tolkien

For Tolkien's seventieth birthday on 3rd January 1962 a memorial volume was prepared by Professors C.L. Wrenn and N. Davis, and entitled *English and Mediaeval Studies: Presented to J.R.R. Tolkien on the Occasion of His Seventieth Birthday*. For it Auden produced 'A Short Ode to a Philologist', in five stanzas of nine lines, on the nature of speech and of the need therein for truth and largeness. Its last stanzas may be quoted in full.

---

16 For all its brevity, its tone and firmness are echoic of Tolkien's 1936 address, '*Beowulf*: The Monsters and the Critics', to the British Academy.

But Dame Philology is our Queen still,
Quick to comfort
Truth-loving hearts in their mother-tongue (to report
On the miracles she has wrought
In the U.K., the N.E.D.
Takes fourteen tomes):[17] She suffers no evil
And a statesman still, so her grace prevent, may keep a treaty,
A poor commoner arrive at
The Proper Name for his cat.
No hero is immortal till he dies
Nor is a tongue,
But a lay of Beowulf's language, too, can be sung,
Ignoble, maybe, to the young,
Having no monsters and no gore
To speak of, yet not without its beauties
For those who have learned to hope: a lot of us are grateful for
What J.R.R. Tolkien has done
As bard to Anglo-Saxon.

Tolkien on Auden

Some five years later Tolkien returned this poetic graciousness by his own contribution to *Shenandoah* (1967a: 96-97), entitled 'A Tribute to Wystan Hugh
Auden on His Sixtieth Birthday', a pair of poems printed facing each other,
where the excellent Old English lines are exactly faced by an idiomatic but not
word-for-word translation. Apart from the fact that this (Old English) poem
– the only one by Tolkien to a living[18] poet – is concerned with their friendship, the text suggests Auden's rich knowledge of books and legends, his link
with (St) Wihsta and that Mercian's heroic line. He rightly drew attention to

---

17 The 'fourteen tomes' is a mistake for the actual thirteen; lines 37-38 are a quotation from the Old
  Norse *Hávamál* ('Sayings of the High One'), a nice touch which likens Tolkien to Othin in his
  capacity as God-inspirer of Norse skalds (poets). See also the translation of the *Hávamál* in *Norse
  Poems* (Auden and Taylor 1981: 147-67).
18 He had written a short tribute to Dr Henry Bradley, the great lexicographer in Old English, within
  his Obituary, 'Henry Bradley, 3 December 1845 - 23 May 1923', published in *Bulletin of the Modern
  Humanities Research Association* 20 (October 1923: 4-5). This poem is edited and annotated by J.S.
  Ryan in his 'Henry Bradley, Keeper of the Works of English, and his Heroic Passing', *Quettar* 27,
  (December 1986: 7-15).

Auden's love of words and ability to inspire other poet-makers (*scopas*). Even as the Bradley poem by Tolkien had likened that great word-smith to both Bede and Caedmon, so this piece[19] defined Auden as the enjoyed wise poet, honoured for his generous heart yet as holy a man as his name saint.

Woruldbúendra sum bith wóthbora,
giedda giffæst; sum bith gearuwyrdig,
tyhtend getynege torhte mæthleth;
sum bith bóca gléaw, on bréosthorde
wísdóm haldeth, worn fela geman
ealdgesægena thæra the úthwitan
fróde gefrugnon on fyrndagum;
sum bith wilgesíth, wærfæst hæle,
fróndrædenne fæle gelæsteth.
Sumne wát ic, secg héahmódne,
the thissa gifena gehwane on geogothféore
him ealdmetod stum gesealde.
Wer wíde cuth Wíhstan hatte,
swilce wæs éac háten on eardgearde
Wægmundinga Wígláfes fæder
secga holdestan, and siththan eft
bearn Wíghelmes the æt beaduwe gecrang
æt Mældúne be his mandryhtne
on gefrægan tham gefeohte. He nú forth tela
níwan stefne thæs naman brúceth
him to weorthmynde, Wíhstan úre.
Swa sceal he á mid mannum mære wunian,
thær sittath searothancle sundor tó rúne,
snyttrum styriath sóthgied scopa.

Ic this gied be thé to grétinge
Awræc wintrum fród, Wíhstan léofa,
theah ic thorfte hrathor thancword sprecan.
    Rægnold Hrædmóding.
        J.R.R. Tolkien

---

19 Reprinted from *Shenandoah: The Washington and Lee University Review*, with the permission of the editor.

Among the people of earth one has poetry in him,
fashions verses with art; one is fluent in words,
has persuasive eloquence sound and lucid;
one is a reader of books and richly stores
his mind with memory of much wisdom
and legends of old that long ago
were learned and related by loremasters;
one is a mate to choose, a man to trust,
who friendship's call faithfully answers.
Another I know of noble-hearted,
to whom all these gifts in his early days
the favour of Fate freely granted.
Now wide is his renown. Wystan his name is,
as it once was also of the Wægmunding
in his far country, father of Wiglaf
most loyal of lieges, and in later time
of Wighelm's son who in war was slain
at Byrhtnoth's side by the Blackwater
in the famous defeat. He follows after,
and now anew that name uses
to his own honour. Auden some call him,
and so among men may he be remembered ever,
where as they sit by themselves by solace of heart
the word-lovers, wise and skilful,
revive the vanished voices of makers.

These lines about you I linked together,
though weighted by years, Wystan my friend:
a tardy tribute and token of thanks.
        J.R.R. Tolkien

Auden on (Tolkienian) Good and Evil

In 1967 Auden composed his last distinctive and insightful essay on Tolkien's creative writings, 'Good and Evil in *The Lord of the Rings*',[20] in the *Tolkien Journal* 3.1 (1967). This essay owes some parts to its writer's antecedent responses to Tolkien, but, rather, expands on the interrelationship between moral judgment, the gift of speech, the presence of good and evil in each of us, and "our deplorable tendency, when our interests, still more the interests of our social group, come into conflict with others, to identify our cause with Good and that of our enemies with Evil" (5). Auden, in a way which would equate Sauron with (Milton's) Satan, argues that "he is a fallen Vala" (an Original Divine Being), like his predecessor, Morgoth. He then notes that the wood-elves of *The Hobbit* have human weaknesses, queries the absolute evil attributed to the Orcs and the Trolls of Mordor, both but "anonymous crowds," and he rather concedes irredeemable wickedness "only to individuals who are nameable or countable" – such as "Sauron, the Lieutenant of Barad-dûr, the nine Nazgûl" (*ibid.* 6).

He then considers good and evil morally and theologically in our Primary World, interrelating our assumptions to a Secondary World like that of Middle-earth, interpreting the similar historical patterns in each and concluding of both:

> As we grow older [...] we realise more and more how much an individual's notions of good and evil and his power to resist temptation depend, not upon his reason and will, but upon the kind of family and society into which he happens to have been born [...]. (*ibid.*)

Thus the good and (excessively?) fortunate Hobbit community is contrasted with the aged Gollum figure, who must seem to have been "exceptionally unfortunate" in the very "wretchedness" of his life, a continuous agony "due to the fact that he has not become wholly evil" (*ibid.*).

External conflict between Good and Evil is defined in terms of physical warfare[21] in the case of larger antagonisms, whereas the moral responsibilities are still

---

20 It was reprinted the following year, in the anniversary Vol. X of the *Critical Quarterly*, which was issued as a book, *Word in the Desert*, edited by C.B. Cox and A.E. Dyson (1968: 138-42).

21 This analysis uses and extends the later portion (pp. 15-17) of Tolkien's paper, 'The Homecoming of Beorhtnoth Beorhthelm's Son', *Essays and Studies by Members of the English Association*, Volume Six, New Series (1953: 1-18), later reissued in *Tree and Leaf* (Tolkien 2001).

with the individual, Frodo in this case. Then the general discussion assesses the instability of all alliances of Evil with Evil, echoing Dr Johnson with Theoden's words, "Oft evil will shall evil mar." The last section includes Tolkien's own famed conception of the *eucatastrophe*[22] (or 'happy up-turn') as the proper ending for a fairy tale and description for the much longer epic, and then moves to the sober appraisal that solutions known as 'victory' are limited, won at personal cost and likely to be overthrown in time. Auden ends very simply:

> If, as I believe, a good story is one which can persuade us to face life neither with despair nor with false hopes, then *The Lord of the Rings* is a very good story indeed. (*ibid.* 8)

Secondary Worlds

At much the same time as he was drafting this last essay, Auden was preparing to give the inaugural T.S. Eliot Memorial Lectures at Eliot College in the University of Kent at Canterbury. This was a most appropriate choice of lecturer since, like Eliot, Auden distrusted the intellect and had often turned to past literatures for his words and forms. The published version (1968) of the lecture is entitled *Secondary Worlds*, which term, like 'Primary World', he explained that he has taken from Tolkien's 'On Fairy Stories'. The four essays are mainly concerned with everyone's

> desire to make new secondary worlds of our own, or, if we cannot make them ourselves, to share in the secondary worlds of those who can (49)

and with the four kinds of human beings, of whom it may be said that their deaths are the most significant event in their lives – the Sacrificial Victim, the Epic Hero, the Tragic Hero, and the Martyr. Necessarily Auden is concerned, as "a twentieth century Christian" (*ibid.* 11) with the intersections of myth, history and literature, and with the difference that any imaginary constructs might make. The primary world he defined as objective, social and political and as containing whatever of man's historical past is still on hand. But our secondary world is one which for its creator will exclude "everything except what we find sacred, important, enchanting" (*ibid.* 52). All true secondary worlds,

---

22 Discussed in his 'On Fairy Stories' (1947), and more widely known from its inclusion in the volume *Tree and Leaf* (Tolkien 2001).

whether in prose or verse, are defined as lying along a spectrum "according to the part played in their composition by the Poet and the part played by the Historian" (*ibid.*).

Then Auden analysed the genre of Old Icelandic saga prose, particularly for its high level of the fictitious,[23] or at least its selective manner in the imaginative presentation of the past. He stressed that industrial society had divorced the marriage of historian and poet, as maker of secondary worlds, leaving as such a true maker only

> the divorced Poet [who] can find materials for building his secondary worlds only in his private subjectivity [...] a sense of the sacred. (*ibid.* 83)

This essay sheds much light on Auden's perception of Tolkien as a prose-poet, Icelandic style, rather than a historian, and one who believed in "the phenomenal world as a realm of sacred analogies" (*ibid.* 144).

Auden and The Elder Edda

In 1969 there was issued *The Elder Edda: A Selection* translated from the Icelandic by Paul B. Taylor and W.H. Auden, dedicated to J.R.R. Tolkien, who is also mentioned specifically for his 'riddle-game' as used by Bilbo Baggins in *The Hobbit*. Many of the introductory comparative points also show close knowledge of Old English literature, as of the poetic *Maxims*. The collection had been embarked upon after Auden's second visit to Iceland in 1965 and would appear again, much expanded, in 1981 as *Norse Poems*. Further Norse materials were included by him in his *A Certain World: A Commonplace Book* (1970: 107), which also featured the passage already cited, on Elrond's wise words to the Fellowship, as it was about to leave Lothlórien:

> The Ring-Bearer is setting out on the Quest [...] On him alone is any charge laid: neither to cast away the Ring, nor to deliver it to any servant to the Enemy [...] The others go with him as free companions [...]

Its category is given as 'Prose and Poetry of Departure', and its text is strongly echoic of the medieval morality play, *Everyman*.

---

23 This dimension became clear after 1945, whereas his early response to the sagas had been to see them as highly democratic and historically accurate.

Auden as Explicator of Tolkien's Purposes

From this chronological account it is clear that we can be illumined in our own pursuit of the meaning and value of Tolkien's major story by following through the various evidences of Auden's response to Dark Age literature in his own poems and in the relevant critical essays. In his review of *The Return of the King*, Auden argued that what produced the immoderate early responses to that book was the question of the validity of purely imagined worlds, deeming them but "light 'escapist' reading" (Becker 1978: 44). He then conceded that the Heroic Quest depicts a pattern of Good against Evil that is not readily discernible in human events, yet this is not more extreme a depiction of man than the realistic novel.

Auden's stress on its 'Heroic Quest' thus draws attention to both the elements of secondary epic that are present in Tolkien's Middle-earth and to the serious nature of the Tolkien construct which is perhaps the last literary masterpiece of the Middle Ages. Aragorn is the traditional epic hero, and Frodo, who is closer to the fairy-tale hero, is a character who

> is not recognizable as a hero except in the negative sense – that he is the one who to the outward eye appears [...] least likely to succeed. (Auden 1954a: 37)

Tolkien's denial that the work was either allegorical or topical still left us his deeper purpose that the epic "would hold the attention of readers, [...] delight them, and at times maybe excite them or deeply move them" (*FotR* ix). The larger questions of the meaning and the relevance of the epic to life he left to the critics, one of the most persistently thoughtful of whom was the poet, W.H. Auden, who, like his teacher, "tried to be a Christian."

Appendix

J.R.R. Tolkien and the *Ancrene Riwle*, or
Two Fine and Courteous Mentors to Women's Spirit

J.R.R. Tolkien and the *Ancrene Riwle*, or
Two Fine and Courteous Mentors to Women's Spirit

> The writer [of these *Ancrene Riwle* group of texts in the feminine anchorite tradition] must have had a high degree of culture, and was familiar with French, [and] with court poetry [...]. He had a sound theological training, with a knowledge of the works of Jerome, Augustine, Gregory, Anselm, and notably of Bernard,[1] from whom he frequently quotes. (Eckenstein 1896: 315-16)

> It is not a language[2] long relegated to the 'uplands' struggling once more for expression in apologetic emulation of its betters or out of compassion for the lewd, but rather one that [...] has contrived, in troublous times to maintain the air of a gentleman, if a country gentleman. (Ancrene Wisse 106).

A too Long Neglected Aspect of the Life and Work of J.R.R. Tolkien

It is little short of the scandalous that there has been such serious omission from the mass of writing about J.R.R. Tolkien of three central issues, which were wholly integrated in his being and so illuminating of this scholarly and committed life and its remarkable achievements, notably

1) his own life-long and passionate commitment to and scholarly and sensitive exploration of God's love for man;

2) the like exploration of his several contemporaries and research students of particular remarkable women's spiritual search and love for God – as revealed

---

1 I.e. Bernard of Clairvaux, a renowned fashioner and collector of similar hagiographic legends, most of which were produced on the continent and reflected on 'hermits' and solitude. Most of these lives were written by older men, clerical instructors, despite their content being aimed at women religious.

2 This is, of course, one of the classic uses by Tolkien of his rich and generous sense of 'language', meaning the whole stylistic, semantic association and all other cultural referents. This glossing is available in print, as was discussed by him in his farewell lecture to the University of Oxford, delivered in Merton Hall in 1959 as reprinted in Tolkien (2006: 224-40).

by the classic West Midlands homilies of the early thirteenth century, customarily known as the *AB* texts;

and, in contrast to that,

3) the popular, or more journalistic, responses to – and even much more recent criticism of – the numerous writings of Professor Tolkien, these last often considering that he was unduly stereotypical towards women and their emotions and not perceptive of their nature, or understanding of the totality of the nature and finer qualities of women.

Two Christian Gentlemen and their Concern for the Spiritual and Devotional Nurture of Women

It is proposed now to treat both of these matters concerning J.R.R. Tolkien as they could be observed, and should have been known and more obvious to the closer Oxford communities generally and, later, to his growing public. Of course, the mediaeval texts and their scholarly interpretation might well have seemed a minor or recherché matter. Yet these constitute two closely linked themes and strangely similar personalities, and so it is possible to compare, in some reflective fashion, the two father figures, the one, the mediaeval monk and spiritual instructor, and the other, the modern mentor and (cultural) guide to so many young women of his own faith. For the reality of the manner of this surprisingly shy man's expressing himself to and about (young) women is far other than it may be assumed – both

1) in relation to his lifelong concern with these several texts of more than scholarly interest and integrity, and with their deeper spiritual significance, and

2) in his compassionate understanding expressed towards the many modestly-financed student lives which he personally assisted, especially academically, they often coming from the lesser women's colleges of the University of Oxford.

Even more significantly, – and in effect, linking the two compassionate Catholics across the intervening centuries – Tolkien himself had always acted with much sensitivity and understanding in both these contexts. For he was ever encouraging and directing the researches of many of these Catholic by nurture students. Most of them would prove to have an often life-long focus on these West Midlands or other (mediaeval) Christian cultural documents and on their deeper moral and eschatological significance.

Over his career he had taught quite inspirationally and otherwise supported in a practical sense – both within the University of Oxford and in the city itself, even over decades – so many of these similar, and deeply committed Christian researchers, both women and men, many of them in religious orders.[3] Similarly, he was, for so many years, supervising closely their work on the various manuscripts associated with this same spiritually reflective and almost incantatory genre, as well as editing and preparing commentaries on and translations of them.[4]

A Short Interlude on the *AB* Texts

The issue of the group of texts produced in the period c. 1180 to 1220 A.D., and often known as the *AB*[5] cluster or texts, and their closely and almost 'standardised' language and style, is a major matter in the history and the tone of the developing and post-Conquest pattern to the native English prose and culture. Indeed, it constitutes a peculiarly fine renaissance of the spirit of Wessex, and one remarkably antithetic to the world of Anglo-Norman writings and its more dubious 'courtliness'.

In this matter of the 'evidence of the texts', apart from the *Ancrene Riwle* itself, there were five closely related pieces known from the title of one of them as the Katherine Group. Three are lives of women saints – St Katherine, St Margaret, and St Juliana – and there are two religious treatises, *Hali Meidenhad* and *Sawles Warde*. The *Ancrene Riwle*, however, is the best known closely related text and written in the same variety of English. While none can be dated precisely, customary scholarly wisdom – as do various inferences – would place them between c. 1180 and c. 1220. The first cluster, the lives, have the primary purpose of

---

3 These tended to be students in or training for Roman Catholic religious orders; to not have the support of adequate scholarships; and/or to be associated with the smaller affiliated University Halls, rather than the larger and much wealthier Colleges (see below). Indeed, many were so modestly affiliated – as with the domestic group that would, later, become St Anne's College – that they were actually or semi-officially known as the 'non-collegiate [women] students'.

4 The prose was so often both alliterative and even rhythmic, and possessed of distinctly euphoneous qualities which did, and still do, make it peculiarly powerful in its impact and haunting resonances.

5 The term was Tolkien's in the context just mentioned. It is also accessibly glossed, and much more recently, by Arne Zettersten in Michael D.C. Drout's *J.R.R. Tolkien Encyclopedia* (2007: 1-2).

extolling virginity, and of showing how the central figures were martyred for their preservation of their maidenhood.

The homily *Sawles Warde* ('The Safeguarding of the Soul'), despite its being found in all three of these related manuscripts, is separate in theme and style, focusing engagingly on the notion of the house as symbolizing the body, and whose master is Wit, and mistress is Will. Clearly the treasure of the house is the soul, ever, as in a castle, guarded by the several inner virtues. The prose style of these legends is marked by the use of much alliteration and by a degree of rhythm. However, the *Ancrene Riwle* is clearly the most influential and important prose work of the early Middle English period. Written originally at the request of three maidens of noble birth who had chosen to withdraw from the world, it was early revised as the *Ancrene Wisse* – *wisse* meaning 'guidance' – for the use of a larger community, (variously) adapted for the use of a male community, and duly translated into French and Latin.

The literary nuances of the texts will be discussed in a moment, but the term *AB* language – Tolkien's own one – is a convenient, now largely a conventional one to describe the seemingly distinctive style, lexis, and, more recently, the consistent pronunciation to be found in all of these texts. What is not at issue is the fact that the *Riwle* is written in an extraordinarily 'consistent' dialect and orthography such as is found elsewhere only in texts which are the holographs of the authors. Even more significant is the use of the same dialect and orthography of the Bodley MS of the Katherine Group – and obviously the language evidence indicates a close connection both in time and place, the Bodley and Corpus MSS having Western antecedents.

And so back to the present larger postulation about two strangely similar figures, namely the intriguingly similar and profoundly illuminating parallels in thought and action, as between the author of the *Ancrene Riwle* and J.R.R. Tolkien himself.

A Rich Spirituality and this Devotional Prose as a True National Heritage, and so the Need for its Close Study and Preservation

Tolkien and the various twentieth century researchers working with him over the years were well aware of what was enshrined in this cluster of highly moral texts, these comprising a genre suffused with the Cistercian spirit and an adaptation of the Benedictine Rule, with the addition of much of the mysticism of Antony and Cassian.[6] They were most concerned with earlier as well as contemporary women living a truly Christian life, and with talking to and communing most meaningfully with God. All of this thought and exhortation had been represented finely and always in a style consonant with the evolution of a devout and native English spirit, one especially flourishing in the far West Midlands.[7]

For that region was one well away from lingering Anglo-Norman etiquettes and the morally dubious contemporary 'knightly' tales based on the shallow and even cynical culture of Courtly Love. It was also close to the location and genres of the last flowering of the finest aspects of the Old English prose homilies and of their influence.

It was in these scholarly traditions and several proximate enclosed church orders – as largely located along the Malvern Hills in the south west of the Midlands, at the beginning of the thirteenth century – that there was able to evolve and be practiced a deep spirituality, one expressed in the most limpid and reflective prose. That body of religious texts Tolkien, a passionate Roman Catholic himself, rightly saw as one of the finest flowerings in England of the mediaeval Christian spirit, as well as a cluster of texts of a high culture and illustrative of the continuity of the traditional West Saxon prose of the Alfredian phase such as that of Æthelwold and Ælfric. And so he strove to obtain the widest recognition for its moral qualities, religious significance – and this, one so

---

6 See for this Vandenbrouck (1968) and Brooke (1964: 32-45).
7 A close examination of his own student period's scheduled undergraduate study courses – see pp. 21-22, in my recent book, *Tolkien's View* (2009) – will indicate that the now cited 13th century materials were largely absent from them, although there was one such regional set text, No 9, in a contemporary textbook, namely Morris and Skeat, *Specimens of Early English*, it being captioned 'The Seven Deadly Sins' and 'Directions how a Nun Should Live' (*ibid.* 21).

extraordinarily influential for mainstream English letters – for its lucid and effective style.[8]

It is also to be observed now that the exploration of the Tolkienian and Tolkien-generated research work in this area affords readers who did not meet him in life a unique perspective on the life and works of this aware, modern, reflective and inspirational Christian father and deeply religious thinker.

Tolkien's Firm and Career-long Focus on the Style and Cultural Significance of the Body of Western Homiletic and Religious Texts of Early Middle English

It is something of a commonplace in the mass of biographic Tolkien research, – as it is of so many more loosely argued critical essays concerned with his career and writings – that his original university studies were very much in the area of the ancient classical languages. Further, the records do show that they were, variously, in those modes or records of linguistic significance deemed essential for work in comparative philology,[9] these ancient European interests being then followed by his many years of labouring in the realms of Old Norse literature, of related folklore, and, similarly, of Old English culture.

However, he had studied closely, when in the 'English' discipline at Oxford between 1913 and 1915, a broad range of the better known, or 'high', and often secular Middle English texts[10] with his tutor, Kenneth Sisam, and would, early on in his career, collaborate with him, to provide the glossary[11] to the

---

8   We may note here T. Shippey's description of the Tolkien essay as "the most perfect though not the best-known of his academic pieces" (1982: 31). In so many mediaeval letters lectures, for Courses I, II, and III, Tolkien would make various subtle links with the language of Shakespeare, another heir to the classic West Midland prose style.
9   Many today forget that the scholar philologist had also completed the Oxford Diploma in Comparative Philology after coming back from World War I.
10 He would refer in lectures to his also very early grappling with J. Hall's uneven clutch of mediaeval prose styles as in his *Selections From Early Middle English 1130-1250* (1920), when he was lecturing on the contents of the Sisam reader, as he would to R.M. Wilson's 1954 issued, *The English Text of the Ancrene Riwle*, from the E.E.T.S., as Old Series, vol. 229. Similarly he would mention the succinct summaries of the related dialectal matters to be found in *Early Middle English Texts*, edited by Bruce Dickins and R.M. Wilson, and first published in 1951.
11 This excellent separate glossary – in effect, a small dictionary – was much issued by the Oxford University Press as *A Middle English Vocabulary*, first in 1922, it then having many re-prints. The standard earlier period reader, Joseph Hall's *Selections from Early Middle English*, would not be issued by the Oxford University Press until 1920.

latter's classic volume, *Fourteenth Century Verse and Prose*. This reader was one which contained sections of the West Midland alliterative verse romance, *Sir Gawain and the Green Knight*, and was certainly responsible for Tolkien's excitedly nurturing – at the beginning of his career and while at the University of Leeds – the teaching of the later periods of Middle English, this work then being generously given over to his close friend, the Canadian, E.V. Gordon. The latter would also collaborate with him for their fine edition of *Sir Gawain and the Green Knight* (1925).

Yet, at the same time, Tolkien would be contributing significantly to the then somewhat meagre scholarship of the less fashionable and earlier phase Middle English homilies, with a significant review,[12] one headed 'Holy Maidenhood', this being his forceful critical response to Furnivall's E.E.T.S. edition of *Hali Meidenhad*, as in *The Times Literary Supplement* of 26 April, 1923 (281). For the body of homiletic and devotional prose, then customarily grouped under the banner of *AB* Language, was, as early on as this, felt by him to be both significant linguistically and culturally, as well as their limpid texts being peculiarly appealing in their lucidly-expressed devotion and wisdom. They would duly become a very obvious syllabus and then research concern for him – once he had succeeded in reforming the Oxford University syllabus[13] for 'English' and much increased the hitherto very small numbers of postgraduates engaged in research in the Faculty, despite the numbers of curious and able Rhodes Scholars from the United States of America wanting only later literature.

By the long existing and defining statute, he was not expected to lecture on such post Old English materials until he had changed, in 1945, to the later-period

---

12 The evidence of his being the author of this unsigned piece is established by reference to his diary, which indicates that the response was written in 1922. See The Tolkien Wiki Community website for this matter. That source also lists the fact that, in 1934, he was writing reflectively for *The Chronicle*, a powerfully expressed cultural journal of the Convent of the Sacred Heart, at Roehampton, in the west of London, as in his poem, 'Firiel' (vol. IV: 30-32).

13 The paper in which he proposed this – and which enabled him to achieve this soon after – was his reformist proposal, 'The Oxford English School', in *The Oxford Magazine* (1930: 778-82). It would go through the various Faculty and University boards and first take effect in the 1931-32 University session.

Less known of today is his subsequent drive to increase the Faculty's research ranks, not least by the regular issue of details of the projects commenced and their supervisors. See further ahead in this essay and the next footnote. 'His' emphatically Christian syllabus would not really last for long after his retirement, but he had enhanced understanding of England's Christian tradition for more than thirty years for all doing the English School.

focussed Merton English chair. However, it may be noted that, in the first ever published official report on postgraduate research in the Faculty of English, as widely circulated in the *University of Oxford Gazette* on 5 October, 1933,[14] he could be referred to as having sole responsibility for – amongst others – these particular research students, with the following and closely linked topics:

> Colborn, A.F., 'A Critical Text of *Hali Meidhad*, together with a grammar and glossarial notes' (from Michaelmas Term, 1933); and
>
> Griffiths, M.E. (Elaine), 'Notes and Observations on the Vocabulary of *Ancrene Wisse*, MS cccc. 402'.

Later, he also supervised

> Salu, M.B. (of Lady Margaret Hall) from Michaelmas Term, 1940, on 'Early English Language', this work being subsequently styled in reports as 'Grammar of the *Ancrene Wisse*';

and, after his war service in the Naval Intelligence section of the Admiralty, then one

> Dobson, Eric John (of Merton College),[15] from Michaelmas 1947, his D.Phil. being awarded in 1951.

But to Return to 1929

In his own already cited longer paper, quoted from now in the form later issued publicly through *Essays and Studies by Members of the English Association* in 1929, he had referred, with much approval, to the identified, limpid, and remarkably consistent mediaeval prose style, one used for various manuscripts of spiritual edification as being consistently produced in the West Midlands

---

14 See the university's first such report in the *University of Oxford Gazette* for 5th October 1933 – its contents discussed by me in some detail in my essay, 'J.R.R. Tolkien's Formal Lecturing and Teaching at the University of Oxford, 1925-1959', in *Seven: An Anglo-American Literary Review* 19 (2002: 45-62). The references are cited exactly as they were given in that significant issue of the *Gazette*. The Belgian student, Simonne d'Ardenne is not listed here, since she had come earlier, and the thesis created with her supervisor, Tolkien, was not, in the end, to be submitted to the University of Oxford.

15 Eric John Dobson (1913-84) was an Australian Harmondsworth Senior Scholar who had attended Tolkien's lectures for the B.A., 1935-37, had obtained a fine first in the much more mediaeval English Course II, and been a research student under him from 1947. Dobson's most significant *Ancrene Wisse* publications will be discussed below.
For his relevant career details and like publications, see the *Merton College Register II, 1891-1989* (1990: 86), edited by Norman and R.H.C Davis (printed for private circulation), and the 'Obituary' as printed in the *Proceedings of the British Academy* 71 (Gray 1985: 533-38).

about the beginning of the 13th century. And he had then focused on the whole style and integrity of such writing, in particular its engaging cultural and moral tone, its hallmarks being

> [...] traditions, and some acquaintance with books and the pen [...] a language at once self-consistent and markedly individual [...] a form of English whose development from an antecedent Old English type was relatively undisturbed. (Ancrene Wisse 106-107)

Long known as the *Ancrene Riwle*, and very much due to his, Tolkien's, insights and career-long championing and furtherance of Oxford teaching and post-graduate research in this regional genre and elegant style, it would be clearly recognized as one of the most influential and important prose works of the Early Middle English period.[16] Undoubtedly it was seen as a centre-piece – both for linguistic and cultural reasons – for the 1930s re-commenced, and progressively, expanded Course II, within the Faculty of English[17] of the University of Oxford.

Previous English Scholarship on these Homilies

In the time of his own undergraduate studies, the main and most accessible literary history in England appraising these same texts was, probably, William Henry Schofield's *English Literature from the Norman Conquest to Chaucer*,[18] a volume which refers pointedly to the numerous Early Middle English "books of edification, rather than didactic [purpose]" (1906: 403), and those content-related ones in Latin, English and French. All of them were engaged in recording and depicting meticulously and compassionately much of contemporary social conditions – in the midst of their religious guidance and instruction – and so producing a number of texts having a "literary interest far greater than one would expect" (*ibid.*).

---

16 Another powerful catalyst to these studies would be the work of the American, Dorothy Bethurum, as in her 'The Connection of the Katherine Group with Old English Prose', *Journal of English and Germanic Philology* 34 (1935: 553-64).
   Some further details of Tolkien's pre-WWI service period's university studies here are given by me in *Tolkien's View: Windows into His World* (2009: 21-22).
17 A more comprehensive illustration of the quickly developed course that he had so furthered and revitalized is given in the 'Appendix 1' to the present essay (pp. 297-99).
18 This text had remained a most helpful and favourite literary and critically interpretive manual for many years.

This last focus was, of course, their common compassion and a remarkable authorial kindliness and graciousness to the enclosed orders of women, a key theme in all these works, as well as being a style manifesting both understanding and a concern of rare integrity and always expressed with an engaging sincerity.

The undoubted favourite amongst them – more than a century ago, as also today – was the *Ancrene Riwle*, or 'Rule of Nuns', now more commonly known as the *Ancrene Wisse*, i.e. 'Instruction for Enclosed Women', a text written early in the thirteenth century by a much older man, a spiritual adviser to three young ladies of gentle birth, they being

> sisters of one father and of one mother, for their goodness and nobleness of mind, beloved of many. (*ibid.*)

Schofield and his generation of scholars had placed the setting of their enclosed 'anchorhold' – a walled-in chamber with two small windows, one into the church, and the other to the outer air – at Tarante in Dorset (*ibid.* 404);[19] and that scholar had also sought to stress the text's emphasis on avoiding the bickering all too common amongst the several orders of nuns; and to distinguish always between the outward and the inner rule; and so it was that

> [h]e [i.e. the mediaeval writer] urges the nuns not to vow to keep anything as commanded except obedience, chastity, and constancy in their abode. (*ibid.*)

A Surprising Wisdom and Compassion to this 'Rule'

It is equally noteworthy that only two of the eight books of the actual mediaeval admonition are occupied with the formal doctrinal matter, or with what the writer and chaplain figure might have been expected to be concerned to inculcate. Much of the advice is more general and reflective, eminently sensible and perceptive, and, certainly, wholly valid for any person withdrawing from the hurly burly of secular society at any time. It was also advised then that the nuns be especially wary of idle and of variously assertive and manipulative priests.

> Believe secular men little, [...] the religious still less. (*ibid.*: 405)

---

19 But see below for Dobson's views on this.

And Schofield had then (*ibid.* 406, ff.) related a gentle parable about a romantic lover from the outer world – one, at first seeming, much like those courtiers to be found in the Breton and other lays of 'Britain'. Now, however, referring directly to the enclosed women he addressed, Schofield continued, explaining the soul's task in a form of chivalrous action, that now the object of their affection was to be the Lord Christ, for

> [t]he king [...] delivered her from all her enemies, and was himself [...] maltreated and at last slain. But by a miracle he arose from death to life. Would not this lady be of a most perverse nature if she did not love him after this above all things? This King is Jesus Christ, the Son of God, who in this manner wooed our soul, which the devils had besieged. And He, as a noble wooer, after many messengers and many good deeds, came to prove his love [...]. He engaged in a tournament, and had, for his lemman's love, His shield everywhere pierced in battle [...]. His lemman beholdeth thereon how He bought her love, and let His shield be pierced, that is, let His side be opened, to show her His heart, and to show her openly how deeply He loved her, and to draw her heart to Him. (*ibid.* 407)

Perceptive American Overviews

Now in the 1920s – and this was the orthodox critical view of his own time – Tolkien had already been much exposed, both when first teaching at the University of Leeds and on his return to Oxford, to the fine and magisterial survey volume from Yale University Press, *A Manual of the Writings in Middle English, 1050-1400*,[20] by John Edwin Wells, as an overview encapsulating the most enlightened scholarship at that time. And we can do no better than to reproduce Wells' own summation of the literary and religious purpose of that redoubtable homilist, as it had appeared to him in the earlier twentieth century:

> The *Riwle* falls into eight parts. The first part, 'Of Divine Service,' and the eighth, 'Of Domestic Matters,' deal with the 'outward rule'; the 'inward rule' is treated in the other six parts, 'On Keeping the Heart,' 'Moral Lessons and Examples,' 'Of Temptations,' 'Of Confession,' 'Of Penance,' 'Of Love.' [...]

---

20 This is especially so in the lucid survey of all these issues (1916: 361, ff.), focusing on the eight important English Manuscripts of the work and their relation to those in other languages. This Olympian work must be read carefully, if only to clarify some of the confusions that, at that time, had long raged over the cluster of texts, their order and primacy, and the parts of likely similarity and/or difference between the various manuscripts.

So, much of the *Riwle* deals with religious themes common in the period.
(1916: 363-64)

The American scholar had also stressed then the more distinctive and personal
qualities of the text, such as the presence in its author of: a fondness for allegory;
his parables; bestiary materials; the concreteness of the images, these beautiful,
tender, humorous, but "always appropriate and illuminating," in which "popular
homely elements abound" (*ibid.* 364); while his sagacious conclusion on the
tone and purpose may be quoted in full:

> It is broad, free, liberal, spontaneous, sincere, fresh, familiar, kindly, tender,
> devout, simple, dignified. But its singular charm resides less in the qualities
> of its matter [...] than in the personality [...] that breathes upon the reader at
> every turn – a fine, elevated, pious, catholic, lovable spirit, full of knowledge
> of the heart, of a mystical and even a romantic nature, wise and good, and rich
> in that love that to him was the center of all. (*ibid.* 365)

Wooing by the Heavenly Lover

Wells then went on to stress, in his definitive last paragraph, that much of this
constituted a powerful reminder of the refined and deeply reflective cultural
tendencies in the South of England at this time that "were advancing and
elevating Women," – notably by the cult of the Virgin, the enthusiastic glori-
fication of the virgin saints, and from the passionate "urgence of the wooing
by the Heavenly Lover" (*ibid.* 365). It may also be observed by us that Wells
had presented this text as defining and inculcating a rare personal worship,
spiritually impressive and an even morally 'heroic' lifestyle for the enclosed
orders, one both insightful and calming. As well, it was one finely challenging
the unduly autonomous spirit too easily available to young Christian women,
in those times of great social change and of both secular and marital threat to
a chaste feminine morality.

Initial Text and its Successor Versions

Written by a much older religious, a male, and, clearly, a close friend to their
family, at the request of three maidens who were sisters and who had elected
to abandon the world to live as anchoresses, the 'Ancrene Riwle' text had been

revised early on as the *Ancrene Wisse* for the use of a larger community, even to be adapted later for the use of a male community and translated into French and Latin.[21] During the 14th and 15th centuries, it would have a remarkable further influence on vernacular devotional literature, for its sincerity and intensity, this merited popularity persisting until well into the 16th century,[22] despite the rise of Puritanism.

The early 13th century text, the one of our concern here, had appealed vastly to Tolkien, a devout Catholic and a young husband and father,[23] for its tolerance and enlightened views – even as it had to so many before him. For it always stressed quietness and a moderation in behaviour, as well as a necessary sensibility in the anchoress's lifestyle – as with all retiring and devout Christian women. Much of the manual was, naturally, focused on the ordinary religious teaching, on the exposition of scripture and on the use of allegory, but then it had, quickly and engagingly, come to life, due to the author's fine and vernacular descriptions, to his plain illustrations and engaging detail as observed from life – the whole being a total and so refreshing contrast to the vapid images that we may well have formed of the women of the time from the secular contemporary Anglo-Norman romances.

While the first and last sections are concerned with the 'outer rule', they are not distinct in tone from the inner rule of the other six. The first is concerned with the more formal and prescribed religious duties as required of the anchoress, while the last contains practical advice as to their daily life, dialogue with their maids, an emphasis on suitable clothing, and practical details of the domestic side of their existence, thus providing a sensible and homely perspective on the realities of the day-to-day pattern of their chosen and now much restricted and cloistered lives.

---

21 It was realized early in modern scholarship that the original composition on this theme – despite the Latin and French versions – was in English, and so see D.M.E. Dymes' views (1923: 31 ff).

22 In this respect, its content and purport have, alike, links with the times and lifestyle as discussed in the fictional John Inglesant text, as treated by me in *Tolkien's View* (2009: 3-15).

23 It is this lived Catholic quality to the pre-war years in the Tolkien family household that is so much stressed by Elaine Griffiths and Simonne d'Ardenne in their various published reminiscences of him then, and as they are discussed below.

The Personality of the Adviser

However, the most interesting aspect of the whole work has long – and rightly – been felt to be the writer's gracious, kindly, and peculiarly engaging focus on the personal spirit of the young Christian woman, the 'inner rule', one which he humanized, even as he had considered:

> the five senses as guardians of the heart;
> the advantages of withdrawing from the world;
> the temptations still to be resisted;
> the times and ways of receiving the Eucharist, and the role and receipt of the sacraments;
> and the power that was always with them, the abiding love of Christ.

As most critics have observed, the gentle personality of the writer comes across strongly and engagingly. For he, a longtime friend of the family, had written this homily as one appropriate to their social position, wealth and temper, and relevant to their obvious excellent previous education – for there are various un-translated references in Latin in his text. And, similarly, the young women are encouraged to read in both English and French, even as he stresses that he has written personally, for them alone.

In short, apart from his warmth and concern, the qualities that impress themselves immediately are his maturity of mind and heart, and his wisdom in focusing on the grace-bestowing inner rule, it imposing genuine piety and the practice of obedience to – and a close knowledge of – one's deeper conscience, as may be heard in quietness and by those with confidence in the Holy Spirit.

He had also exhorted the need for their obedience to their confessor, but – to avoid possible contention as to the technicalities of their prescribed observance as between the various orders – he advised them, if questioned on these (potentially argumentative and doctrinal) issues, to ascribe their practices, as appropriate as they should be assigning themselves to 'the rule of St James'. This fictitious order[24] was one which he had explained and defined as being concerned with

---

24 This is an engaging device, the shrewdly intended effect of which was clearly to confuse the carping and the all too likely doctrinally aggressive, and particularising critics, and so divert their attack.

assisting widows and fatherless children, reflecting on the general state of society, and as one keeping the novices busy, pure and unstained by the world.

And the Matter of Pité both in the Texts and in one Tribute to J.R.R. Tolkien

The caring and compassionate tone adopted throughout the *Ancrene Wisse* is one firmly expressed, and of a gentle and kindly moderation, advising the novices to only be:

taking communion fifteen times a year;
praying less frequently than others might have enjoined;
and reading much more than repeating formal devotions;

– while the author displays a remarkably sympathetic understanding of their chosen pattern of existence, and indicates a determination to lighten its rigours as far as possible. Indeed, he expresses a gentle form of 'pité', or the quiet and Christ-like concern for all that was so much like the core of Geoffrey Chaucer's writings in the later fourteenth-century.

Interestingly, it is, surely, no accident that Tolkien's Course I student from 1954 -56, – and in due course to be the initial Tolkien Professor, Douglas Gray (b. 1930), later a Professorial Fellow of Lady Margaret Hall – would offer as his contribution to the mentioned 'tributary volume' of 1977 an essay entitled 'Chaucer and "Pite"'. For, of course, that same gentle quality was one peculiarly central to Tolkien's own genuinely shy personality and his obvious caring for all, as so many of his closer students have always affirmed, rather than the common notion of his being 'bluff' or even eccentric, as the New York and London press alike are delighted to suggest.

And now we may also recall in this discussion of (homiletic) manner in a particular context what Professor Albert C. Baugh[25] had observed long ago of the author of the *Ancrene Wisse* that:

---

25 In many ways, Baugh (1891-1981), whom the present writer had met in North Europe in 1965, was a/the American scholar of kindred spirit to Tolkien, both in age, and in his main dates and interests, as in his formal career and in his deep commitment to the tradition of philology with its twin concerns with the language and the history of literature. Similarly, he had rather focused on the

he was completely candid and free from any trace of hypocrisy. Without being of the world, he was not remote from it or ignorant of its ways. Above all, he was a kindly, benevolent spirit, one in whom a genuinely large nature was united with a becoming modesty and true simplicity of soul. (1948: 134)[26]

Tolkien's Research Conclusions in the 1920s on the *AB* Matter

After this very lucid description of the temper of the *Ancrene Wisse* and, perforce, of its writer, we can do no better than consider more closely Tolkien's finely nuanced grammatical and interpretive essay (as cited initially), delivered to a (perhaps religious or denominational)[27] study group somewhat before 1929 – when it was finally published in a bound yearbook volume that went out[28] to the many thousands of members of the cultural organization, the English Association, worldwide. Essentially in its content, this pondered appraisal is a most powerful, quantified and thoughtful reflection on the authentic and closely consistent and confident lexis, grammar, and the quietly dignified verbal style of the linguistic vehicle that conveys that measured and wise text.

However, its immediately seeming focus is a modest one, foregrounding his own (painstaking) analysis of the grammatical forms so consistently used in the studied text, and, essentially, comprising a daunting but quietly confident piece of meticulous research, one based on the modern exegetical writer's encyclopedic

---

literature produced in England in the Middle English period (1100-1500), so writing that volume in the vast and authoritative *Literary History of England* of which he was the co-editor. His *A History of the English Language*, with five careful revisions, is still the preeminent account of English's career from Germanic language to world *lingua franca*.

26 He would soon expand on this in his own related edition, *The English Text of the Ancrene Riwle, British Museum MS Royal 8 C.i* and issue it for the E.E.T.S. in 1956, as their publication Number 232.

27 There were various such groups, most of those that Tolkien attended would be involved with the religious thought of Christopher Dawson and/or Fr. Thomas Corbishley, S.J., a former student of Campion Hall, ordained in 1936, duly Master of the Hall, 1945-58, and then moving to the significant pulpit of Pound Street Church in London. Works by the latter which were known to Tolkien included *Roman Catholicism* (1950), *Religion in the Modern World* (1952), as well as various contributions to the *Catholic Commentary on Holy Scriptures* (Orchard *et al.* 1953). For such a dialoguing group, see especially Ryan (1969: 59, ff) and Appendix 2 to the present essay.

28 This particular selection was one made by H.W. Garrod (1878-1960), (resident) Fellow of Merton College for more than sixty years, and also a former Professor of Poetry at the University of Oxford. Much later than this, from 1945 on, Garrod would meet up with Tolkien on a daily basis when they were neighbours in Fellows' Quad in Merton (see the 1955 group in a photo illustration in the present volume).

knowledge of the cluster of works loosely styled as being from this area. Additionally, it also indicates and presents an almost total familiarity with (all possible) Old English and Late Old English choices of forms and of variant spellings – witness his juggling and classifying meticulously some 2,355 relevant forms derived from Old English weak verbs, and then categorizing them (1929: 124).

Of course, this close report on his own research is much more than an early and apparently careful computational exercise, since he was then able to postulate a number of exciting cultural and author-illuminating axioms – none of them disputed in the eighty and more years since – namely:

> 1) the particular stage of the consistent language of "AB cannot , in the west, [...] be put much before 1225, if as far [back]" (*ibid.* 120);[29]
>
> 2) that Kentish and Northern influences [i.e. also those of Canterbury and of the Church in the former north-east, the Danelaw – and also of those texts' lexis and dialectal features] may be excluded;
>
> 3) that one dare "not [...] apply my linguistic theory to the questions 'by whom' and 'for whom'" the text had been so shaped (*ibid.* 116); and / but that
>
> 4) it MAY be possible to find a trace of the identity[30] of "[t]heir instructor" (*ibid.* 116).

And so to this Amazingly Researched Presentation of his Mind at Work

This encomium to the text's very moving compassion comes from the heart of the eager young neo-mediaeval man, Tolkien, and himself a loving father, as well as the Catholic professor, and even then about to re-focus and more "mediaevalise/illumine from the truly Christian centuries"[31] the Oxford English School. This eschatological purpose is made clear from his closely linked reflective – if unexpected – musing on mortal existence in the same period and later –

> If one considers the throngs of folk in the fair field of the English centuries, busy and studious, learned and lewd, esteemed and infamous, that must have

---

29 This indicated a prose tradition of 300 years or more, despite all the upheavals of the 10th and 11th centuries.

30 This was a task appealing to many, and particularly to E.J. Dobson (see below).

31 This was a comment made to me by several clergy, both Roman Catholic and Church of England, during my various times in Oxford, as well as when I was visiting the Dominicans at Blackfriars in Cambridge (see below).

lived without leaving a shred of surviving. For they have left no sign of their passage on and from this earth. (1929: 116.)

And so it was his deepest wish and purpose in 1929[32] that he might be able to offer both Oxford and England a close and in depth scholarly treatment of the most attractive religious texts of this same period, in effect, in his planned new syllabus, one making available to all so attracted – a training in the close editing and interpreting of so many as yet ill-presented and early Middle English homiletic texts from his antecedent region, the beloved west of England. For this pondering on the legions of those folk – i.e. the mass of the quietly living and God-fearing people from that region and elsewhere – who, apart from their speech-patterns and thoughts have left no enduring worldly record,[33] is a compassionate and William Langland-echoing phrasing of his love for all men and women who have ever lived *sub specie aeternitatis*.

And so it is to be recognized as a reflective comment on the ordinary English 'folk' and one to embody his perception of them, then living in their customary devout fashion, well away from the disliked Norman influence. Here, too, he might ponder on all those long gone devout souls, who have left so little evidence of their mortal existence – (or is it a scholarly challenge for what had already happened to the Christian Church in England, particularly in the Norman-dominated abbeys in the east and south-east?).

There then follows a somewhat wry but reflective thought as to the common lot of an isolated group of humanity being forgotten by men of political power

---

32 Many of these opinions have been confirmed to me by various religious friends, notably by
   1) Father Edward Booth of Blackfriars in Cambridge, a priest who, long ago, had ministered to Tolkien's farmer brother in the Cotswolds;

   2) Father Thomas Gilbey, the Head of the same house in the 1960s and who propounded like views on his visit to Australasia in the later half of that decade;

   3) Professor David Knowles, historian, of Peterhouse; and, also, by

   4) various other practicing Catholics who were Fellows of Peterhouse, Cambridge, then, and also by

   5) the celibate Anglican cleric, Canon Maycock, of Little St Mary's Parish in Cambridge, and his brother, Hugh, the Head of Pusey House in Oxford in the later 1950s, when the latter would invite Tolkien to give sermon-type addresses on his religious purposes in writing *The Lord of the Rings*.

33 More recent scholarship has been aware of just how much of wise insight is communicated in the *Ancrene Wisse*, as in the interpretation offered by Kari Kalve in her 'A Virtuous Mouth: Reading and Speaking in the *Ancrene Wisse*', in: *Essays in Mediaeval Studies* 14 (1997: 39-49).

and 'business' – but not by God. Tolkien then goes back to the activities of the earlier spiritual guide and sensitive man of letters speaking to us of that same West Midland place and literary mode, and then concluding that –

> The 'dear sisters' are as little likely to have left a record in this world. Their instructor is in more hopeful case [...]. (*ibid.*)

A Cultural – and Georgian – Significance to Tolkien's Essay beyond the Biographical, the Empathetic, and the Religious?

And then, after reflecting on the eschatological content of the early 13th century text, the excited and meticulous language and dialect scholar takes over from the compassionate Catholic scrutiny of the authentic and nuanced manuscript, leaving this resounding and challenging observation on the survival and continuity of a distinguished, consistent, widely respected, and uplifting standard for English prose: one miraculously coming from so far before the advent of printing, it had offered a culture –

> [w]here two different scribes could write a common language in the same spelling, two different authors could conceivably have written under the influence of a common training, reading, and tradition. (*ibid.* 117)

For, indeed, and once again, he was focusing on the like thought of his early mentor and older and devout Roman Catholic friend, R.W. Chambers (1874 –1942),[34] who had, since 1922, been the Quain Professor of English at University College, London. Chambers was then – and is still – deservedly renowned for his

---

34 Chambers had written much about the *Ancrene Wisse* around the time of Tolkien's early work, e.g. in
    1) *The Review of English Studies* 1.1 (1925: 4-23);
    2) in the same journal, vol. 2.5, responding to a reply by Father Vincent McNabb (McNabb and Chambers 1926: 82-89); and
    3) and together with Herbert Thurston in the following issue in reply to some new arguments by Father McNabb (McNabb, Chambers and Thurston 1926: 197-201).
While this matter of the scholarship of a widely accepted style and lexis before the time of print is reported in various places – and so of others discussing it with Tolkien, Tom Shippey has made this point best (2001). Similarly, Douglas A. Anderson has more recently, in 2006, been exploring the relationship between Tolkien and Chambers, especially as indicated in the style of *The Hobbit*, as in a note in *Tolkien Studies* 3 (2006: 142-43).
And see also Sissons, Charles Jasper, and Hilda Winifred Husbands, *Raymond Wilson Chambers, 1874-1942* (1945). Chambers had also linked to this tradition the several non-London versions in English of the finely Christian life of Thomas More, statesman and martyr.

authoritative work on the theme of 'The Continuity of English Prose' (published first in 1932). That was a mediation on the influence of West Saxon prose moving on into Early Middle English, and on the stylistic and cultural consequences of this outreach, and so producing his essays on the same but somewhat further developed (western) style of various records of Sir Thomas More (1927), these helpful texts for their morality also so close to Tolkien's own.

For Chambers had argued, powerfully and impressively, for its distinctive limpid clarity – and one long practiced in the land – as this owing much to the Anglo-Saxon writers of Wessex, and to their highly cultured Christian followers, rather than they being obligated to the Normanised court, to London, or to other seemingly Europe-derived styles of writing, lexis, semantics and (secular) themes.

Ongoing Research Work by Tolkien and his Various Catholic and Largely Women Researchers into these Western Texts

Simonne T.R.O. d'Ardenne[35]

The first such researcher-colleague was the Belgian student, Simonne d'Ardenne, (1908-86), a young woman of an aristocratic Walloon family, who had studied Middle English with Tolkien in the early 1930s, when she first completed a small 'western' project for the B.Litt. training, and been very close to the Tolkien family during the preparation of the edition that constituted her B.Litt. thesis, a work which has always been said to owe much to her supervisor, Tolkien. In due time, this was followed by a larger project, one best described as originally published:

> *An edition of the Liflade and te Passiun of Seinte Iulienne.* Bibliothèque de la Faculté de Philosophie et Lettres de L'Université de Liège 64. Paris: Droz, 1936.

Despite the title, this fine edition also provides a full and detailed study of the language of the *AB* group in general, and not merely of Seinte Julienne. There

---

35 Her full name was Simonne Rosalie Thérèse Odile d'Ardenne. My comments on this scholar and friend to the Tolkien family were written independently of the entry in the *J.R.R. Tolkien Encyclopedia*, ed. Michael D.C. Drout (2007), in which reference work she is discussed briefly on pp. 117-18.

are significant sections on the literary and linguistic setting of all of the *AB* group, and their style and punctuation. The long final section (*ibid.* 177-250) discusses first the general character of the *AB* language, and then it treats of its phonology and of its accidence. In order to obtain a tenured post in her own home university of Liège, she had finally not submitted this, her doctoral thesis[36] to the University of Oxford, but, rather, at her home university in 1936. There she was promoted quickly (in 1938) to a full professorship – of 'comparative grammar', – while an expanded version of the thesis would be issued by the Early English Text Society in 1961.[37] Further, her other work with Tolkien – on St Katherine – would finally be issued by E.J. Dobson in 1981 (*v.infra*), and then later, in her career in Liège, too, she would write many such scholarly pieces as 'The Old English Inscription on the Brussels Cross',[38] a piece of fine research about the holy relic which forms part of the present cross, and explaining intriguingly how it had found its way from Westminster Abbey to the Netherlands, where it had – and has – long been in the treasury of the Church of SS. Michel and Gudde.

In addition to this doctoral thesis done by Simonne D'Ardenne and her own close and long-running association with the Tolkien household (see below), we may first note other evidence of the Oxford professor's continuing concern with this cluster of texts in 'Language *AB*', he being variously listed for :

1) (with S.T.R.O. d'Ardenne) ' "Ipplen" in Sawles Warde', *English Studies* 28.6 (December 1947: 168-70); or,

---

36 Printed in Belgium in 1936, in order to make her eligible for a chair there, it would, finally, appear in England, with a few corrections, in 1961, as 'The Life and the Passion of Saint Juliene', in the E.E.T.S. sequence (Old Series), as volume 248.

37 This then, under the name *The Liflade ant te Passioun of Seinte Iulienne*.

38 This was published in *English Studies* 21 (1939: 14-64). There is an excellent synopsis of her more numerous – and variously Tolkien-linked contributions to Middle English in *Annotated Bibliographies of Old and Middle English Literature: I. The Language of Middle English Literature*, by David Burnley and Matsuji Tajima (1994). See its contents' items for her, as, e.g.:

    1) 'The Devil's Spout' in *Transactions of the Philological Society* 45.1 (1946: 31-55);

    2) 'Smithes in *The Owl and the Nightingale*', *Review of English Studies* 9.33 (1958: 41-43);

    3) on 'Breatewil'- in *Katherine*, 1974;

    4) her edition of the Katherine Group, from Bodley M. 34, [Paris, 1977];

    5) on *Sawles Warde*, in 1978, etc., etc.

After Tolkien's death in 1973, she would continue such work, and offering 'Two Notes on Early Middle English Texts', to *Five Hundred Years of Words and Sounds*, a festschrift for her research-follower, Eric John Dobson, that volume ed. by Douglas Gray and E.G. Stanley (1983: 21-22).

2) (in collaboration with S.T.R.O. d'Ardenne), his 'MS Bodley 34: A Re-collation of a Collation', in *Studia Philologica* 20 (1947-48: 65-72).

Closely linked to her 1930s thesis, further work of Tolkien's includes:

1) his strong support for M. Day's edition, *The English Text of the Ancrene Riwle*, by the Early English Text Society, and published by it as text O.S. No. 225 (in 1952);

2) his succinct but penetrating 'Preface' to *The Ancrene Riwle*, as translated into Modern English by M.B. Salu (1955);

and his own last work on the texts of the group,

3) Tolkien's editing – and, unintended initially, but much delayed into his retirement – completion work for his definitive edition of *Ancrene Wisse: The English Text of the Ancrene Riwle*, as from MS Corpus Christi College, Cambridge 402, it being the volume for the Early English Text Society, No. 249, with an introduction by N.R. Ker (1962).

This last item – like her doctorate itself – was, in some considerable part, a joint production with Tolkien, and they had intended to do much more collaborative editing and interpretation together, but the 1950s pressures from his creative writing after the publication of the *The Lord of the Rings* seems to have precluded that;[39] and yet she continued with texts associated with the Walloon-Germanic contact area, as well as with her *The Katherine Group*, as edited from MS Bodley 34 (1977), and with supplying notes of interpretation in many continental and British academic journals, until the last on the Katherine Group in *Notes and Queries* in 1982.

Interestingly, it is also the case that d'Ardenne had quite early been the initiator of a campaign for an honorary doctorate from her own university for Tolkien, as is variously recorded by Humphrey Carpenter and by several web postings in 2010, these referring to files of the Archives of the University of Liège, the essence of which is the following cluster of facts:

1) D'Ardenne had written to the Faculty of Letters at Liège on 27 May, 1953, proposing a doctorate for Tolkien, this being duly – and unanimously – endorsed by her colleagues there, that degree being conferred on him in person

---

39 There are extant several somewhat embarrassed comments by the professor on his falling behind in this work, and so disappointing his eager Belgian collaborator, this matter referred to Carpenter (1981b), e.g. "[...] I'm also in serious trouble with the Clarendon Press; and with my lost friend Mlle. Simonne d'Ardenne [...]" (114).

on Saturday October 2, 1954, for having established the continuity of English prose from 10th century Anglo-Saxon, while the citation finely said that he is "a man of learning who is also a poet and a charming storyteller." (Vanhecke 2007: 55)

Perhaps the most significant aspect of this oration was that it was the pre-war text, *The Hobbit*, and Tolkien's academic work, that were the case for the degree, and not the vast prose epic which had as yet to have its first volume printed; and

2) D'Ardenne reading, teaching and then perhaps editing into French versions various parts of Tolkien's earlier creative writing.

Much more recently, and from 2005 onwards, entries on web-sites refer to Tolkien-linked items in the University of Liège's archives, viz.: the various much earlier gifts of academic books from Tolkien to d'Ardenne, notably a letter which had been sent to Simonne, with a copy of *The Hobbit* "[w]ith love from all my family & affectionate remembrance from your collaborateur. JRRT" (*ibid.* 52).

Finally it should be mentioned that, in 1975, Simonne herself published a translation of her own of 'Farmer Giles of Ham' with the Association des Romanistes de l'Université de Liège, with a delightful cover illustration by Jacques Liénard on it:[40]

And so to the Teaching about 'Middle-earth' in the 1960s at the University of Liège

In a gently reflective correspondence with the present writer, from c. 1965 to 1969, Professor d'Ardenne had referred to her several 1950s attempts to have Tolkien again visit Liège, but that he had not been able to travel, largely because of his wife's poor health. Simonne had also stated, with a certain quiet pride, that, for many years, she had been teaching at many levels Tolkien's *The Hobbit* and *The Lord of the Rings* to both her mediaeval and literary students, and, indeed, even to community groups in the surrounding and the general

---

40 The illustration by Jacques Liénard is reprinted on p. 284 with the kind permission of the Association des Romanistes de l'Université de Liège.

Cover illustration by Jacques Liénard for the French translation of 'Farmer Giles of Ham', translated by S.T.R.O. d'Ardenne, published by the Association des Romanistes de l'Université de Liège.

Walloon area of Belgium. She wryly observed that there had not been evinced the same interest in the master fantasy writer by the much more ancient and earlier assertively Catholic University, in the west of Belgium, in Leuven.

Mary B. Salu and some other Catholic Research Students from the 1930s and 1940s

As any biographic account of the domestic and family life of J.R.R. Tolkien will make clear, he had long been concerned with the formal studies in English of all young Catholic women in the University, and so, to this end, he had been working very positively, particularly with the Association for the Education of Women, the first institution in Oxford to assist non-collegiate women with their undergraduate and graduate studies there. This long-struggling group had progressed very slowly, it being poorly endowed, and yet remaining remarkably caring of its members, many of whom were practicing Roman Catholics from schools not usually easily sending pupils to or training them for Oxford.

The best known young person in this group – first to study under, and then, later, to lecture beside Tolkien in the Faculty of English – was M. Elaine Griffiths (1909-96), who had matriculated as a Home Student in 1928, then duly started to undertake research under J.R.R. Tolkien. It was she who, as a family friend of the Tolkiens, had read the long unpublished manuscript of *The Hobbit* and, duly, had caused it to reach Sir Stanley Unwin, in a handwritten form, the publisher's young son Rayner then excitedly endorsing the tale, so that Allen & Unwin would publish it, and soon realise that they has a 'classic' on their hands.

And then later, having become a college Tutor in English in 1938, Elaine would move to the more prestigious and demanding University level of official teaching, and would have a long career, lecturing brilliantly for the Faculty of English, as would her older friend from St Anne's College, Dorothy Bednarowska (1915-2003). Both were inspiring lecturers, especially on Dark Age cultural and like mediaeval matters,[41] and held in enormous affection throughout the university.

---

41 Dorothy Bednarowska was long remembered for excellent classes on William Langland, and her help with Middle English for Americans struggling with the few compulsory earlier period texts.

They are but two of the very large numbers of such Catholic students who had not come through the more 'prestigious' women's colleges[42] in the between-the-wars period.

And so to the Tolkien-influenced supervision of her research from 1940, and, in due course, his ongoing contribution to the career of Sister Mary B. Salu of Lady Margaret Hall at the University of Oxford. Apart from assisting her research work, he would support her preparation of a fine – and now standard – translation of the *Ancrene Wisse*,[43] as well as arranging that it would become a set resource text for 'English' mediaevalists within the university.[44]

It may now be appropriate to quote Tolkien's summarising – but strong and authoritative – 'Preface' to this same volume:

> For her new translation Miss Salu has chosen the version which names itself *Ancrene Wisse*, or "Guide of Anchoresses". It is one of the oldest, possibly the oldest, surviving copy so far as the date of actual writing goes; though it is not original, and presents a form that already shows the processes of editing and expansion to which this Rule, destined for a long popularity, seems at once to have been subjected. It is, however, for a translator probably the best text to use, since it was made by a scribe who not only wrote a beautiful and lucid hand but seems also to have been perfectly at home with the language (the spelling, the grammar and the vocabulary) with which he was dealing.[45]

---

42 For the Oxford system was one of College posts first – these not appointed by the University or the relevant Faculty – and then, if one was lucky, a like post at the University. However, the professor would not 'head a department' or control the appointment of academic staff as has been the norm worldwide since the passing of that customary Oxbridge style or college phase of organizing the face to face teaching and tutoring of disciplines.
    Thus it was that many of this group owed their slow but steady academic progression to his encouragement and courtesy, and to a fine concept of equity and the burning desire to remove this long lingering discrimination.
    Significantly, his air-raid-precautions work in World War II was at St Hugh's College, a 'middle range' women's society.

43 This was published by the religious publishers Burns and Oates in 1955, and also by the University of Notre Dame Press, Notre Dame. The English edition had affixed a 'Nihil Obstat' from Westminster, i.e. the Roman Catholic Archdiocese – as was, incidentally, the case for most of the books of the Tolkien friend, Christopher Dawson's work. This body of text is discussed in my *Tolkien's View* (2009).
    In due course, the translation would have many reprints in both the United Kingdom and the United States of America. Later facsimiles have come from the University of Exeter Press. Quotations from this text are from the 1990 edition.

44 See the appendix at the end of this essay.

45 This situation would suggest that there was a widely respected standard there – a situation almost unique in Middle English, or later, in the centuries prior to the printing press.

This language now appears archaic, almost "semi-saxon" as the term once was, after nearly seven and a half centuries; and it is also "dialectal" to us whose language is based mainly on the speech of the other side of England, whereas the soil in which it grew was that of the West Midlands and the Marches of Wales. But it was in its day and to its users a natural, easy, and cultivated speech, familiar with the courtesy of letters, able to combine colloquial liveliness with a reverence for the already long tradition of English writing. It has been the endeavour of the translator to represent this in modern terms: a difficult task, which Miss Salu fitted by long familiarity with this text and research into peculiarities of its idiom, has carried out with great success. (Salu 1990: vi)

The Actual Faculty of English in Oxford's Use of this Version of the Text

Because of the translator's then lesser 'status', it was not possible for her to give lectures on this text, these for several years being assigned to the Master of St Benet's Hall, Dom Gerard Sitwell who had contributed to the volume – pp. vii-xxii, and also pp. 193-96. Tolkien would himself attend in the smaller lecturing room for at least one of these offerings of the book version in Modern English.[46]

* * *

Mary Salu would long remain a family friend, and would also, in due course, become the co-editor with Robert T. Farrell of the posthumously issued *J.R.R. Tolkien: Scholar and Story-teller: Essays in Memoriam* (1979), at the same time as she had published/edited the finely sympathetic volume, *Essays on 'Troilus and Criseyde'* (1979).[47] As indicated, she had been well known to Tolkien as a researcher in the Faculty, even as he would ensure that her work on the text was recommended – or effectively set – for Courses I and II in English.[48]

---

46 The present writer had attended such a series in either 1955 or 1956, with the excited Tolkien present in the largely clerical and Roman Catholic orders' audience.

47 The text would be printed again in 1991 and in 2007.

48 This is indicated in the Lecture Lists as printed in the *University of Oxford Gazette* for several years after 1955. The lecturer was usually Dom Gerard Sitwell, OSB, long time (1947 to 1959) the Master of St Benet's Hall, Oxford, and a friend to Tolkien for much of his life. Dom Sitwell (1906-93) had lectured for a number of years in the English School, at the University of Oxford, being also long and deservedly remembered for his classes on the spiritual classic, Walter Hilton's *Scale of Perfection*. See the subtle obituary for him in the *London Times* for Dec. 21, 1993 (15).

And so, after many years of mutual friendship and respect, in due course, she had suggested the compilation of a volume of tributary essays to Tolkien, herself playing a significant part in the assembling of these same essays. And, like her mentor, she would long continue to be fascinated with the developing and/or persisting 'traditional' manner, or English preferred (traditional) stylistics, as, for example, in her work as co-author of the shrewdly perceptive *Attitudes to English Usage* (Mittins *et al.* 1970).[49]

Again, however – Simonne d'Ardenne (1908-86)

Culturally speaking, the voice that most significantly recalls the distinctive – and distinguished – student following that Tolkien had obtained for a research focus on these remarkable religious texts is, rightly, that of Simonne d'Ardenne. And so, from the University of Liège, in 1977 she contributed to the same commemorative volume the insightful opening essay, 'The Man and the Scholar' (Salu and Farrell 1979: 33-37), a fine piece which stresses eloquently the welcome that she had always had from the Tolkien household. She also refers with charm to the family man and the warmth of his home in the later 1920s and 1930s, that family being particularly accepting of her as a foreign research student in Middle English and a fellow Roman Catholic.

And so to – Eric John Dobson (1913-84)

This impressive scholar,[50] also a Roman Catholic, and born in Sydney, New South Wales, had obtained a University–topping degree through the English

---

49 See the helpful review of the same book, and comments on her excellent ear for significant and historically nuanced tones, as is discussed in *The Modern Language Journal* 55.4 (Povey 1971: 253). Of like significance for its freshness and the probing of deeper meanings, see also her edited *Essays on Troilus and Criseyde*, 1979 and 1991, both published by Boydell and Brewer.

50 A very fine obituary for him was contributed to the *Proceedings of the British Academy* 71 (1985: 533-38), by Professor Douglas Gray, by then his much younger colleague, and himself a late student under Tolkien. The first of his, Dobson's Colleges, Merton, had been particularly welcoming throughout the twentieth century to Pacific-nurtured students of English language – to Australians like G.A. Wilkes and R. Bruce Mitchell; or to New Zealanders such as Kenneth Sisam, Norman Davis (Tolkien's successor in the Merton chair), and to the same just cited Douglas Gray, he to become the first 'Tolkien Professor' in the University (see also above, as well as the *curriculum vitae* for him in the *Merton College Register II, 1891-1989* (1990: 84)).

School, with First Class Honours (through Merton) in Course II of English 1937, to become a prestigious Senior Scholar there from 1938, and then a lecturer at Reading University; returning to Merton, after war service, to complete his D.Phil. in 1951. He then achieved a meteoric career elsewhere in Oxford – to earn the title of Professor in 1961, and be the Professor of English Language from 1964-80.[51] Apart from his outstanding work in phonetics and philological circles,[52] he had produced a steady stream of definitive research related to the *AW* group of texts, notably:

1962 his festschrift piece for one of his most significant mentors, 'The Affiliations of the MSS of the *Ancrene Wisse*', in *English and Mediaeval Studies Presented to J.R.R. Tolkien* (128-63);

1966 'The Date and Composition of the *Ancrene Wisse*', Gollancz lecture to the British Academy. See the *Proceedings of the British Academy* 52 (1967: 181-208);

1972 *The English Text of the Ancrene Riwle: Edited from B.M. Cotton MS. Cleopatra C.vi, for the Early English Text Society.* – This work has a 173-pages long 'Introduction' containing extended discussions of the dialectal forms and spellings used by the three scribes of the MS., and making many pertinent comments on the scribal and spoken influences in the mss.;

1974 'Two Notes on Early Middle English Texts [i.e. in the *AW*]' in *Notes and Queries* 21.4, (1974: 124-26);

1975 *Moralities on the Gospels - A New Source of 'Ancrene Wisse'*;

1976 *The Origins of the Ancrene Wisse* – The third chapter of this work is taken up with the dialectal location of the *AB* language, of MSS CCCC402 of Ancrene Wisse and Bodley 34 of the Katherine Group, this analysis leading him to the conclusion that *AW* and its group were written in northern Herefordshire or southern Shropshire, and, more specifically, at Wigmore Abbey (this ascription has since been deemed to be 'too precise');

1979 (in collaboration with F.L. Harrison), *Mediaeval English Songs*;

1981 *Seinte Katerine* (an E.E.T.S. edition, in collaboration with Professor S. d'Ardenne of Liège);

– while he was still engaged on a critical edition of the *Ancrene Wisse* when he died.

---

51 In many ways, he was the closest successor to Tolkien's own scholarly work on hitherto more simplistically treated texts in this influential field of the Western homilies of Early Middle English, – this identification being now made despite the period of Neville Coghill with such a title, as well as another New Zealander, Norman Davis following the master in Tolkien's second Oxford chair.

52 He, too, was prominent in and generously serving (inter-)nationally the Philological Society, as had been Tolkien, and Harold Bailey – see the 'Prequel' to this present book, ie. pp. 15, 18 and 19.

In 1983, he had received a Festschrift for his seventieth birthday, a volume entitled *Five Hundred Years of Words and Sounds*, and it is more than appropriate
to quote here Douglas Gray's last comment in the volume on the recipient's
distinguished and hugely focused career –

> his work on the manuscripts of the *Ancrene Wisse* had [...] made him expert in
> the craft of editing but also deeply interested in the theory of textual criticism.
> (Gray and Stanley 1983: 536)

– this last a comment that was, – and is, – even more true of his inspirational
mentor.

*   *   *

However, for the purposes of my general argument about this text, Tolkien's
insights concerning it, and Dobson's most subtle and nuanced insights into the
Ancrene Wisse are to be found in his 1966-presented essay to the British Academy,
some twenty-eight pages of closely reasoned argument about the style, date,
and significance of the text. While we do not know if Tolkien was present for
this address, he would certainly have read the address and savoured hugely the
numerous subtle insights, from which these precise phrases may be selected:

> the language was a [...] cultivated literary one (182);

> Christ, like a noble wooer, '[...] showed through knightliness that he was worthy
> of [his followers'] love' (184);

> [Dom Gerard Sitwell] remarks on certain features of the devotions prescribed
> for the anchoresses, especially the comparative modernity of the purely private
> devotions (187);

> the interest in penance and confession [indicates the period of composition as]
> between 1215 and 1222 (192);

> *Ancrene Wisse* is a most carefully and explicitly planned work. [...] Despite the
> liveliness of the style and the ease with which the transitions are managed,
> *Ancrene Wisse* is from first to last an ordered book, conceived and written as
> a unity. (193);

and

> the whole process [of writing] must fall within a comparatively short span of
> years (203).

An Interlude – Tolkien's Tastes in Lecturing from circa 1954 until his Retirement

As a perspective comment on his lecturing style and manifest enthusiasms within the Faculty of English, – and this was written some time after leaving Oxford, – my own earlier reflective observation – in 1969 – may have a certain relevance here:

> It is perhaps fair to state that Ronald Tolkien's greater interest as a lecturer [as far as I could see] was in Middle English, rather than Old English.[53] The early period offered a limited corpus of verse – less than 10,000 lines actually survive – and the society was Christian and heroic but in many ways strangely pagan, harking back to that quiet lull before the dawn which conversion to Christianity brought. Whereas the later period gave him a vast body of material [over which to range] [...]. (Ryan 1969: 21)[54]

Then, too, the syllabus texts that he handled when occupying the Merton Chair were virtually all Christian ones and thus it was possible to probe or glance at the religious texts and faith of the nation in earlier times, as well as the cultural purpose of writers on spiritual issues much more than possible with the largely 'heroic' texts from Old English poetry. Indeed, his lecturing became more reflective and serious to the point of being muted, deeply moral and eschatological, as the years progressed, with so much less of the early performance style commented on by W.H. Auden, when famously recalling the mid-1920s style of the young professor.

---

53 For he did give the odd lecture here, as I discussed in my long article of 2002, 'J.R.R. Tolkien's Formal Lecturing and Teaching at the University of Oxford, 1925-1959' in *Seven* 19 (45-62).

54 This much earlier book of mine was published by the University of New England, Armidale, New South Wales, and then released in North America and elsewhere through the (1960s-1970s) University of New England Reprints Series.

　Another aspect of his early and ongoing interest in Norse and Middle English was his catalyzing and founder membership of the General Editorial Board of the Oxford English Monographs, before and after World War II, while he was still in the Anglo-Saxon professorship.

　These volumes included, amongst others:

　　1) an edition of *Víga-Glums Saga*, ed. by G. Turville-Petre in 1940;

　　2) *Elizabethan Acting*, by B.L. Joseph, in 1951; and

　　3) *The Peterborough Chronicle, 1070-1154*, ed. by Cecily Clarke, in 1958; etc. etc.

But – an Occasional Form of Zestful – and Neo-mediaeval Escape?

It is also interesting that, as Sub-Warden of Merton College in the 1950s, he was more than glad to go with the College Bursars on official visits of inspection to the College's Estates in various southern and eastern counties, Lincolnshire being so toured by him. On one occasion when the present writer had suggested that such travel might perhaps be exhausting, he had quickly denied this, exclaiming that he really enjoyed the various farms, especially for the chance to again 'see the pigs'.[55] It was also the case that he would take the opportunity when so touring in East Anglia, to visit Peterhouse in Cambridge as Merton's brother institution, and many senior fellows of the Cambridge institution had colourful tales and recollections of his visits and enunciated opinions on so many mediaeval and doctrinal matters.[56]

Tolkien's Fascination with the Spiritual Lives of English Women under Monasticism – and with the Roman Catholic Orders in the University of Oxford

In the most recent account of Tolkien and the *Ancrene Wisse* – that by Arne Zettersten[57] to be found in the *J.R.R. Tolkien Encyclopedia* (2007: 15-17), as edited by Michael D.C. Drout – there is some reference to the heroic efforts of the Professor and others to edit the many manuscripts of the *Ancrene Riwle*, rather than giving stronger emphasis to the charm of the whole, its freshness, and the warm justification of the chosen life of anchoresses.

Accordingly, one must now re-stress the thrust of the core chapters, those concerned with the Inner Rule, viz.:

> 2) protecting the Heart through the Senses – this really concerned with Christian ethics;

---

55 Some of this love may well have come from the farming activities of his brother Hilary, and Hilary's son, especially in the Cotswolds area. (Information supplied to me by Fr. Booth, O.P., of Blackfriars, Cambridge, who had served in a parish in some proximity to Tolkien's brother and his family).

56 My informants here include the theological and history disciplines' Fellows of Peterhouse, notably Master Herbert Butterfield and Professor David Knowles, O.P. who wrote the 'Introduction' to Ælred of Rievaulx, *Treatises & Pastoral Prayer* (1971).

57 See also his *Middle English Word Studies* (1964).

3) birds and Anchorites; the Inner Feelings – much of this derived from the Psalms, notably 101; significantly there are echoes of those passages concerned with 'the path' – presumably for all men and women;

4) the various Temptations and the Comforts, and Remedies for the same, with a particular concern for lethargy or 'sloth' – is largely centred on the lapsing of personal morals; while

5) confession and 6) penance are both straightforward in their content; and

7) 'The Pure Heart and the Love of Christ' – explains the process of 'exchange' [58] operating between the two, so that there is a continual flow, this embodying the attainment of grace, the whole process presented in a most engaging fashion, the steps for mediaeval folk to take to practice and so to the obtain of a true state of Christian Spirituality.

Distinct Cautiousness in Readers of the Tolkien Stories, despite their Coming from a deeply Religious and Traditional Roman Catholic

It is perhaps of significance to readers that such doctrinal matters as touched on above, and his public reflections in answer to eager questions, had been the focus of Tolkien's explications – nominally on *The Lord of the Rings* – as given during his lecture-seminars to devout Christian groups, as at Pusey House in Oxford in the later 1950s.

The Complex Matter of Tolkien, the (likely) Translating of 'The Book of Job', and 'The Book of Jonah' as in *The Jerusalem Bible* [59]

For those seeking evidence of the writer's thoughts and opinions, it is eminently clear that there are many clues as to the mind and spirit of J.R.R. Tolkien beyond his creative writings, his scholarly editions, as, for example, in the textual notes

---

58 This was a key critical term used amongst the Inklings in Oxford, Charles Williams and C.S. Lewis were writing much about this process, whereas Tolkien illustrated it rather in reciprocity of action.

59 This section of my present book is written late in 2010, with an awareness of the confusions of 2009-10, as to whether this Bible's 'The Book of Job' would be published as a separate 'Tolkien' book, and at the time of a process of advertising its likely appearance and cover, followed by its sudden withdrawal from the impending list of Tolkien's further, new, or re-edited, and other publications.

and phrasings[60] as originally supplied by him, but seemingly modified prior to publication to *The Jerusalem Bible.*

There are now quoted some of my earlier (published) comments on some of his associations with *The Jerusalem Bible* text then, as we note that the principal collaborators of the work had included J.R.R. Tolkien and his Dominican friend, Kenelm Foster, O.P. The whole project was intended as an authoritative translation into current English, made from Greek and Hebrew texts, in a style neither overly traditional nor self-consciously modernistic. Tolkien's responsibility was both 'Jonah' and, it is believed,[61] some portion of the 'Introduction to Job' (Jones 1968: 726-28), and perhaps an oversight of *Job* itself (*ibid.* 729-78). Much of that was verse and speeches, all in poetry – firstly, the long dialogue poem between four voices, then the hymn in praise of wisdom, the conclusion of the dialogue, then the speeches of Elihu, and, finally, the speeches of Yahweh.

And so to 'The Book Of Job', as Published in *The Jerusalem Bible.*

The framework is prose, where, as it is believed, Tolkien had observed, "in this prose narrative the author has preserved the flavour of a folk tale" (*ibid.* 729).

Although it may seem a little subjective – to relate the form of words used by the translator to his own glosses on other (mediaeval) texts and to his creative writing – the following quotations would clearly indicate Tolkien's or a like fascination with religious traditions and the spiritual experiences and so inheritance apt to be bound up with such texts. Thus they may well give some clue

---

60 There are now quoted above my own remarks on the matter of Tolkien and *Job*, as taken from my *Tolkien: Cult or Culture?* (1969: 25-26), comments that I had 'run past' various Roman Catholic and/or Church of England figures in those Oxford circles in 1968.

61 This matter of Tolkien and his contribution to *Job* has never been clarified satisfactorily, but it was also reported as fact to the Tolkien Society, and so recorded in their bulletin, *Amon Hen* 26 (Kemball-Cook 1977: 12) – namely that they had been told by the publisher, Darton, Long, and Todd, that Tolkien had worked on the 'Book of Job', providing its initial draft and playing an important part in establishing its final text.
The same information was given to me variously in 1967-68 when in Oxford, and so I followed this view – and am now paraphrasing it – a general glossing which is hard and perhaps impossible now to substantiate fully.

as to the ways in which Tolkien was thinking in the later 1960s and had then handled the literary and theological aspects of his allotted task.[62] And so we may note here the following sequential excerpts from the text, its translation respectively, as originally cited or slightly modified by me in the later 1960s:

> The Book of Job is the literary masterpiece of the wisdom movement [...] After this introduction the long dialogue poem begins which constitutes the body of the book [...] In a series of three speeches Job and his friends oppose their different conceptions of divine justice [...] All three, however, defend the traditional thesis of retribution on earth [...] Job confronts this theorizing with his own sad experience and with the universal experience of injustice. He comes back to this repeatedly, and as repeatedly is brought against the mystery of a God of justice who makes the good man suffer [...].
>
> Job was traditionally regarded as a model of virtue, whose loyalty to God remained unshaken despite grievous trials. Our author has used this old story as the framework of his book.
>
> The author of Job is known to us only from his work [...] His date is conjectural. The prose narrative smacks of patriarchal times [...] and even here, traditional sources or literary imitation may explain the style. The book is later than Jeremaiah [...] and its language has a strong Aramaic flavour. We are therefore in post-exile times when absorption in the destiny of the nation as a whole was giving way to interest in the individual.
>
> The writer puts the case of the good man who suffers. This is a paradox for the conservative view then prevalent that a man's actions are rewarded or punished here on earth [...] Job protests against (the) rigorous theory of cause and effect with the vigour of conscious innocence. He does not deny the principle of earthly recompense, indeed, he lives in hope of it, and God gives it in the end [...] But the recompense is, here and now, withheld; this is Job's problem and he seeks in vain for the meaning of it all.
>
> [...] When God does appear it is to tell him how inscrutable are his person and his designs, and Job falls to silence. This is the book's lesson: faith must remain even when understanding fails. At this stage of divine revelation, the author could go no further. More light cannot be thrown on the mystery of suffering innocence until God opens up the prospect of a future life in which recompense is made, and until man learns the worth of suffering when it is united with the suffering of Christ. (Ryan 1969: 726-28)

---

62 The extracts following here, are largely as they were published in my *Tolkien: Cult or Culture?* (1969: 26-27).

Some Later Personal Reflections on Tolkien, his Life as it was Lived, and its Religious Core

The various sections patterned in this long and reflective essay are concerned to treat – and in some degree of hindsight – of a topic largely eschewed by critics and interpreters of the ever-increasing bulk of the opera of J.R.R. Tolkien. All of these matters illuminate, as they should, his full awareness of the original Catholic Christianity of England and of the practice of such a Saviour-remembering compassion in his own daily life and work. These were the qualities of the man behind the shy scholar whom few of his students saw at close range, or pondered very much on the real life of witness as lived so privately by their inspired lecturer.

Clearly in both the academic life and in his accompanying writings and the daily round, he was responsible for a new awareness of the sacredness of the person and of the imminence of the supernatural, as, concurrently, as he worked through his numerous books[63] in order to validate a possible literary and spiritual withdrawal from the so deeply flawed surrounding society. This was ever of an heroic sort, and one which has proved more durable than those contemporary movements of both nihilism and of anger. His stress was always on the individual, his responsibilities to others and his ultimate destiny, as well as on his service to his fellows, rather than the postwar adulation of the intellect, of the organization man or the technocrat. For John Ronald was concerned with the truths to be found in the traditional atmosphere of England and in the transmitted-through-story experience and so with the awesome heritage of the race.

In short, so much of the life he lived in Oxford with his family and his students and his colleagues was a triumphant vindication of non-naturalism, as well as a luminous re-statement of an order which maintains the whole universe, even as it represents Man's task as a Christian. His own Christian and Roman-Catholic stance gave him imaginative concepts as to the nature of myth and history, a

---

63 For we now know, by reason of Christopher Tolkien's efforts in publishing so much, that, even in the 1920s, there were innumerable discovered and intuited tales, legends and retellings in his mind as a totally obsessed philologist, and so compulsive 'maker' of story.

joy and ecstasy in living, an awareness of the epic and the heroic really possible in the life of Everyman and Everywoman.

For it is now ever clearer to this present writer that the life that Tolkien lived out in the daily round was a form of Christian witness ever more difficult for a Roman Catholic in England in post-Reformation times, let alone in the largely secular Oxford of the 20th century. He resented and defied so many societal changes in his own lifetime and set his back on much that was accepted and practiced in his own time. And we know all too well now that he had good reason for all his fables of burden-carrying, and selfless religious philosophies – as enshrined so memorably in his life and work as a Christian 'Maker'.

Appendix 1: The Rise of the Truly Mediaeval Course II in the Faculty of English, University of Oxford and its Style as Shaped by Professor J.R.R. Tolkien

While this has been referred to above, it is clear that the Tolkien and C.S. Lewis-inspired early 1930s reforms to the syllabus for the Final Honours School to a much more exciting focus on 'provenance' and genre and so on the traditional 'culture'/'body of story' in the best sense, as they had both savoured from their early nurture in the ancient classics. This freshly-shaped syllabus, and humane and richer cultural core to the studies of the earlier periods, had transformed the Faculty's work after the Old English period from a study of sounds – hitherto phonetic and palaeographic matters, and perhaps excessive grammar and the like[64] – to a depth study of a number of Western European languages, their literatures and their cultures, all usually sympathetically integrated.

Thus they, together with the Scottish Professor Nichol Smith,[65] had effectively welcomed the grand themes and methods as earlier presented in the *Literae Humaniores* courses and in the Taylorian Institute for Modern Languages to occupy a significant and interactive place in the English Faculty. This was, quite

---

64 One may well note here the earnest tomes from his Merton predecssor, H.C. Wyld, as contrasted with the thoughts of Merton's Tolkien-inspiring and very language-focussed Professor George Gordon – the latter is so interpreted for his influence on Tolkien in Leeds and Oxford in my *Tolkien's View* (2009: 61-70).

65 He, too, was one of the editors of the focused, incisive, fresh and 'manageable' theme scholarship of the Oxford English Monographs. See fn. 51 above.

simply, the beliefs, the writings, and indeed the 'high culture' of the mediaeval and profoundly Christian periods, as well as allowing a place for the like ages' recorded folk culture, through the prominent place already regularly given to ballad and to 'story'.[66]

To show this refreshed 'Course II' in its developed form, there is now appended, for illustration of this, the pattern of normal papers for the various clusters – following the rubrics in the University of Oxford Examination Statutes as revised to the end of Trinity Term 1968 (i.e. to the end of the 1967-68 academic year, for it had survived that long and beyond):

> Course I. Largely Dark Ages, with emphasis on Old and Middle English, 9 papers in all; while
>
> Course III, also had 9 papers. This largest undergraduate aspect of the School was really for 'literary' students', with earlier periods' texts serving as a somewhat skeletal background.

The distinctively Tolkien and Lewis-thrust – and long their ongoing creation – was

> the much enriched Course II in the School of English (as all such, a selection of 9 papers), with the following ones now compulsory –
>
> A 1. Old English Philology
>
> A 2. Middle English Philology
>
> A 3. Modern English Philology
>
> B 1. Old English Texts
>
> B 3. Middle English Texts
>
> B 5. Chaucer and his Contemporaries
>
> B 6. Shakespeare – special study of 2 plays, both with large cultural debts to an earlier society.
>
> B 7. English literature, only coming down to pre-1550, if so wished.
>
> There was also to be one paper chosen from Old English Literature; Middle English Literature; Old Norse; Old French; Mediaeval Welsh; and Spenser and Milton.

---

66 As a single example here, one may cite the innumerable folk-type researches by the prolific story-teller, if less well-known, Inkling and long-time Mertonian, Roger Lancelyn Green (1918-87). The latter's most memorable work is his fine B.Litt. thesis on Andrew Lang and story – personally supervised by Tolkien and published in 1946. Tolkien also much savoured Green's history of the Lancelyn family in Poulton (1948).
Other works by Green include *Tales from Shakespeare* (2 vols., 1964, 1965a); *A Book of Myths* (1965b); *The Tale of Ancient Israel* (1969); or in collaboration with Walter Hooper, *C.S. Lewis: A Biography* (1974). See also the following references to him in Carpenter (1978: 223, 230, 239f and 247f).

Clearly this could and should be seen as a Pre-Reformation Course, peculiarly focused on the reflective experience, spirituality and understanding of earlier religious ages, and one therefore savoured by many High Anglicans and/or Roman Catholic men and women,[67] not least by those in – or training for – Holy Orders, especially in the years before Vatican II. Certainly there were still many such students in these classes in both the 1950s and 1960s.

Without being in any sense formally conducted for adherents of the Catholic Church, the classes, open to all in the university, were so often focused on the more Christian times in England, the texts full of helpful homilies, and – especially in the case of the *AB* texts – centred on healing, forgiveness and a renewed dedication of the person to the service of one's God.

The potential or actual Catholic religious, if matriculated, were able to attend the University lectures in the Examination Schools, in the High Street, usually the women religious being accompanied by another of their order.

The smaller denomination-based Colleges and Halls from which many came were indeed affiliated to the University, but often located somewhat on the perimeter of the University buildings for the Arts and Social Sciences, these normally located in or about the centre of the University – and so of the city.

Thus the Course focused on above may be said to have given a strongly Catholic – if ecumenical – aspect to the undergraduate teaching of the Faculty of English during Tolkien's years as a professor, 1924-59.

---

67 Many, like Tolkien's eldest son, would duly proceed from such university training in Oxford, to teach in intellectually prestigious Church Schools, much as John Tolkien did later, at Ampleforth College, a Benedictine College-School in North Yorkshire (more recently that institution has become co-educational).
   There would also be the smattering of Course II students from the Continent, almost all of them graduates already. S.T.R.O. d'Ardenne and others would seem thus to be part of a fruitful source of recruitment for the English School, undergraduate and graduate, which Tolkien very much supported.

Appendix 2: And the Roman Catholic Presence / Orders in the University City and the Non-Collegiate Women

References in the Roman Catholic periodical, *The Month*, in *Time and Tide* in 1954, and elsewhere – as also in *The Chestertonian* – confirm Tolkien's association and sympathetic contact with such Roman Catholic Oxford religious, as at

Campion Hall, the Masters there and so involved being

> Martin D'Arcy, 1933;[68]
> Thomas Corbishley, 1945;
> Anthony Denis Doyle, 1958;
> Father Deryck Hanshell, 1962;
> Edward John Yarnold, 1965;
> Benjamin Winterborn, 1972;

St Benet's Hall

> Francis Gerard Sitwell 1947;
> Cyril Louis James Forbes 1964.

Other individual heads of women's groups of Catholic significance known to Tolkien included, as mentioned, the more modest grouping namely

St Anne's – a non-denominational Women's Society till 1960, when it became a College, it was still nominally secular – the Principals of his time, there then, now given as commencing office, were

> The Hon. Elenor Mary Plummer, 1940;
> Lady Mary Helen Ogilvie, 1953;
> Nancy Kathleen Trenaman, 1966f.

---

68 Fr. Martin Cyril D'Arcy (1889-1978), priest, writer and literary friend to Evelyn Waugh, Dorothy Sayers and J.R.R. Tolkien. He was the Provincial of the English Province of the Society of Jesus from the 1930s until his death and perhaps England's foremost Catholic public intellectual from the 1930s until his death. While at Princeton he participated in public discussion of the Tolkien Corpus. However, it is his friendship with academics and writers that is the hallmark of his mastership, as many have stressed. Particularly notable here is his *The Mind and Heart of Love, Lion and Unicorn* (1945), a text published by T.S. Eliot at Faber and Faber. See Harp (2009), and Sire (1997).

ADAM, Lucien, 1874, 'Une Genèse Vogoule', In: *La Revue philologique et d'ethnographie* 1 (1874), 9-14.

ADAMS, Robert M., 1960, 'The Origins of Cities', In: *Scientific American* 203.3 (1960), 153-68.

AELRED OF RIEVAULX, 1971, *Treatises & Pastoral Prayer*, ed. by Dom. David Knowles, transl. by Sister Penelope, Kalamazoo, MI: Cistercian Publications.

ALEXANDER, Henry, 1912, *The Place-names of Oxfordshire: Their Origin and Development*, Oxford: Henry Frowde.

ALLAN, Jim, 1978, *An Introduction to Elvish*, Hayes: Bran's Heath Ltd.

ANDERSON, Douglas A., 2006, 'R.W. Chambers and 'The Hobbit'', In: *Tolkien Studies, An Annual Scholarly Review* 3 (2006), 137-147.

ANDERSON, R.B., 1891, *Norse Mythology: Or The Religion of Our Forefathers Containing All the Myths of the Eddas Systemized and Interpreted with an Introduction, Vocabulary and Index*, Chicago: S.C. Griggs & Co.

ANDRAE, Walter, 1936, 'The Story of Uruk', In: *Antiquity* 10.38 (1936), 133-45.

ANTONACCIO, Carla Maria, 1955, *An Archaeology of Ancestors: Tomb Cult and Hero Cult in Early Greece*, London: Rowman & Littlefield.

ARIOSTO, Ludovico, 1974, *Orlando Furioso, A New Prose Translation by Guido Waldman*, Oxford: Oxford University Press.

ATTENBOROUGH, Frederick Levi (ed.), 1922, *The Laws of the Earliest English Kings*, Cambridge, Cambridge University Press.

AUDEN, John Ernest, 1912, *Little Guide to Shropshire*, London: Methuen & Co Ltd.

AUDEN, W.H., 1937, *Letters from Iceland*, London: Faber and Faber.

1954a, 'The Hero Is a Hobbit: A Review of 'The Fellowship of the Ring' by J.R.R. Tolkien', In: *New York Times*, 31 October 1954, 37.

1954b, 'A World Imaginary, but Real: A Review of 'The Fellowship of the Ring' by J.R.R. Tolkien', In: *Encounter* 3 (November 1954), 59-62.

1961, 'The Quest Hero', In: *Texas Quarterly* 4 (1961), 81-93.

1963, *The Dyer's Hand and Other Essays*, London: Faber and Faber.

1967, 'Good and Evil in *The Lord of the Rings*', In: *The Tolkien Journal* 3.1 (1967), 5-8.

1968, *Secondary Worlds: The T.S. Eliot Memorial Lectures Delivered at Eliot College in the University of Kent at Canterbury, October 1967*, London: Faber and Faber.

1970, *A Certain World: A Commonplace Book*, New York: Viking Press.

1988, *Paid on Both Sides*, In: Edward Mendelson and Christopher Isherwood (eds.), 1988, *The Complete Works of W.H. Auden. Plays and Other Dramatic Writings, 1928-1938*, Princeton, New Jersey: Princeton University Press, 3-34.

AUDEN, W.H. and Paul B. TAYLOR, 1969, *The Elder Edda, A Selection, translated from the Icelandic*, London: Faber.

1981, *Norse Poems*, London: Athlone Press.

AUSTIN, D. and Thomas, J., 1990, 'The 'Proper Study' of Medieval Archaeology: A Case Study', In: D. Austin and L. Alcock (eds.), 1990, *From the Baltic to the Black Sea: Studies in Medieval Archaeology*, London: Routledge, 43-78.

BAILEY, H. W. and Alan S.C. Ross, 1961, 'Path', In: *Transactions of the Philological Society* 60.1 (November 1961), 107-142.

BAKER, Ernest Albert and Herbert E. BALCH, 1907, *The Netherworld of Mendip: Explorations in the Great Caverns of Somerset, Yorkshire, Derbyshire and Elsewhere*, Kent: Baker/Simpkins, Marshall, Hamilton.

BALCH, Herbert E., 1926, *The Caves of Mendip*, London: Folk Press.

BARFIELD, Owen, 1926, *History in English Words*, London: Methuen & Co. Ltd.

BARING-GOULD, Sabine, 1865, *The Book of Were-Wolves: Being an Account of a Terrible Superstition*, London: Smith, Elder and Co.

BARKER, Ernest, 1947, *The Character of England*, Oxford: Clarendon Press.

BARKER, Philip, Roger H. WHITE, Kate PRETTY and M. CORBISHLEY, 1997, *The Baths Basilica Wroxeter: Excavations 1966-1990*, English Heritage Report 8, London: English Heritage.

BARNEY, Stephen A., 1977, *Word-Hoard: An Introduction to Old English Vocabulary*, New Haven: Yale University Press.

BARRON, W.R.J. (ed.), 1974, *Sir Gawain and the Green Knight*, Manchester: Manchester University Press.

BARROWMAN, Rachel C., Colleen E. BATEY, and Christopher D. MORRIS, 2007, *Excavations at Tintagel Castle, Cornwall: 1900-1999*, London: Society of Antiquaries of London.

BARTHOLOMEW, John G. 1972. *Gazetteer of the British Isles*, Edinburgh: J. Bartholomew & Son Ltd.

BASSETT, S.R. 1989, 'Churches in Worcester Before and After the Conversion of the Anglo-Saxons', In: *The Antiquaries Journal* 69 (1989), 225-56.

BATHURST, William Hiley, 1879, *Roman Antiquities at Lydney Park, Gloucestershire: Being a Posthumous Work of the Rev. William Hiley Bathurst, M. A.*, (with Notes by C.W. King), London: Longmans, Green and Co.

BAUGH, Albert C. (ed.), 1948, *A Literary History of England*, London: Routledge & Kegan Paul.

1956, *The English Text of the Ancrene Riwle, British Museum MS Royal 8 C.i*, Early English Text Society 232, London: Oxford University Press.

BECKER, Alida (ed.), 1978, *The Tolkien Scrapbook*, New York: Grosset, Dunlap.

BENNETT, J.A.W. and Douglas GRAY, 1986, *Middle English Literature*, edited and completed by Douglas Gray, Oxford: Clarendon Press.

BESSINGER, Jess B., 1960, *A Short Dictionary of Anglo-Saxon Poetry*, Toronto: University Press.

BESTER, Alfred, 1980, *Golem 100*, New York: Simon & Schuster.

BETHURUM, Dorothy, 1935, 'The Connection of the Katherine Group with Old English Prose', In: *Journal of English and Germanic Philology* 34 (1935), 553-64.

BINYON, Laurence,1928, *Episodes from the Divine Comedy Rendered in Verse*, London: Ernest Benn.

BIRCH, Samuel, 1873-1881, *Records of the Past: Being English Translations of the Assyrian and Egyptian Monuments Published under the Sanction of the Society of Biblical Archaeology*, 12 vols., London: S. Bagster and Sons Ltd.

BLACKMORE, Richard D., 1869, *Lorna Doone: A Romance of Exmoor*, London, etc: Chambers.

BLACKWELDER, Richard E., 1990, *A Tolkien Thesaurus*, New York and London: Garland Publishing.

BLAIR, J., 1995, 'Anglo-Saxon Pagan Shrines and their Prototypes', In: *Anglo-Saxon Studies in Archaeology and History* 8 (1995), 1-28.

BLAKE, William, 1794, *The Book of Urizen*, Mineola, NY: Dover Publications, 1997.

1797, *Vala, or The Four Zoas: a facs. of the ms. A Transcript of the Poem and a Study of its Growth and Significance by Gerald E. Bentley, Jr.*, Oxford: Clarendon Press, 1963.

BLISS, Alan J. (ed.), 1954, *Sir Orfeo*, London: Oxford University Press.

BLOCH, Oscar and Walter VON WARTBURG, 1950, *Dictionnaire Ètymologique de la Langue Française*, 2nd edition, Paris: Presses Universitaires de France.

BOBERG, Inger M., 1966, *Motif-Index of Early Icelandic Literature*, Copenhagen : Munksgaard.

BOSWORTH, Joseph and T. NORTHCOTE TOLLER, 1898, *An Anglo-Saxon Dictionary*, London: Oxford University Press.

1921, *An Anglo-Saxon Dictionary, Supplement III,* Oxford: Clarendon Press.

BOWRA, Cecil Maurice, 1952, *Heroic Poetry*, London: MacMillan.

BRACHET, Auguste, 1882, *Etymological Dictionary of the French Language*, 3rd edition, Oxford: Clarendon Press.

BRADLEY, R., 1987, 'Time Regained: The Creation of Continuity', In: *Journal of the British Archaeological Association* 140 (1987), 1-17.

BROOKE, Christopher, 1964, 'The Church and the Welsh Border in the Tenth and Eleventh Century', In: *Flintshire Historical Society Journal* 21 (1964), 32-45.

BROOKS, D.A., 1986, 'A Review of the Evidence for Continuity in British Towns in the Fifth and Sixth Centuries', In: *Oxford Journal of Archaeology* 5 (1986), 77-102.

BROWN, Arthur, 1968, 'Albert Hugh Smith', In: *Onoma, Journal of the International Council of Onomastic Sciences* 13, (1968), 177-190.

BUCHAN, John, 1915, *The Thirty-nine Steps*, Edinburgh and London: William Blackwood and Sons.

BUCK, Samuel & Nathaniel, 1732, *The North West View of Tewkesbury Abby, in the Country of Gloucester* [Image with text], London: Buck Brothers.

Burgess, Michael, 1985, 'Of Barghest, Orc, and Ring-Wraith', in: *Amon Hen 75* (1985), 15-16.

BURNLEY, David and Matsuji TAJIMA, 1994, *The Language of Middle English Literature*, Cambridge: D.S. Brewer.

BYNON, Theodora, 1966, 'Concerning the Etymology of English *path*', In: *Transactions of the Philological Society* 65.1 (1966), 67-87.

CAMERON, Kenneth, 1961, *English Place Names*, London: B.T. Batsford.

CAMPBELL, Roy, 1924, *The Flaming Terrapin*, London: Cape.

1939, *Flowering Rifle: A Poem from the Battlefield of Spain*, London and New York: Longmans, Green, and Co.

1969, *Light on a Dark Horse: An Autobiography, 1901-1935*, London: Hollis & Carter.

CARLSON, C.M., 1998, ' 'The Minstrels Song of Silence': The Construction of Masculine Authority and the Feminised Other in the Romance *Sir Orfeo*', In: *Comitatus* 29 (1998), 62-75.

CARPENTER, Humphrey, 1977, *J.R.R. Tolkien: A Biography*, London: George Allen & Unwin.

1978, *The Inklings – C.S. Lewis, J.R.R. Tolkien, Charles Williams and Their Friends*, London: Allen & Unwin.

1981a, *W.H. Auden: A Biography*, London: George Allen & Unwin.

(ed. with the assistance of Christopher TOLKIEN), 1981b, *The Letters of J.R.R. Tolkien*, Boston: Houghton Mifflin.

CASHMAN, Ray, 2000, 'The Heroic Outlaw in Irish Folklore and Popular Literature', In: *Folklore* 111.2 (October 2000), 191-215.

CAVENDISH, Richard, 1983a, *Man, Myth & Magic : The Illustrated Encyclopedia of Mythology, Religion, and the Unknown*, Vol. 4: Eye - Grea, New York: Marshall Cavendish.

1983b, *Man, Myth & Magic : The Illustrated Encyclopedia of Mythology, Religion, and the Unknown*, Vol. 11: Time - Zurv, New York: Marshall Cavendish.

CAVILL, Paul (ed.), 2004, *The Christian Tradition in Anglo-Saxon England: Approaches to Current Scholarship and Teaching*, Cambridge: D. S. Brewer.

CHADWICK, Nora, 1946a, 'Norse Ghosts (A Study in the Draugr and the Haugbui)', In: *Folklore* 57.2 (1946), 50-65.

1946b, 'Norse Ghosts II (continued)', In: *Folklore* 57.3 (1946), 106-27.

CHADWICK, Hector Munro, 1899, *The Cult of Othin, An Essay in the Ancient Religion of the North*, London: C.J. Clay and Sons.

CHALMERS, Patrick Reginald, 1933, *Kenneth Grahame : Life, Letters and Unpublished Work*, London: Methuen.

CHAMBERS, Raymond W., 1925, 'Recent Research upon the *Ancren Riwle*', In: *The Review of English Studies* 1.1 (1925), 4-23.

1927, *The Saga and the Myth of Sir Thomas More*, London: Oxford University Press.

1932, *On the Continuity of English Prose from Alfred to More and his School*, London: Milford.

CHANEY, William A., 1962, 'Grendel and the Gifstol: A Legal View of Monsters', in: *PMLA* 77.5 (1962), 513-20.

1970, *The Cult of Kingship in Anglo-Saxon England: The Transition from Paganism to Christianity*, Manchester: Manchester University Press.

CHAUDHURI, Nirad C., 1914, *Scholar Extraordinary: The Life of Professor the Rt. Hon. Friedrich Max Mueller, P.C.*, London: Chatto and Windus.

Chesterton, G.K., 1913, 'A Song of Temperance Reform', in: *New Witness*, 25 September 1913, 658.

CHILDE, Vere Gordon, 1940, *Prehistoric Communities of the British Isles*, London, Edinburgh: W. & R. Chambers.

1946, *What Happened in History*, London: Penguin Books.

CLARK, Ronald, 1960, *Sir Mortimer Wheeler*, New York: Roy Publishers.

CLARK HALL, John R. (trans.) and C.L. WRENN (ed.), 1940, *Beowulf and the Finnesburg Fragment: A Translation into Modern English Prose*, London: George Allen & Unwin (Rev. ed., first published in 1911).

1950, *Beowulf and the Finnesburg Fragment: A Translation into Modern English Prose*, London: George Allen & Unwin (Rev. ed.).

CLARKE, Cecily, 1958, *The Peterborough Chronicle, 1070-1154, ed. from Ms Bodley Laud Misc. 636*, Oxford: Oxford University Press.

CLAY, R.G., 1927, 'Some Prehistoric Ways', In: *Antiquity* 1 (1927), 54-65.

COBBETT, William, 1967, *The Autobiography of William Cobbett: The Progress of a Plough-Boy to a Seat in Parliament*, Ed. by William Reitzel, London: Faber and Faber.

and Ian DYCK (ed. and intr.), 2001, *Rural* Rides, London [et al.]: Penguin Books.

COCKAYNE, Thomas Oswald (ed.), 1865, *Leechdoms, Wortcunning, and Starcraft of Early England*, Vol. II, London: Longman, Green, Longman, Roberts, & Green.

COLE, E. Maule, 1905, 'On the Place-Name Wetwang', In: *Saga-Book of the Viking Club, Society for Northern Research* 4 (1905), 102-106.

COLLINGWOOD, Robin George, 1930, *The Archaeology of Roman Britain*. London: Methuen.

1932, *Roman Britain*, 2nd edition, Oxford: Oxford University Press.

1937, *Roman Britain and the English Settlements*, 2nd ed., Oxford: Oxford University Press.

COLERIDGE, Samuel Taylor, 1975, *Biographia Literaria, Or, Biographical Sketches of My Literary Life and Opinions*, reprint, London: Dent.

COLLINS, Rob and James GERRARD (eds.), 2004, *Debating Late Antiquity in Britain, AD 300-700*, BAR: British Series, Oxford: Archaeopress.

CONAN DOYLE, Arthur, 1911, 'The Blighting of Sharkey', In: *Pearson's Magazine* 31 (1911), 353-62.

THE CONCISE OXFORD DICTIONARY, 1982, 7th edition, ed. by J.B. Sykes, Oxford: The Clarendon Press.

COOK, Albert S. and Chauncey B. TINKER (eds.), 1908, *Select Translations from Old English Prose*, Boston: Ginn & Co.

COOPER, James Fenimore, 1827, *The Prairie: A Tale*, London: Colburn.

CORBISHLEY, Thomas, 1950, *Roman Catholicism*, London, New York: Hutchinson's University Library.

1952, *Religion in the Modern World*, London: Allen & Unwin.

COX, C.B. and A.E. DYSON, 1968, *Word in the Desert*, Oxford: Oxford University Press.

CRAIGIE, William Alexander (sel. and trans.), 1896, *Scandinavian Folk-Lore: Illustrations of the Traditional Beliefs of the Northern People*, Paisley: Alexander Gardner.

DANIEL, Glyn, 1975, *A Hundred and Fifty Years of Archaeology*, 2nd edition, London: Gerald Duckworth & Co. Ltd.

D'ARCY, Martin Cyril, 1945, *The Mind and Heart of Love, Lion and Unicorn: A Study in Eros and Agape*, London: Faber & Faber.

D'ARDENNE, S.T.R.O., 1936, *An Edition of Þe liflade ant te passiun of Seinte Iuliene, Þe uie of Seinte Iuliane, passio Sancte Iuliane*, Liège [et al.]: Fac. de Philosophie et Lettres [et al.].

1939, 'The Old English Inscription on the Brussels Cross', In: *English Studies 21* (1939), 145-64, 271-72.

1946, 'The Devil's Spout', In: *Transactions of the Philological Society* 45.1 (1946), 31-55.

1958, 'Smithes in *The Owl and the Nightingale*', In: *Review of English Studies* 9.33 (1958), 41-43.

1961, *Þe liflade ant te passiun of Seinte Iuliene*, London: Oxford University Press.

1977, *The Katherine Group. ed. from Ms. Bodley 34*, Paris: Soc. d'Éd. "Les Belles Lettres".

1981, *Seinte Katerine [Catharina Alexandrinensis] ; Re-ed. from MS Bodley 34 and the Other Manuscripts*, ed. by Eric J. Dobson, Oxford: Oxford University Press.

1982, 'Two Words from Ancrene Wisse and the Katherine Group', In: *Notes and Queries* 227 (1982), 3.

1983, 'Two Notes on Early Middle Texts', In: E.G. Stanley and Douglas Gray (eds.), 1983, *Five Hundred Years of Words and Sounds, Festschrift for Eric John Dobson*, Cambridge: Brewer, 21-22.

DASENT, G.W. (ed.), 1859, *Popular Tales from the Norse* (transl. from: ASBJÖRNSEN, Peter Christen and Jørgen MOE, *Norske Folkeeventyr*), Edinburgh: Edmonston & Douglas.

DASS, Rhonda, Anthony GUEST-SCOTT, J. Meryl KRIEGER and Adam ZOLKOVER (eds.), 2007, *Over the Edge: Pushing the Boundaries of Folklore and Ethno-Musicology*, Cambridge: Cambridge Scholars Publishing.

DAUZAT, Albert, 1947, *Dictionnaire Étymologique de la Langue Française: avec un Supplément Lexicologique et un Supplément Chronologique*, Paris: Librairie Larousse.

DAVIDSON, Hilda R. Ellis, 1950, 'The Hill of the Dragon – Anglo Saxon Burial Mounds in Literature and Archaeology', In: *Folklore* 61.4 (1950), 169-85.

DAVIS, Norman and C.L. WRENN (eds.), 1962, *English and Medieval Studies Presented to J.R.R. Tolkien on the Occasion of His Seventieth Birthday*, London: George Allen & Unwin.

DAY, David, 1979, *A Tolkien Bestiary*, London: Mitchell Beazley.

DAY, Mabel, 1952, *The English Text of the Ancrene Riwle, edited from Cotton MS. Nero A xiv*, (on the basis of a transcript by J.A. Herbert), Early English Text Society 225, London: Cumberlege .

DE GUBERNATIS, Angelo, 1872, *Zoological Mythology or The Legends of Animals*, London: Trübner.

DE HOUGHTON, C., 1971, 'Parsival', In: *Man, Myth and Magic* 76, London: Purnell, 2141-43.

DICKINS, Bruce, and Richard M. WILSON (eds.), 1951, *Early Middle English Texts*, Cambridge: Bowes & Bowes.

DICTIONARY OF THE OLDER SCOTTISH TONGUE, FROM THE 12TH CENTURY TO THE END OF THE 17TH, FOUNDED ON THE COLLECTIONS OF SIR WILLIAM A. CRAIGIE, 1983, Ed. by A. J. Aitken, Part 5, O-Pn, Aberdeen: University Press.

DILLON, Myles and Nora CHADWICK, 1967, *The Celtic Realms*, London: Weidenfeld & Nicolson.

DIRINGER, David, 1962, *Writing*, London: Thames & Hudson.

Dobson, Eric John, 1962, 'The Affiliations of the MSS of the *Ancrene Wisse*', In: Norman Davis and C.L. Wrenn (eds.), 1962, *English and Mediaeval Studies Presented to J.R.R. Tolkien*, London: Allen and Unwin, 128-63.

1966, 'The Date and Composition of the *Ancrene Wisse*', Gollancz lecture to the British Academy, In: *Proceedings of the British Academy* 52 (1966), 181-208.

1972, *The English Text of the Ancrene Riwle: Edited from B.M. Cotton MS. Cleopatra C.vi*, Early English Text Society 267, London et. al.: Oxford University Press.

1974, 'Two Notes on Early Middle English Texts [i.e. in the *AW*]', In: *Notes and Queries* 21.4, (1974), 124-26.

1975, *Moralities on the Gospels – A New Source of 'Ancrene Wisse'*, Oxford: Clarendon Press.

1976, *The Origins of the Ancrene Wisse*, Oxford: Clarendon Press.

and Frank L. HARRISON, 1979, *Mediaeval English Songs*, London: Faber.

DONALDSON, Dwight M., 1953, *Studies in Muslim Ethics*, London: S.P.C.K.

DRONKE, Ursula (ed.), 1969, *The Poetic Edda, Vol. 1: Heroic Poems*, Oxford: Clarendon Press.

DROUT, Michael D.C. (ed.), 2007, *J.R.R. Tolkien Encyclopedia. Scholarship and Critical Assessment.* New York et. al.: Routledge.

DU CHAILLU, Paul, 1889, *The Viking Age: The Early History, Manners, and Customs of the Ancestors of the English-speaking Nations*, New York: Charles Scribner's Sons, London: Murray.

DUBOIS, Arthur E., 1954, 'Gifstol', in: *Modern Language Notes* 69.8 (1954), 546-49.

DUFF, John Wight, 1910, *A Literary History of Rome: From the Origins to the Close of the Golden Age*, 2nd ed., London & Leipzig: T. Fisher Unwin.

DUMÉZIL, Georges, 1973, *Gods of the Ancient Northmen* (ed. by Einar Haugen, introduction by C. Scott Littleton and Udo Strutynski), Berkeley, California: University of Berkeley Press.

DUNKLING, Leslie Alan, 1983, *The Guinness Book of Names*, Enfield: Guinness Superlatives.

DYMES, D.M.E., 1923, 'The Original Language of the Ancrene Riwle', In: *Essays & Studies* IX (1923), 31-49.

EARLE, John, 1892, *The Philology of the English Tongue*, (5th ed.), Oxford: Clarendon Press.

ECKENSTEIN, Lina, 1896, *Women under Monasticism. Chapters on Saint-Lore and Convent Life between A.D. 500 and A.D. 1500.* Cambridge: Cambridge University Press.

EISLER, Robert, 1949, *Man into Wolf,* London: Spring Books.

EKWALL, Eilert, 1951, *The Concise Oxford Dictionary of English Place-Names*, 3rd ed., Oxford: Clarendon Press.

ELTON, Oliver and Frederick Y. POWELL (trans.), 1894, *The First Nine Books of the Danish History of Saxo Grammaticus*, London: Nutt.

ENCYCLOPÆDIA BRITANNICA, 1968a, vol. 13, London: The Encyclopædia Britannica.

1968b, vol. 16, London: The Encyclopædia Britannica.

EREMIN, Igor P., 1966, *Literatura drevnej Rusi (The Literature of Old Rus)*, Moskow: Izdat. Nauka.

ERLINGSSON, Thorsteinn, 1899, *Ruins of the Saga Time: Being an Account of Travels and Explorations in Iceland in the Summer of 1895*, London: David Nutt.

ERNOUT, Alfred, 1916, *Recueil de textes latins archaïques*, Paris: ed. Klincksieck.

ERNOUT, Alfred and Antoine MEILLET, 2001, *Dictionnaire Etymologique de la Langue Latine: Histoire des mots*. 4ème éd. rev., corr. et augm. d'un index, Paris: Klincksieck.

ESTRICH, R.M., 1944, 'The Throne of Hrothgar – *Beowulf*, ll. 168-169', in: *Journal of English and Germanic Philology* 43 (1944), 384-89.

EVANS, Jonathan, 2000, 'The Dragon-Lore of Middle-earth: Tolkien and the Old English and Old Norse Tradition', In: George Clark and Daniel Timmons (eds.), 2000, *J.R.R. Tolkien and his Literary Resonances: Views of Middle-earth*, Contributions to the Study of Science Fiction and Fantasy 89, Westport, Connecticut, etc.: Greenwood Press, 21-38.

FARMER, David Hugh, 1978, *The Oxford Dictionary of Saints*, Oxford: Clarendon Press.

FARNOL, Jeffery, 1910, *The Broad Highway, A Romance of Kent*, London, Sampson Low & Co. Ltd.

FAST, Howard Melvin, 1966, *Torquemada: A Novel*, Garden City, New York: Doubleday & Company.

FLEMING, Robin, 2010, *Britain after Rome: The Fall and Rise, 400-1700*, London: Penguin/Allen Lane.

FOSTER, Robert, 1978, *The Complete Guide to Middle-earth*, London: Allen & Unwin.

FOX, Cyril, 1952, *The Personality of Britain, Its Influence on Inhabitant and Invader in Prehistoric and Early Historic Times*, Cardiff: National Museum of Wales.

FULLER, Edmund, 1968, 'The Lord of the Hobbits', In: Neil Isaacs and Rose Zimbardo (eds.), 1968, *Tolkien and the Critics: Essays on J.R.R. Tolkien's The Lord of the Rings*, Notre Dame and London: University of Notre Dame Press, 17-39. First published in: Fuller, Edmund, 1962, *Books with Men Behind Them: a Companion to Man in Modern Fiction*, New York: Random House, 169-96.

Fuller, John, 1970, *A Reader's Guide to W.H. Auden*, London: Thames & Hudson.

FURNIVALL, Frederick J., 1923, 'Hali Meidenhad', In: *The Times Literary Supplement*, 26 April, 1923, 281.

GARLICK, K.J., 1976, 'Foreword', In: *Drawings by J.R.R. Tolkien*, Oxford: The Ashmolean Museum (jointly with the National Book League), 5.

GEOFFREY OF MONMOUTH, 1903, *Historia Regum Brittaniae* (trans. by Sebastian Evans), London: Everyman.

GIDDINGS, Robert and Elizabeth HOLLAND, 1981, *J.R.R. Tolkien: The Shores of Middle-earth*, London: Junction Books.

GILLIGAN, Kathleen E., 2011, 'Temptation and the Ring in J.R.R. Tolkien's *The Fellowship of the Ring*', In: *Student Pulse* 3.05 (2011), retrieved from: <http://www.studentpulse.com/a?id=534>, last access: September 27th 2011.

GOLDING, William, 1954, *Lord of the Flies*, London: Faber and Faber.

GOUGH, John Wiedhofft, 1930, *The Mines of Mendip*, Oxford: Clarendon Press.

GORDON, Robert Kay, 1926, *The Anglo-Saxon Poetry*, London: Dent, 1954.

GRAHAME, Kenneth, 1928, *The Golden Age*, London: Lane.

1968, *The Wind in the Willows*, London: Methuen.

and Peter HAINING (ed.), 1983, *Paths to the River Bank: The Origins of 'The Wind in the Willows'*, illustr. by Carolyn Beresford, London: Souvenir Press.

GRAY, Douglas, 1979, 'Chaucer and "Pite"', In: Mary Salu and Robert T. Farrell (eds.), 1979, *J.R.R. Tolkien, Scholar and Storyteller*, Ithaca and London: Cornell University Press, 173-203.

1985, 'Obituary for John Eric Dobson', In: *Proceedings of the British Academy* 71 (1985), 533-38.

GRAY, Douglas and Eric G. STANLEY (eds.), 1983, *Five hundred years of words and sounds: A festschrift for Eric Dobson*, Cambridge: Brewer [et al.].

GRAY, Harold St. George, 1925, 'Excavations at Ham Hill, South Somerset, part I', In: *Proceedings of the Somerset Archaeological and Natural History Society* 70 (1925), 104-116.

1926, 'Excavations at Ham Hill, South Somerset, part II', In: *Proceedings of the Somerset Archaeological and Natural History Society* 71 (1926), 57-76.

GREBSTEIN, Sheldon Norman (ed.), 1968, *Perspectives in Contemporary Criticism*, New York: Harper and Row.

GREEN, Dennis Howard, 1970, 'Irony and the Medieval Romance', In: *Forum for Modern Language Studies* 6 (1970), 49-64.

1977, 'The Pathway to Adventure', *Viator* 8 (1977), 145-188.

1979, *Irony in the Medieval Romance*, Cambridge: Cambridge University Press.

GREEN, Peter, 1959, *Kenneth Grahame, 1859-1932: A Study of his Life, Work and Times*, London: John Murray.

GREEN, Roger Lancelyn, 1946, *Andrew Lang: A Critical Biography*, Leicester: Ward.

1948, *Poulton-Lancelyn: The Story of an Ancestral Home*, Oxford: Oxonian Press.

1964, *Tales from Shakespeare, Vol.1, The comedies*, Foreword by Christopher Fry, London: V. Gollancz.

1965a, *Tales from Shakespeare, Vol. II, The Tragedies and Romances*, London: V. Gollancz.

1965b, *A Book of Myths, Selected and Retold*, London: J.M. Dent.

1969, *The Tale of Ancient Israel*, London: Dent et.al.

and Walter HOOPER, 1974, *C. S. Lewis: A Biography*, London: Collins.

GRIMALDI, Patrizia, 1981, 'Sir Orfeo as Celtic Folk-Hero, Christian Pilgrim and Medieval King', In: Morton W. Bloomfeld (ed.), 1981, *Allegory, Myth and Symbol*, Cambridge, Massachusetts: Harvard University Press.

GRIMM, Jacob, 1808, 'Entstehung der Verlagspoesie', In: *Zeitung für Einsiedler* 7, 23 April, 1808, 56.

1888, *Teutonic Mythology, translated from the fourth edition with notes and appendix by James Steven Stallybrass*, vol. 1, New York: Dover Publications, 1966.

GRINSELL, Leslie V., 1936a, *The Ancient Burial-Mounds of England*, 2nd ed. revised and reset (1953), London: Methuen & Co.

1936b, 'Analysis and List of Berkshire Barrows', In: *The Berkshire Archaeological Journal* 40.1 (1936), 20-58.

1958, *The Archeology of Wessex: An Account of Wessex Antiquities from the Earliest Times to the End of the Pagan-Saxon Period, With Special Reference to Existing Field Monuments*, London: Methuen.

1976a, *Folklore of Prehistoric Sites in Britain*, London: David & Charles.

1976b, 'The Legendary History and Folklore of Stonehenge', In: *Folklore* 87.1 (1976), 5-20.

GUTTELING, J.F.C., 1924, 'Demogorgon in Shelley's Prometheus Unbound', In: *Neophilologus* 9.1 (1924), 283-85.

HAGGARD, Henry Rider, 1885, *King Solomon's Mines*, London: Cassell.

HALL, Joseph (ed.), 1920, *Selections from Early Middle English 1130 – 1250*, 2 vols., Oxford: Clarendon Press.

HAMILTON, Mary, 1906, *Incubation or the Cure of Disease in Pagan Temples and Christian Churches*, London: Simpkin, Marshall, Hamilton, Kent & Co.

HAMMOND, Wayne (with the assistance of Douglas A. ANDERSON), 1993, *J.R.R. Tolkien: A Descriptive Bibliography*, Winchester: St Paul's Bibliographies.

HARP, Richard, 2009, 'A Conjuror at the Xmas Party', *Times Literary Supplement*, Dec. 11th, 2009.

HASTINGS, James (ed.), 1908-26, *Encyclopædia of Religion and Ethics*, 13 vols., Edinburgh: Clark.

1908, *Encyclopædia of Religion and Ethics: Volume I: A-Art*, Edinburgh: Clark.

1915, *Encyclopædia of Religion and Ethics: Volume VIII: Life and Death-Mulla*, Edinburgh: Clark

1920, *Encyclopædia of Religion and Ethics: Volume XI: Sacrifice – Sudra*, Edinburgh: Clark.

1921, *Encyclopædia of Religion and Ethics: Volume XII: Suffering – Zwingli*, Edinburgh: Clark.

HATTO, Arthur T., 1980a, *Parzival*, Harmondsworth: Penguin Classics.

1980b, *Traditions of Heroic and Epic Poetry, Vol. 1: The Traditions*, London: Modern Humanities Research Association.

HAVERFIELD, F.J., 1906, 'Romano-British Somerset', In: William Page (ed.), *The Victoria History of the County of Somerset*, Vol. I, Haymarket: James Street, 207-371.

Hawkes, Christopher, 1932, 'Reviews', In: Antiquity: A Quarterly Review of Archaeology 6.24 (December 1932), 488-90.

HAWKES, Jacquetta, 1982, *Mortimer Wheeler: Adventurer in Archaeology*, London: Weidenfeld and Nicholson.

HEDGES, Ned Samuel, 1968, *The Fable and the Fabulous. The Use of Traditional Forms in Children's Literature*, Lincoln, Nebraska: University of Nebraska (Diss.).

HIGHET, Gilbert, 1949, *The Classical Tradition: Greek and Roman Influences on Western Literature*, Oxford: Oxford University Press.

HILTON, James, 1933, *Lost Horizon*, London: MacMillan.

HILTON, Walter, 1991, *The Scale of Perfection* [1494], transl. from the Middle English, with an Introduction and Notes by John P.H. Clark, New York [et al.]: Paulist Press.

HODGKIN, Robert H., 1935, *A History of the Anglo-Saxons*, vol. 2, London: Oxford University Press.

HOLDSTOCK, Robert, 1984, *Mythago Wood*, London: Victor Gollancz.

HOLTHAUSEN, Ferdinand, 1934, *Altenglisches Etymologisches Wörterbuch*, Heidelberg: Carl Winters Universitätsbuchhandlung.

HOSKINS, William George, 1955, *The Making of the English Landscape*, London: Hodder and Stoughton.

HYNES, Samuel, 1976, *The Auden Generation, Literature and Politics in England in the 1930s*, London: The Bodley Head.

ILIOWIZI, Henry, 1897, *In the Pale: Stories and Legends of the Russian Jews*, Philadelphia: Jewish Publication Society of America.

ISAACS, Neil D. and Rose A. ZIMBARDO (eds.), 1968, *Tolkien and the Critics: Essays on J.R.R. Tolkien's 'The Lord of the Rings'*, Notre Dame, Indiana: University of Notre Dame Press.

(eds.), 1981, *Tolkien: New Critical Perspectives*, Lexington, Kentucky: The University Press of Kentucky.

ISHERWOOD, Christopher, 1937, 'Some Notes on Auden's Early Poetry', In: *New Verse* 26/27 (Auden Double Number, November 1937), 4-9.

JACKSON KNIGHT, William Francis, 1944, *Roman Vergil*, London: Faber and Faber Ltd.

JACKSON, William Thomas Hobdell, 1960, *The Literature of the Middle Ages*, New York: Columbia University Press.

JENKIN, Alfred Kenneth Hamilton, 1927, *The Cornish Miner: an Account of his Life Above and Underground from Early Times*, London: George Allen & Unwin.

JOHNSON, Walter, 1908, *Folk-Memory*, Oxford: Clarendon Press.

JOHNSTON, James B., 1892, *Place-Names of Scotland*, Edinburgh: D. Douglas.

JOLLIFFE, J.E.A., 1937, *The Constitutional History of Medieval England from the English Settlement to 1485*, London: A. & C. Black.

JONES, Alexander (gen. ed.), J.R.R. TOLKIEN et al. (eds.), 1968, *The Jerusalem Bible*, Garden City, N.Y: Doubleday.

JONES, Diana Wynne, 1993, *Hexwood*, London: Methuen.

JONES, Siân, 1997, *The Archaeology of Ethnicity: Constructing Identities in the Past and Present*, London: Routledge.

JOSEPH, Bertram L., 1951, *Elizabethan Acting*, London: Oxford University Press.

JUNG, Carl G., 1933, *Modern Man in Search of a Soul*, transl. by W.S. Dell and Cary F. Baynes, New York: Harcourt.

KALVE, Kari, 1997, 'A Virtuous Mouth: Reading and Speaking in the Ancrene Wisse', In: *Essays in Mediaeval Studies* 14 (1997), 39-49.

KEIGHTLEY, Thomas, 1878, *The World Guide to Gnomes, Fairies, Elves and Other Little People*, New York: Macmillian.

1968, *The Fairy Mythology*, London: Bohn.

KELLETT, E.E., 1914, *The Religion of our Northern Ancestors*, London: Charles H. Kelly.

KEMBALL-COOK, Jessica, 1977, 'Books', In: *Amon Hen* 26 (1977), 11-12.

KERSHAW, Nora (ed. and trans.), 1922, *Anglo-Saxon and Norse Poems*, Cambridge: Cambridge University Press.

KEYNES, Simon and Michael LAPIDGE (eds.), 1983, *Alfred the Great, Asser's 'Life of King Alfred' and Other Contemporary Sources*, Harmondsworth et. al.: Penguin Books.

KHALIFATUL MASIH II, 1949, *Introduction to the Study of the Holy Qur'an*, London: The London Mosque.

KIPLING, Rudyard, 1906, *Puck of Pook's Hill*, Leipzig: Tauchnitz.

KIRBY, D.P., 2000, *The Earliest English Kings*, rev. ed, London: Routledge.

KIRK, Geoffrey S., 1970. *Myth: Its Meaning and Functions in Ancient & Other Cultures*, Sather Classical Lectures, Vol. 40, Cambridge: Cambridge University Press.

KLAEBER, Frederick (ed., with introd., biography, notes, glossary, and appendices), 1936, *Beowulf and the Fight at Finnsburg*, Boston et al.: Heath.

KNIGHT, Francis A., 1915, *The Heart of Mendip*, London: J.M. Dent & Sons Ltd.

KNIGHT, Jeremy K., 1999, *The End of Antiquity: Archaeology, Society and Religion, AD 235-700*, Stroud, Gloucestershire et al.: Tempus.

KNOWLES, Dom David, 1973, 'Christopher Dawson, 1889-1970', In: *Proceedings of the British Academy* 57 (1973), 439-52.

KOCHER, Paul Harold, 1973, *Master of Middle-earth: The Achievement of J.R.R. Tolkien*, London: Thames & Hudson.

KRAMER, Samuel N., 1957, 'The Sumerians: Their History, Culture and Character', In: *Scientific American* (1957), 18-30.

KUSKOV, Vladimir Vladimirovič, 1980, *A History of Old Russian Literature*, (translated by Ronald Vroon), Moscow: Progress Publishers.

LABAT, René, 1948, *Manuel d'épigraphie akkadienne: Signes, Syllabaire, Idéogrammes*, Paris: Imprimerie Nationale.

LAMBERT, Wilfred G., A.R. MILLARD and Miguel CIVIL, 1969, *Atra-Hasīs: The Babylonian Story of the Flood*, Oxford: Clarendon Press.

LANE, Edward, 1908. *An Account of the Manners and Customs of the Modern Egyptians*, London: Everyman's Library, Dent.

LAPIDGE, M., J. BLAIR, S. KEYNES and D. SCRAGG (eds.), 1999, *The Blackwell Encyclopaedia of Anglo-Saxon England*, Oxford: Blackwell.

LASATER, Alice E., 1974, *Spain to England: A Comparative Study of Arabic, European, and English Literature of the Middle Ages,* Jackson: University Press of Mississippi.

LEGUIN, Ursula K., 1971, 'Vaster than Empires and More Slow', In: *The Wind's Twelve Quarters: Short Stories,* 1975, New York, N.Y.: Harper & Row.

LEIVICK, H., 1921, *Der golem, a dramatiše poeme in acht bilder,* New York: Farlag Amerike.

LEONARD, William Ellery, 1934, *Gilgamesh: Epic of Old Babylonia,* New York: Viking Press.

LEWIS, Clive Staples, 1939, 'To the Author of *Flowering Rifle*', In: *Cherwell,* 6 May 1939, 35.

    1945, *That Hideous Strength,* London: Bodley Head.

    1955, 'The Dethronement of Power', In: *Time and Tide,* 22 October 1955, 1373-74.

    1964, 'To the Author of Flowering Rifle', In: W. Hooper (ed.), *Poems* [by C.S. Lewis], New York and London: A Harvest / HBJ Book, Harcourt Brace Jovanovich, 65 [1st publ. as: Whilk, Nat (pseud.), 'To Mr. Roy Campbell', In: *The Cherwell,* May 6th, 1939, 35.]

LEWIS, Warren Hamilton (ed.), 1966, *The Collected Letters of C.S. Lewis, Edited with a Memoir,* New York: Harcourt, Brace, World.

LIVELY, Penelope, 1972, *The Driftway,* London: Heinemann.

LOCAS, Claude, 1973, 'Christopher Dawson: A Bibliography', In: *Harvard Theological Review,* April (1973), 177-206.

LOFTUS, William Kennett, 1857, *Travels and Researches in Chaldaea and Susiana,* London: James Nisbet and Co.

LOOMIS, Roger Sherman (with Laura Hibbard LOOMIS), 1957, *Medieval Romances,* New York: The Modern Library.

    1959, *Arthurian Literature in the Middle Ages,* Oxford: Clarendon Press.

LOTSPEICH, Henry Gibbons, 1932, *Classical Mythology in the Poetry of Edmund Spenser,* Princeton: Princeton University Press.

LUCY, Sam J., 2000, *The Anglo-Saxon Way of Death: Burial Rites in Early England,* Stroud: Sutton.

MacDonald, Duncan Black, 1909, *The Religious Attitude and Life in Islam*, (Haskell lectures in comparative religion at the University of Chicago), Facsimile Reprint of the 1909 edition, Beirut: Khayats, 1965.

MacDonald, George, 1954, *The Visionary Novels: Lilith; Phantastes*, ed. by Anne Fremantle, with an introduction by W.H. Auden, New York: Noonday.

MacDonald, George, 1872, *The Princess and the Goblin*, Philadelphia: J.B. Lippincott & Co.

McClure, Edmund, 1910, *British Place-Names in Their Historical Setting*, London: Society for Promoting Christian Knowledge.

Manwood, John, 1592, *A Brefe Collection of the Lawes of the Forest*, privately circulated.

Mason, Eugene (transl.), 1932, *French Mediaeval Romances from the Lays of Marie de France*, London: Dent.

McNabb, Vincent, and Raymond W. Chambers, 1926, 'Further Research upon the *Ancren Riwle*', In: *The Review of English Studies* 2.5 (1926), 82-89.

McNabb, Vincent, Raymond W. Chambers and Herbert Thurston, 1926, 'Further Research on the *Ancren Riwle*', In: *The Review of English Studies* 2.6 (1926), 197-201.

Mellaart, James, 1970, 'The Earliest Settlements in Western Asia From the Ninth to the End of the Fifth Millenium B.C.', In: Edwards, I.E.S., Cyril John Gadd and Nicholas Geoffrey Lemprière Hammond (eds.), *The Cambridge Ancient History Vol. I Part 1: Prolegomena and Prehistory*, Cambridge: University Press.

Mellinkoff, Ruth, 1980a, 'Cain's Monstrous Progeny in *Beowulf*, part I, Noachic Tradition', In: *Anglo-Saxon England* 8 (1980), 143-60.

1980b, 'Cain's Monstrous Progeny in *Beowulf*, part II, Post-Diluvian Survival', In: *Anglo-Saxon England* 9 (1980), 183-97.

Merit, H.D., 1954, *Fact and Lore About Old English Words*, Stanford, California: Stanford University Press.

Merton College Register, 1891-1989, 1990. edited by Norman Davis and Ralph Henry Carless Davis, privately circulated.

Meyrink, Gustav, 1915, *Der Golem*, Leipzig: Wolff.

1928, *The Golem*, translated by Madge Pemberton. Boston: Houghton Mifflin.

MILES, David (ed.), 1986, *Archaeology at Barton Court Farm, Abingdon, Oxon: An Investigation of Late Neolithic, Iron Age, Romano-British and Saxon Settlements*, London: Oxford Archaeological Unit and the Council for British Archaeology.

MILLETT, M., 1990, *The Romanization of Britain: An Essay in Archaeological Interpretation*, Cambridge: Cambridge University Press.

MILNE, Alan Alexander, 1952, *Toad of Toad Hall, A Play from Kenneth Grahame's Book 'The Wind in the Willows'*, London: Methuen.

MITTINS, W.H., Mary Salu, Mary Edminson, and Sheila Coyne, 1970, *Attitudes to English Usage: An Enquiry by the University of Newcastle upon Tyne Institute of Education English Research Group*, London: Oxford University Press.

Monaco, Richard, 1977, *Parsival or a Knight's Tale*, New York: MacMillan.

MONTAGUE, Robert, 1954, *Havelok and Sir Orfeo*, Leicester: Edmund Ward.

MORRIS, Richard (ed.), 1872, *An Old English Miscellany Containing a Bestiary, Kentish Sermons, Proverbs of Alfred, Religious Poems of the Thirteenth Century: From manuscripts in the British Museum, Bodleian Library, Jesus College Library, etc.*, London: Trübner.

MORRIS, Richard and Walter W. SKEAT, 1885, *Specimens of Early English, Part I: From "Old English Homilies" to "King Horn" [A.D. 1150-A.D. 1300]*, Oxford: Clarendon Press.

1898, *Specimens of Early English, Part 2: From Robert of Gloucester to Gower [A.D. 1298-A.D. 1393]*, 4th ed., Oxford: Clarendon Press.

MORROW, Jeffrey L., 2005, 'J. R. R. Tolkien as a Christian for our Times', In: *Evangelical Review of Theology* 29.2 (2005), 164-77.

MÜLLER, Friedrich Max, 1854, 'The Last results of the Researches respecting the Non-Iranian and Non-Semitic Languages of Asia and Europe, or the Turanian Family of Languages', In: Bunsen, Charles Christian Josias, 1854, *Outlines of the Philosophy of Universal History, applied to Language and Religion*, vol. 1, London: Longman, Brown, Green and Longmans, 263-521.

1868, *On the Stratification of Language*, Sir Robert Rede's Lecture, Delivered in the Senate House before the University of Cambridge on Friday, May 29, 1868. London: Longmans Green, Reader, and Dyer.

1873, *Lectures on the Science of Language delivered at the Royal Institution of Great Britain in April, May, and June*, vol. I, 7th ed., London: Longmans Green.

MÜLLER, Georgina (ed.), 1902, *The Life and Letters of Friedrich Max Müller*, 2 vols., London, etc.: Longmans, Green and Co.

MUNCH, Peter Andreas, 1926, *Norse Mythology: Legends of Gods and Heroes*, translated by Sigurd Bernhard Hustvedt, New York: The American-Scandinavian Foundation.

MURPHY, Paul, 1984, 'Song of the Sybil', In: *Book of Mazarbul* 1 (1984), 18-19.

MURRAY, Paul, 2004, *From the Shadow of Dracula: A Life of Bram Stoker*, London: Jonathan Cape.

MUSTARD, Helen M. and Charles E. PASSAGE, 1961, *Parzival by Wolfram von Eschenbach*, New York: Vintage Books.

NEEDLE, Jan, 1981, *Wild Wood*, London: Andre Deutsch.

Nelson, Brent, 2008, 'Cain-Leviathan Typology in Gollum and Grendel', In: *Extrapolation* 49.3 (2008), 466-85.

NICHOLLS, Henry George, 1858, *The Forest of Dean; An Historical and Descriptive Account, Derived from Personal Observation, and other Sources, Public, Private, Legendary, and Local*, London: John Murray.

NICHOLSON, Reynold Alleyne, 1907, *A Literary History of the Arabs*, London: T.F. Unwin.

NOEL, Ruth S., 1977, *Mythology of Middle-earth*, Boston: Houghton Mifflin.

    1980, *The Languages of Tolkien's Middle-earth*, Boston: Houghton Mifflin.

NORMAN, Philip, 1967, 'The Hobbit Man', In: *The Sunday Times Magazine*, 15 January 1967, 34-36.

NORTH, R., 1957, 'Status of the Wark Excavations', In: *Orientalia*, N.S. 26, (1957), 185-256

Obituary: Professor J.R.R. Tolkien, 1973, In: *The Times*, September 3, 1973.

OBITUARY: PROFESSOR MAX MUELLER, 1900, In: *The Times*, October 29, 1900.

Obituary: Dom. Francis Gerard Sitwell, In: *London Times,* December 21, 1993, 15.

O'DONNELL, Elliott, 1969, *Casebook of Ghosts*, edited by Harry Ludlam, London: W Foulsham & Co. Ltd.

OHLGREN, Thomas H. (ed.), 1998, *Medieval Outlaws: Ten Tales in Modern English*, Stroud: Sutton Publishing.

OLRIK, Axel, 1919, *The Heroic Legends of Denmark*, (trans. and rev. in collaboration with the author Lee M. Hollander), New York: American-Scandinavian Foundation.

O'NEILL, Timothy R., 1979, *The Individuated Hobbit, Jung, Tolkien, and the Archetypes of Middle-Earth*, Boston: Houghton Mifflin.

ONIONS, Charles T. (ed.), 1966, *The Oxford Dictionary of English Etymology*, with the ass. of G.W.S. Friedrichsen and R.W. Burchfield, Oxford: Clarendon Press.

1933, *The Shorter Oxford English Dictionary on Historical Principles: Vol. 2: N-Z*, Oxford: Clarendon Press.

OPPERT, Julius, 1876, 'Inscription of the Annals of Sargon', In: Samuel Birch (ed.), 1876, *Records of the Past: Being English Translations of the Assyrian and Egyptian Monuments*, Vol. VII, Assyrian Texts, London: Society of Biblical Archæology, 21-56.

O'RAHILLY, Thomas Francis, 1957, *Early Irish History and Mythology*, Dublin: Dublin Institute for Advanced Studies.

ORCHARD, Bernard , Edmund F. SUTCLIFFE, Reginald C. FULLER and Ralph RUSSELL, 1953, *A Catholic Commentary on Holy Scripture,* London et al.: Nelson.

ORWELL, George, 1999, *Animal Farm*, ed. by Wanda Opalinska, Harlow: Longman.

OSBORNE, Charles, 1979, *W.H. Auden: The Life of a Poet*, New York: Harcourt Brace Jovanovich.

OXFORD ENGLISH DICTIONARY, 1933, 12 vols. with supplement, Oxford: Clarendon Press.

OXFORD ENGLISH DICTIONARY, 1989, ed. by J.A. Simpson, Part 20, Wave - zyxt., Bibliography, Oxford: Clarendon Press.

SUPPLEMENT, 1972, vol. 1, A-G, Oxford: Clarendon Press.

SUPPLEMENT, 1976, vol. 2, H-N, Oxford: Clarendon Press.

SUPPLEMENT, 1982, vol. 3, O-SCZ, Oxford: Clarendon Press.

PALGRAVE, Francis, 1832, *The Rise and Progress of the English Commonwealth, Anglo-Saxon Period*, London: Murray.

PARKER, M. Pauline, 1960, *The Allegory of the Faerie Queene*, Oxford: Clarendon Press.

PARKER PEARSON, Mike, 1999, *The Archaeology of Death and Burial*, Stroud: Sutton.

PARRY, Thomas, 1955, *A History of Welsh Literature*, translated from the Welsh by H. Idris Bell. Oxford: Clarendon Press.

PARTRIDGE, Eric, 1958, *Origins: A Short Etymological Dictionary of Modern English*, London: Routledge & Kegan Paul.

PEAKE, Arthur S., 1919, *A Commentary on the Bible*, suppl. by A.J. Grieve, London: T.C. and E.C. Jack.

Perrault, Charles, 1697, *Histories, or Tales of Past Times*, London: Printed for J. Pote and R. Montagu.

PERRING, D., 1991, 'Spatial Organisation and Social Change in Roman Towns', In: J. Rich and A. Wallace-Hadrill (eds.), 1991, *City and Country in the Ancient World*, London: Routledge, 273-293.

PETERS, Robert Anthony, 1961, *A Study of Old English Words for Demon and Monster and Their Relation to English Place-names*, Philadelphia, Pennsylvania, University of Pennsylvania, Diss.

PETTS, D.,2004, 'Burial in Western Britain AD 400-800: Late Antique or Early Mediaeval?', In: R.Collins and J.Gerrard (eds.), 2004, *Debating Late Antiquity in Britain AD 300-700*, BAR Brit. Ser. 365, Oxford: Archaeopress, 77-87.

PHELPS, Humphrey, 1982, *The Forest of Dean*, Gloucester: Alan Sutton.

Philipps, D. 'Wardale, Edith Elizabeth (1863–1943)', *Oxford Dictionary of National Biography*, Oxford University Press, 2004, 397.

PINCHES, Theophilus Goldridge, 1886, 'The Erechite's Lament over the Desolation of his Fatherland.' In: *The Babylonian and Oriental Record*, 1886, vol. 1. London: D. Nutt, 84-85.

1890, 'A New Babylonian Version of the Creation Story', In: *The Academy: A Weekly Review of Literature, Science and Art* 38 (1890), 508-509.

1891, 'A New Version of the Creation-story', In: *Journal of the Royal Asiatic Society* (New Series) 23.3 (1891), 393-408.

PLUQUET, Frédéric, (ed.), 1834, *Contes Populaires, Préjugés, Patois, Proverbes, Noms de Lieux*, de L'arrondissement de Bayeux, 2nd ed., Rouen: Edouard.

POAG, James Fitzgerald, 1961, *'Minne' and 'Gradualismus' in the Works of Wolfram von Eschenbach: A Study of Wolfram's Development of the Problems of Courtly and Religious Love in the Light of Medieval Ordo*, Urbana: University of Illinois, Diss.

1972, *Wolfram von Eschenbach*, New York: Irvington Pub.

POVEY, John F., 1971, 'Review of *Attitudes to English Usage* by W. H. Mittins; Mary Salu; Mary Edminson; Sheila Coyne', In: *The Modern Language Journal* 55.4 (1971), 253.

RAU, Heimo (ed.), 1974, *F. Max Mueller: What He Can Teach Us*, Bombay: Shakuntala Publishing House.

READY, William, 1968, *The Tolkien Relation: A Personal Inquiry*, Chicago, Ill.: Regnery.

ROSS, Anne, 1967, *Pagan Celtic Britain: Studies in Iconography and Tradition*, London: Routledge and Kegan Paul.

ROTHBERG, Abraham, 1970, *The Sword of the Golem*, New York: McCall Publishing Co.

RUTTER, John, 1829, *Delineations of the North Western Division of the County of Somerset, and of its Antediluvian Bone Caverns: with a Geological Sketch of the District*, London: Longmans, Rees and Co.

RYAN, J.S., 1963, 'Othin in England: Evidence from the Poetry for a Cult of Woden in Anglo-Saxon England', In: *Folklore* 74 (1963), 460-80.

1966, 'German Mythology Applied – The Extension of the Literary Folk Memory, In: *Folklore* 77.1 (1966), 45-59.

1969, *Tolkien: Cult or Culture?* (revised edition 2012), Armidale, N.S.W., Australia: University of New England.

1978, 'And What May Britain Be? – the Fiction Field of Roman Britain', In: *Orana* 14.3 and 14.4 (1978): 79-122.

1978, 'Tolkien's Language and Style', In: *Ipotesi*, 4, no. 9-12 (1978), 361-68.

1981, 'J.R.R. Tolkien: Lexicography and other Early Linguistic Preferences', In: *Mallorn* 16 (1981), 9-12, 14-15, 19-26.

1983a, 'Woses: Wild Men or "Remnants of an Older Time" ', In: *Amon Hen* 65 (1983), 7-12.

1983b, 'The Wild Wood – Place of Danger, Place of Protest', In: *Orana* 19.3 (1983), 133-40.

1983c, ' "B.B." Delineator of England's Natural Glories', In: *Orana* 19.1 (1983), 11-24, plus four illustrations.

1983d, 'Before Puck – the Púkel-men and the puca', In: *Mallorn* 20 (1983), 5-10.

1985 , 'The Barghest as Possible Source for Tolkien's Goblins and Ring-Wraiths', In: *Amon Hen* 73 (1985), 10-11.

1986a, 'Henry Bradley, Keeper of the Works of English, and his Heroic Passing', In: *Quettar* 27 (December 1986), 7-15.

1986b, *The Nameless Wood: Victorian Fantasists, Their Achievement, Their Influence, Proceedings of the Second Annual Conference of The Inner Ring: The Mythopoeic Literature Society of Australia*, Armidale, N.S.W., Australia: University of New England.

1986c, 'Warg, Wearg, Earg and Werewolf', In: *Mallorn* 23 (1986), 25-29.

1986d, 'Ancient Mosaics from out the West: Some Romano British 'Traditional' Motifs', In: *Minas Tirith Evening Star* 15 (1986), 13-17.

1986e, 'Dwarf's Hill', In: *The Book of Mazarbul* 7 (1986), 12-14.

1988, 'Mid-Century Perceptions of the Ancient Celtic Peoples of 'England' ', In: *Seven: An Anglo-American Literary Review* 9 (1988), 57-66.

2002, 'J.R.R. Tolkien's Formal Lecturing and Teaching at the University of Oxford, 1925-1959', In: *Seven: An Anglo-American Literary Review* 19 (2002), 45-62.

2009, *Tolkien's View: Windows into his World*, Zurich and Jena: Walking Tree Publishers.

SACKER, Hugh, 1963, *An Introduction to Wolfram's 'Parzival'*, Cambridge: University Press.

SALU, Mary B. (ed.), 1979, *Essays on Troilus and Criseyde*, Cambridge: Boydell & Brewer.

1990, *The Ancrene Riwle*, (The Corpus MS. *Ancrene Wisse* translated into Modern English), London: Burns and Oates.

1991, *Essays on Troilus and Criseyde*, reprint. ed., Cambridge: Boydell & Brewer.

and Robert T. FARRELL, 1979, *J.R.R. Tolkien: Scholar and Story-teller. Essays in Memoriam*, Ithaca: Cornell University Press.

SANDARS, Nancy K., 1960, *The Epic of Gilgamesh*, Harmondsworth: Penguin.

SAYCE, Archibald Henry, 1880, *Introduction to the Science of Language*, 2 vols., London: Kegan, Paul, Trench, Trübner.

(ed.), 1888, *Records of the Past: Being English Translations of the Ancient Monuments of Egypt and Western Asia*, vol. I, London: S. Bagster and Sons Ltd.

(ed.), 1888-1892, *Records of the Past: Being English Translations of the Ancient Monuments of Egypt and Western Asia*, 6 vols., London: S. Bagster and Sons Ltd.

1892a, *The Principles of Comparative Philology*, 4th ed. revised and enlarged, London: Kegan Paul, Trench, Trübner, reprinted Oxford: Kessinger, 2004.

1923, *Reminiscences*, London: Macmillan.

SCARTH, H.M., 1859, 'Some Account of the Investigation of Barrows on the Line of the Roman Road between Old Sarum and the Port at the Mouth of the River Axe, Supposed to be the 'Ad Axium' of Ravennas', In: *The Archeological Journal* 16 (1859), 146-57.

1875, 'Notes on the Roads, Camps, and Mining Operations of the Romans on the Mendip Hills', In: *Journal of the British Archaeological Association* 31 (1875), 129-42.

1879, 'On the Roman Occupation of the West of England, Particularly the Country of Somerset', In: *The Archeological Journal* 36 (1879), 321-36.

1883, *Roman Britain*, London: E. & J.B. Young/SPCK.

SCHOFIELD, William H., 1906, *English Literature from the Norman Conquest to Chaucer*, London: Macmillan.

SCHOLEM, Gershom, 1960, *Zur Kabbala und ihrer Symbolik*, Zürich: Rhein-Verlag.

1965, *On the Kabbalah and its Symbolism*, London: Routledge and Kegan Paul.

SCHÜCKING, Levin Ludwig, 1915, *Untersuchungen zur Bedeutungslehre der angelsächsischen Dichtersprache*, Heidelberg: Winter.

SCOTT, Walter, 1816, *The Antiquary*, In Three Volumes, Vol. II, Edinburgh: Archibald Constable and Co.

1820, *The Monastery: A Romance*, In Three Volumes, Vol. II, London: Hurst, Rees, Orme, and Brown.

1839, *Minstrelsy of the Scottish Border*, London: Tegg.

SEAL, Graham, 2011, *Outlaw Heroes in Myth and History*, London, New York: Anthem Press.

SEDGEFIELD, Walter John (ed.), 1899, *King Alfred' Old English Versions of Boethius De Consolatione Philosophiae*, Oxford: Clarendon Press.

(transl. and ed.), 1900, *King Alfred's version of the Consolations of Boethius, Done Into Modern English with an Introduction*, Oxford: Clarendon Press.

SEMPLE, S., 1998, 'A Fear of the Past: The Place of the Prehistoric Burial Mound in the Ideology of Middle and Later Anglo-Saxon England', In: *World Archaeology* 30 (1998), 109-26.

SHELLEY, Percy Bysshe, 1820, *Prometheus Unbound: A Lyrical Drama in Four Acts With Other Poems*, London: C. and J. Ollier.

SHIPPEY, Tom, 1979a, 'Creation from Philology in The Lord of the Rings', In: Mary Salu and Robert T. Farrell (eds.), 1979, *J. R. R. Tolkien, Scholar and Storyteller: Essays in Memoriam*, Ithaca: Cornell University Press, 286-316.

1979b, 'Wealth and Wisdom in King Alfred's Preface to the Old English Pastoral Care', In: *English Historical Review* 94.371 (1979), 346-55.

1982, *The Road to Middle-earth*, London: George Allen & Unwin.

2001, *J.R.R. Tolkien, Author of the Century*, London : HarperCollins.

2004, 'John Ronald Reuel Tolkien', In: *The Oxford Dictionary of National Biography*, vol. 58, Oxford, etc.: Oxford University Press, 903-04.

SIRE, H.J.A., 1997, *Father Martin D'Arcy: Philosopher of Christian Love*, Leominster: Gracewing.

SISAM, Kenneth (ed.), 1921, *Fourteenth Century Verse and Prose, With a Middle English Glossary by J.R.R. Tolkien*, Oxford: Clarendon Press.

SISSONS, Charles Jasper and Hilda Winifred HUSBANDS, 1945, *Raymond Wilson Chambers, 1874-1942*, London: Cumberlege.

SKEAT, Walter W. (ed.), 1881-85, *Ælfric's Lives of Saints: Being a Set of Sermons on Saints' Days Formerly Observed by the English Church*, vol. I, 2, London: N. Trübner & Co.

1882, *A Concise Etymological Dictionary of the English Language*, Oxford: Clarendon Press.

1891, *Principles of English Etymology*, second series, Oxford: Clarendon Press.

(ed.), 1915, *The Lay of Havelok the Dane*, (rev. by Kenneth Sisam), Oxford: Oxford University Press.

SMITH, Albert Hugh, 1928, *The Place-Names of the North Riding of Yorkshire*, Cambridge: University Press.

1937, *The Place-Names of the East Riding of Yorkshire and York*, Cambridge: University Press.

1956a, *English Place-name Elements; Part 1, Introduction, Bibliography, The Elements Á – Iw, Maps*, Cambridge: University Press.

1956b, *English Place-name Elements; Part 2, The Elements Jafn - Ytri, Index and Maps*, Cambridge: University Press.

1961-63, *The Place-names of the West Riding of Yorkshire*, Cambridge: University Press.

1964-65, *The Place-names of Gloucestershire*, Cambridge: University Press.

SOUTHEY, Robert, 1808, *Chronicle of the Cid*, London: Longman, Hurst, Rees, and Orme.

SPENSER, Edmund, 1869, *Book I of The Faery Queene*, Oxford: Clarendon Press.

STARKIE, Enid, 1954, *Petrus Borel the Lyacanthrope, His Life and Times*, London: Faber & Faber.

STARRETT, Vincent, 1934, 'The Dead Man's Chest, A Stevensonian Research', In: *The Colophon* 17 (June 1934).

STENTON, F.M., 1943, *Anglo-Saxon England*, Oxford: Oxford University Press.

STEVEN, Henry Marshall and Alan CARLISLE, 1959, *The Native Pinewoods of Scotland*, Edinburgh [et al.]: Oliver & Boyd.

STEVENSON, Robert Louis, 1883, *Treasure Island*, London: Cassell and Company.

1896, *Songs of Travel and Other Verses*, London: Chatto & Windus.

STEWART, Hugh Fraser, 1891, *Boethius: An Essay*, Edinburgh and London: Blackwood.

STOKER, Bram, 1897, *Dracula*, Westminster: Archibald Constable and Company.

2008, *The Lair of the White Worm, reprint*, London: William Rider and Son Ltd.

STRACHEY, Barbara, 1981, *Jouneys of Frodo: An Atlas of J.R.R. Tolkien's The Lord of the Rings*, London: Unwin Paperbacks.

SWEET, Henry, 1896, *The Student's Dictionary of Anglo-Saxon*, Oxford: Clarendon Press.

1967, *Anglo-Saxon Reader in Prose and Verse*, edited by Dorothy Whitelock, 15th edition, London: Oxford University Press.

SZEMERÉNYI, Oswald J. Lewis, 1962, *Trends and Tasks in Comparative Philology*, An Inaugural Lecture Delivered at University College, London, 23 October 1961, London: HK Lewis & Co. Ltd.

TAIT, Charles, 2011, *The Orkney Guide Book*, Fourth Edition, St Ola: Charles Tait.

THE AUSTRALIAN ENCYCLOPÆDIA, 1958, Vol. 2, Sydney: Angus and Robertson.

THE CONCISE OXFORD DICTIONARY, 1982, ed. by J. B. Sykes, 7th edition, Oxford: Oxford University Press.

TENNYSON, Alfred, 1859, *Maud and Other Poems*, London: Edward Moxton & Co.

THOMPSON, Stith, 1955-1958, *Motif-Index of Folk-Literature: A Classification of Narrative Elements in Folk-Tales, Ballads, Myths, Fables, Mediæval Romances, Exempla, Fabliaux, Jest-Books and Local Legends*, 6 vols., Copenhagen: Rosenkilde and Bagger.

THOMPSON, William Irwin, 1981, *The Time Falling Bodies Take to Light: Mythology, Sexuality & the Origins of Culture*, New York: St. Martin's Griffin.

TODD, M.(ed.), 1989, *Research on Roman Britain, 1960-1989*, Britannia Monograph Series 11, London: Society for the Promotion of Roman Studies.

TOLKIEN, Baillie, 1976, 'Introduction', In: *Drawings by J.R.R. Tolkien*, Oxford: The Ashmolean Museum (jointly with the National Book League), 6-7.

TOLKIEN, John Ronald Reuel, 1915, 'Goblin Feet', In: G.D.H. Cole and T.W. Earp (eds.), *Oxford Poetry* (1915), Oxford: B.H. Blackwell, 64-65.

1922, *A Middle English Vocabulary, Designed for use with Sisam's Fourteenth Century Verse & Prose*, Oxford: Clarendon Press.

1923, Obituary: 'Henry Bradley, 3 December 1845 - 23 May 1923', In: *Bulletin of the Modern Humanities Research Association* 20 (October 1923), Cambridge: Assoc., 4-5.

1924, 'Philology: General Works', In: *Year's Work in English Studies*, vol. IV, no. 1 (1923), 20-37.

1925, *Sir Gawain and the Green Knight*, (ed. by J.R.R. Tolkien and E.V. Gordon), Oxford: Clarendon Press.

1926, 'Philology: General Works', In: *Year's Work in English Studies*, vol. V, no. 1 (1924), 26-65.

1927, 'Philology: General Works', In: *Year's Work in English Studies*, vol. VI, no. 1 (1925), 32-66.

1929, '*Ancrene Wisse* and *Hali Meiðhad*', In: *Essays and Studies by Members of the English Association* XIV (1929), Oxford: Clarendon Press, 104-26.

1930, 'The Oxford English School', In: *Oxford Magazine* 48.21, 29 May, 1930, 778-82.

1932, 'The Name 'Nodens'', In: R.E.M Wheeler and T.V. Wheeler, 1932, *Report on the Excavation of the Prehistoric, Roman and Post-Roman Site in Lindney Park, Gloucestershire*, London: Printed at the University Press by John Johnson for The Society of Antiquaries, 132-37.

1934, 'Firiel' (poem) In: *The Chronicle* 4. Roehamptom: Covenant of Sacred Heart.

1934, 'Chaucer as a Philologist: The Reeve's Tale', In: *Transactions of the Philological Society* (1934), London: David Nutt, 1-70.

1951, *The Hobbit or There and Back Again*, 2nd ed., London: Allen & Unwin.

1953, 'The Homecoming of Beorhtnoth Beorhthelm's Son', In: *Essays and Studies by Members of the English Association* 6 (New Series), 1-18.

1955, 'Preface', In: Mary B. Salu, (trans. into Modern English), 1955, *The Ancrene Riwle*, London: Burns and Oates.

1962, *Ancrene Wisse. The English Text of the Ancrene Riwle, ed. from MS. Corpus Christi College Cambridge 402*, with an introd. by N.R. Ker, Early English Text Society 249, London: Oxford University Press.

1965a, *The Fellowship of the Ring: being the first part of The Lord of the Rings*, 2nd ed., Boston: Houghton Mifflin.

1965b, *The Two Towers: being the second part of The Lord of the Rings*, 2nd ed., Boston: Houghton Mifflin.

1965c, *The Return of the King: being the third part of The Lord of the Rings*, 2nd ed., Boston: Houghton Mifflin.

1967a, 'For W.H.A. - in Modern and Old English', In: *Shenandoah: The Washington and Lee University Review* 18.2 (1967), 96-97.

1967b, *Smith of Wootton Major*, London: George Allen and Unwin.

1975a, 'Guide to the Names in *The Lord of the Rings*' (ed. by Christopher Tolkien), In: Jared Lobdell (ed.), 1975, *A Tolkien Compass*, La Salle: Open Court, 153-201.

1975b, *Maître Gilles de Ham*, 1re Version, traduit de l'anglais par S. d'Ardenne, Liège: Association des Romanistes de l'Université de Liège.

1977, *The Silmarillion* (ed. by Christopher Tolkien), London: George Allen and Unwin.

1980, *Unfinished Tales of Númenor and Middle-earth* (ed. by Christopher Tolkien), London, etc.: George Allen & Unwin.

1982, *Finn and Hengest, The Fragment and the Episode*, ed. by Alan Bliss, London: Allen & Unwin.

1984, *The Book of Lost Tales Part I* (ed. by Christopher Tolkien), *History of Middle-earth*, vol. 1, Boston: Houghton Mifflin.

1985, *The Book of Lost Tales Part II* (ed. by Christopher Tolkien), *History of Middle-earth*, vol. 2, Boston: Houghton Mifflin.

2001, *Tree and Leaf: Including the Poem 'Mythopoeia' and 'The Homecoming of Beorhtnoth'*, London: HarperCollinsPublishers.

2006, *The Monsters and the Critics and other Essays* (ed. by Christopher Tolkien), London: HarperCollinsPublishers.

and Simonne T.R.O. D'ARDENNE, 1947, ' "Ipplen" in Sawles Warde', In: *English Studies* 28.6 (December 1947), 168-70.

and Simonne T.R.O. D'ARDENNE, 1947-48, 'MS Bodley 34: A Re-collation of a Collation', In: *Studia Philologica* 20 (1947-48), 65-72.

and Eric V. GORDON, 1936, *Songs for the Philologists*, London: G. Tillotson, A.H. Smith, B. Pattison and other members of the English Department, University College, London.

Eric V. GORDON and Norman DAVIS (eds.), 1967, *Sir Gawain and the Green Knight*, Oxford: Clarendon Press.

TUCKER, Thomas George, 1931, *A Concise Etymological Dictionary of Latin*, Halle (Saale): Niemeyer.

TURVILLE-PETRE, Edward Oswald Gabriel (ed.), 1940, *Víga-Glúms Saga*, London: Oxford University Press.

1953, *Origins of Icelandic Literature*, Oxford: Clarendon Press.

1964, *Myth and Religion of the North: The Religion of Ancient Scandinavia*, London: Weidenfeld and Nicolson.

1972, *Nine Norse Studies*, London: The Viking Society for Northern Research.

TYLER, J.E.A., 1976, *The Tolkien Companion*, London: Macmillan.

THE UNIVERSITY OF OXFORD GAZETTE, various issues, Oxford: University of Oxford Press.

VAN DE NOORT, R., 1993, 'The Context of Early Mediaeval Barrows in Western Europe, In: *Antiquity* 67 (1993), 66-73.

VANHECKE, Johan, 2007, 'Tolkien and Belgium', In: Dorine Ratulangie (ed.), 2007, *Lembas Extra. Proceedings of the 5th Unquendor Lustrum*, Wapenveld: Unquendor, 51-62.

VANDENBROUCK, Francois, 1968, 'Lay Spirituality in the Twelfth Century', In: Jean Leclercq, François Vandenbrouck and Louis Boyer (eds.), 1968, *The Spirituality of the Middle Ages*, London: Burns & Oates.

VICTORIA COUNTY HISTORY, A HISTORY OF THE COUNTY OF SOMERSET, 1906, Vol. I, ed. by W. Page, Haymarket: James Street.

VICTORIA COUNTY HISTORY, A HISTORY OF THE COUNTY OF GLOUCESTERSHIRE, 1965, Vol. VI, ed. by C.R. Elrington, Oxford: Oxford University Press.

1968, Vol. VIII, ed. by C.R. Elrington, Oxford: Oxford University Press.

1976, Vol. XI, ed. by N.M. Herbert, Oxford: Oxford University Press.

1981, Vol. VII, ed. by N.M. Herbert, Oxford: Oxford University Press.

1988, Vol. IV, ed. by N.M. Herbert, Oxford: Oxford University Press.

1996, Vol. V, ed. by N.M. Herbert: Oxford, Oxford University Press.

2010, Vol. XII, ed. by A.R.J. Jurica, Woodbridge et al.: Boydell & Brewer.

VIGFUSSON, Gudbrand and F. York POWELL (eds.), 1883, *Corpus Poeticum Boreale, part I: Eddic Poetry*, Oxford: Clarendon Press.

WAGNER, Heinrich, 1971, *Studies in the Origins of Celts and of Early Celtic Civilization*, Belfast: Institute of Irish Studies.

WALLER, Gregory A., 1986, *The Living and the Undead: From Stoker's Dracula to Romero's Dawn of the Dead*, Urbana Ill., University of Illinois Press.

WALTERS, Brian, 1992, *The Archaeology and History of Ancient Dean and the Wye Valley*, Cheltenham: Thornhill Press.

WALSHE, Maurice O'Connell, 1962, *Medieval German Literature: A Survey*, Cambridge, Mass.: Harvard University Press.

WARDALE, Edith Elizabeth, 1922, *An Old English Grammar*, New York: Dutton.

1935, *Chapters on Old English Literature*, London: Kegan Paul, Trench, Trubner.

1937, *An Introduction to Middle English*, London: Kegan Paul, Trench, Trubner.

WARDLE, W.L., 1968, 'Nimrod', In: *Encyclopædia Britannica*, Vol. 16, London: The Encyclopædia Britannica.

WATKINS-PITCHFORD, Denys (Pseud. "B.B."), 1955, *The Forest of Boland Light Railway*, London: Eyre & Spottiswoode.

1959, *The Wizard of Boland*, [London]: Edmund Ward.

WEEKLEY, Ernest, 1921, *An Etymological Dictionary of Modern English*, London: Murray.

WELLS, H.G., 1896, *The Island of Dr. Moreau*, New York: Modern Library, 1996.

1910, *The History of Mr. Polly*, London et al.: Thomas Nelson and Sons.

WELLS, John Edwin, 1916, *A Manual of the Writings in Middle English 1050-1400*, New Haven: Yale University Press.

WESTON, Jessie L., 1901, *Arthurian Romances Unrepresented in Malory's 'Morte D'Arthur', No. 4, Morien, A Metrical Romance, Rendered into English Prose from the Mediaeval Dutch*, London: David Nutt.

1906, *The Legend of Sir Perceval, Studies upon its Origin, Development and Position in the Arthurian Cycle*, 2 vols., London: David Nutt.

WHEELER, Robert Eric Mortimer and Tessa Verney WHEELER, 1932, *Report on the Excavation of the Prehistoric, Roman and Post-Roman Site in Lydney Park, Gloucestershire*, London: Printed at the University Press by John Johnson for The Society of Antiquaries.

WHITE, Terence H., 1958, *The Once and Future King*, London: Collins.

WHITELOCK, Dorothy, 1952, *The Beginnings of English Society*, Harmondsworth: Penguin.

WHITTAKER, C., 1994, *Frontiers of the Roman Empire: A Social and Economic Study*, Baltimore: John Hopkins University Press.

WIENER, Norbert, 1950, *The Human Use of Human Beings, Cybernetics and Society*, London: Eyre & Spottiswoode.

1964, *God and Golem, Inc., A Comment on Certain Points Where Cybernetics Impinges on Religion*, Cambridge, Mass.: M.I.T. Press.

WIERSMA, Stanley Marvin, 1961, *A Linguistic Analysis of Words Referring to Monsters in 'Beowulf'*, Ann Arbor, Mich.: University Microfilms Int.

WILLIAMS, Charles, 1947, *War in Heaven*, London: Faber and Faber. First edition London: Victor Golancz, 1930.

1952, *Arthurian Torso*, Oxford: Oxford University Press.

1982, *The Arthurian Poems of Charles Williams*, Woodbridge: Brewer.

WILLIAMS, David, 1982, *Cain and Beowulf: A Study in Secular Allegory*, Toronto: University of Toronto Press.

WILLIAMS, Howard M.R., 1997, 'Ancient Landscapes and the Dead: The Reuse of Prehistoric and Roman Monuments as Early Anglo-Saxon Burial Sites', In: *Mediaeval Archaeology* 41 (1997), 1-31.

1998, 'Monuments and the Past in Early Anglo-Saxon England', In: *World Archaeology* 30 (1998), 90-108.

1999a, 'Placing the Dead: Investigating the Location of Wealthy Barrow Burials in Seventh-Century England', In: M. Rundkvist (ed.), 1999, *Grave Matters*, BAR, Int. Ser. 781, Oxford: Archaeopress, 57-86.

1999b, 'Identities and Cemeteries in Roman and Early Mediaeval Britain', In: P. Barker, C. Forcey, S. Jundi and R. Witcher (eds.), 1999, *TRAC 98: Proceedings of the Eighth Annual Theoretical Roman Archaeology Conference*, Oxford: Oxbow, 96-107.

2006, *Death and Memory in Early Mediaeval Britain*, Cambridge: Cambridge University Press.

WILLIAMS, Margaret Anne, 1946, *Word Hoard: Passages from Old English Literature from the Sixth to the Eleventh Century*, London: Sheed & Ward.

WILLOUGHBY, L.A., 1935, 'Coleridge as a Philologist', In: *Transactions of the Philological Society* 34.1 (1935), 75.

WILSON, Edmund, 1956, 'Oo, Those Awful Orcs', In: *Nation* 182, 14 April 1956, 312.

WILSON, Richard M., 1954, *The English Text of Ancrene Riwle*, (edited from Gonville and Caius College MS. 234/120, with an introduction by N.R. Ker), London: Oxford University Press.

WILSON, Roger J.A., 1980, *A Guide to the Roman Remains in Britain*, 2nd revised edition, London: Constable.

WOODWARD, Ian, 1979, *The Werewolf Delusion*, New York and London: Paddington Press.

WRENN, Charles Leslie, 1953, *Beowulf: with the Finnesburg Fragment*, London et al.: Harrap et al.

and Norman DAVIS, 1962, *English and Mediaeval Studies: Presented to J.R.R. Tolkien on the Occasion of His Seventieth Birthday*, London: Allen and Unwin.

WRIGHT, Elizabeth Mary, 1913, *Rustic Speech and Folk-Lore*, London: Oxford University Press

1932, *The Life of Joseph Wright*, 2 volumes, London: Oxford University Press.

WRIGHT, Joseph (ed.), 1898, *English Dialect Dictionary*, vol. I, London: Henry Frowde.

(ed.), 1900, *English Dialect Dictionary*, vol. II, London: Henry Frowde.

(ed.), 1902, *English Dialect Dictionary*, vol. III, London: Henry Frowde.

(ed.), 1903, *English Dialect Dictionary*, vol. IV, London: Henry Frowde.

(ed.), 1905, *English Dialect Dictionary*, vol. VI, London: Henry Frowde.

WRIGHT, Judith, 1966, *The River and the Road*, Melbourne: Lansdowne Press.

ZETLER, L.A., 1974, 'Chesterton and the Man in the Forest', In: *Chesterton Review* 1 (1974), 11-18.

ZETTERSTEN, Arne, 1964, *Middle English Word Studies*, Lund: C.W.K. Gleerup.

ZEYDEL, Edwin H., 1951, *The Parzival*, Chapel Hill: University of North Carolina.

ZIMBARDO, Rose A. and Neil D. ISAACS (eds.), 2004, *Understanding The Lord of the Rings: The Best of Tolkien Criticism*, Boston and New York: Houghton Mifflin Company.

The index contains mentions of authors, works and places with the exception of fictional characters and places as well as works by J.RR. Tolkien himself. A number of key themes studied in these books are also included in the index.

Works are placed with the author where possible. Crossreferences leading to the author are put under the letter with which the first word begins – ignoring definite or indefinite articles.

Tolkien's View: Windows into his World

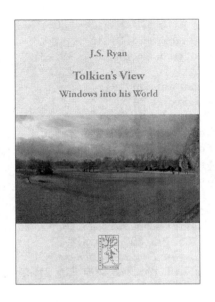

The present book is published as the second of a pair collecting the essays of J.S. Ryan. The accompanying first volume, *Tolkien's View: Windows into his World* is equally available from Walking Tree Publishers.

J.S. Ryan, *Tolkien's View: Windows into his World*, Zurich and Jena 2009 (Cormarë Series 19), ISBN 978-3-905703-13-9.

The book is available from reputable Tolkienia retailers, or directly from the publishers at www.walking-tree.org or by email from sales@walking-tree.org.

Walking Tree Publishers

Walking Tree Publishers was founded in 1997 as a forum for publication of material (books, videos, CDs, etc.) related to Tolkien and Middle-earth studies. Manuscripts and project proposals can be submitted to the board of editors (please include an SAE):

Walking Tree Publishers
CH-3052 Zollikofen
Switzerland
e-mail: info@walking-tree.org
http://www.walking-tree.org

Cormarë Series

The *Cormarë Series* collects papers and studies dedicated exclusively to the exploration of Tolkien's work. It comprises monographs, thematic collections of essays, conference volumes, and reprints of important yet no longer (easily) accessible papers by leading scholars in the field. Manuscripts and project proposals are evaluated by members of an independent board of advisors who support the series editors in their endeavour to provide the readers with qualitatively superior yet accessible studies on Tolkien and his work.

News from the Shire and Beyond. Studies on Tolkien
Peter Buchs and Thomas Honegger (eds.), Zurich and Berne 2004, Reprint, First edition 1997 (Cormarë Series 1), ISBN 978-3-9521424-5-5

Root and Branch. Approaches Towards Understanding Tolkien
Thomas Honegger (ed.), Zurich and Berne 2005, Reprint, First edition 1999 (Cormarë Series 2), ISBN 978-3-905703-01-6

Richard Sturch, *Four Christian Fantasists. A Study of the Fantastic Writings of George MacDonald, Charles Williams, C.S. Lewis and J.R.R. Tolkien*
Zurich and Berne 2007, Reprint, First edition 2001 (Cormarë Series 3), ISBN 978-3-905703-04-7

Tolkien in Translation
Thomas Honegger (ed.), Zurich and Jena 2011, Reprint, First edition 2003 (Cormarë Series 4), ISBN 978-3-905703-15-3

Mark T. Hooker, *Tolkien Through Russian Eyes*
Zurich and Berne 2003 (Cormarë Series 5), ISBN 978-3-9521424-7-9

Translating Tolkien: Text and Film
Thomas Honegger (ed.), Zurich and Jena 2011, Reprint, First edition 2004 (Cormarë Series 6), ISBN 978-3-905703-16-0

Christopher Garbowski, *Recovery and Transcendence for the Contemporary Mythmaker. The Spiritual Dimension in the Works of J.R.R. Tolkien*
Zurich and Berne 2004, Reprint, First Edition by Marie Curie Sklodowska, University Press, Lublin 2000, (Cormarë Series 7), ISBN 978-3-9521424-8-6

Reconsidering Tolkien
Thomas Honegger (ed.), Zurich and Berne 2005 (Cormarë Series 8),
ISBN 978-3-905703-00-9

Tolkien and Modernity 1
Frank Weinreich and Thomas Honegger (eds.), Zurich and Berne 2006 (Cormarë
Series 9), ISBN 978-3-905703-02-3

Tolkien and Modernity 2
Thomas Honegger and Frank Weinreich (eds.), Zurich and Berne 2006 (Cormarë
Series 10), ISBN 978-3-905703-03-0

Tom Shippey, *Roots and Branches. Selected Papers on Tolkien by Tom Shippey*
Zurich and Berne 2007 (Cormarë Series 11), ISBN 978-3-905703-05-4

Ross Smith, *Inside Language. Linguistic and Aesthetic Theory in Tolkien*
Zurich and Jena 2011, Reprint, First edition 2007 (Cormarë Series 12),
ISBN 978-3-905703-20-7

How We Became Middle-earth. A Collection of Essays on The Lord of the Rings
Adam Lam and Nataliya Oryshchuk (eds.), Zurich and Berne 2007 (Cormarë
Series 13), ISBN 978-3-905703-07-8

Myth and Magic. Art According to the Inklings
Eduardo Segura and Thomas Honegger (eds.), Zurich and Berne 2007 (Cormarë
Series 14), ISBN 978-3-905703-08-5

The Silmarillion - Thirty Years On
Allan Turner (ed.), Zurich and Berne 2007 (Cormarë Series 15),
ISBN 978-3-905703-10-8

Martin Simonson, *The Lord of the Rings and the Western Narrative Tradition*
Zurich and Jena 2008 (Cormarë Series 16), ISBN 978-3-905703-09-2

*Tolkien's Shorter Works. Proceedings of the 4th Seminar of the Deutsche Tolkien
Gesellschaft & Walking Tree Publishers Decennial Conference*
Margaret Hiley and Frank Weinreich (eds.), Zurich and Jena 2008 (Cormarë
Series 17), ISBN 978-3-905703-11-5

Tolkien's The Lord of the Rings: Sources of Inspiration
Stratford Caldecott and Thomas Honegger (eds.), Zurich and Jena 2008 (Cormarë
Series 18), ISBN 978-3-905703-12-2

J.S. Ryan, *Tolkien's View: Windows into his World*
Zurich and Jena 2009 (Cormarë Series 19), ISBN 978-3-905703-13-9

Music in Middle-earth
Heidi Steimel and Friedhelm Schneidewind (eds.), Zurich and Jena 2010 (Cormarë
Series 20), ISBN 978-3-905703-14-6

Liam Campbell, *The Ecological Augury in the Works of JRR Tolkien*
Zurich and Jena 2011 (Cormarë Series 21), ISBN 978-3-905703-18-4

Margaret Hiley, *The Loss and the Silence. Aspects of Modernism in the Works of C.S. Lewis, J.R.R. Tolkien and Charles Williams*
Zurich and Jena 2011 (Cormarë Series 22), ISBN 978-3-905703-19-1

Rainer Nagel, *Hobbit Place-names. A Linguistic Excursion through the Shire*
Zurich and Jena 2012 (Cormarë Series 23), ISBN 978-3-905703-22-1

Christopher MacLachlan, *Tolkien and Wagner: The Ring and Der Ring*
Zurich and Jena 2012 (Cormarë Series 24), ISBN 978-3-905703-21-4

Renée Vink, *Wagner and Tolkien: Mythmakers*
Zurich and Jena 2012 (Cormarë Series 25), ISBN 978-3-905703-25-2

The Broken Scythe. Death and Immortality in the Works of J.R.R. Tolkien
Roberto Arduini and Claudio Antonio Testi (eds.), Zurich and Jena 2012
(Cormarë Series 26), ISBN 978-3-905703-26-9

Sub-creating Middle-earth: Constructions of Authorship and the Works of J.R.R. Tolkien
Judith Klinger (ed.), Zurich and Jena 2012 (Cormarë Series 27),
ISBN 978-3-905703-27-6

Tolkien's Poetry
Julian Eilmann and Allan Turner (eds.), Zurich and Jena 2013
(Cormarë Series 28), ISBN 978-3-905703-28-3

O, What a Tangled Web. Tolkien and Medieval Literature. A View from Poland
Barbara Kowalik (ed.), Zurich and Jena 2013 (Cormarë Series 29),
ISBN 978-3-905703-29-0

J.S. Ryan, *In the Nameless Wood*
Zurich and Jena 2013 (Cormarë Series 30), ISBN 978-3-905703-30-6

Paul H. Kocher, *The Three Ages of Middle-earth*
Zurich and Jena, forthcoming

Beowulf and the Dragon

The original Old English text of the 'Dragon Episode' of *Beowulf* is set in an authentic font and printed and bound in hardback creating a high quality art book. The text is

illustrated by Anke Eissmann and accompanied by John Porter's translation. The introduction is by Tom Shippey. Limited first edition of 500 copies. 84 pages.

This high-quality book will please both Tolkien fans and those interested in mythology and Old English. It is also well suited as a gift.

Selected pages can be previewed on: www.walking-tree.org/beowulf

Beowulf and the Dragon
Zurich and Jena 2009,
ISBN 978-3-905703-17-7

Tales of Yore Series

The *Tales of Yore Series* grew out of the desire to share Kay Woollard's whimsical stories and drawings with a wider audience. The series aims at providing a platform for qualitatively superior fiction that will appeal to readers familiar with Tolkien's world.

Kay Woollard, *The Terror of Tatty Walk. A Frightener*
CD and Booklet, Zurich and Berne 2000, ISBN 978-3-9521424-2-4

Kay Woollard, *Wilmot's Very Strange Stone or What came of building "snobbits"*
CD and booklet, Zurich and Berne 2001, ISBN 978-3-9521424-4-8

Ossie felt the back of his neck go prickly....

Lightning Source UK Ltd.
Milton Keynes UK
UKOW03f2252220913

217667UK00001B/2/P

9 783905 703306